Beyond the Valley

Beyond the Valley

NO EYE HAS SEEN BOOK 1

ROANNE L KING

This publication is a work of fiction. Names, characters, places, and incidents are either products of the author's imagination or are used fictitiously.

Roanne King
https://roanneking.com/

Copyright © 2021 Roanne L King

All rights reserved.

ISBN-13: 9798589837056

DEDICATION

To all who desire to use your hardships for good as you strive to benefit others.

May you believe in what you cannot see and persevere with faith built upon truth until the fullness of what God has prepared for you comes to pass.

Beyond the Valley

PROLOGUE

"If anything happens to me, this is the only proof that Lydia exists . . ." Emelyn Sinclair held out her partially completed diary to Miss Hastings.

When Miss Hastings reached for the diary, Emelyn kept her hold on it and grasped the older woman's wrist with her free hand. She pressed her fingers into leathered wrinkles and sought the assurance of her midwife's gaze. "And proof that she's a Sinclair."

Her former midwife and current confidant was a fixture of ancient wisdom in the splintered wooden rocking chair near the fireplace in Emelyn's cabin. She was the only person, besides Emelyn that five-year-old Lydia had ever known or seen. But now, Miss Hastings would become a memory Emelyn prayed faded faster than her daughter's attention span.

Lydia was taking her late afternoon nap on a rumpled quilt at Miss Hastings' feet. The glow of fireplace flames spilled across the child's plump cheeks in a display of pure peace. Miniature fingers clutched the dingy-white linen quilt corner, a contrast to the bold silk-velvet patchwork design that made up the rest of her makeshift napping place.

Once Emelyn let go, Miss Hastings nodded and slipped the diary into the pocket of her charcoal-black dress. Then she leaned down, smoothed her palm over the top of Lydia's head, and tucked a golden curl behind the child's ear.

Emelyn wrung her fingers together. "I've prayed for another way, but it's all I can do to make sure she remains safe and with me." Light-headed, she turned away from the fireplace to draw in a breath of cooler air. "If you don't stop your visits now, she'll start asking even more questions about you and the other *angels* I've told her about. She's already so curious. I don't want to put you in a position where you must also lie to her."

Emelyn needed to protect her daughter from the unforgiving circumstances that had brought her and Lydia's father to these mountains in the first place. Hiding Lydia from the world beyond the Valley was crucial. A dense forest climbed a vertical hillside to the sky and surrounded the small valley where they lived. It created the perfect setting for a secluded life.

"I see your concern." Miss Hastings' voice wavered with age. She shook her head. A strip of silver hair slipped below the front of her navy-blue bonnet and settled along scattered creases on her forehead. For a moment, her eyes narrowed, and she stared into the flames. Then she turned back and smiled. "Let's have faith. You're still so young and have a fervor I haven't seen in a city girl since . . ."

"Since?" Emelyn spun back around to face Miss

Hastings.

But the midwife waved as if a bee had swarmed in front of her, then pinched her hanger-thin lips closed. She rarely spoke more than a few words at once. And never about anyone else.

Emelyn shook her head and sighed. Then she grabbed an apple crate containing a dozen jars of blackberry jam from the kitchen table and hugged it against her hip. Though there wasn't time to question the meaning behind Miss Hastings' stifled comment, Emelyn pondered it. How had she come to trust this woman whom she knew nothing about aside from her midwifery services?

Was it more than Miss Hastings' call to midwifery that had prompted the woman to make her home in French Corral, high above the canyon and rushing waters of the Yuba River and Bridgeport?

Those seeking gold or refuge had flocked to these hills for almost forty years. Layered valleys dotted with mossy boulders, stiff-leaf Manzanita bushes, and groves of poplar and oak were bordered by evergreens that created the perfect oasis—or escape for those seeking solitude.

Yet, what mattered now was that Miss Hastings had been faithful well beyond her midwife obligations. They wouldn't have survived Lydia's birth, let alone the winter of 1887 without her. Yet, if Emelyn were to succeed in continuing to raise Lydia apart from the world, she needed to succeed alone.

Emelyn took the apple crate to Miss Hastings' wagon. A light, yet brisk early autumn breeze shook infant limbs on the oak tree near her cabin. Honey-hued leaves clapped and then parted from crooked limbs. Emelyn watched as leaves landed around a bucket of rusty scraps that leaned against the weathered side of the barn. Near hidden by the overgrown vines climbing up the unsealed grayed boards, the sight of the bucket caused Emelyn to wince at all she'd lost.

She wasn't going to lose her daughter as well.

Emelyn strode over and tugged at the metal handles to pry the bucket's base from where it had sunk into hardened mud. The only value of the bucket's contents lay in her memories of Lydia's father. Still, it needed to go with Miss Hastings even if it ended up in a junk pile outside of town.

After adding the bucket of memories and scraps to the load in Mrs. Hastings' wagon, Emelyn hurried back inside. She tiptoed over to the fire where Miss Hastings watched over Lydia for the last time. Emelyn spoke in a hushed, even tone that prompted order over her emotions. She apologized for the work this final trip to and from the Valley entailed.

"My pleasure, dear one. Mr. Roberts and his son are expecting me to return with plenty of goods for their store. They'll find a use for it."

The confidence in Miss Hastings' words eased part of Emelyn's worries. She took a sealed envelope from her pocket. "Here's the summer payment for Mr. Sinclair. By God's grace he still believes that Lydia's father is generating income from a vineyard on this land."

As far as Emelyn could tell, Lydia's unbeknown grandfather had no clue the only thing planted on his land was a vegetable garden grown to sustain Emelyn and Lydia through winter months. Anything left over was used to trade for animal feed, hay, and other supplies Emelyn was unable to grow on her own.

Lydia stirred and flopped onto her back. She released a huge sigh, but her eyes remained closed. Innocence and contentment emanated from the child's parted pink lips to her bare feet poking out from the hem of an oversized mint-green gingham dress. It seemed a lifetime since Emelyn had worn that dress, dreams vast and alive at the prospect of a future life in America.

"You should go before she wakes." Emelyn nodded toward the door to hint that they continue their goodbyes outside.

Miss Hastings leaned forward. "What of your uncle in the city?"

Emelyn shook her head, wishing now that she hadn't told her about the telegram she'd received from her father's brother last spring. "I'll continue to write so he knows we're well, but I won't burden him . . .unless it becomes necessary."

A sigh seeped from the older woman's lips. Flames reflected in the tears pooling in the deep recesses of her muddy brown eyes.

Miss Hastings left her seat and crouched, then kneeled one leg at a time and braced herself with hands on either side of Lydia. "May the Lord protect you and keep you from harm dear one . . ." She hummed a moment, then sang only part of the hymn she'd used time and again when she would rock Lydia to sleep. "Safe in the arms of Jesus, safe from corroding care, safe from the world's temptations, sin cannot harm you there . . ." When her voice cracked beyond evidence of age, she sighed again and stood. This time tears streaked her cheeks and traced the lines that etched her face.

The weight of keeping secrets wasn't fair for either of them to bear.

In every way, Miss Hastings had been Emelyn's

angel of mercy and grace for the past five years. Now, they had to say goodbye. Emelyn's heart wrenched as her chest swelled with gratitude.

A brick of regret settled in Emelyn's stomach. She could continue to convince Lydia that Miss Hastings was an angel bringing them supplies. But then how would she explain things if Miss Hastings should pass away? Angels didn't die.

Moments later, they walked outside, keeping the cabin door ajar in case Lydia woke.

"I'll come to town to trade gowns and other goods for fabric and farming supplies as soon as I can leave Lydia alone. I'll include my regular telegrams and a satchel of scraps. That way you'll know we're still well."

Miss Hastings stepped onto the porch and nodded. "The Lord will keep you well, just as he has done for me all my years."

Miss Hastings' endurance was worth admiration. The only midwife for miles around, she'd developed a tolerance over decades to traverse the uneven terrain in every season to reach countless women on the brink of childbirth.

Emelyn averted her gaze to a gap between weather-worn floorboards, the knowledge of her own lack of stamina burning her throat. At twenty-one years old, a single trek to town every few months wore her down for weeks. But she hadn't been living this pioneer life for as long as Miss Hastings or other women such as Madame Penn, who'd owned hundreds of acres and from where the town of Penn Valley got its name. In time, and with Lydia now old enough to help with basic chores, she was sure she'd grow stronger. She had to if she were to survive here alone with her daughter.

Details of Emelyn's plans rolled off her tongue more for her own mind's sake than for Miss Hastings'. "The last time I was in town, Mrs. O'Shea and I arranged to keep our trading spot at the well for the rest of autumn and through the winter." Emelyn pressed her palm into her chest and bowed her head. "At the general store, Mrs. Roberts said that Alice Sinclair purchased one of my more recent gowns for her engagement party from a boutique in the city, unaware it was made from the same seamstress who made her debutante ball gown." She patted her heart and stifled a grin. She would never wrap her mind around the bittersweet irony that her oblivious sister-in-law caused her father-in-law's money to run in a circle.

Miss Hastings shook her head and glanced at the ajar cabin door. "How will you manage all that sewing with Lydia at your apron strings?"

The young mother smiled, pride puffing out her chest. "Hasn't Lydia shown you her quilt squares?" She whispered though Lydia wouldn't hear a shout from where Emelyn stood. "She's taken to basic hand stitching much faster than I did and looks forward to sewing every night. I may have a seamstress prodigy on my hands."

Miss Hastings smiled, nodded, then glanced at the darkening sky above as if to acknowledge God's divine hand in the matter. Then she climbed onto her wagon seat with ease. Once she settled, Emelyn checked that her diary remained secure inside her midwife's pocket.

Emelyn continued, confirming the confidence in her plan with each word. "Once she's mastered more complex patterns and can complete an entire dress on her own, we'll more than double our income. Then I can save our money instead of handing it all off to Mr. Sinclair. Lydia will need an inheritance since her grandfather wouldn't give her a penny—even if he discovers she exists."

Emelyn looked once more inside the cart filled end-to-end with items representing her past. Aside from holding back a carton of her old clothing that Lydia would eventually use, she'd have to part with Lydia's father's belongings, photographs of Emelyn and her parents, and tools and household items that were of no use for gardening, sewing, or cooking.

Was there anything else that may lead to Lydia asking questions? Emelyn threw up her hands. "Wait!"

Miss Hastings knit an already wrinkled brow and nodded.

Emelyn raced inside, glanced around the kitchen to her right, then grabbed another apple crate from below the counter. Careful not to disturb Lydia, Emelyn entered her room to the left through a curtain that represented a door. She eased into a squat to avoid creaking boards and set the crate on her mattress on the floor.

One-by-one she picked up each book from by her bed and placed them into the crate. She'd miss the stories and adventures by Charles Dickens, Mark Twain, Louisa May Alcott, and Jane Austin. She stifled a bittersweet chuckle as she placed each of the three volumes of *Sense and Sensibility* on the top of the stack.

Oh, the irony as she was acting without sense and with all sensibility. She no longer had the luxury of adhering to the common rules of the common world when the survival of herself and her daughter were at stake. From now on, stories would be limited to those Emelyn had memorized since her own childhood, and they'd have a purpose beyond mere entertainment.

Lastly, she placed the few remaining sheets of paper she'd used for writing letters, and her ink well and pens, in the spaces between book bindings. She'd buy replacements once she could hide them from Lydia. For now, she'd stick with telegrams for required communication with the outside world.

"Mama, what are you doing with our stories?" Lydia's voice started as a whisper, then strengthened to her sweet childish pitch as the patter of her bare feet grew near.

Emelyn sucked in her breath and held it, unsure of how to answer her daughter.

When the child's fingers grazed the back of Emelyn's shoulder, she turned and exhaled, forcing a small smile.

With sprawled fingers, Lydia brushed loose strands of hair out of her wide blue eyes, blinked, then wrinkled her forehead. "Why are you putting our stories in the butter box?"

Of course, that's what Lydia called it since it's where they stored fresh-churned butter each morning. She'd never seen or eaten an apple. The only food Lydia ate was made, grown, or slaughtered at home.

A cooling autumn breeze pushed open the cabin door and Miss Hastings' horse whinnied.

Lydia scurried to the doorway and squealed. "Bye Angel Lady!" Lydia waved and bounced on her bare toes.

Emelyn stood and strode across the floor and in between Lydia and the doorway. Her heart thumped at least a dozen times with each step to the wagon. Breathless, she nestled the crate of books, paper, and pens between a cedar chest and the tailgate.

"Mama, is Angel Lady going to read our stories now?" Lydia hollered from the doorway, having been taught not to leave the house without putting on her boots or slippers.

Emelyn sighed as tension released. "Yes, Lydia, it's her turn to read them now." Her words came out dry as her tongue parted with the roof of her mouth. What did it matter to add one more lie to the list of things her daughter believed?

She turned away from Lydia to untie the reins from the porch post and hand them to Miss Hastings. She mouthed the words *thank you*, sure that if she spoke them aloud, she'd also have to explain to Lydia why her and Miss Hastings were crying.

Miss Hastings waved to Lydia but turned her head in a way that her dark-blue bonnet shaded her face.

Several minutes passed before the dust settled between the barn and chicken coop where Miss Hastings had departed. A single worn path no wider than a wagon wheel marked the trail that led across the Valley to the north and the pond that lie before the forest's edge. It was all that remained of the road that used to head west and be the easier passage into town but was now overgrown with wild grass and wandering blackberry bushes.

Miss Hastings' wagon bounced over uneven ground and up a hill, then passed a solitary grove of sycamore and cottonwood trees with tops glowing gold, crimson, and flame-orange in the light of the lowering sun.

Though the wagon disappeared over the hill, Emelyn knew the route Miss Hastings would take. After reaching the dense evergreens that made up the forest's edge and the perimeter of the Valley,

Miss Hastings would follow the brook until the path grew steep toward the top of the mountain. If she kept a good pace, despite the weight of the load, she should make it to town before dusk.

Emelyn wiped her eyes with the edge of her apron and turned back toward Lydia, who now sat cross-legged inside the doorway playing with her yarn doll. Plump purple toes didn't care that the autumn air had grown brisk. The child was enamored with the little world she had created for herself and her doll.

Desiring to preserve the love and security of the life she'd made for them, Emelyn's resolve dug deeper roots and gave her the strength she'd need to do whatever it took to keep it that way.

Beyond the Valley

PART 1

But as it is written, Eye hath not seen, nor ear heard, neither have entered into the heart of man, the things which God hath prepared for them that love him.
1 Corinthians 2:9

ONE

"Mama, wake up!" Lydia giggled while she crouched and reached through shadows toward her mama's shoulder illuminated in the setting moonlight.

Mama swatted at Lydia's hand and groaned. "Is it morning already?"

"I heard birds, Mama, birds!" Lydia was sure Mama was teasing her. "We've got to take our first walk of spring today. I don't care if it's near freezing."

"Grab my walking stick." Mama sighed and pointed to a dark corner of her room.

Lydia clapped and hopped up from the side of Mama's bed. "I promise I won't run too far ahead of you, but Mama . . . it's so close to my seventeenth-year transition I think I might burst." She grabbed the stick and leaned it on the foot of Mama's bed. Then she left to start a fire in the stove for warming water upon their return.

By the time flames roared inside the belly of the stove, Mama emerged from her room, her boots laced over snagged black stockings. A wool sweater covered her apron and work dress.

"That was fast. I'll be ready in a moment." Lydia raced to her bedroom. She yanked off her nightgown and reached for last year's spring dress, which she'd laid out the night before. She smiled when the dress sleeves felt snug and the hem fell several finger widths above her bare knees. She had grown over the autumn and winter, despite their limited food rations.

Mama shook her head when she saw Lydia's attire. "You'll freeze. You know where my old dresses are in the barn. Why didn't you grab one when you locked it up last night?"

"Because this is proof I've grown out of my girl clothes." She tugged the dress hem and stepped near the stove to warm her legs, hoping Mama wouldn't notice her goosebumps.

"Yes, you have." Mama's voice faded, and she turned to the door. "Let's get going then."

Lydia ignored the sadness that lingered with Mama's words. Then she slipped her bare feet into her boots without bothering to lace them, grabbed her spring shawl from a nail on the wall, and followed Mama out the door.

Between the dawn light and setting moon, the path leading from their yard to the edge of the Valley was lit well enough they didn't need a lantern. Lydia kept pace with Mama until they passed the fig trees at the edge of the garden bed and reached the base of the first hillside. Neither of them had been this far past their cabin and barn since Mama had taken offerings to the angels before winter set in.

Lydia tugged a fistful of threadbare woolen shawl loops and pulled them tighter around her shoulders. She rubbed a tingling palm along her arm to ward off the cool air that seeped past shawl threads to her sleeve. She willed her legs to move faster against the numbing air. Shadows of shrubs reached toward the faded path, still veiled in early dawn's haze and remnants of a long winter. Icy morning air licking every spot of bare skin was worth the sacrifice. Finally, she could roam beyond the gap between the cabin and barn.

Mama grunted from behind, her walking stick clicking in staggered jabs against rock and dirt. "No need for you to hurry. It's a morning stroll, not a sprint."

Lydia didn't slow, convinced they both needed movement after months of cabin confinement. Without Mama in tow, Lydia could walk the path from home to the far side of the pond in less time than it took to milk their cow, Megan.

Lydia's boots crunched along at twice the rate of the gnarled oak-branch cane that led Mama a few paces back. "I've got to stretch my legs, Mama."

The forest came into view from the top of the hill beyond a trio of smaller rolling hills. Like a ring of cooled coals inside a fireplace, dense evergreens encircled the Valley against a steep dirt-red mountain slope. Mama said somewhere between the forest's edge and where entangled trunks climbed to the top of the mountain, a chasm divided the Valley from the Holy Place.

A shudder skittered up the nape of Lydia's neck. It had been three winters since their horses had run off and met their doom in that chasm.

"Are you getting too cold? I don't think your shawl is enough." Mama breathed hard between words, the distance between them lengthening.

"I'm almost to the pond and that sunny patch. The sun will warm me when I get there."

When Lydia approached the end of the trail, she strode south around the pond. Was it too early to discover a budding orange poppy, its brilliant petals like a soft flame against crisp, waxy green Manzanita leaves? Or perhaps she'd find lupine instead, with tall, narrow buds that reminded her of a string of knotted yarn stained with blackberry juice. But those were the common flowers of spring.

What she hoped for was the discovery of an anemone—pale purple or snow-white flowers that hadn't pressed past the Valley's soil for several springs. Mama said their blooms signaled protection from evil and the expectation of a good year ahead.

Chirps and clicks of insects sang a welcome song while Lydia slipped between stalks of cattails. Before Mama caught up, Lydia crouched along the muddy bank and stole a glance at her own reflection.

She would transition into womanhood at the end of spring. Had the winter months removed all signs of girlhood? Though it was hard to tell in the muddled view, she thought her high cheekbones and straight nose resembled Mama's more than ever. Her hair had always matched the same shade of dried grass as Mama's, which lightened in spring and summer months.

Mama approached, her cane clicking in pace with the scoot and scratch of her boots. "We need more warm days before the flowers bloom, Lydia. We should head back."

To avoid a lecture about how looking at her reflection could cause her heart to stray from God's work, Lydia sat in haste and removed her boots. Though the act would only lead to a different rebuke.

Mama gasped. "Your legs are purple. You want your toes to freeze too?"

"Please, Mama—my toes need to breathe." Lydia hung her boots by their tied laces over her arm and searched behind a mossy rock for flower buds. "I'm not seeing any flowers here. Can I check the other side of the pond?"

Mama pursed her lips then nodded. "Stay on the path and clear of the forest's edge."

"Yes, I know." Why did she always remind her of the boundaries?

Mama jabbed the ground twice with her stick. "I won't make it that far. I'll be at our picnic spot near the boulder. These tired legs can't keep up."

The bottoms of Lydia's toes stung as she padded over uneven ground and a mixture of sharp rock, stiff grass blades, and icy earth. Though fingertip-like shadows reached toward her ankles, she did her best to ignore them and searched the border of the narrow trail to find tender shoots. Standing so close to the forest reminded her of the consequences of disobedience.

Her stomach tightened. She should not have glanced at her reflection.

A black cluster came into view beneath broken, straw-hued grass blades. She skipped forward. Though facing the forest, she kept her head turned down while she curled her numbing toes into softening earth. She stooped and tucked the hem of her dress behind her bent knees, hoping to discover a rare flower bud.

When she pushed the grass blades aside, jagged, dark green leaves stretched and opened along a thick dandelion stem topped with a tightly enclosed bud. Now closer to the ground with her sight adjusted to the shadows, she discovered several dandelion clusters scattered along the forest's edge. She grinned. Dandelion wasn't rare, but it was a sure sign spring was upon them. As she plucked her discovery and turned back toward Mama, the chorus of insects and bird songs hushed.

Lydia halted at the rare sudden silence. Something rustled among the trees behind her.

Mama couldn't hear or see activity inside the forest from where she stood. She leaned on the boulder and waved at Lydia, the glimmer of dew melting in buttery shards of sunshine behind her indicated that it was time to return for morning chores.

Leaves rustled louder, followed by snapping branches and the echoes of clanging rocks from deeper within the forest.

Lydia's heart pounded. She dared look up, straining to decipher what creature made the commotion among the shadows.

Was God returning a horse as a reward for their diligence over the long winter?

A large shadow shifted between the tree trunks, too tall to be a horse.

Lydia stood paralyzed.

Then the figure vanished toward the abyss.

She choked down a scream and scrambled to Mama.

"Did you see any lupine or poppy shoots? What's the matter?" Mama leaned on her cane and pulled herself upright.

"No . . . it was just . . . a . . . a dandelion." She shoved the dandelion into Mama's free hand. "But I heard something. I saw it moving in the trees. I thought God was bringing us a horse, but it wasn't a horse, and then it disappeared. What else could it be?" She grasped Mama's shoulders and forced eye contact.

Mama glanced behind Lydia and stuffed the dandelion leaves into her sweater pocket. She tightened her lips and pulled her shoulders back. Her chest heaved once, then she blinked and let her shoulders sink into Lydia's grip. "You must have strained your eyes. It was probably a squirrel."

Lydia let go.

Mama turned away and then kept a faster pace than Lydia as they marched home. Each jab of Mama's cane disregarded Lydia's fright, leaving it with the futile puffs of dust that trailed behind her.

Inhaling until her lungs ached, Lydia sped past Mama when they reached the fig tree line and headed straight for the barn to milk Megan.

By afternoon, the day had warmed up enough to begin preparing the garden for spring planting. Lydia yanked a hard-toothed rake through dead roots and leaves as if clearing the debris of winter could erase the image of the figure from the forest.

Would whatever it was enter the Valley? Why had Mama dismissed it, despite her warnings about the forest's dangers? She wanted to ask, but Mama's pressed lips had told her she wasn't in the mood for explaining.

In the same fierceness of Lydia's raking, Mama plunged the pitchfork into the loosened pile and then scooped the decayed remnants of last year's harvest into a wheelbarrow for the compost bin.

Lydia thought back to their horses' demise. Only

thirteen summers old then, she'd been devastated at the thought of never riding Jasper again. He'd been her horse since her ninth year.

While she pushed the wheelbarrow across the yard, she recalled the talk Mama had given her, which seemed more like a reproof than an explanation.

"Why didn't they know not to go into the forest?" Sobs had wracked Lydia as she slumped in her seat at the kitchen table across from Mama.

"Animals aren't capable of understanding God's boundaries."

Although Mama was the one who had forgotten to secure the barn door, Lydia felt responsible. If only she'd helped Mama secure the yard the evening before, perhaps the horses would not have escaped.

"Why would God allow this to happen? We need horses to do our work." Lydia's sorrow turned to anger.

"We can't be certain." Mama frowned. Her red-rimmed eyes contrasted her flat voice. "God gives and he takes away. Tears will not bring them back. We must move on. Max is a strong ox and is very capable of pulling the wagon with our offerings up the mountain."

Lydia scrubbed her palms against her eyes and nodded.

The discussion had ended when Mama reached across the table and cupped Lydia's face in her frigid fingertips. "Let this be a lesson for us. The forest is dangerous for those God hasn't allowed there. Our place is in the Valley. We can understand our boundaries more than the animals can." Mama exhaled and stood, a signal that meant she was done.

Mama hadn't been the same since that day the

horses disappeared. She'd put off tasks, and no longer nagged Lydia about striving toward perfection in her chores or crafts. On more than one occasion, sewing and loom work sat half-done while Mama rocked on the porch, stared across the Valley, and moved her lips in silence. The memory also marked the beginning of Lydia giving up on asking Mama to explain things that still failed to make sense about their life in the Valley.

Why didn't God bring more people to care for the land and animals? Others would ease the burden and add interest to their life. Instead of a gentle, but vague answer, Lydia's questions had led to Mama's rants which accused Lydia of discontent and a lack of gratitude for the peace and provision God never failed to provide. So, Lydia eventually chose to work unto God and find joy in her evening sewing—the one task she had freedom to use her imagination. Gowns for angels had no boundaries and never led to rebuke.

When the wheelbarrow Lydia pushed collided with the compost bin, it jolted her back to the present. She had hoped that all the confusion of her childhood would end with her summer transition, so there was no point in questioning Mama about God's purposes again. What if God saw her discontentment and decided she wasn't ready? She couldn't risk that. She'd waited too long for the opportunity to deliver offerings and receive blessings from the angels on the top of the mountain.

The desire for change gnawed like a beetle burrowing into a fallen tree branch. If things went as planned with the spring offering, Mama would ask permission for Lydia to join her for delivering offerings when summer began. She hoped God would accept the request and provide a child to train, who in time would ease the burden of work for them both.

A sheet of thin clouds chased away a pink and orange sky, bringing on an early dusk. With sunset, the air cooled in haste while Lydia and Mama completed their normal end-of-day outdoor chores. Brisk twilight stirred anxious thoughts in Lydia as fragments of her and Mama's morning walk surfaced. Long shadows lurched from the sides of buildings and trees in the distance, creating the perfect hiding places for a creature from the forest. Lydia hurried to pump water and gather wood chips and bark for stove and fireplace kindling in the morning, then waited on the front porch for Mama to finish her chores.

A chorus of crickets filled the chilly air, their chirps multiplying like stars as darkness enveloped the Valley. Mama fluttered like a moth in the yard, floating from building to building to secure the barn door, henhouse, and sheep fences. A lantern dangled over one arm, illuminating her dingy gray nightgown while twilight cast long shadows around her feet. When she was done, Mama hung the lantern on the porch hook, snuffed the flame, and went inside without pause or comment.

Evening meant sewing until the fire died and they could no longer see their stitching by candlelight alone. This used to be Lydia's favorite part of the day. They'd work needles and thread to bind and adorn satin, silk, and velvet while Mama told of a complicated world where many more people had once lived and experienced adventures, struggle, and heartache. The stories that angels told Mama when she delivered offerings helped to explain God's ways and purposes. But tales of love, war, and another people called men only led Lydia to long for a life beyond the Valley's edge. She didn't care if it would lead to her suffering and being tempted by sin.

But Mama had stopped telling angels' stories during Lydia's thirteenth year. Ever since, they sewed in silence except for when Mama inspected Lydia's work or taught her a new pattern.

"I will head out with our offerings before the full moon." Mama broke the silence, her eyes remaining focused on her needle and thread.

What? She never brought offerings so early. "The moon's only half full and we haven't sheared the sheep for yarn yet." The full moon warded off dangerous forest creatures and was God's sign that Mama's journey up the mountain was safe.

Not to mention I saw a frightening creature in the forest this morning.

"Within the week. Our supplies are running low after the long winter. We have plenty of goods for offering, even without wool. Besides, it's time to petition for your transition." Mama stopped sewing and stared at Lydia.

Lydia's chest swelled and she held her breath and waited for Mama to show some sign of joy, of relief of the prospect of sharing in the duty of delivering offerings. But Mama's frown deepened while her hands fell limp on her lap.

"Does this mean..." Lydia hesitated. Would Mama dash her hopes? "Will God deliver another child to the Valley soon? You said God delivered me during your seventeenth year, and my seventeenth year will begin with summer."

Mama inhaled, her shoulders rising only a moment. She set her sewing aside, stood, and folded arms against her gut. Then she walked to the window and stared into the darkness. "At this point, I'm uncertain of God's plan." Her voice trailed into whispers. "I've prayed for answers, for direction. Yet, I fear I've failed God, and as a result, I've failed you."

Lydia set her sewing aside and joined Mama at the window. The glow of a half-moon cast pale blue light over the Valley that stood peacefully oblivious to the stirring in her soul. Whether Mama's words stemmed from sorrow, remorse, or fear, Lydia needed to be diligent for them both now—even if she didn't get the answers or change she craved.

"You haven't failed me, Mama. You've taught me to love the Valley and to honor God with my hands and my heart. Whatever God has planned, I'll accept it without question, just as you have." She rested her head on her mama's shoulder and hugged her waist.

Firelight flickered in the window's reflection, revealing a trail of tears flowing down Mama's cheeks.

TWO

Images of dozens of people overwhelmed Lydia's dreams that night. Some wore the gowns of angels, though they were people like her and Mama. Others had bodies with the strength of an ox and coarse hair on their faces. The people tried to speak, but only screeched in an unfamiliar language. Though they frightened her, she somehow understood they wanted to help. Their presence penetrated like the weight of a dozen wool blankets on her chest. The voices grew louder until the oak branch scratching the window woke her.

Robin whistles joined finch chatters. Although darkness still cloaked most of the Valley, the morning song signaled the onset of spring. Lydia pushed open the window and took in a deep breath of air that tasted of sweet dew and bitter soil. Though cool, it held a hint of coming warmth. In moments, the sounds and smells of morning dissolved the chaos that clung from her dream.

"Lord, lead me this day in serving you with all my heart and soul. Help me to fulfill my purpose with everything within me. Amen."

Lydia pulled on a wool sweater over her nightgown but left her boots at the foot of her mattress. Once outside, cool earth clung between her toes while thawing grass blades prickled her feet and revived her senses.

Careful to avoid splinters, she tiptoed up the wooden ramp to the henhouse enclosure. Her numb fingers fiddled with the wire latch while gurgling clucks and eager scratches vibrated the wooden door slats.

Once inside, Lydia checked for eggs, taking only a few for their breakfast and leaving the rest. For the past few weeks, she'd kept the lantern lit through the day and evening to stimulate egg production—an approach Mama suggested during longer winters. They'd lost two hens during a blizzard at the onset of winter, so the earlier they could breed chicks for spring, the better.

"You girls are so well behaved this morning," Lydia told her hens while they fluttered their feathers and gently poked their beaks into her hands and wrists in reply. "Something tells me that soon enough, you'll be out of this cage and free to roam outside. You aren't the only ones longing to run free from confining winter walls."

When she finished, she turned out the lantern and opened the side windows to let in sunshine and warmth and to air out the dank and dusty henhouse. Then, clutching the end of her wound apron bib that held the eggs, she mimicked the songs of robins with echoing whistles and skipped toward the kitchen doorway along the west side of the cabin.

Mama balanced a pile of chopped logs in one arm while adding to the stack of firewood against the wall of the lean-to with another. Two logs tumbled from Mama's grasp and bounced from the porch to the dirt, barely missing her feet.

Lydia hurried up behind Mama. "Would you like some help?" All winter Mama's tasks took longer and required more effort even though she acted as if they didn't, never complaining and never asking Lydia to assist her.

"Good morning." Mama turned with a slight smile. She focused on the eggs Lydia held out in her apron for her to count, and then returned to stacking logs.

Lydia set the eggs in the basket outside the kitchen door, and then turned back to pick up the wood that had fallen off the porch in Mama's failed effort.

"Stop. I'll get them." Mama pulled the logs from Lydia's arms and tossed them to the top of the stack. "We have much to do to prepare me for tomorrow's journey. Now go milk Megan."

Lydia ignored the strained look on her mother's face, brought the basket of eggs into the kitchen, and headed back out toward the barn. After last night, she was more determined than ever to work hard. She wanted to earn God's approval for her transition, but she also wanted to relieve the pain her mother endured without complaint.

"Good morning, Megan," Lydia said as she caressed the cow's moist nose and patted its round belly. She slid the bucket under the cow, gathered her skirt, and sat on a three-legged stool. "These barn walls don't do much to keep out the cold, but as long as I sit close enough, you sure keep me warm."

Megan snorted a puff of white air in response and stood in reverence.

"Poor girl." Lydia pulled gently on the cow's cracked, dry teats. "This dry, frigid winter hasn't treated you well. Sorry if this hurts girl, but it will be worse if I don't empty you. Then I'll rub on a thick layer of salve."

Seconds later, warm milk streamed up Lydia's arms and soaked the bunched sleeves at her elbows. She adjusted her grip and soon milk shot into the bucket, darting between the sides then flowing into a foamy, white pool that rose steadily from the bottom. Mesmerized by the methodical task, Lydia's thoughts strayed back to Mama.

What's the matter with her, Lord? Why won't she let me help? The pain I see in her eyes is more than physical. Why won't she tell me what's making her so sad?

When Lydia was younger, she often asked Mama if God would ever create more people for their world. Mama's eyes would glaze over before she'd answer in her usually vague manner. "God created the Valley specifically for us. He finds joy in watching us love the land and the animals. God's ways are not our ways, Lydia. But we must accept them all the same."

Once Lydia was old enough to distinguish between male and female animals, her questions grew more curious. "Why doesn't God bring us a male human, Mama?"

This was around the same time that Mama's answers and patience grew thin. "Why must you question everything, Lydia? We have everything we need here in the Valley. We don't need a man. God's provision is enough."

The last couple of years had tested them in many ways. When the summer sun scorched and forced sweat from every limb or the sun lost its fight with the bitter wind and winter kept Lydia's fingers from grasping the ax handle as she chopped wood for the fire—she couldn't help but complain. God's reasoning became less clear now that she noticed

Mama struggling. Did it bring God joy to see them strain and toil without relief?

What did Mama mean last night about failing God and me? She was sure she heard Mama crying after they went to bed. Was it possible that Mama failed to follow through on something God told her to do? What would happen if she couldn't complete her purpose in the Valley? Would God call her spirit home as he had for the older, injured animals over the years?

Lydia's breath caught at the thought.

She tightened her jaw as heat flooded from the center of her chest through her arms and legs. If Mama returned from delivering offerings without answers, Lydia would find a way to get the answers from God herself. She wouldn't let Mama continue to suffer without a good reason.

"Lydia." Mama's voice startled her.

Milk sprayed over the edge of the bucket and warmed her tingling toes.

"You're daydreaming again. The bread is nearly done, and we haven't any butter. Come now, the sun is already peeking above the treetops." Mama spun around. The barn door slammed, leaving Lydia with the echo of Mama's boots pounding earth as she trudged back to the cabin.

Early the next morning, Lydia secured their ox to the wagon while Mama loaded the last box of their offerings—blackberry jam and the remainder of their wool cloth and yarn.

"My prayers will be with you the whole time,

Mama." Lydia handed Mama a large jar of fresh water from the well.

"I'll be fine. God and his angels always provide." Mama's eyes glistened. She sighed and climbed onto the narrow, splintered wagon seat.

"What we need are answers, Mama." Lydia handed the reins over and firmly grasped Mama's wrists.

Mama pressed her lips together and faced away. "Yes," Mama whispered. "It's time for answers." She turned back, leaned down, and kissed Lydia's forehead. She lingered for a moment and then snapped the reins and led Max around the Valley's edge toward the mountain path.

Lydia stood still until Mama and Max disappeared. She ignored the wisps of her hair blowing around her face, clasped her hands, and closed her eyes until she could find the words. "I don't want to question your ways, God. I pray you show Mama what to do. Give her the answers she needs, the answers I need. If it's time for me to transition, I'm willing to do whatever I must to fulfill my purpose. If it's your will—and you have mercy on Mama and me despite our failures—I pray you provide us with another person to help us in the Valley before . . ."

Before you take Mama to be with you for eternity.

The breeze shifted and knocked an empty milk bucket from the top of the fence. Lydia tucked her loose strands of hair beneath her bonnet and scooped up the bucket. She sighed and started her work, knowing it was the remedy for passing time while Mama was away.

By early afternoon, Lydia had tilled the compost into the garden bed, churned two batches of butter, and washed and hung the bed linens to dry. As she went to milk Megan for the second time, ashen clouds gathered above the treetops to the east, eclipsing the sunlight and late afternoon warmth. She quickened her pace when the breeze turned into a steady wind. A spring rainstorm would douse the Valley before evening.

Upon entering the kitchen with a fresh bucket of milk, Lydia's stomach gurgled. All morning, she'd never stopped to eat. She grabbed the loaf of bread from the windowsill, broke off a piece and slid it across the butter in the box beneath the counter. Then she sunk her teeth past the hard crust into the soft center. Fresh bread with a dab of churned butter was one of Lydia's favorite foods. She wrapped the remainder of the loaf in a muslin cloth for later and returned it to the windowsill.

Pale green blades of grass danced in the breeze. Lydia pulled the kitchen window shut. Clouds shadowed the clothesline where the sun had shone earlier, prompting Lydia to gather the linens before rain drenched them. She glanced around the yard, making sure anything that couldn't withstand a little spring rain was under shelter.

She checked that the sheep had food and water, nuzzled the lambs, and told them to stay close to their mama during the storm. While holding a basket of wool she'd found from last summer's shearing, Lydia struggled to close the gate with one hand. She let the gate hang open for an instant while she set the wool down outside the fence. But when she turned back toward the gate, one of the lambs scurried past her and bolted in the direction of the pond.

Lydia's heart thumped.

She pulled the gate shut with both hands. Her legs, weary from garden and laundry work, didn't care to run, but she pushed them anyway.

Would the pond's edge stop the lamb long enough for her to catch up?

When the lamb came up to the cattails, it darted around them and ran straight toward the forest's edge. Still dozens of steps ahead, the lamb's hooves carried it faster than Lydia could run.

Within seconds, the blur of bobbing white wool disappeared beyond the trees. The lamb's bleats faded as fast as any hope Lydia had of capturing it. Dare she enter the forest to rescue the lamb before it met the same fate their horses had years before?

Lydia stopped under the shade of a towering cedar tree. The intense spicy scent of bark burned her nostrils. She'd never been this close to the edge of the forest. Were those faint cries of the lamb, or were they simply echoes in her mind? After a few seconds, her eyes adjusted to the darkness, and she could see further into the forest.

A squirrel scurried over a mound of rocks and a patch of pine needles. A chorus of chattering birds, croaking frogs, and chirping insects hushed while leaves whispered, and a brook babbled between shiny round rocks and drenched branches. It didn't seem possible this forest would bring death.

Mama's fearful warnings vanished from Lydia's mind. Her feet pressed forward. After she passed the first cluster of trees, the staggering bleats of the lamb grew louder. Lydia stepped forward gingerly. She squeezed between the bowing branches of a pine tree and a boulder covered in cool, yellow moss.

The lamb now stood a few feet in front of her. Its nose nudged at something under a pile of dried leaves. Lydia tiptoed toward it and the lamb jerked its head in her direction. She reached her hand out as the undisputable sound of a horse's neigh and hooves rumbled behind her. She stopped but her heart pounded in her chest.

"Whoa!" A voice thundered.

Lydia spun around and froze.

A strange person sat on a pale horse. Thick, bulging arms tugged back reins that stopped the horse short of trotting over Lydia.

The lamb scurried under Lydia's skirt.

She grabbed the creature and cradled it to her chest in a feeble attempt to feel protected. Then she dropped to her knees.

THREE

Terrified at the fate that Lydia may have cost herself and the lamb, she pressed her forehead into the sharp, chilly forest floor.

"Hello, ma'am?" The person's voice was husky, more like the grunt of a strange animal than it was like her or Mama's. "I apologize if I've startled you. Your lamb spooked my horse. I didn't expect to find a young woman wandering alone through these woods."

Lydia remained prostrate, forcing her face further into the earth. The weight of the words took root in her mind. Why wouldn't she be alone? Mama was delivering offerings.

"Ma'am? We mean you no harm. Bailey and I were just going for an evening ride. We didn't mean to venture onto your property."

Property?

Lydia raised her head, the breeze drying the tears she hadn't realized were streaming down her face. She squeezed the squirming animal in her arms and slowly brought herself to her feet.

"Are you . . . an Israelite?" Lydia breathed. Maybe he was a man—a man sent by God in answer to her prayers for help.

He wrinkled his forehead, joining thick eyebrows. "Israelite?"

"Yes . . . are you from . . . the Promised Land?"

"No, ma'am." He shook his head. Wisps of acorn-brown hair fell from beneath the brim of his wide hat and onto his forehead. "The only Israelites and Promised Land I know of are from my Bible studies. I live in French Corral on the other side of the mountain with my parents Andrew and Jaina Prescot. I'm Dylan Prescot." He climbed off his horse and grasped the reins with one of his hands while extending his other hand toward Lydia.

Frenchcorral? Parents?

"Dylan. Prescot." Lydia repeated his names, wondering why he had two of them. Was she supposed to do something to his hand?

After a moment, he drew his hand back and sighed. "Ma'am, would you be so kind as to tell me your name?"

"Um . . . My name?" Her voice shook and heat rushed from her chest to her face. "I only have one . . . It's Lydia. My name is Lydia." Her words muffled beneath the pounding of her chest. "Are you . . . a man?"

"A man?" he chuckled. "Well, most would say I still have some growing up to do. But yes. Miss Lydia, I am a man for practical purposes."

He was taller than Mama or Lydia. His thick arms, legs, and neck muscles etched firm bulges into the fabric of his clothing. Odd, thick stockings tucked into his boots. Lydia couldn't tell what color his eyes were in the shadows of the tree branches, but she could tell they were lighter than Mama's dark blue eyes. His wide nose fell even between a distinct jawline and full lips surrounded by shadows.

In the few quiet seconds Lydia took to observe their differences, she realized this man before her was like the visions of men she'd seen in her dreams. Dreams she never dared tell Mama. Each feature from the wavy locks of hair falling across his brow to the way he held himself with ease and strength—all of him looked like she'd imagined.

Mama and Lydia were no longer alone. Had God finally sent them a man?

Dylan Prescot said he knew the stories of the Israelites, so he must know God too. If Mama had known about his arrival, she would have prepared Lydia for their encounter. Perhaps God would tell Mama while she delivered offerings.

But why didn't this man know of her? Didn't he know they would meet?

A crack of lightning shot white light through the stirring leaves and thunder vibrated the ground. The lamb Lydia held captive in her arms squirmed loose and scurried back toward the pond. The slow tap of raindrops on the tree limbs and leaves became a steady pelt on the forest floor.

"Well, Miss Lydia, may I give you a ride to shelter?" Dylan Prescot mounted his horse and drew his hand toward her. He glanced through the branches toward the sky which hovered over them like a heap of heavy wool blankets.

Lydia's confusion had dampened her discernment. Mama warned her about men her whole life. God never allowed any in the Valley. Men would cause them pain and bring sin into their world. Fear of Mama's warnings overrode the fear of dashing through a thunderstorm.

She attempted to dart around Dylan Prescot and his horse and race toward the shelter of home. However, before she could take two steps, he leaned over, scooped her sideways into his lap, and set the horse galloping at a pace where Lydia risked broken limb if she dared jump off.

She squeezed her eyes shut, held her breath and leaned into his chest to brace herself. She clutched the firm arm wrapped around her waist as her legs dangled helplessly off one side of the horse. The pounding of her heart methodically joined the pounding of horse hooves until they were of one accord.

Thunder rolled across the sky.

Rain drenched them.

Yet, she only felt his warm, firm, chest against her cheek.

In moments, they came to a halt in front of her cabin. With gentle care, Dylan Prescot lowered her to the ground. He brushed sopping hair out of his eyes and back under his hat.

Lightning flashed, revealing Dylan Prescot's eyes flecked with green and gray that glowed like willow leaves against an overcast sky. What she thought were shadows on his face when they stood in the forest were stubs of hair, like in her dreams. Mama never told her that men grew hair on their faces. Did this make them strong like in the story of Samson?

Dylan Prescot started to turn his horse around to leave.

"Wait." Feeling bolder under the safety of her porch, Lydia dared speak over her racing heart. "I don't understand. I thought God sent you here to live with us in the Valley. Tell me about *Frenchcorral?*" Had God made a new land?

He turned his horse back around to face Lydia and nodded. "French Corral is the former hydraulic mining town from the '49 gold rush. You haven't

Beyond the Valley

heard of it? Just a few dozen faithful families remain since the flooding of the dam in '83, but we make do."

"I don't understand. And what did you mean by *parents* and *property*? Mama said *nothing* lies beyond the forest but the edge of the Valley—nothing but certain death and the Abyss besides the Holy Place."

He widened his eyes below his wrinkled brow and leaned closer to her. "Ma'am, I don't mean to jolt you, but beyond this valley and over that steep mountainside of forest lies a valley much larger than this one. What you see here—this land—it's only a hint of the splendor of this great state of California."

"Has God created another world?" Could this be an answer to her prayers? "Please don't leave." She yelled over the crackling and swishing of the thunderstorm.

Dylan Prescot climbed off his horse again and then tied it to the side of the porch.

Lydia sighed and pulled her shaking hand to her throat. He was going to stay and give her answers.

"I don't understand," Lydia said when he didn't speak. "Mama told me we were the only people—that others lived in different lands, long ago, but no longer existed. All God's stories . . . did those things really happen beyond the forest?"

He crossed his arms and brought one hand to his chin. After several silent moments, he shifted his gaze from Lydia to the cabin, then the other buildings and beyond the garden.

Before he answered, the lamb managed to make its way back to the sheep pen's gate. It bleated in protest as rain beat down on its head and back. Needing a moment to allow this stranger's presence to resonate, Lydia ran over to let the lamb through the gate. It ran immediately to the shelter and warmth of its mother.

Lydia dashed back through the rain toward this man standing on her porch while the heavens drowned out any certainty about her and Mama's life in the Valley.

Dylan Prescot cupped her elbow and led her toward the bench near the front door. He took the quilt draped over the back of the bench and wrapped it around her while she sat. Then he stepped back to the edge of the porch.

His voice was soft, yet firm. "Miss Lydia, there's much more to this world than what your Mama has told you. Beyond this valley lie rolling hills, a great river, and a variety of people and towns . . ."

She sat silent while he described the vast world that existed beyond the boundaries of the Valley. She didn't understand the meaning behind many of his words. All she knew was that with his words, each flash of lightning revealed a little more truth, each snap of thunder cracked like a whip on her heart.

Dylan Prescot told Lydia about French Corral, the town, using words she didn't understand like gold, mining, and river.

Then he talked about Mama. "I've heard of an Emelyn of the Mountain who has lived secluded in these parts for over sixteen years." His spoke soft and slow, pausing until Lydia nodded for him to go on. "The town people say she is a harmless widow who keeps to herself. She lives off the land she used to share with her husband. Every couple of months she comes off the mountain to trade goods and crops for supplies. I haven't heard mention of you, Lydia, or that Emelyn lived with anyone else. As far as the town people know, she lives alone and has made it clear that she doesn't want visitors. Is this Emelyn of the Mountain your mama?"

Lydia wanted to understand everything he was saying, but his words confused her. "Is my mama, Emelyn? Yes, Emelyn is the name God called her before I was delivered to the Valley. I call her Mama. Like the mama sheep that care for their lambs, Mama cares for me too. But she never had a husband . . . God no longer allows them."

His brows wrinkled, and he looked out toward the barn. "This is going to take more time to explain than I thought."

Lydia's head pounded and her eyes burned. What he was saying didn't make any sense. Why didn't he understand anything about their life here? Maybe he wasn't from God. Maybe he was what Mama had warned her about—pain and sin and— "No. No! I don't understand what you're saying. Who are you? Why are you here and why didn't Mama tell me you would arrive while she was gone?" Her voice quivered with each word as she tried to hold back sobs. "Mama must have a reason for not telling me. Why didn't she tell me?" Lydia leapt up and the quilt around her shoulders flew back into the muddy stream flowing beneath the porch.

Maybe she was imagining the whole thing and the rain would wash away this stranger and his words at any moment. Instead, like rushing waters changing the landscape, the only thing she understood was that her life was about to change forever.

She covered her face with her hands and shook as she wept.

After several minutes, the downpour retreated to a gentle drizzle. Dylan Prescot stayed silent and didn't try to approach her.

She contemplated this stranger on her porch and focused her thoughts on God. *I thought I wanted this, Lord. I thought Mama and I needed a man here. Yet, in only minutes, he's already bringing me pain. I prayed for answers, Lord. Not more questions.*

"Miss Lydia." Dylan took a step forward, his hat in his hands. "I apologize for upsetting you. I shouldn't have said so much before asking about your life here. Tell me more about yourself and your mama."

Lydia pulled her hands away from her face and twisted the end of her braid between her fingers. She sighed and looked out across the Valley. "First, tell me how many. How many people live beyond the forest?" She made no effort to wipe away the tears slipping down her cheeks.

"About four hundred in French Corral but—"

She uttered a sob. "Four hundred?" She shuddered, unable to imagine that many people—alive and near them.

"What has your mama told you? You said something about Israelites and the Promised Land before." His voice remained calm, soothing.

"The angels tell her the stories of people who lived in other lands long ago. The stories help us understand our purpose in the Valley." Lydia stepped toward him. "You've heard these stories as well?"

"Yes, I have. I'm not sure of which stories you know, but many stories about the Israelites are in the Bible. And like your mama said, the stories help us to understand God's plan for mankind and how he works through all of us to fulfill a purpose. May I sit?" He opened his palm toward the porch bench.

Lydia nodded. Hearing this brought some relief

and her fear began to dissipate. At least this man was familiar with God. She sat next to him and stuffed her distress aside in hopes of finally getting answers. He scooted away when her leg brushed against his. The bench usually only fit Mama and her if they sat hip to hip.

"Whenever I ask Mama why God never put more people in the Valley, she says it's to protect us from pain and sin. She says God needs us to care for the animals and the land and that he sees no need for other people—especially men—to live here with us." While she spoke, she coiled her shaking fingers in her apron. Why would such subtle details—like the warmth of his knee near hers or the edge of his thick boot nudging her toe—create an odd sensation in her chest?

"I think your mother may have suffered from a broken heart, Miss Lydia." He glanced out at the buildings and land before them. When he turned back to her, Lydia caught a whiff of his warm, minty breath. A ray of sunshine peeked through the dissolving clouds and cast a white beam of light across his face.

"If it were a broken heart, why wouldn't she tell me? Why couldn't she tell me about other people? I used to ask her so many questions, but she made me feel . . . ungrateful. Do you know why she wouldn't tell me about other people?"

"I can't tell you why your mama has kept you up here away from the world, Lydia. She may be trying to protect you. However, she must know that one day soon she'll have to tell you that there's more to this world than this valley."

"She lied to protect me? You said the people thought she lived here alone. If nobody knows about me why would I need protecting?"

The horse whinnied and stomped his hooves.

"Miss Lydia, it would be my honor to help you sort this out. Nevertheless, I must get back to my home before nightfall." He stood and untied the horse reins from the porch post.

Even though Lydia had many more questions, this man brought the hope of answers.

"Once your mama returns, you'll have to act as you always have and not tell her about our encounter or our conversation."

"You don't want me to tell Mama of our meeting?" She finally had a reason to press Mama for answers.

"For your safety and hers it would be best. I've overstepped my bounds enough as it is. Allow me to find some answers so that our meeting doesn't cause anyone harm." He tugged his hat on his head and tightened the strap on the saddle.

Lydia nodded and her throat tightened. *Now I must lie to Mama?*

"Tomorrow, I'll send a message to the city and see what I can find out about Miss Emelyn's life before settling here." He mounted his horse and pulled the reins tight so that he'd continue to face the porch.

Perhaps, when Mama returned from delivering the offerings, something would compel her to tell the truth on her own. Mama had said it was time for answers before she left. If Dylan Prescot were right, maybe Mama was making sure they would be safe before she told her.

Lydia pushed herself up from the bench, walked over to Dylan Prescot and his horse, and touched his arm one last time for assurance that she was not dreaming. "Dylan Prescot, I'm afraid. The only thing I've ever kept from Mama were my own *thoughts . . ." and dreams about a man coming to the Valley.*

"Just call me Dylan . . . no need to say my surname. I'll explain the reasons for two names later." He patted her hand resting on his arm and smiled. Behind him, the sky above the treetops turned shades of pink and purple as dusk settled.

"How will I know what you find out?"

"While I wait for a return telegram, I'll learn what I can from the store owners and locals. It may take some time. Would it be possible for you to meet me between the pond and the forest without your mama knowing?"

Her heart raced in anticipation of meeting him again. "I normally don't have time alone when Mama's not delivering offerings. She'd have to be sleeping for me to get there without her noticing." This was beginning to feel like one of the angel's stories. "You won't hurt us, will you?" She had to ask.

"Of course not, Miss Lydia. I want to help you." His smile and the glimmer in his eyes put her at ease.

Did she have any choice but to believe him? "I'll try to meet you." She spoke with a confidence that surprised her. "There's a tall bunch of cattails on the east side of the pond. We can meet there the first night of the full moon."

"Perfect. That'll give me enough time to get some answers. You better get inside now, Miss Lydia. You're shivering from those wet clothes." He pinched the rim of his hat and nodded, then faced his horse toward the forest. Turning to Lydia once more, he said, "If this brings you comfort in the meantime, of all your Mama has told you be assured that the God she speaks of is real. And I will be praying for His guidance in this matter."

In moments, he and his horse sped off through the glistening grass blades and vanished beyond the hills toward the forest's edge that used to symbolize the walls of her secluded life—walls that were dissolving like the sun setting behind the mountaintop.

That evening, the knowledge of all that possibly lie beyond the Valley made Lydia feel more alone than ever before. While firelight flickered low, chills and fatigue encompassed her body long after she changed into dry clothes. Though her eyes grew heavy while she rocked in Mama's chair, her thoughts spun faster than Mama's fingers at the loom. A dying ember popped as the fire died, and darkness tried to lull her to sleep.

Delighted and frightened at the prospect that there was more to this world than the Valley, one question kept repeating in her mind.

Mama must know of the world beyond the Valley. So why keep it from me?

FOUR

"Lydia," Mama shouted. She nudged Lydia's shoulder. "Wake up."

"I can't, Mama." Lydia mumbled, trying to pull the blankets up to her neck. A pointless effort since her limbs felt like sacks of wet wool.

Mama pressed her palms against Lydia's cheeks and sighed. "You have fever, honey. Sit still. I'll grab you a dry gown to change into, and then help you to your bed."

Mama shuffled off.

Lydia's thoughts whirled. *I'm not in my bed?* She searched her memory for the last thing she remembered. Images of a man and his horse ran through her mind. She felt queasy and her mouth tasted sour.

"Sit forward a bit. There you go. Oh no—"

"Sorry Mama . . ." Lydia whispered, staring at the blur of contents from her stomach now in a puddle on the floor.

Mama sopped up the mess using the sweat-soaked nightgown. "It's all right honey. It was going into the wash pile anyway. Let's hurry and get this dry gown on you before you catch a chill."

A few moments later, Mama managed to help

Lydia into bed without further incident.

After lying flat for a few moments, the spinning in Lydia's head stopped and she was able to open her eyes.

Mama placed a cool rag on Lydia's forehead. "I know this is cold but we've got to break that fever."

Tears burned into Lydia's already hot cheeks. Her heart raced. How could she act as if nothing had happened while Mama was away?

"Don't cry sweetheart. You must have worked yourself into a fever with all I had for you to do while I was gone. And I missed the thunderstorm by a day. You didn't keep working in the rain, did you?"

How would she avoid telling Mama about meeting a man in the forest? She'd exhausted herself trying to make sense of what he'd told her. Should she believe any of it? Now she was too ill to talk. A blessing, perhaps.

"No . . . I finished before the rain . . . came, but—"

"Shhhh, honey you don't have to talk right now. Rest your eyes. Shhhh." Mama dried Lydia's tears with her fingertips and kissed her cheek.

Closing her eyes, Lydia's thoughts returned to Dylan Prescot. Had their meeting been a dream? During their conversation on the porch, he'd said far more than she could have made up on her own.

Lydia remained in bed while Mama to tended to her every need. Was her sudden illness God's way of protecting them? Although she felt some frustration toward Mama for lying, she wanted to believe it was for a good reason. Mama bathed her with cool rags, changed her bed linens and nightgown, prayed, and sung Psalms at her bedside.

Why would Mama take such care if she'd meant me harm?

The next morning, a cool breeze drifted in through the open window. It reminded Lydia of their first walk that season. She'd seen something in the forest that day. Could it have been that man?

If it was, then why did he speak as if he had never been to their Valley before?

A few days later, the cheerful melody of birds broke through the darkness. Lydia sat up, full of strength and energy. Her eyes adjusted to the early morning light. Everything around her was exactly as it was before Mama left to deliver offerings.

The shadows of oak tree branches sprouting leaf buds fell onto her bedspread, bordered in hazy light. Flames from the fire danced behind the outline of Mama's shadow on the cloth that divided her room from the rest of the house. Lydia lifted her arms, reached toward the ceiling, and arched her back to stretch her shoulders. Inhaling, her mouth watered at the aroma of sizzling bacon, scrambled eggs, and sliced strawberries.

The encounter with a man in the forest and a conversation with him on the porch seemed a distant, muddled memory. Surprised to feel her lips curve into a smile, she shook her head to rid it of uncertain thoughts. *I must have dreamed up the whole event.* She felt foolish thinking that her fantasies led to such a vivid dream.

"Good morning." Lydia approached Mama from behind and wrapped her in a hug. Mama's slender, yet familiar frame diminished any lingering thoughts of uncertainty.

"Good morning." Mama spun around, returning Lydia's embrace. "Well, I think you've made a full recovery. Thank our Father in Heaven. You must be starving. You've hardly consumed more than chicken broth and mint tea for two weeks. I hadn't realized how much you ate until the basket outside overflowed with all the eggs I couldn't eat myself."

She generously filled Lydia's plate with eggs and bacon. "Signs of spring are everywhere, Lydia. I had to clear out spider nests in the strawberry patch yesterday. Flowers are blooming across the Valley and the oak tree is budding." Mama rattled on.

Lydia sat quietly, savoring every bit of her breakfast.

Mama continued. "It's good we have not had another storm with all the laundry I have had to do. The thunderstorm must have been stronger than I thought. It blew the porch quilt clear off into the mud. I wouldn't have seen it, except—"

Lydia inhaled quickly, nearly choking on a piece of bacon. Her face grew hot and her heart raced. *It wasn't a dream.* And it wasn't the storm that caused the blanket to fall behind her on the porch—unless the storm inside her counted.

"Sweetheart, I know you're hungry, but you should take it slow. Here I'm going on and on about all the work I've been doing, and I forgot to pour you some tea."

Lydia cleared her throat. She used the edge of her nightgown sleeve to soak up the tears trying to escape.

During the remainder of breakfast, Mama's voice faded into the background. Echoes of Lydia's illness lasting nearly two weeks put a sense of urgency in her heart. Did she miss the full moon? If she had, would the man, Dylan come back again the next time Mama brought offerings? Would Mama tell her the truth before then?

Did God tell Mama it was time for Lydia's transition? If what Dylan said was true, maybe Mama was trying to make sure Lydia was safe before telling her about the people and the world beyond the Valley walls. The rest of the morning, she listened more intently.

Mama explained how far she'd gotten on the garden and the weeding, the pile of wool that needed spun, and the warmth and sunshine Lydia had missed. Not a word about what happened while she delivered offerings. Normally, Mama would share, especially since she left earlier than usual with the intent to get answers.

By evening, exhaustion took over despite Lydia doing very few chores.

While Lydia drew the last bucket of water from the water pump for an overdue bath, the sky grew dark and thunder rumbled beyond the back edge of the forest.

Fear enveloped Lydia. Her heart raced.

Images of Dylan and his horse galloping through the rain filled her mind. She drew up the water in haste and ran to the shelter of the cabin. By the time she started pouring the water into the cauldron on the stove, her hands shook violently.

"Lydia, what's wrong dear? Are you all right?" Mama took the bucket from Lydia and led her to the rocking chair.

"I'm . . . fine. It's only a thunderstorm. I hadn't noticed the clouds coming in and the thunder startled me."

Mama didn't look convinced. "But you love

thunderstorms. You probably need more rest. You worked hard for the first day back on your feet. You may take a bath before me tonight and go right to sleep."

"What about the spinning, Mama? We'll never have enough done in time for—for the next offering." She stared at the fire, avoiding eye contact with Mama. It felt strange to say those words—a forced lie—and to encourage Mama to continue her own lies.

Mama walked around to the back of the rocking chair and unwove Lydia's braid. She cleared her throat. "The days are getting longer and soon it will be warm and light enough for us to spin on the porch. We'll even have the light of the full moon tomorrow and the next evening."

Nothing about getting answers from God while she was gone. At least the full moon hadn't passed yet.

"Besides, the gardening is complete aside from watering, the sheep are sheared, and we have enough smoked venison to get us by until next moon. You know, it was not too many years ago that I did most of the work around here by myself."

And you have years of experience in skirting around telling me the truth.

Lydia rolled her eyes. "I know, Mama, I know. You used to hoe with me tied onto your back, cook with me clinging to your ankles—" She drew in a deep breath, too tired to press Mama for details about the offering.

Flashes of light and smacks of thunder shook the walls, revealing the storm's fast approach. Lydia's hands started shaking again, but she managed to slip them under her legs before Mama noticed.

Mama poured the hot water from the stove into

the cool water already in the tub. Moments later, Lydia sunk into the warm water. She draped loose hair over the backside of the tub. The flames of the fire danced with the sounds of the storm. She really did meet a man in the forest that early spring evening. He told her there was more to this world than the Valley she lived and worked all her life. He said he was coming back to tell her more. She and Mama were not the only people. The reality of it hit her like an ax splitting a brittle log. Had he seen the desperation in her face? Had he seen that she wanted to know the truth, even if it hurt?

Lydia closed her eyes and pressed a soaked muslin cloth along her neck. Warm water drizzled down her back. Rain pelted the rooftop in bursts that muffled out the crackling fire. Lydia imagined herself back on the porch, face to face with Dylan. This time she felt warm and didn't shake with fear. Dylan stood beside his horse, the storm drifting away behind him. Fat drops of water fell from the porch overhang and splashed into the muddy stream flowing along the sunken earth surrounding the cabin. He didn't seem dangerous—even if his presence made a place inside her flutter like a hummingbird's wings. Surely, Mama wasn't keeping her away from him.

Lydia decided to wait for Mama to come around in her own time, believing she had reasons for keeping the outside world a secret. In the meantime, Lydia knew she was betraying her mother to find answers on her own.

The next night, at Lydia's request, Mama told one of her stories. Searching for new meaning, Lydia pondered the truth behind these people, the Israelites.

". . . and Joshua led the Israelites into the Promised Land, following the Lord's instructions and how to distribute land between the tribes. God promised Joshua that he would be there wherever Joshua went. God commanded Joshua to be strong and courageous, even during times of doubt." Mama sighed, concentrating intently on her needlework.

Did Mama even hear herself speaking?

Lydia carefully laid her dress aside, noting the placement of her needle in the seam of the wristband, and then stood to tend the fire. She piled on another log and blew a few long breaths into the hot coals. The flames arched over the top and crackled as they devoured the dry bark.

She recalled the last time Mama told her the story of Joshua, and the last time she asked Mama about men.

"But why does God always tell you stories about men?" Lydia was twelve and beginning to wonder more about the "why" of their solitary existence.

"To help us understand why he created the Valley without them. They're not needed here. We have God himself, and without war and greed, we need no man to rescue us."

Lydia wouldn't mind a war if it gave her the thrill of being rescued. Still, she kept her thoughts to herself and sighed. Clearly, God's purpose was different for Mama and her, or so she thought at the time.

Back then, Lydia's questions didn't seem to matter at all. Now, her curiosity felt like a prompting in her heart that knew there was something beyond the life they lived of tending the land and sewing dresses for angels. All the stories Mama told seemed real. Lydia couldn't explain how, but deep inside, she knew there was something beyond the forest. Maybe it was evil, and the only safe place was here. If that were so, how had Mama brought offerings year after year and always returned safely?

Before encountering Dylan, Lydia imagined the Israelites still lived and that they lived nearby. Yet, for some reason, their Promised Land was out of reach. During those first moments in the forest, she assumed she was right when she asked Dylan if he was an Israelite. Though he was not one of them, he knew of their stories.

Somehow, Mama had come to know of these same stories. But how?

Lydia stared at Mama, trying to make sense of her possible motives.

As if Mama could read Lydia's thoughts, she suddenly perked up from her sewing and met Lydia's gaze.

"Lydia," Mama sang with a small smile and raised eyebrows. "Isn't it great that we don't have to endure the hardships that Joshua and his people did?"

"Yes, Mama."

"Aren't you grateful for all we have . . . food, warmth, clothing, and the comfort of God's Spirit with us wherever we are here in the Valley?"

"Yes, Mama."

"Don't you feel safe each evening as we say our prayers and fall asleep to the sounds of whispering trees and chirping insects, without the threat of war, famine, or enemy attack?"

"Yes, Mama."

With each question, Lydia's answers grew louder and she fought back tears. She knew what Mama was getting at.

Contentment.

Why couldn't Lydia be content with her life? Why was it that Lydia wanted answers to everything? She had grown tired of fighting it. She had grown weary of battling the voice inside that wanted more to life. She had long given up her desire for wars, famine, and enemies to experience something new and different.

Now, with the prospect of her desires becoming a reality, Mama was still trying to keep her here, keep her from experiencing anything outside of their solitary life. Did she hope Lydia would still choose this life after discovering the truth?

Lydia rinsed the soot off her hands in the basin. Slowly, silently, she dried them on her apron, and avoided Mama's eyes by focusing on the fire.

Realizing the moon would be rising soon, Lydia shifted her gaze to Mama. "You look as tired as I am." That was the truth. She retrieved the needle and thread from Mama's swollen fingers. "You don't usually have to work so much after coming back from delivering offerings. Let's save our strength, get a solid night's rest, and plan on finishing our sewing in the moonlight on the porch tomorrow."

Mama nodded and cooperated without protest.

Surprised at Mama's willingness to agree with her plan, Lydia didn't hesitate to finish the evening tasks. The moon poured gray-blue light across the Valley while she gathered logs for the morning fire. *How soon will Dylan be there waiting for me?* Her insides went hollow at the thought of seeing him again, alone, with the night air surrounding them.

Her thoughts churned.

Did he find anything about Mama? What sort of a man was Dylan? Was he anything like Joshua or Samson? Did he really believe in and serve the same God they did? If so, why would God permit Mama to raise her alone?

FIVE

Lydia brought the wood inside. Mama went to her room to say prayers. Then Lydia made sure the cabin was in order so Mama wouldn't find a reason to leave her bed. She stayed in the kitchen long enough to make Mama believe she secured the door with the wooden plank. Leaving it up would ensure Lydia didn't make too much noise when she left.

"Dear Father in Heaven," Lydia whispered at her bedside a few minutes later. "I don't know what will come from this evening, but I pray for your protection over me and Mama. Please, Lord, help me to find the truth, and help Mama to forgive me for trying to find it without her. Lord, I pray that you are still real in some way because right now the only hope I have is in what I cannot see. Amen."

She wanted to pray on and on but feared Mama would hear her whispers and awaken. She kept praying in her heart as she removed her nightgown and stuffed it next to the wool blanket rolled under the quilt on her bed. She slid on her dress and apron, and then slipped her fingers into the tops of her boots she'd put on after she stepped off the porch.

She listened at the foot of the doorway for Mama's slow, deep breathing. Lydia stood there for several breaths, making sure Mama slept deeply enough to ignore any commotion as she left the cabin. Avoiding the creaking floorboards, she tiptoed along the wall to the door and opened it enough to slip her body through.

She dashed across the moonlit valley, past small hills of grazed grasses and the sweet scent of poppies and lupine lingering above the gray quilted pattern of their closed blossoms. The still night air was refreshing and cool.

The overgrown path Lydia followed was where she and Mama used to ride their horses. Lydia had loved taking the horses on an evening trot after they'd worked hard pulling the plow or hauling firewood all day. She also savored the freedom of riding Jasper, the wind brushing her face and dancing with her hair. She guessed he would prefer to gallop at full speed, without her weight or the confines of a harness holding him back. Nevertheless, Mama said horses didn't have the self-control people did. They would surely wander into the forbidden forest, unknowingly entering their doom. Now, Lydia doubted truth existed in any part of Mama's explanation.

Maybe Mama told her the horses had died to frighten her. Considering that the horses possibly faced another fate, Lydia recalled more details from that day as she slowed to a walk and approached the pond and the edge of the forest. Perhaps Mama had revealed some hint of the truth.

Would Dylan know about the horses and what happened to them? Did they really run away, or did Mama get rid of them willingly?

When Lydia reached the side of the pond where

the cattails grew tallest, Dylan wasn't there yet. Her heart sunk and she wondered if he would still come. She plucked a few blossoms from a honeysuckle bush and sucked out the sweet nectar. She peered into the forest and listened for a hint of the sounds of a horse, but all she heard was a chorus of chirping and buzzing nighttime insects.

The sounds reminded her about the first time she had seen a cricket. It was also the first time she remembered Mama warning her about the forest.

It was the first walk Lydia remembered, long before she was old enough to ride a horse. The midsummer air hung low, wrapping her in heat. Lydia crept along the sides of the pond, finding relief in the cool shadows of the cattails, which had towered above her six-year-old head.

"Not too close to the edge, Lydia," Mama had warned. "The pond is for the fish and the geese, not for young ladies—"

"Mama, what's that? What's that?" Lydia shrieked, pointing to some grass blades sprouting from a large rock. Among them, a small, black insect glistened in the orange sunlight.

"Why, that's a cricket. Do you recall the chirping songs you often hear at your window after dark? This cricket is the maker of those songs. I haven't seen one in years. If you sit quiet and still, you might be able to watch it play a tune."

The discovery had nearly caused her heart to burst. Lydia wanted to take the cricket back to her bedroom. She had wanted to construct a small house for it out of pieces of bark from the oak tree.

In her eagerness, she had charged toward the cricket—ignoring Mama's suggestion to observe the creature where it sat—and scuffed her palms and wrists on the edge of the rock.

The cricket sprang from her reach.

Lydia picked herself up and chased after the creature without looking back.

"No, Lydia!" Mama called from behind her.

Lydia held her hands cupped in front of her to ensure a quick retrieval. The cricket stayed several paces ahead of her efforts. She lost sight of it as it jumped into the darkness between tree trunks.

Before she ventured further, Mama grabbed her by the underarms and spun her around, a look of horror across her face.

"What are you doing?" Mama shouted. "You could have been . . . you could have been . . . killed!"

"The cricket could kill me? I didn't think anything could kill us in the Valley." Tears stung Lydia's eyes. Her chest tightened. Mama never raised her voice.

"Oh no, you must never go into the . . . the . . . forbidden forest." Mama pulled her away from the shadows and onto the path that still glowed with fading rays of sunlight.

"Why, Mama?" Uninhibited tears streamed down her cheeks.

"I'm sorry I didn't tell you before. You've always stayed right by my side, so I didn't feel the need." Wiping Lydia's tears with her apron, Mama showered her damp cheeks with kisses. Then she grasped Lydia's hand in hers and started back to the cabin. "I'll explain everything on the way home."

All those years ago, Lydia listened carefully. Mama told her that beyond the forbidden forest lie the edge of the Valley—the edge of their world. There were creatures that lived in the forest, harmful creatures that God created to instill enough fear that neither she nor Mama would ever wander far enough in to fall off the edge.

Before that day, Lydia had not thought much of the forest surrounding the Valley. When she watched the sun rising from the garden, her six-year-old mind only saw the treetops climbing up toward the horizon on all sides. She never considered what did or did not lie beyond what she could see. Back then, she had lived her life moment by moment. She never considered her future beyond completing chores and her special times with Mama.

Over time, the comfort and satisfaction Lydia had known up until then started to fade. After a while, she realized that every time she asked, *why*, the answer would always produce another question. "Why would God make a place so dangerous?" "Why does there have to be an edge of the Valley?"

Mama's answers were always vague.

Lydia learned that when Mama was finished answering questions she would say, "God's ways are not our ways."

Instead of asking another question, Lydia learned to reply with the response Mama expected. ". . .Because we were made to live and work in the Valley."

For the ten springs that had passed since, they played out this ritual. Soon, it meant nothing more to Lydia than any other methodical task required of their life in the Valley.

Now, as Lydia sat waiting for this man called Dylan to bring her answers, the holes in Mama's feeble explanations seemed larger than ever. Would he finally reveal the truth she longed to hear?

On the other hand, would Mama's warnings prove true, even if she cloaked them in lies? Would he bring pain with uncovering the truth?

Just then, the insects hushed under clicking

hooves and a deep voice penetrating the darkness.

As soon as his horse trotted into the moonlight, he got down and connected the horse to a low oak tree branch behind the cattails. His smile grew the closer he came to Lydia. He held a strange object.

Lydia stood. What could she do or say as he approached?

"I'm glad to see you made it safely, Miss Lydia." He removed his hat and nodded his head. Then he handed her the object.

She slowly reached out her hand. She tried to keep her fingers from shaking while she touched the top of it.

Lydia jerked back her hand. "It's cold."

"It's all right, Miss Lydia. Take it." He pushed the object forward until she took it from his hand.

It was hard and round. Part of it glowed in the moonlight.

"It's an apple from one of the trees on our property. Haven't you seen an apple before?"

"*Anapple*? What is it for?" Lydia stepped back, wanting a little more information.

Dylan laughed and revealed dimples bordering straight, white teeth. "It's for eating. It will make a nice snack. But first, I want to show you something."

He held out his hand toward the apple. "May I?"

She returned the apple to his open palm.

He stepped beside her and his arm brushed across her shoulder. He held the apple up and placed his thumb over part of it.

"See this spot here, the lighter patch about the size of my thumb?"

Lydia nodded, leaning closer to the apple and to Dylan.

"It's not exactly proportionate, but this spot is

close to the size of the United States of America, the country where we live. The rest of the apple is like miniature version of the planet Earth, where all of creation resides."

She did not understand.

"Miss Lydia, I am sure it will be difficult for you to fully grasp everything until I can bring you some photographs. However, I wanted to give you an idea of how much larger our world is than this valley."

Unable to voice a response, Lydia hoped he would continue to explain.

He twisted the small brown stick on the top of the apple until it came off. Figs were the closest thing to this apple that Lydia could think of, but they were smaller, softer, and oblong.

"The tip of this stem is about the size of French Corral, Bridgeport, and the land and other towns of Nevada County, the part of the state of California where we live." He pressed the stem into the apple, making an indentation. Then he took his thumbnail and outlined a crescent shape around it.

"That would be the state of California. So, we have the world," he held the apple in his palm.

. . . the country of the United States." He pointed to the light patch.

. . . the state of California—the Nevada County area, for the mark of the stem here and finally, French Corral, which is only a speck of a town compared to the larger cities of Grass Valley and Nevada City. They lie about a one-day journey on horseback from here."

Lydia closed her eyes and pulled her hands to her face. Her mind spun trying to understand it all. The life Mama and she lived here in the Valley used to seem so important and big. Even with hearing all the stories about the Israelites, Lydia never felt as small as she did in that moment. She didn't comprehend all he said, but one thing was clear—the world that Lydia knew was just a speck.

As valuable as Mama made their lives seem all these years, there was a whole world managing an existence without them.

"Miss Lydia, perhaps you should sit down for a moment." Dylan stepped over, pulled a blanket off Bailey, and laid it down on the patch of grass behind where Lydia stood. Then he gently guided Lydia to a sitting position. After handing her a handkerchief to wipe her tears, he sat down in the grass across from her and waited without a word.

She shook her head, trying to hold back the sobs. "I—I have so many questions—I don't know which to ask first." She opened the sopping handkerchief. "Like this hanky. I know what this is even if it does have a different pattern on it than what we embroider on ours. Why would Mama let me know about a handkerchief and not an apple? Why would she let me know anything if she wanted me to be here my whole life?"

She sniffled and wiped her nose. "And how did she keep others like you from coming here until now?"

He set the apple on the blanket between their crossed ankles. "I can see you're overwhelmed and with good reason. It will take more than a single evening to answer all your questions. However, I can provide some general answers."

"You can?" Lydia sighed deeply, blew her nose once again, and wiped her eyes with the dry corners of the handkerchief.

"Yes, about this land. In these parts, men and women respect private property. The Sinclair family once owned this valley, and much of the forest surrounding it. I'm still looking into how it all happened, but at some point in the last twenty years, your mama came into possession of this land. There are 'No trespassing' signs surrounding all entrances, and most men, including what Indians remain in these parts, respect those signs as a warning. See, venturing on to someone else's property gives the owner a right to take whatever means necessary to scare or even hurt the person trespassing."

She didn't know what he meant by signs, but if other people saw them and stayed away, why didn't he? "But you—"

"Yes, I ignored the signs. Sometimes my curiosity gets me into trouble and you have no idea how relieved I was when I saw you, an unarmed woman."

"Unarmed woman?"

"Sorry, Miss Lydia. . . uh. . . unarmed means without a shotgun. Have you or your mama ever had use for guns, such as to defend yourself against wild animals?"

"No, I have never heard of guns. Mama and I set traps and dig holes around the backside of the barn and sheep pen. We always store our food on the rafters in the barn. During the past few years there has only been one or two times a bear wandered through here, and Mama said it was best for us to lock ourselves in the cabin until it passed through."

Lydia tucked the handkerchief into her apron pocket and reached for the apple as if holding it would somehow bring revelation. A cool breeze whisked through the cattails. The moonlight disappeared behind a cloud. They sat silent in the darkness for a few moments.

When the cloud moved again, Dylan stood and reached for Lydia's hand to pull her up. For an instant, he pulled her close enough that Lydia felt the warmth emanating from his chest. He stepped back and released her hand. She looked up to search his eyes, but with the moonlight behind him. Shadows cloaked his face.

"Well, Miss Lydia, we should get going before your mama wakes up and finds you gone. I am sorry I could not find out more. It would be difficult for me to explain why, but there might be a chance that your mama kept your existence a secret to protect you from the Sinclair family. There is no record of your birth in the town records."

"Sinclair . . . family?" She gritted her teeth, wishing she didn't have to ask. How else would she understand?

"Sinclair is the surname, like my surname is Prescot." He grabbed the blanket off the grass. "It's a way of identifying the people that belong to a family. Rather like . . . the Israelites. Explaining modern day families will take a whole night on its own." His laugh sounded constrained. "We must meet again. As soon as I find out anything more, I'll leave a sign—I'll leave an apple, here in the cattails."

Her stomach sunk at the thought of sneaking out again, but her heart longed to know more about the world beyond the forest walls, and once she had the courage to ask—more about this man standing before her. "But a raccoon or squirrel could take it before I find it."

"True," he said. "And we also don't want your mother to find it first. What if I put the apple under this rock here?" He patted a rock about the size of a milk bucket. It lay nestled halfway between the edge of the pond and the worn, grassy path Mama and she used to ride their horses along. He tugged on the rock several times before it lost its grip on the earth. He proceeded to dig a small hole, and then replaced the rock.

"There. This way, neither animals nor your mother will know to look but it should be loose enough for you to lift it easily. When you find the apple, we can meet the next time your mother comes to French Corral. She usually stays the night at the Inn. How long before she leaves again?" He pulled his shoulders back, resting his fists on his hips.

"She usually goes once a season, so in a few weeks, when signs of summer begin to show and we have spun enough wool and jarred enough jam for offering. This last time she was supposed to petition for my transition. She was going to ask God if it was time for me to bring offerings. Although, she hasn't said a word about it since she returned. I grew ill the evening after you left, so we have not had time to talk about it."

Dylan wrinkled his forehead and pressed his lips together. "Ill? I'm sorry to hear that. In my eagerness to share my side of things, I failed to ask you about how things have gone." He sighed and folded the blanket, then draped it over Bailey's rump. "It sounds like she is in the process of finding a way to explain things to you soon. I'll see if she spoke to anyone aside from the usual folks and go from there. In the meantime, how do you feel about continuing to keep our meeting a secret?"

There went those butterflies in her belly again. A part of her felt satisfaction in being the one keeping the secrets for once. Another part was afraid that if Mama found out, she would make sure Lydia never saw Dylan again. After all, Dylan promised to find answers while Mama created more questions.

"I'm not sure how I feel about any of this. However, I am more uncertain of Mama's reaction in knowing." Lydia twisted the end of her braid with her free hand and held the apple tightly in the other. "Maybe there is a way I can get her to tell me the truth without revealing what I know."

"God willing, that would make things easier for us all." He untied the knot connected Bailey to the tree branch. "But no matter, I have sent word to the city to find out more about how the Sinclair family fits into all of this."

"Dylan?" Her voice cracked as she fought tears.

"Yes?" Dylan mounted the horse.

"Thank you. Thank you for helping me."

"You are very welcome," he said, dimples and teeth soaking up the moonlight. "I only pray that once we find the answers we are searching for, that both of you can find peace in the truth. For now, I really must go. Eat that apple. I think you will enjoy it." With the tip of his hat, he disappeared into the forest before she could say good-bye.

Lydia held the apple in her hands, pondering all that had transpired.

How could she take a bite of something so hard?

Finally, she pressed her teeth into the part where Dylan had marked it with the stem.

Hot tears flowed.

She hoped the sweet and crunchy taste of this apple was a sign that though learning the truth might be hard, the answers would lead to a sweet future.

SIX

Lydia's curiosity of the world beyond the Valley blossomed along with the spring. Mornings held a fresh fragrance in the cool air that promised a warmer day ahead. Lydia kept busy with various outdoor tasks. Mama stayed indoors, spinning wool, mending stockings, and dresses, or preparing food. This allowed plenty of time apart from Mama and relief since Lydia couldn't decide how to ask Mama any questions without revealing her encounters with Dylan.

What was this world like beyond the forest? If Mama was trading their goods for the things with people and not angels, did other people make the things she brought home from offerings?

Lydia spent hours examining the items she had used without thought or question for most of her life. The spoon she ate from, the spade she weeded with, the nails that held the sheep pen's logs together. If the angels didn't make them, then somewhere another person made these things. How did they form each spoon to the exact same size and shape? Where did they get the hard metal? How did they shape it? What tools did they use? How did they make it smooth and shiny?

She pondered fixtures too, such as her bedroom window. Smooth, hard, and clear, it seemed sturdy. Yet, the bottles in the kitchen that contained their salt and lard, which were also glass, would easily break if not handled carefully. How was it that the window was flat and the bottles were round? What were those raised markings of lines, ovals, and squares? Did they represent the person who created them? Were they simply decorative? Although the weeks went by quickly, they could not come fast enough. Would Dylan be able to answer all her questions?

Mama also seemed consumed in her own thoughts, and rarely prompted a conversation beyond comments about their tasks. Did her silence mean she knew something happened while she was gone? Mama worked more slowly than ever. She no longer masked a wince while she carried in logs or lifted a large pot of water onto the stove. Yet, she never complained. She pretended as if she were as capable of doing her work in the same manner she had since Lydia was a small girl.

Lydia could not recall a dryer spring in all her life. The days and nights grew steadily warmer. Soon the bright green grasses surrounding the barn and pond dried up and turned a dirty shade of yellow. The second storm during the evening of her recovery had provided the most rainfall of the season. There had been only a few more days of light showers since. Forced to give up nearly all the well water for the animals and the garden, they had little left for cooking, and none for their monthly baths.

Even the pond water receded, leaving a muddy ring of moss and rock between the murky water and crispy cattails. Lydia checked beneath the rock whenever she could without Mama noticing, but there was never a sign of the apple Dylan promised to leave there.

"I must deliver offerings before summer begins," Mama declared over frog croaks and cricket chirps. They were sitting on the porch, trying to stay cool while using the last of the daylight to complete their evening sewing. "I know I usually only go once per season, but we have plenty of goods for the offering. Perhaps if my prayers are fervent enough, God will send us one last rainstorm to wet the garden and fill the well before summer."

Lydia's heart began to pound. Her palms grew moist in anticipation of Dylan's promise. He said he would return once he knew Mama was in town. He had not left the apple to signal he had more information.

Would he still meet me?

Although uncertain of how his findings would alter her future, she held onto the promise of his return—the promise of truth she hoped would set her free. It took everything within her to swallow the lump in her throat, and to keep her hands still in response to Mama's announcement.

"Of course. I've been thinking that you should go early as well." Lydia couldn't believe the words spilled so easily from her mouth. *Now I'm making things up.* "Rather, I was thinking we should pray and ask God to bring us rain. I cannot remember such a dry spring."

Mama shot up from the bench and smoothed out the wrinkles in her skirt. "Well, then, I guess it's settled. I thought you might be apprehensive for me to leave again so soon. I'm sure God is impressed with your hard work the past few weeks.

I will insist you are now ready for your transition." She spoke in haste and then disappeared into the house before Lydia could even respond.

Did those words hint that Mama would confess all upon her return?

Lydia closed her eyes and offered a silent prayer. *Please, let it be that Mama will tell me the truth first. Please, let this be a sign that she knows she cannot keep me secluded here any longer. Please, God, help me not to be angry with her, for I can't deny this knowledge inside of me that she does not mean me any harm . . . that somehow she believes she is doing what is best for both of us.*

Daylight faded into blues and purples. In silence, Lydia and Mama prepared themselves for bed.

Mind swirling, palms sweating, and heart thumping—sleep eventually took Lydia into restless dreams full of strange places and people she had never seen. Morning came too soon. She forced herself to forget about the images in her head. She must help Mama pack up the cart with offerings and the supplies she would need for her journey.

With the warm and dry morning air, Lydia insisted that Mama take an extra jar of water. When Mama protested, Lydia said she would be fine drinking the juice from crushed tomatoes or cantaloupe to quench her thirst.

Before the sun rose enough to shed more heat onto the Valley floor, Mama and the cart vanished beyond the small clearing of trees.

For many years, Lydia envisioned the clearing led to a path surrounded by angels, a path forbidden for her to enter. That morning, a new vision of a wide clearing opening to a vast valley dotted with dozens of cabins much like their own, filled her mind. She envied the freedom Mama had to come and go. Even though nothing but her own will now kept her there, Lydia still felt chained within the forest walls.

Although anxious to learn of the world outside, fear overcame her. Mama had taught her how to survive here and nowhere else. Was there any truth to what she'd said about the dangers and hurtful people God had never allowed in the Valley?

Will it be difficult to speak and act with other people? When Dylan returns, will he still want to help me? What has he learned of Mama and her life here? What if his findings endanger us all?

Her concerns moved aside when she turned to face the barn.

Thin gray clouds rose above the tops of the trees in the distance. At first, Lydia's heart leaped at the prospect of rain clouds. Then, she realized what she saw were fine pillars of smoke. Mama once warned that a forest fire could burn their home in the Valley.

As a precaution, each summer, they would make a clearing around the barn and cabin, burn rotten wood and grass clippings in the fireplace, and carefully dispose of hot ashes in a pit of water.

If this smoke were a concern, Mama would return right away . . . wouldn't she?

Unable to do anything about it, Lydia busied herself with chores until the heat forced her inside the muggy cabin walls. The clouds of smoke beyond the treetops grew thicker. As the day progressed, the sky became hazy, like early morning. Wherever Mama was, either she didn't know of the smoke, or she didn't realize Lydia could see it from here.

Lydia ate the last of the strawberries and cream for supper, and then pulled out a summer dress that needed mending from the sewing basket. She wished she could do something about her soiled hands and fingernails. Wiping her forehead with her apron, a layer of dirt and sweat clung to it. She felt uncomfortable about Dylan seeing her in such a filthy state. She could soak a muslin cloth in the pond and try to clean up, but then she would smell like pond water. How did other people stay clean while water was scarce?

She worked by the light of the window, occasionally glancing out at the pond in search of Dylan and his horse. Though she assumed he would not return until after sunset, she hoped that he would arrive sooner.

Caught up in her thoughts and sorting the images from her dreams earlier in the week, her senses perked at the sudden intense odor of smoke—much stronger than what came from their stove. It seemed like only moments had passed since she last glanced outside, yet a banner of smoke now blocked her view of the pond. She could not even see the forest's edge past the clouds hovering above the grassy plain.

A moment later, billows of smoke broke away to reveal Dylan galloping on his horse straight toward the cabin. Again, Lydia's heart nearly flew from her chest.

She dropped her sewing and ran directly toward him.

Within seconds and without words, the two met.

Dylan pulled Lydia onto the horse and into his lap.

He snapped the reins, jerking the horse in a direction opposite the cabin and the smoke-enveloped forest.

Lydia squeezed her eyes shut. She buried her face into the comforting and firm confines of Dylan's chest.

It seemed an eternity before he finally stopped. Lydia looked around her with hesitation. Her arms and legs stung from the scratches of tree branches. Her eyes burned from the smoke still floating around them. They were in a clearing on a wide path of worn grass.

"We must try to find your mama before she heads back home."

The panic in Dylan's voice jolted Lydia. "But how?"

"Can you think of anything she might have said about her journey? She must take another way aside from the main road ahead since I didn't see her on my way."

"No, I have never . . . I don't know—" she gagged and coughed. Her mouth and throat burned as if she'd swallowed a cup of ashes from the fireplace. "Mama said she went through the forest, and up the mountain." She did not know if her description of the path Mama took was even accurate.

"Then back through the forest it is," he said and urged Bailey on. "This fire moved much faster than we thought it would. I'd hardly heard the news that Emelyn was in town when I saw the smoke in the direction of your property. The fire's heading around the mountain, and away from French Corral." He yelled over pounding horse hooves and thrashing branches.

Tears sprung from Lydia's eyes at the reality of his words.

Mama is in danger. She will try to rescue me. She will come back home when she knows the fire is on its way. She will have to tell me everything. And she's weak, possibly ill. What if she injures herself trying to come back? Oh, why Mama? Why didn't you tell me more? All these years you have tried to protect me and take care of me, and now you need me to help you and I don't know how. God—

"We'll find her, Lydia, don't you worry." He must have felt her tears soaking into his shirt, her shaking sobs as she clung to his waist.

The smoke grew thicker. She could taste it mixing into her tears.

When they both began to cough violently, Dylan turned Bailey back around. Then, thundering horse hooves surrounded them.

"Jack, Benjamin, any sign of Emelyn?" Dylan shouted.

Lydia looked up to see four other men on horses and pulling them to a stop.

"No sign." One of the men answered Dylan. A red and white cloth wrapped around his mouth and nose. "The smoke is getting too heavy now...the flames are making the heat unbearable." He handed Dylan two similar-looking cloths.

The men continued to discuss options. Dylan tied one handkerchief around his nose and mouth, and then tied one on Lydia's face.

She inhaled deeply, grateful that the cloth filtered out most of the smoke.

"Take the girl into town," one of the men said. "We'll keep searching. Meet us at Wells Fargo in half an hour." Then, he and the other men took off on their horses into the smoke-filled forest.

Dylan guided Bailey on the wide, dirt path, away from the forest and the smoke.

Lydia felt like she was in a dream, caught up in one of the stories Mama used to tell her. Yet, she knew this was not a dream. Instead of feelings of excitement and the fluttering in her heart she had imagined, she felt paralyzed.

The thought of living without Mama terrified

her.

The prospect of never seeing her home in the Valley again frightened her.

Were all the horrible things Mama had tried to protect her from happening at once?

SEVEN

Dylan slowed the horse to a trot. Lydia's insides might as well have been the center of a butter churn. The ground changed from a path of dried and flattened grass into a wide clearing of pale brown dirt and gray rocks, bordered with pine trees and manzanita bushes. Bailey stirred up clouds of dusty earth, which coated the smoke lining Lydia's nose and throat. The sun beat down on her head and back, feeling more intense the further they moved onto open terrain. She loosened her grip around Dylan's waist enough to see beyond the front of the horse's lurching head.

A red building with green doors spanning porch to roof stood at the bend. An odd black board with crossed and curved white lines spread along the roof's shingles above the porch awning. The road curved at the building, and after rounding the corner dozens more buildings came into view. Each one had a pale gray roof, all varied in height with different types of windows and doors. Behind those building were more rolling hills, filled with grazing sheep and cows, as well as other buildings. Some looked like their cabin. Others had white walls, instead of wooden ones. Several barns and stables dotted each plot of land.

Did people really live this close to one another with such a vast amount of land untouched?

People—varying as much as the buildings did in size, shape, and coverings—strode in and out of buildings. Others rode on carts covered with canopies and pulled by horses. They all appeared to be men, wearing thick two-legged stockings tucked into pointed, knee-high boots like Dylan's attire. The brown wide-brimmed hats and long-sleeved shirts they wore seemed awfully heavy and hot. Some of the men tipped their hats, while others stared as Dylan guided Bailey slowly past.

Shocked by the strange sights and number of people, Lydia avoided eye contact until she caught sight of a woman sitting in a rocking chair on a porch. The woman rocked with ease. Her dress spilled onto the wooden floorboards, flowing in several layers of green and white fabric. Her white and green bonnet matched the exact color of her dress. Though she sat in the shade, she fanned her pale, glistening face furiously with a thin, flat board.

Dylan pulled the horse to a stop. More people stopped their tasks and looked up at Dylan and Lydia. One of the men who had been unloading a cart rushed over and offered his hand to Lydia. She looked at Dylan, unsure of what to do. He turned to her, nodded and he removed the cloth from her face, careful not to disturb the layer of dust and ash threatening to fly into her eyes.

"Go ahead, Lydia. This is Jason Roberts. We call him Mr. Roberts. He'll bring you to his wife across the way. They run the general store and do most of the trading of goods with your mama. I'm heading back down the mountain to help the other men try

Beyond the Valley

and find your mother before the fire spreads."

Believing she had no choice but to comply, Lydia followed his instructions. Mr. Roberts' hand was hard and rough, but firm and comforting as he lifted her down from the horse. Once she was down, he gripped his waist, and turned out his elbow.

He pinched the front of his hat with his other hand and nodded. "Miss Lydia."

Confused by his gesture, she stood still, staring at his arm. After a moment, he took her hand and placed it inside his elbow. Lydia wasn't sure if it was the sun's heat or all the eyes burning with curiosity that caused her face to burn with each speechless step.

They walked toward the woman rocking on the porch. She stood, brushed down her skirts, and clasped her hands together.

There was some relief from the heat beneath the covered porch. In seconds, Lydia's vision adjusted to the shadows and she was able to observe the full beauty of the only other woman she had ever seen besides Mama.

The woman's smooth face paled against sky-blue eyes, and berry-red lips. She smelled of primrose blossoms. Ringlets of pale blond hair fell evenly above her eyebrows and tapered in a frame around her face. The rest of her hair swept up beneath her bonnet.

"Welcome to French Corral, Miss Lydia!"

The woman's voice was almost sweeter than her scent—like the melody robins sang each morning.

The woman took Lydia's hands in hers, squeezing them before she pulled Lydia into a welcoming hug. "You may call me Clara, though most everyone around here refers to me as Mrs.

Roberts." She pulled a thin white handkerchief from the fabric belt around her waist, and gently wiped the tears from Lydia's cheeks.

Lydia stood still, unable to speak through the burning in her throat. What would she say even if she could?

Clara didn't seem bothered by her lack of response as she led Lydia inside.

A mixture of strange and familiar aromas bombarded Lydia. Tables and shelves of various sizes contained dozens of items from rolls of fabric to jars of powder and dried herbs. Most of the other items Lydia could not begin to describe. Some were familiar, such as sacks of salt piled under the window, and balls of spun wool that looked identical to the ones her and Mama spun for their offering each season. Was this a storage building of some kind?

"I'm going to grab a few things for you to use once you get settled into your room at the Inn. Mrs. O'Shea already prepared a room for you and your mama. Let's see, you'll need a fresh bar of lye and some talc and . . ." Clara filled a basket with several more items, naming each one and showing it to Lydia as if she had never seen any of them.

Grateful at Clara's efforts to explain everything, Lydia was also relieved that she recognized most of the items. Mama had at least allowed her to become familiar with some of the things other people used. Then her thoughts paused.

How selfish am I? Mama is probably searching for me in the smoke and flames and I'm focused on the fact Clara also uses lye soap.

At that thought, fear flooded her mind. The new sights surrounding her seemed distant and insignificant. "My mama . . ." Lydia choked and pulled her hand away from Clara's grasp.

She pressed bare feet firmly into the floor.

"Don't worry about your mama, now, sweetheart. Half the men in town are searching for her." Clara grabbed Lydia's hand again and took her out the door and into another building.

Clara guided Lydia to sit at a small round table covered with a cloth of blue and white squares. She introduced her to another woman who poured her a cup of tea and took a seat. Mrs. O'Shea stood shorter than Clara did and had dark-brown hair streaked with white.

What will Mama think when she arrives at the cabin and can't find me?

Clara gently unraveled Lydia's knotted braid, then she brushed her hair carefully, and pinned it up in a bun.

If the fire burs up the cabin, will Mama think I perished in the blaze?

A girl about Lydia's age smiled softly and placed a plate of steaming food in front of Lydia. She had dark, smooth skin, black-brown eyes and even darker hair tied back in a single, thick braid, which ran down the center of her back. Lydia couldn't help but stare at the contrast in their skin tones. She had no idea other people could look as varied as a field of wildflowers.

"Dylan just told us this morning that he met you at the end of winter," Mrs. O'Shea said. "When the signs of the fire crept over the hills, he realized he had to tell us that someone other than Ms. Emelyn lived on the mountain."

Clara took a seat at the table. "Ms. Emelyn never hinted she had a young lady living with her. How long have you lived with her?"

Lydia remained silent.

Mrs. O'Shea nodded at the dark-skinned girl, waved her on and then faced Clara. "The circumstances are complicated, Clara. Dylan informed me that Lydia has not been beyond the Sinclair property lines until today."

Clara rested her fists under her chin and leaned into the tablecloth. "Did your mama ever mention who your father was?"

"Shush, Clara! Don't you think she is in enough turmoil with the fire and being brought to French Corral? You should not be bringing up such private matters." Mrs. O'Shea shook her head and turned to Lydia. "You'll soon find Clara is our town gossip. Don't mind her."

Lydia sat there, slowly eating, with no clue how to respond. These two women didn't seem to know much more than Lydia did about her mama. Yet, their conversation made her consider things she never thought of before. She recalled stories about the Israelites—how men and women married and how God blessed them with children. Had Mama been married in this way? Had Lydia been a blessing to Mama and a man? If she did have a father at one time, where was he now?

Despite Mrs. O'Shea and Clara's efforts, Lydia felt even more helpless than in the isolation of the Valley. Hundreds of questions filled her head, but she couldn't utter a single word. By the time, she finished her food, the conversation shifted to other people in town. They stopped discussing Lydia or Mama.

"You know Jack is the best rider in the county," Clara said.

"And Dan knows every inch of the woods that is not private land," added Mrs. O'Shea. "I am sure he will have no trouble locating your mama's path to your property. He's familiar with the terrain from the north fork of the river down to Bridgeport."

Only part of what they said made any sense. Instead, Lydia focused on Mama's survival. She couldn't recall the threat of fire to the Valley before. Had Mama ever faced a fire?

Did she go back to rescue me? Are her fears of me knowing the outside world great enough that she would be willing for us both to perish? Will Mama come back to town, or will she head into the burning mountains, making it more difficult for the men to find her? What if they can't find her?

Lydia no longer cared about knowing why they lived apart from other people for so long. She only cared about hearing Mama's voice, feeling the comfort of Mama's arms around her.

She had to believe Mama would be okay.

She imagined their life would go on as usual, with the exception that Lydia would join her as she went into town each season. Yes, she wanted to know more about the town, Dylan and the other people who lived here. She wanted to learn about life outside of the Valley. However, she wanted Mama to be part of it. Lydia never once dreamed of a life that didn't include Mama.

Yet, the more time that passed in that unfamiliar room, and the more Clara and Mrs. O'Shea talked about the men and their ability to find Mama and bring her to town safely—the more Lydia doubted she would ever see Mama again.

Occasionally, Lydia's heart pounded at the sound of clopping hooves and mumbling of voices coming from outside. When nobody came in to announce Mama had been found, Lydia's chin quivered and she bit her tongue.

Clara lit several candles, signaling evening would be upon them shortly. Until then, Lydia hadn't noticed how the light coming in from the window had faded into dusk.

The hours that passed suddenly felt like minutes.

Just after dark, several men's voices bellowed outside the door.

The dark, quiet girl refilled Lydia's teacup, then took the empty supper plate, and disappeared into the kitchen.

The front door flung open.

Two men entered, soil and soot emphasized their wan expressions. Each glanced between Clara and Lydia. Then they removed their hats and stared at the floor.

Lydia jolted, biting her lip hard enough to taste salty blood.

"No . . . no . . . no . . ." Tears flooded Lydia's face.

The men stepped aside and turned toward the doorway. Dylan walked in, carrying Mama in his arms.

Mama's head hung back. Her bonnet, tangled in strands of hair, revealed a blackened face and closed eyes. Her arms dangled like the branches of willow trees in the breeze. Her hair draped to the floor in knotted strands like unwoven wool.

Tears streaked white, ragged lines down Dylan's dirty cheeks. His eyes blazed red and glassy.

Lydia held her breath.

Dylan laid Mama on a bench near the door.

"Mama!" She ran over and buried her face into Mama's neck.

Dust and ash blended into salty tears. The charred remains of Mama's dress smeared Lydia's freshly washed face.

Lydia sobbed and held tightly to Mama's frail and lifeless body.

She didn't care about the people surrounding her. She didn't care about knowing them or their world.

She didn't care about any of it if it didn't include Mama.

EIGHT

Eventually, Clara and Dylan managed to pry Lydia away from Mama's body, and Clara guided Lydia upstairs to the room Mrs. O'Shea had prepared.

"Sit on the bed dear." Clara kept a tight hold on Lydia's shoulders as they sat together.

Too weak to protest, Lydia stared at the floor. She tried to comprehend the reality that Mama was dead. She couldn't erase Mama's lifeless face from her mind, the strange feel of her cold, limp hand unresponsive to Lydia's pleas for her to wake up. She hadn't wanted to leave her side.

Clara dabbed Lydia's tears. "God Almighty, help me help her," she whispered, rocking Lydia gently.

"God?" Lydia choked and shook her head. She couldn't attempt to consider what part God played in this moment.

"Oh, Lydia, I'm sorry. Times like this demand we have faith until God reveals His purposes."

Lydia glanced around the room. Ignorance about the name and purpose of every unfamiliar object only added salt to her wounds. "Will God's purposes ever make sense to me? Everything Mama ever told me was that God wanted what was best.

Beyond the Valley

How is this best? Now ... now she can't even tell me why. Why? Oh, God—why?" She grew limp in Clara's arms.

"You'll make yourself crazy trying to answer that question, sweetheart." Clara grabbed a crisp, white nightgown from the crate containing the goods she brought from the general store. "Let me help you change into this nightgown and wash—"

"No." Lydia turned away and crossed her arms. The scent of soot wafting from her dress was overwhelming. Yet, she wasn't ready to remove it and remove what trace it held of Mama.

Clara draped the gown over the arm of the rocking chair and walked around the bed to push open the window. It let in mostly warm air laced with smoke. "Normally I don't care to speak of it, but perhaps you will find comfort in knowing I have suffered loss as well. My daddy died—drowned—when the dam broke and flooded back in '83. I was only three."

Lydia turned to face Clara, who stood looking out the window. She heard the hurt in Clara's voice. She'd cared for this daddy.

Lydia flashed to Clara's bright smile, the sense of joy she saw when they met hours earlier.

Is it possible to feel happiness after a loved one dies?

Lydia couldn't imagine feeling happy again. "I don't know how I can go on without her, Clara. I can't see my life without Mama."

Clara walked back over to Lydia and cradled her hands. "What you're feeling is very normal. You're grieving. You have lost your mother and you'll need time to mourn her. Under these circumstances, only God knows how long that'll take."

The glisten in Clara's eyes contrasted with the faint smile on her lips.

"For tonight, you need rest. There is a washcloth, water, and a rinse bowl over there if you feel the need." She nodded at the back corner of the room. "I'll be back in the morning to help you prepare for the funeral." Clara squeezed Lydia's hands, releasing them slowly as she turned to the door. "Lydia, I'm sorry for your loss, so sorry." She whispered a prayer, and then closed the door.

A cool and steady breeze began to blow through the window, though it still reeked of smoke. Lydia laid back crossways on the bed and stared at the stark white ceiling. Although grief bound her like an ox's yoke, sleep would not take over. She wanted to blame God for allowing it. What if Mama's death was her fault?

She relived every moment of the past few weeks in her mind. Why didn't she tell Mama she'd met Dylan? Why didn't she insist on answers instead of allowing Mama to make excuses? Maybe all her questions caused this. If she had only been content, willing to accept their life as it was without wanting more.

What if she didn't let Dylan take her when the fire came through? Would both she and Mama have perished? Would Dylan have stayed until Mama returned?

She couldn't find words for the feelings turning in her stomach. The aching in her chest made it difficult to breath.

Should she be angry with God, herself, or Mama? It didn't feel right to be angry with Mama, but she was. Admitting it made her wish she were dead as well.

She threw the soggy handkerchief onto the floor and buried her face in the pillow.

Someone knocked at the door, and then opened

it slightly.

Lydia kept her back facing the door. She didn't want to talk to anyone.

"Sorry to bother you dear," Mrs. O'Shea said. "Mr. O'Shea and I want to be sure you're all right before we turn in for the night. Clara didn't want to leave you, but she was at a loss. I suppose we all are. The whole town is in shock. Is there anything else you need, Lydia?"

Lydia didn't move or speak. The door creaked, and the gentle tap of footsteps indicated Mrs. O'Shea approached.

"Lydia?"

Lydia sighed and pulled her face out of the pillow. She fixed her eyes on the hazy moonbeams floating through the window behind Mrs. O'Shea's silhouette.

Mrs. O'Shea sighed. "Here is a lighter quilt, if that one on the bed is too heavy for you in this heat. There is also a dress here for you to wear tomorrow."

Out of the corner of her eye, Lydia watched Mrs. O'Shea step back around to the foot of the bed and drape the items over the wooden fence that held the bed up off the floor.

Mrs. O'Shea lit a candle. The glow cast out the moonbeams. "May I pray for you Lydia?"

Why did everyone want to bring God into this?

God's ways are not our ways. Mama's words echoed in her mind. *Do not be afraid. Be strong and courageous. I will always be with you.*

Lydia surrendered. "Yes, please."

Mrs. O'Shea kneeled near the bed. It was then Lydia noticed the same worn lines around her eyes that Mama had, the same thin, bony hands, and fingers. White strands streaked dark-brown hair in a tight bun on top of her head.

"O God, from whom all holy desires, all good counsels, and all just works do precede . . . Give unto thy servant, Lydia, that peace which the world cannot give. Be with her this night and for the days to come. Amen."

A chill ran through Lydia's back and her arms tingled, despite the hot and stuffy room.

Mrs. O'Shea stood and left Lydia behind the closed door. The silent glow of candlelight threw odd shadows across the wall. Lydia listened for the sounds of crickets or the scratch of a small animal scurrying outside. She couldn't hear anything except the breeze flapping the curtains. She thought of all the stairs she climbed to get up there, at least a dozen of them. She was probably too high above ground to hear the nighttime sounds that normally lulled her to sleep.

She glanced at the bowl and water pitcher in the corner of the room. Maybe washing would help her feel better. Soot and dust coated her hands and clung to her face where the tears had not washed it away. Sighing, she peeled back the quilt, stood, and stripped off her apron and dress, leaving them in a heap beneath the window.

She walked over to the bowl and pitcher. Startled at the sight of a woman's face appearing on the wall, she uttered a cry, and drew her hand to her mouth in fright.

The woman cried and drew her hand up at the same time.

When Lydia pulled her hand down, so did the woman.

It is my reflection!

It was like looking at herself in the pond, only she her face wasn't distorted by small ripples of water or muddled by tree limbs or a cloudy sky. She touched the wall, thinking it would ripple as with pond water, but it was hard and cold like a bedroom window.

Though shadows cast across her face between the candlelight, she could see clearly enough to wash away the black smudges across her forehead and along her neck.

Why hadn't Mama brought something like this home?

Once Lydia washed off as much of the ash and dirt as she could, she observed her reflection carefully. Her skin was mottled red and pink, with brown speckles showering her cheeks and nose. It was nothing like Clara's smooth, white skin. Why was it so different?

Seeing a brush on the table next to the bowl and pitcher, Lydia took the pins out of the bun Clara had twisted up earlier. Her hair fell around her shoulders, flowing to her waist. In the candlelight, it looked like dried grass in the setting sun, not nearly as soft and smooth as Clara's appeared. Then Lydia looked closer at her face. Her straight nose, thin lips, and dark blue eyes were more like Mama's than she could tell from the pond's reflection. She pressed her hand against the wall near her reflection. Her mind flooded with all that had happened since that first walk of spring. Searching her own eyes only brought more confusion. Maybe this was why Mama hadn't wanted them to see themselves.

Lydia pulled on the clean nightgown Clara had draped over the rocking chair. The soft, cool fabric felt comforting in contrast to her wool dress. She climbed under the covers, and found comfort in their heaviness, despite the warmth still cloaking the room. She blew out the candle on the table near the bed and buried her head back into the pillow.

In the darkness, her eyes grew heavy. Unable to comprehend what tomorrow would hold, she willed her thoughts to a time long before she questioned Mama about their life in the Valley—a time when she easily found joy in the moment.

"Now hold your hand very still and it won't fly away."

A bright orange and black butterfly sat in between the lines on Lydia's sweaty palm. Its wings slowly opened and closed. Her heart fluttered at the thought of it flying away at any moment. Mama cupped her coarse hands beneath Lydia's and kneeled in the dry dirt near the garden. Mama's breath was sweet from the mint leaves she had been chewing.

"It's tickling me!" Lydia squealed and started to giggle. Her hand jiggled with her laughter, but the butterfly stayed.

"Now let it go. Slowly lift up your hand and let it go."

"But it's so beautiful. Can't I keep it?" Lydia pleaded. If she tried to touch its wings, it would die.

"No, honey. God made the butterfly with wings so it could fly and be free. Go on and let it go."

When Lydia tried to lift her hand, the butterfly felt heavy.

Its wings spread out over her palm until Lydia couldn't see her hand any longer.

Then, her hands and arms transformed into wings. She had become the butterfly!

Yet, she was unable to fly. Mama held onto her and wouldn't let go. She stretched out her wings with a sudden force and broke free. She soared up into the sky, above the Valley. She was free. Her mind and body felt a surge of energy—as if she were limitless.

Then the heat from the sun began to beat down on her back. She glided down to the garden in search of Mama and the shade. When Lydia got there, Mama was gone.

Mama was gone. The words rang out in her mind. The heat of the sun became a heavy weight on her chest.

"Mama! Mama!" Her screams brought her back into the strange bed she slept in, the strange room with a solid door.

A thick, bright ray of sunshine shot through the window onto her face and chest.

Lydia pushed the heavy blanket off her chest and tried to sit up.

Outside, the clatter of horse hooves and muffled men's voices reminded her that she was no longer in the solitude of the Valley. Dread filled her with the weight of a tub of dirty wash water as she allowed the images of Mama's lifeless body to flood her mind again.

Lydia turned toward a faint creaking, expecting to see Mama emerge from the other side of the door.

Mrs. O'Shea peeked around the door. "You awake, hon?" She whispered.

Lydia nodded, the smell of food she would normally devour putting a lump in her throat and a knot in her stomach. Mrs. O'Shea brought in a large tray filled with strawberries, biscuits, scrambled eggs, bacon, and a cup of very dark looking tea. She set it next to Lydia on the bed and handed her a linen napkin.

Lydia gathered up her unbraided hair and tossed it behind her back. Without saying a word, she grabbed the biscuit and nibbled.

She didn't feel hungry, but if she ate, she might not have to speak.

"Miss Wilson has offered to donate a shroud to cover your Mama, and Mr. O'Shea is out back fitting together a proper, pine coffin . . ." Mrs. O'Shea's delicate voice soothed Lydia, despite her confusing words.

How would Lydia ever learn the meaning of everything she didn't understand? If only Mama were at her side, finally willing to explain it all. Frustrated and lamenting tears burned her eyes.

Mrs. O'Shea did not press her to eat or speak while she described to Lydia the things involving Mama's burial. The words became a meaningless jumble of sounds while Lydia tried to grasp a life without Mama at her side.

Lydia considered her options. Part of her wanted to find her way back to the Valley. She would pretend Mama was delivering offerings and continue life as usual. She would tend to the animals and maintain the garden. The thought of being among familiar surroundings, though alone, brought some relief to her grieving spirit.

Then, she recalled the bits of conversation between the men last night. There were unsure if the cabin or barn were intact. They had rescued the cow and found the ox on the edge of the river, but there was no sign of the chickens or sheep. Going back home now was not an option—even if she could find her way back.

Lydia took a sip of the strange looking tea to

ward off tears. She could hardly swallow the bitter taste and scrunched her face at Mrs. O'Shea.

"It's coffee." Mrs. O'Shea laughed and took the cup from Lydia. "Would you prefer tea?"

All these people wanted to do was help. How could she run from their kindness? Maybe in time, they would help her to find out more about how she and Mama ended up in the Valley. A small voice inside reminded her of a Psalm of David Mama used to recite.

Be still, and know that I am God.

Then she recalled another, repeating it as a prayer in the quiet of her heart.

Preserve me, O God, for in thee I put my trust.

For if she could not trust God now, there was no point in facing another day.

NINE

Mrs. O'Shea didn't press Lydia for another response. "I will send Clara with tea when she arrives to help you prepare for the funeral service. We have closed the Inn to travelers until later this evening. In the meantime, I am preparing food for a small gathering after the funeral. Only those who personally knew your mother will be present."

Lydia nodded and forced a small smile. "That sounds nice, Mrs. O'Shea. I am grateful, even if I don't understand what's happening."

"Don't be hard on yourself, dear." Mrs. O'Shea lifted the tray from Lydia's lap and headed into the hallway. "Have faith that the Lord will guide you one day at a time."

One day at a time? Oh, Lord, I need you by the hour.

It took only a single day for her life to float away like ashes in the wind. Lydia dragged herself out of bed.

She took a closer look at the dress she was supposed to wear. It wasn't like the simple dresses she and Mama wore. Yet, it was not nearly as glorious as the ones they had made for the angels. It was black, with many buttons and folds—the fabric, cool and soft like her nightgown. Several white garments lay beside it, and a shiny pair of boots and black stockings sat on the floor below the foot of the bed.

When she heard clopping coupled with Dylan's voice outside, her stomach turned. She laid the dress down and stepped over to the window. Three men sat on horses facing Clara standing on the wide path below.

"She was still jolted when I left her last night." Clara faced Dylan and petted Bailey's nose.

"What did you expect, Mrs. Roberts? In time, she will fit into life here. She's a smart young woman, more than I expected."

"Well, it's not like she was raised by wolves. Mrs. O'Shea told me her mother used to live in the city." Clara waved her hands around as she spoke. She no longer wore a green and white dress. Instead, her black attire included covered hands and a black bonnet.

"I wish we could put off the funeral for a few days to allow her time to rest and take in all that's happened. However, this heat demands a quick burial. We must lay Emelyn to rest and spare Lydia from unnecessary grief." Dylan spoke firmly.

Everyone in the group nodded at his words.

"Mr. Prescot, you are taking this seriously." Clara fanned her face with an oval-shaped black object she retrieved from her waistcoat. "One would think you have feelings for Miss Lydia."

Dylan cleared his throat. "Mrs. Roberts, I'm only taking responsibility for the matter. I feel partially responsible for what has happened."

"Clara," Mrs. O'Shea's voice rang from the porch. "Miss Lydia is awake whenever you are ready to assist her."

Lydia drew away from the window when she heard her name. What did Dylan mean about her being smarter than he expected? What did Clara mean about Dylan having feelings for her? Although Lydia understood each word on its own, she had no point of reference for their combined meaning. It was like hearing her chickens clucking away—making noise and nonsense. A few moments later, Clara was at her door.

"Okay, now, first you need to put on this undergarment." Clara handed Lydia a thin white slip with narrow shoulder straps bordered by thin pink ribbon. It was much prettier than the plain, gray slip Lydia normally wore.

Clara pointed to a tall, folding wall in the corner. "You may change over there."

Lydia hadn't noticed the folding wall before. Shadows concealed it in the corner opposite the bowl and pitcher. Stepping behind it, she noticed another reflecting wall and gasped. This one reflected from the top of her head all the way down to the floor.

"What's the matter, honey, did you see a spider?"

"No, I'm all right. I have never seen a reflecting wall like this before. What do you call it?"

"Really?" Clara laughed. "That is a mirror. You and your mama lived all those years without mirrors? Poor thing."

More confusing words Lydia ignored, too enthralled at the vision before her. "A mirror," she repeated, looking herself over. "This is far better than trying to see my reflection in the pond." She exchanged her soiled, rough, gray slip for the silky white one.

Seeing the soft cloth gently hugging her sides gave her an odd sensation. She shifted her gaze from the mirror, then smoothed her hands across the slip and stepped out of the corner.

"That must feel heavenly." Clara clapped her hands together once. Her eyes sparkled.

A few moments later, Clara stood behind Lydia, tugging on corset strings. "You're such a dainty thing. I'm going to have to cut the extra cord. Do you know about corsets?" She cinched it once more.

Lydia winced. "No, Miss Clara. Is that right to call you Miss Clara?"

"Since we are both ladies, you can call me Clara. Whenever a lady goes out in public, she wears a corset under her garments," Clara said. "Don't ask me why. It's the proper way in these parts."

Clara buttoned and tied and pulled some more, naming the corset cover and two petticoats while she wrapped them around Lydia.

The fabric was a finer wool than any she or Mama had worn, but not nearly as elegant as the satin or silk they'd used to hand-stitch gowns for the angels. She admired the fine stitching that could not have possibly been done by hand. Was there a special tool that could achieve such a consistent pattern?

Then Clara brushed Lydia's hair into a loose bun, allowing her hair to frame her face in a soft circle.

"As a final touch, will you allow me to apply some facial powder to your nose and cheeks? It will smooth out the redness and hide those freckles." Clara took a small metal can out of a flower-embroidered bag she had brought to the room.

This must be how she keeps her face so smooth and white.

Lydia closed her lips and eyes while Clara applied the powder with a round, fuzzy cloth.

It was hard for Lydia to understand why women would go through so much trouble to dress and arrange their hair. Worse, how could they remain in these clothes for an entire day? Although the corset relieved the aching in her back, the layers of clothing stifled her. When she walked back over to the mirror behind the folding wall, she hardly recognized her reflection. She looked and felt like the other women. She began to understand why they would take so much time to dress and prepare.

Lydia followed Clara outside to the front porch, descending the stairs and taking care to avoid tripping over the yards of fabric cascading from her waist to the floor. A slight breeze welcomed them, only hinting of the heat threatening to take over later in the day. The busy town she entered on horseback the afternoon before lay barren of people, carts, and even horses.

"Come on." Clara hooked her arm around Lydia's. "Everyone's at the schoolhouse waiting to pay their respects." Clara proceeded to lead Lydia away from the cluster of buildings and up a wide-trodden dirt path on a grassy hill.

They approached a white building at the top of a hill nestled in clusters of manzanita bushes.

Bursts of yellow, orange, and purple wildflowers speckled the dried grass. To the right of the building, at least two dozen people—all dressed in black—stood under the shade of a towering oak tree.

Lydia's heart thumped against the confines of her corset.

"We won't overwhelm you with introductions prior to the eulogy." Clara squeezed Lydia's hand inside her arm. "Mr. Miller will say a few words and a prayer on your Mama's behalf and then bless her soul as she joins the saints in the presence of our Lord Jesus. Afterward, people will want to pay their respects..."

Lord Jesus? Mama never called God by this name.

The wooden box where Mama's body lay had been placed on a low table in the center of the crowd. At the sight of it, Lydia released her grip on Clara, raced forward, and fell to her knees in front of the box. Whispers and voices blended into the rustling tree branches.

"Oh, Mama." Lydia rested her elbows onto the box and pressed her face into her palms. "Why did you have to leave me?" She whispered, ignoring the cool tears that rolled down her lips. "Why would God take you now, when I was finally getting answers? I'm sorry . . . so sorry I didn't tell you about what I knew, about meeting a man in the forest. Mama, I only wanted to understand. What were you afraid of that you didn't think I could understand?"

She could stay there for hours. An odd feeling of freedom resonated within her. She could finally ask or tell Mama anything without fear. Yet, she said nothing more. Her secret thoughts, her many questions—they didn't matter anyway.

Forgetting there was a crown of people standing behind her, she shuddered as a heavy hand rested on her shoulder. Then, another hand, with firmness she recognized, cupped her elbow, gently nudging her to stand. Lydia stood, welcoming Dylan's embrace without hesitation. Was it wrong to feel relief in his arms during this moment of grief?

He led her to the edge of the crowd and stood close by her as Mr. Miller spoke words of comfort and farewell on behalf of Mama. Lydia found some of his words confusing, but others echoed Mama's teachings about God and His plan. At least Mama gave her something in common with these people. It seemed they held a similar understanding about God.

After he finished speaking, the people lined up before Lydia.

"We looked forward to your mother's jams every autumn."

"Emelyn was a sweet soul and a hard-working woman."

"Your mama provided many needs to French Corral. We will miss her dearly."

"I'm sorry for your loss, Miss Lydia. Take comfort in knowing we are willing to help you in your time of need."

Dylan remained at Lydia's side, his hand resting on the small of her back. His parents were on a trip to another town, so he said he would arrange for Lydia to meet them at another time. Clara stood on Lydia's other side, whispering each person's name and their role in French Corral as they approached.

Lydia was astonished that Mama had interacted with so many people. They must be the *angels*—the ones who provided for them beyond what they could do for themselves in the Valley.

One by one, everyone left the shade under the oak tree and made their way down the hill back to town. When only Dylan, Clara, and Lydia remained, the three of them started to stroll down the hill back toward the Inn.

"Clara, wait," bellowed a man's voice.

Clara turned around to face her husband running toward them. "Jason, what is it? I thought you were getting the wagon and men needed to head to the cemetery."

Breathless, Mr. Roberts caught up with them, holding a crate in his arms.

"This crate has your mother's clothes, Miss Lydia. They were drying on the line behind the schoolhouse. My apologies for not considering this earlier—this heat is really getting to my head."

Clara wrinkled her eyebrows and snatched the crate from Mr. Roberts. "Jason, this really could have waited. Well, what's done is done. Dylan, would you mind carrying this?" Clara glared at her husband while shoving the crate toward Dylan. "Mr. Roberts should be making the final preparations for moving Miss Sinclair's casket to the cemetery."

Mr. Roberts wiped the sweat from his brow, tipped his hat, and took off back up the hill without another word.

Once they were back on the wide, dirt path and under more tree cover, Dylan looked at the items in the crate.

"Miss Lydia." His eyes raised and stopped, holding up a handkerchief. "Did you have this with you last night?"

At first, Lydia didn't realize its significance. She and Mama had many handkerchiefs. This one looked similar until she noticed the gold embroidery bordering the edge and the strange gold markings in the corner. Those same gold markings were on the handkerchief Dylan gave her the night they had met by the pond. That night, after she returned home, she hid the handkerchief at the bottom of a jar of dried wildflower petals in her room.

"What's so shocking about a handkerchief, Mr. Prescot?" Clara held her waist with one hand and fanned her face with the other.

Dylan looked wide-eyed at Lydia, rubbed the back of his neck, and dropped the handkerchief back into the crate.

"Yes," Lydia lied. "Yes, I did have it with me. I must have left it with Mama by accident."

Turning away from Clara's curious gaze, Lydia quickened her pace into town. She took a deep breath and hoped she wouldn't faint under the weight of the blaring sun and the shock of what Dylan discovered. What did this mean?

If Mama had found the handkerchief, what exactly did she know and how long had she known it?

TEN

"May I introduce you to someone else I think you'll be glad to meet?" Dylan led Lydia out to the back patio at the Inn.

Overwhelmed at already having met so many people, Lydia was ready to head upstairs to the solace of her room. Most everyone who attended the small gathering at the Inn had gone home. She hoped she would finally be able to rest. Yet, when she saw the woman Dylan was leading her to, her heart flipped and weariness fled.

A crocheted, black shawl draped over the white hair of a small woman standing alone under the branches of a willow tree. The lines on her face buried small, black eyes, and a round, lumpy nose. She leaned on a walking stick, like Mama's cane, and watched Lydia and Dylan approach.

"This is Miss Hastings," Dylan said.

Miss Hasting nodded at Lydia, a slight smile crossing her closed lips.

"Hello." Lydia found something familiar about this woman. How was that possible?

"Miss Hastings knew your mother better than anyone else here in French Corral," Dylan explained. "She normally doesn't attend public gatherings but insisted on seeing you right away. I'll leave the two of you alone. Mrs. O'Shea is in the kitchen if you need anything. The other men and I are going to see if we can locate any animals that survived the fire and collect whatever un-charred belongings we can from your cabin."

Lydia nodded, smiling slightly before he turned away. A light breeze played with the willow branches. Dylan's footsteps faded while Lydia waited for Miss Hastings to speak first.

"Your mama asked something of me many years ago when you were a small child." Miss Hasting spoke barely above a whisper. "When you were much smaller, I used to visit you and Emelyn. Until Dylan approached me a few weeks ago, I thought I was the only one in French Corral who knew about you."

"Visit us?" A faded memory of an angel sitting by the fireplace surfaced in Lydia's mind.

"When you were too small for your mama to leave you alone on her trips into town, I secretly cared for you. Other times I brought supplies to the edge of the forest."

"You know why, then? You know why she kept me from knowing about life and people beyond the Valley?" Lydia pressed her hand to her chest as hope flooded her heart.

Miss Hastings nodded and then shook her head. "I know more than I should, sweetheart. However, I vowed to provide you with only this for answers." She handed Lydia something that appeared to be layers of thin cloth pressed between two tattered black boards. "Many of the answers you seek are in here, in your mama's diary."

Lydia didn't know what it was, but she clung to it anyway. It had belonged to Mama.

Beyond the Valley

Miss Hastings patted Lydia's hands over the diary. She gazed at Lydia with moist eyes for several moments. Then, without a word, she steadied her steps with her cane and inched her way between the stables and the side of the Inn.

How could this diary have answers? Holding it in one hand Lydia found the boards came apart at one end, the thin slips of cloth in between them covered in row after row of small black shapes. Catching a glimpse of Mrs. O'Shea through the window, Lydia headed inside.

After breakfast the following morning, Lydia joined Mrs. O'Shea at a table in the dining area.

"Books come in many sizes and are filled with sheets of paper." Mrs. O'Shea explained, after Lydia told her she had never seen or heard of a *book* before. "These pages are filled with rows of words that tell a story or explain something." Mrs. O'Shea took one of the books she had stacked on the table.

"Words? These rows of black lines and circles are...words?" Lydia said, dumbfounded.

"Yes." Mrs. O'Shea smiled. "Each word we speak can be written by hand or imprinted with a printing press onto paper."

"How do you know what they mean?" Lydia's intrigue grew as she tried to grasp the concept.

Mrs. O'Shea sighed. "This is one of those things you may understand better if I show you. This one is a story written by Charles Dickens, called *David Copperfield*. It is a novel, a made-up story for the purpose of entertainment, for enjoyment. Listen as

I read you a few lines to give you an idea." Mrs. O'Shea opened the book and ran her finger along the rows of words as she spoke.

Lydia sat amazed for several minutes, listening to Mrs. O'Shea. Though many of the words were strange, Lydia still felt she understood. This was like the stories her mama told her—the stories from God.

"Mama told me stories like this, Mrs. O'Shea. Do you think her stories could be in this diary?"

"A diary holds more than a story, my dear. It records one's personal journey—places they go, people they meet, and their feelings and thoughts about life."

Lydia handed Mama's diary to Mrs. O'Shea. "Then re...r-*read* it to me, please. Read it all to me. Miss Hastings said this held the answers—or most of the answers—to why Mama raised me alone."

"Oh, I don't know. A diary is a very personal thing." Mrs. O'Shea held her hands up and shook her head. "I hardly knew Emelyn and wouldn't feel right reading something so personal."

"But Mrs. O'Shea, I can't read it myself. Please—it's the only way I will know the truth. Mama must have known someone would have to read it to me." Lydia surprised herself at the desperation in her voice.

She thought God had answered her prayer. How could Mrs. O'Shea refuse to read this diary to her?

Sighing and looking around the empty Inn, Mrs. O'Shea nodded. "I don't feel right about this, but I suppose there is no other way." She grasped Lydia's hands and looked her straight in the eye. "I vow," she whispered, "for my own consciences' sake that I will not repeat any of what I read to another soul."

Lydia nodded—surprised to feel her cheeks

tighten with a grin.
　Mrs. O'Shea began.

April 15, 1886
How strange to write these words. I have wanted a diary for so long. Mama and Papa gave me this yesterday, for my sixteenth birthday. It was all they could give me. They are such wonderful parents even though we don't have much in the likes of things or money. Mama also promised to give me my own dress project—a gown ordered by Mr. Sinclair for his daughter's debutante ball! Now that I am a young woman, I can put my studies aside for a while to perfect my skills in our family trade. However, Mama says I never know when I might be called on, and a man wants a wife who can cook and sew over one who can read and recite Bible stories. Well, Papa just got back to the apartment from his deliveries. Mama is calling me to supper.

April 18, 1886
I am grateful to have a place to write my thoughts. I have nobody else to talk to, at least not until today. I was delivering newly mended dinner jackets at the Sinclair's house when I met him. Yes, him—Charles Sinclair. He is not arrogant like his father. The housemaid let me in and directed me to deliver the jackets upstairs. I have never been inside and found myself gawking at their large paintings and ornate furniture. Then I turned a corner and walked right into a low table holding a large white vase—and it toppled to the floor, breaking into a dozen or more pieces!

　I was fighting tears at the thought of the consequences when Charles rushed to my side from the other room. He helped me clean up the mess without another soul in the house noticing. He even offered to hide the porcelain fragments and promised not to tell his father. He also gave me his handkerchief.

Mama's reminding me to conserve lamp oil, so my time here is done.

Lydia listened to each word, staring out at waves of heat rising from the dust surrounding the corral behind the Inn. Dylan led Megan into the barn. Lydia's mind barely noted the relief of seeing the tan and brown velvety swirls of Megan's hide. Her heart and mind struggled to comprehend what Mrs. O'Shea had read from Mama's diary.

Lydia had heard that name, Sinclair before. Dylan said something about their land belonging to them. Could this Charles person be responsible for bringing Mama to the Valley?

"It looks like Dylan found some survivors." Mrs. O'Shea nodded and looked up from the diary. "Go on now and see what else he has piled in his wagon."

Her mind still on Mama's diary, Lydia went outside in a daze.

Dylan's wagon held a crate overflowed with kitchen supplies and their loom.

"It's a miracle the house and barn are still standing." Dylan handed her a salt sack filled with some of her clothes, the bitter scent of smoke emanating from it. "But the sheep pen burned along the north side. We've put the word out for anyone finding stray farm animals to bring them into town. Mr. O'Shea says they can stay in surrounding stables or the barn with your cow for the time being." He turned and grabbed something else out of the wagon.

"And I thought you might want this." He was careful to keep it folded, waiting for Lydia to have a good grasp on it.

"My quilt," Lydia cried, and unfolded it to examine a tattered corner. She rubbed her fingers over the frayed stitches and she knew for the first time why one square was different from the rest of them—the square Lydia would tuck under her chin on cold nights.

Something was special about it. She had always thought of the blue stars as angels protecting her and giving her hope of a life beyond the Valley. At the time, Lydia thought of that life as being in Heaven with God.

Could this quilt square be what remained of the handkerchief Charles Sinclair had given her Mama?

"If there is anything else you need, anything from the cabin, anything at all . . . let me know." Dylan heaved the loom over the edge of the wagon and carried it to a corner of the back patio.

Lydia began to feel like Ruth from one of Mama's stories. Who was the kind young man who so willingly accepted her and so generously offered his help in any way he could? His bright green eyes sparkled. They seemed to see right through her—reading the questions simmering in her mind and recognizing the confusion stirring in her heart.

In the story of Ruth and Boaz, one of the few stories Mama had told her that involved a woman—Ruth had lost her husband and moved to another land with her mother-in-law. Ruth met Boaz, who owned the land where she collected the leftover wheat. He fell in love with her, had compassion for her, and eventually married her. Lydia had been captivated at how Boaz still loved Ruth even though she was different and had lived in another land all her life.

Lydia never completely understood the family dynamics of Mama's stories. But she did understand that God had made man and woman to be husband and wife at one time. Together they had children and populated other lands. The stories Mama told were about those people, but somehow seemed to reflect bits of truth about those in this land called French Corral. Maybe Mama hadn't only told those stories to teach Lydia to be content in the Valley. Maybe she told those stories to prepare Lydia for the outside world she would eventually encounter.

Men only bring pain. The echo of Mama's words crushed her heart. *They bring war and greed and heartache. The only man we need is God, Lydia. God is all we need.*

Suddenly Lydia felt ashamed for the feelings bubbling up inside of her. Was she giving in to the sinful ways of men because she enjoyed Dylan's presence? The men in the stories Mama told her were not all bad. Most of them served God with all their hearts and loved and honored the women in their lives. The conflict between Mama's words and the stories disturbed Lydia.

How was she supposed to react to Dylan's kindness? How could she know the difference between a man who could bring pain and one who would bring joy? As Dylan returned to the cart, tears stung Lydia's eyes. She clutched her smoke-smoldered belongings.

"Thank you," Lydia choked, hiding her tears by staring into the heat rising from the dust.

She ran inside, seeking solace in her temporary

room for the remainder of the day. Surprised to see a stack of books at the foot of her bed, she quickly changed into her nightgown and braided her hair.

Her heart raced. She flipped open the cover of the large black book at the top of the stack. She gasped at the sight of miniature images of people and things, buildings and landscapes, machines, and tools.

These must be what Mrs. O'Shea called photographs.

Lydia held her breath and took in every detail of a world that had been so close—but had seemed so far away until that moment.

ELEVEN

The next morning, Lydia's mind swirled with images from photographs and drawings. She ignored the heaviness bearing down on her again. She had to do something, anything to keep her hands busy and her mind from straying to the past and the things she could not change. As if she were waking in her small room in the Valley, Lydia pushed back her covers and stretched her hands toward the ceiling.

"Lord, lead me this day in serving you with all my heart and soul. Help me to fulfill my purpose with all that is within me. Amen."

After she made her bed, braided and wrapped up her hair beneath her bonnet, and gathered the stack of photograph books to return to Mrs. O'Shea, she made her way to the kitchen.

Lydia placed the books on a wooden crate and pushed open the swinging kitchen door.

Mrs. O'Shea was bending over the front of the massive stove, feeding it with a shovel full of black rocks.

"Good morning Mrs. O'Shea."

Mrs. O'Shea scooped once more, set the shovel down, and secured the stove door before turning to face Lydia. "Good morning. I didn't expect you to awaken so early or I would have prepared your breakfast." She wiped the black dust from her hands onto the underside of her apron and grabbed a cast iron pan from the shelf.

"Oh, I don't expect you to keep serving me as a guest here. I'm used to working and serving and would like to assist you in the kitchen today. I understand that travelers exchange their own goods in trade for sleeping and eating here. Since my possessions are few, I am happy to work in trade until I figure out what I will do about my own home."

Mrs. O'Shea raised her brows, eyes sparkling with a smile stretching across her withered cheeks. "Of course you can help me. I've always got plenty of work to do."

Lydia took a deep breath. "Thank you. I feel the need to keep my hands busy. I am not used to having nothing to do. Where can I start?"

Mrs. O'Shea showed Lydia around the kitchen, pointing out where she could find the flour and lard, explaining how coal burned hotter and lasted longer than wood. Since the wagon trains no longer came through in droves, they usually cooked and baked more than they needed. No matter, each morning entailed baking several loaves of bread, a few dozen rolls, and at least five pies. By noon, the top of the stove would hold two large pots of lamb stew, chili, and boiling jars ready for jam.

"You can start with kneading that batch of dough there, and then take that basket to fetch enough blackberries for a pie and six jars of jam. Do you know where the blackberry bushes are behind the barn?"

Lydia nodded. Then she pulled up her sleeves

and thrust her knuckles into the ball of dough. The ball deflated. Lydia folded the dough in layers over itself, pressing down and folding again until it stopped sticking to her fingers. Making bread had been Mama's job. Lydia treasured completing the task now, as if it made Mama's memory more alive—more significant to the outside world.

"Oh, that reminds me." Mrs. O'Shea said a few minutes later. "Dylan has your cow settled into her own stall. One of the servants already milked her this morning, but you're more than welcome to check on her and milk her this afternoon."

Megan!

Lydia felt a twinge of guilt for forgetting about one of her daily companions. She hastened her work with the dough, torn between cherishing the task and desiring to embrace the familiar sounds and scents of her cow.

Cool air hung in pockets of shadows inside the barn, hiding from threads of warm morning sunlight streaming through cracks in the wood-slatted walls. Lydia paced herself, slowing to glance into each stall until she came across Megan's. It wasn't hard to recognize the pattern of her hide, the clusters like brown clouds against a cream-colored sky.

"Good morning Megan." Lydia's eyes stung with tears. She wrapped her arms around the cow's head and pressed her forehead into the folds of velvety skin on Megan's neck. "Oh, I've missed you . . ." her voice cracked.

Megan snorted softly and shifted her hooves a tad, as if she leaned her head into Lydia's to return the embrace.

After a few moments, Lydia sighed and pulled back. "I wish I could stay here with you longer, but I promised Mrs. O'Shea I would help her today. I'll be back to milk you in a couple of hours. Then, I will tell you how different our life looks to be from now on."

She took a moment to search for the blackberry basket she hadn't even realized she'd dropped at the entrance to Megan's stall. Then she went around to the back of the barn where the blackberry bushes grew in fat clusters against the fence. The shade and silence gave her momentary solace. Would her tears continue to arrive in unexpected bursts like this? Was it normal for a person to feel sad and joyful at the same time?

A while later, Lydia returned to the kitchen with red and purple stained fingers and scratched hands and wrists. "Will this be enough?" She lifted the basket, blackberries spilling over the sides.

Mrs. O'Shea looked up from the cubes of potatoes she was cutting on the counter. "My goodness, yes—that's plenty. I was wondering what was taking you so long."

Lydia frowned and lowered the basket.

"Oh, but it's fine, dear, simply fine. Clara just informed me a wagon train is due to come through tomorrow. We'll make some blackberry cobbler too, but we need to get this stew on the stove first."

While Mrs. O'Shea and Lydia hung the bedding on the clothesline that afternoon, a young man and woman who looked no older than her own sixteen years, came by to introduce themselves. Dan and Hattie Logan had missed the funeral as well. Lydia remembered Dan from the day of the fire.

Hattie held a small person in her arms.

The adorable little person—a baby, was named Olive. She enthralled and enchanted Lydia. Her fine hair was the shade of pine nuts, her skin as soft as rose petals. Lydia couldn't contain her laughter as Olive pulled at her hair and gurgled and slobbered on her blouse. It felt good to laugh. It felt good to hold a little life, young and innocent. Olive had a hope for a future with a mama and papa whom Lydia could tell loved her very much.

After bidding good evening to the Logans and expressing gratitude to the O'Shea's, Lydia headed upstairs to her room, eager to slip into the loose-fitting comfort of her nightgown.

"There are twenty-five adults, three servants, and six children," Mrs. O'Shea explained as Lydia removed a second batch of rolls from the oven. "Mr. O'Shea is assisting with the horses. He will bring the crates and boxes containing the items they will need through the morning into the upstairs hall. You've done well here today. I must say your mama taught you skills I've not seen in some time. However, I'm going to send you upstairs now to help Lucy prepare the beds and then you both need to report to the dining room."

"Of course," Lydia said, glad to get relief from the heat of the kitchen. She removed her apron and tucked loose strands of sweat-saturated hair behind her ears. She hadn't spoken with Lucy yet—the dark-skinned servant girl who had served her the day she arrived—and was curious to know her.

The heat upstairs was hardly a reprieve from the kitchen. Nevertheless, she welcomed the change of scenery.

"Miss Lydia." Lucy curtsied, a small smile hovering over her lips. Lydia could drown in the deep, dark pools of her eyes that resembled those of a newborn deer.

"It is nice to meet you, Lucy." Lydia mimicked the curtsy and repeated the greeting dozens had given her in recent days.

"Now, we get to work. Three rooms and thirty-one peoples need fold-up beds on floors. Other servants sleep in the wagons so we don't worry 'bout them. This closet has clean quilts and bed covers. Dustin' rags are over there. Windows stay open while we work so dust flies out. Got it?" Lucy nodded again and again until Lydia responded.

"Where are the fold-up beds?"

"You listen good! We get those in shed out back." Lucy's smile revealed two missing teeth, and several discolored ones.

With a few more instructions, Lydia got to work on preparing the room next to her own. Across the hall, Lucy stripped the beds and pushed the mattresses together. As she worked, she hummed and sang words Lydia didn't understand. Yet, the beauty of her voice soothed her like the caress of a gentle breeze melting across her shoulders.

By the time they finished preparing the last bedroom, the wagon party had settled into the shade of the yard behind the Inn. A chorus of voices, children's squeals, and other sounds Lydia couldn't identify floated up through the open window. Lydia took a moment to look down, observing the crowd from a distance.

A group of women stood under the willow tree. One held a baby similar in size to Olive. The other rested her hands on the shoulder of a thin child clinging to her legs. A third woman rested a glass of lemonade on her swollen belly and wiped her forehead and neck with a tattered handkerchief.

Right below the window, several men sat in a circle on an assortment of crates, folding chairs, and a bench. One of them scratched and patted the head of what looked like a wolf. Lydia caught her breath.

"Why is that man petting a wolf?" Lydia called to Lucy.

"Wolf? What wolf?" Lucy tucked a quilt corner around the end of a bed and joined Lydia at the window. "Oh, ha ha!" Lucy giggled. "That no wolf, Lydia. That's a dog. Lots of men have dogs 'round here. Dogs protect and keep company I s'pose. Never really thought 'bout it much."

"They don't bite people?"

"Uh, well they can bite people if they are a threaten'n. But you're not a threaten'n Miss Lydia. A good dog will know that." Lucy patted Lydia's shoulder. "Now, it's time to go down and set the tables."

The following hours became a blur between serving, cooking, and cleaning. When dusk settled, the women with smaller children headed upstairs while the men's voices grew louder with each gulp of ale. After gathering empty pie plates from the porch, Lydia headed to the kitchen to see what else Mrs. O'Shea needed from her for the evening. Arms sore and feet throbbing, she hoped she could rest soon.

Yet, before she crossed the dining room, she

recognized Dylan's voice.

Hugging the plates to her chest to avoid dropping them, she took in a shallow breath and held it. Dylan stood facing Mrs. O'Shea at the doorway to the kitchen. Their voices were low and sounded serious.

"Is something wrong?" Lydia stepped toward them.

Dylan turned on his heel and pulled off his hat, shaking his head. "Good . . . good evening, Miss Lydia." His eyes shifted to Mrs. O'Shea and back to Lydia.

Mrs. O'Shea leaned back into the door, casting light from the kitchen into the dining room that shadowed her and Dylan's faces. She shook her head and briskly rubbed a towel over the platter she held. "Nothing wrong, dear. Dylan was just . . . updating me on a delivery due in tomorrow."

"Oh." That seemed odd. Didn't Mr. and Mrs. Roberts handle deliveries? But it wasn't her concern.

Dylan stepped away from the doorway as Lydia approached. His silence troubled her.

Mrs. O'Shea raised her brow and tilted her chin up to Dylan. "I'll finish the clean-up. Our guests won't need our services for the rest of the night. Such a nice evening—"

Lydia set the soiled dishes into the washtub and began to untie her apron. Her stomach tightened now that she had a clear view of him from the inside of the kitchen.

"Eh—yes, it is Mrs. O'Shea—a very nice evening." Dylan placed his hat back on the coils of brown hair that framed his flushed cheeks. Willow-green eyes locked with Lydia's gaze.

Clearing his throat, he reached a hand toward

Lydia. "Would you like to join me for a walk to the schoolhouse before you turn in for the night? We haven't a moment to visit since the funeral. And it looks like Mrs. O'Shea will be keeping you busy from here on out."

Why did that smile of his seem to put a lump in her throat and make her insides flutter? If this was how Boaz affected Ruth, how did she bear to sleep at his feet? Had she been drawn to him too, despite the emotions he stirred within her?

Lydia wiped clammy hands on her bunched-up apron before tossing it into the heap of soiled linens in the corner.

"A walk would be wonderful." Lydia took Dylan's hand and tried to recall the last time she had gone on a walk.

Though only days had passed, Mama and her strolling around the pond picking wildflowers seemed more a muddled dream than a memory.

In moments, she and Dylan walked along the quiet road, sounds of the men outside of the Inn fading into the distance. The tap of their boots hitting the dry ground encouraged scurries among the creatures hiding in the brush. Muted orange light flickered from inside the windows of a several houses throughout the hillside. Peace hovered around them like the mist of clouds surrounding the rising moon.

"Dan told me that you met Hattie and Olive yesterday," Dylan began.

"Yes, I did." Lydia sighed, relieved at his chosen topic. "I've never seen a baby before—at least not a human baby. Hattie seems kind too."

"Hattie will make a good friend. I imagine she'll make her way to the Inn sometime tomorrow after the folks from the wagon train head out."

"Friend? Hmm . . . Mama used to call our animals friends." Lydia pondered the thought. "I wonder what the difference will be having a friend that can talk back."

Dylan laughed and stopped to face Lydia, keeping a strong grasp of her hand nestled inside the crook of his arm. "You must be worn from the inside out, yet you still find energy to consider the differences between animal and human companions."

Lydia searched his eyes. The evening shadows made it difficult to read the intent of his words. "Is that wrong?"

"It's not wrong at all. It's exactly what this town needs—a new perspective." He winked, one side of his lips curling up in a quick smile. "Now, tell me about the Inn and assisting Mrs. O'Shea."

While she shared, Dylan guided her up the hill where they sat on the schoolhouse steps and watched the moon ascend above the treetops.

Lydia spoke with ease as Dylan mostly listened. When she wasn't sure how to describe something, he would provide the words. The woman with the swollen belly was *pregnant* or *with child*. Some of the words she heard the men blurting out were *curse words*—better not to repeat—especially by a young woman. The round, hollow wooden object with a flat handle that made interesting yet beautiful sounds was a *banjo* and the sounds were *music*.

By the time Dylan walked Lydia back to the Inn, the whole town seemed to be sleeping. A single candle sat lit by the entrance, ready to lead her upstairs to her long-awaited slumber. As worn as she'd been prior to the unexpected evening walk, the weight of her long day had lifted.

Random memories floated in and out while she

prepared for sleep. Working backward from Dylan's hesitant goodbye, she cherished each moment of their walk and all he had taught her in their brief time together. But somehow, that instant she first noticed Dylan in the kitchen speaking with Mrs. O'Shea unsettled her. Had she seen Dylan slip something into his coat pocket as he faced her? Her surprise in seeing him overshadowed her observation. So, why did the image of his hand lingering inside his coat enter her mind as she drifted to sleep?

TWELVE

Over the following weeks, Mrs. O'Shea patiently showed Lydia everything involved in running the Inn. Lydia wanted to be of use and gladly followed her lead. Gradually, she became accustomed to greeting guests and making keen observations that helped her to understand the ways of these people of French Corral. Hattie would come by often with Olive to chat and share tidbits about life to connect the gaps between what Lydia assumed and how things were.

When the afternoon heat thickened the air too much inside the Inn, Mrs. O'Shea would make up a huge pitcher of lemonade and they would sit under the shade of the poplar tree behind the Inn, facing the corral. Lydia would fan her face with a folded newspaper and sip on her drink while listening to Mrs. O'Shea read more entries from Mama's diary.

April 25, 1886
Why must social caste be so important? I have all the skills of a good wife. I have manners and know how to groom myself. However, none of this seems to matter to Mr. Sinclair. Charles only wanted to take me to the theatre, share part of his society life and

culture with me. Mr. Sinclair refused to acknowledge me as nothing more than a servant. He does not even care that I know how to read and write.

My parents are no different. They do not think it appropriate for an employer's son to be pursuing the company of an employee—despite the future happiness or welfare of their only daughter. They claim they want the best for me, but only for what they see as best. Why does it not matter that Charles sees me for who I am and not what I am?

Once again, I am short on time and lamp oil, so I must go.

Mrs. O'Shea set the diary on her lap. "What did your Mama tell you about people? Do you understand what she meant by 'social caste' and 'employee'? I don't want to assume you understand, nor do I want to make you feel foolish for lack of knowledge."

Mrs. O'Shea must have guessed from her wrinkled face that Lydia was confused. Yes, Lydia wanted to know everything.

"I know nothing of people other than the stories Mama told me that God gave her when she brought offerings. Stories about men and women in other worlds God created. Each story was meant to help us be content in the Valley." Lydia sighed, fighting the tears welling up in her eyes. "But somehow, I think she was trying to tell me about people like you and Dylan and Clara, or Hattie and Dan. I think Mama was trying to help me understand people."

Mrs. O'Shea nodded and sipped her lemonade, inviting Lydia to continue.

"But I'm confused. The people Mama told me

about fought in wars and battled evil. Harsh kings and men who did not honor God's word ruled them. They seemed to live the opposite kind of life than the one you live here in French Corral. It's as if they lived in a different world than this one."

Mrs. O'Shea nodded again and wrinkled her forehead. "Tell me about one of the stories your Mama told you. Perhaps I can help you understand her possible intentions." She shifted in her rocking chair and leaned toward Lydia.

A wave of warm air rustled through the branches, drying the thin layer of sweat on Mrs. O'Shea's brow.

"You would like me to tell you a story?" It was a good thing Lydia was used to repeating Mama's stories to Megan. Which one could she tell? "There are so many stories—such as the one of a shepherd boy called David, who defeated a giant named Goliath. In another story, she told me of a man named Samson who gave into his sinful ways and allowed a woman named Delilah to deceive him. She told me of a woman named Ruth who . . ." Lydia eagerly spilled out the stories she held closest to her heart.

Mrs. O'Shea sat quietly fanning herself with her own folded paper. She nodded with a small smile. "I think I understand, now. Wait here a moment." Mrs. O'Shea stood and went inside.

When she returned, she held a thick brown book. "This is one of the most blessed books ever written in the history of the world. This is the Holy Bible. It contains many of the stories your Mama told you. They are not just stories—they are true accounts of men and women whom God called for a higher purpose. They happened thousands of years ago, in this world, though in places far away from French

Corral."

Lydia held the Holy Bible in her hands. She turned the delicate pages carefully, in awe at the number and small size of the words each page held. The heaviness that lifted from her heart, lifted from her face as well—as if a shroud of wool had been preventing her cheeks from fully expressing joy until that moment.

Mama had not made up those stories.

Ever since Lydia had learned they were not the only people, she wondered how much truth was in what Mama told her about God. This Holy Bible would take an awfully long time to read. She wanted to learn to read it on her own. If she did, maybe one day she could fully understand why Mama chose to reveal this one truth among the many lies.

"Now, back to your Mama's diary. I can't tell for certain where she lived when she wrote this, but I think it was San Francisco."

"San Francisco?"

"Unfortunately, one of the problems in a big city is that you face society stigmas, such as social caste. San Francisco is a huge city, much bigger than French Corral. I think there is a photograph or two in the albums I brought to your room. It is several days journey by wagon from here."

Perplexed, Lydia twirled strands of hair at the end of her braid.

Mrs. O'Shea frowned and then smiled. "You are familiar with David and Goliath?"

Lydia nodded. Mama told her that story one night after a bear wandered into the garden.

"It's not exactly the same thing, but there were some who did not think David could slay a giant because he was a shepherd boy and not a warrior—"

The back door squeaked.

Mrs. O'Shea slyly slid Mama's diary behind the pillow on her chair and jumped to her feet. Mr. O'Shea approached them.

"Dylan Prescot is here to speak with you, Miss Lydia." Mr. O'Shea nodded once, and then left as quickly as he had appeared. His boots whispered across the grass as he returned to the sheep pen.

Lydia looked back at Mrs. O'Shea. "May I? I won't be long and I'll get right back to work."

Mrs. O'Shea smiled and nodded toward the patio door. "Go ahead. The laundry won't mind a bit more sunshine."

The churning feeling arrived in her belly once again. Inside, Dylan stood before the front window, his hat in his hands. He was not wearing his normal, dusty, working clothes. Instead, he wore a crisp brown button-up shirt with a vest and dark slacks. He raised his arm, elbow out, as Lydia approached.

She slid her hand into the crook of his elbow, proud that she was now accustomed to this gesture, and allowed him to lead her out to the front porch.

Standing under the shade of the overhang, Dylan nodded, fingers playing with the edges of his hat. "Miss Lydia, I would like the honor of escorting you to your first dancing party this evening. We're not only about mining and farming in French Corral. We all get together from time to time, play music and games, and enjoy each other's company. My father, Mr. Prescot will be joining us so you will finally be able to meet him."

Lydia couldn't tell if it was the heat or her heart that made her head feel fuzzy. She hugged herself with one arm and reached for Dylan with the other as the heaviness crept back into her chest.

Dylan clasped her arm. "Are you all right?"

A dancing party? Meeting Dylan's father? It sounded fantastic and frightening.

"I don't know what you mean by play music and games. And the only dancing I ever did was with Mama in the garden."

He smiled and gave her hand a reassuring squeeze. "There's nothing to worry about. You can sit and enjoy watching everyone. Hattie and Dan will be there. And Mr. and Mrs. Roberts—err—Jason and Clara will also be there."

"Will I have to wear one of those corsets again?" Lydia grimaced at the thought and held her breath. She'd been wearing her own clothing, wearing two slips if needed, to avoid the confines of that corset ever since Mama's funeral.

Dylan chuckled. "I'll leave that up to you and Mrs. O'Shea. Or would you like for me to send Hattie over to help you find something to wear?"

She exhaled at the suggestion. "I would like that very much. You don't think Mrs. O'Shea will mind?"

"Not at all. It's the very sort of thing you younger ladies do. For now, please excuse me, I must attend a meeting with my father regarding the vineyard." He stepped off the porch and placed his hat on his head. "After the meeting, I will tell Dan to send Hattie to come assist you. The dancing party will begin immediately after supper." He tipped the brim of his hat. Then he smiled and revealed the dimples that made Lydia's heart flutter every time she saw them.

Lydia sat in the shade of the porch for several minutes, even though the heat surrounding her felt as suffocating as a heavy blanket. Her heart pounded and her hands shook at the thought of yet another experience among strangers. Even if Mama had told her about people like those in French Corral, nothing would have prepared her for living among them. She still desired to learn all she could about this new world beyond the Valley, regardless of the uncertainty she had of ever learning their ways. Avoiding participation in their rituals would only make it that much harder.

After supper, Hattie promptly arrived at the door to Lydia's room. She toted Olive in one arm, a half-dozen dresses draped over the other. Hattie freely exhibited all the excitement Lydia didn't know how to express. She might as well have been an infant like precious Olive, grabbing at and drooling over everything. She tried on dress after dress. Hattie chatted and giggled without stopping. Olive squealed and bounced on the bed and seemed to agree with her mama's enthusiasm.

"May I tell you something?" Lydia had just removed a dress of green calico that Hattie announced brought out the blue in her eyes.

"Of course, you may. You can tell me anything you want to." Hattie scooped up Olive and sat on the bed. The baby's gurgles suddenly turned into whines, a sign Lydia had learned meant the child was ready to nurse and take a nap.

Lydia sat on the bed in only her petticoat, holding the next dress on her lap. "You know none of this is easy for me. Everyone has seemed willing and eager to showing me how to live here in French Corral. Yet, I keep wondering how long I can do this. Mama only told me about people from Bible stories. Yet, you are nothing like those people. Can you tell me more about this dancing party? I don't think that is something the people did in the Bible stories."

Hattie shushed Olive, swaying, and lowering her voice to a whisper. "Actually, the Bible is full of stories of singing and music and celebrating unto God. However, tonight, our dancing party is about gathering in the cool of the evening and enjoying each other's company. The girls and boys will dance together to the rhythm of banjos and other instruments."

"That is what I mean. I remember the banjo from the wagon train, but what are instruments? When Mama and I danced in the garden, she would sing to me what she called 'the joyful noise'."

Hattie giggled. "I don't know if I can explain it to you. I'm sure you will love it. Music is a form of expression for people. It has been for thousands of years. Here, you want me to show you how to waltz?" She tucked sleeping Olive between the pillows and quilt. Then she stood and grabbed Lydia's hands.

"Oh, no. I think I'll just watch tonight." Lydia shook her head and pulled her hands away and clasped them behind her back so Hattie wouldn't take them again. "What about the games Dylan mentioned? Will I have to do that?"

"Of course not. No one is expecting you to know how to play games. You're perfectly welcome to sit and watch. I'm happy to show you how if you change your mind." Hattie raised her brows and smiled with a wink. "But if you want, I'll sit with you. We can keep watch over the food and shoo the night bugs out of the tea."

"Thank you. Please, stay with me the whole time and explain everything, no matter how simple it seems."

"I'll try, but I'm warning you, sometimes over a hundred folks show up and it gets pretty loud and rowdy. We can always come back here if you're feeling overwhelmed. Now, what about Dylan? After all, he did ask you to the party."

Lydia sighed. "I'm especially worried about meeting his father. Is Mr. Prescot nice? Will he ask me many questions? How do I act around him? I haven't really spoken to any other men besides Dylan and the miners who stop at the Inn for pie and coffee."

Hattie waved her hand and grinned with one cheek. "Mr. Prescot is extremely kind. He is quiet, though. I don't think he'll ask you many questions. He might ask if you are enjoying French Corral and make sure Dylan has been a gentleman with you. You'll be fine. I can't think of anything that could ruin your night."

After that, Lydia tried on the rest of the dresses. They kept the conversation hushed so Olive would stay sleeping. When they'd first met, Lydia thought maybe her upbringing would hinder their ability to become friends. But Hattie didn't seem to care. She embraced each of Lydia's questions, going to great lengths to answer her. Though grateful for Hattie's enthusiasm, Lydia couldn't help but feel a twinge of hurt. Why had Mama been so unwilling to share such things?

This hurt only continued into the evening as Lydia watched men, women, and children dance, laugh, and enjoy the company of one another. Dylan eventually brought his father over for introductions. Although Hattie had tried to assure her, Lydia hoped that this "social caste" that Mama wrote of in her diary wouldn't be something she had to endure.

"Father," Dylan yelled over the strumming of instruments and the squealing of children running circles around the barrel where Lydia sat. "This is Lydia, the young lady who lived alone with Emelyn of the Mountain until the fire a couple of weeks ago."

Mr. Prescot tilted the wide, worn brim of his hat. His eyes moved slowly from her white, lace bonnet down to her pink calico dress and tightly tied black shoes. At first, his face was solemn. Then a huge grin formed, revealing worn teeth and dimples identical to those Lydia had grown accustomed to seeing on Dylan. Thick, brown hair sprinkled with white, wrapped around the bottom of long, leathery cheeks. He reached down, grasped her gloved-covered hand, and drew it to his mouth. Even through her gloves, she could feel the rough callouses snagging the fabric and his whiskers pricking the tops of her fingers.

"It is a pleasure to meet you, Miss Lydia." With his words, he firmly kissed her hand and then let it go. "Are you enjoying French Corral, even in this awful heat?"

Hattie had been right. Lydia sighed and smiled back at Mr. Prescot. "It is a pleasure to meet you as well," Lydia mimicked, unable to hide the relief in her voice. "Yes, everyone here has been very kind to me, very kind." Lydia glanced up at Dylan and allowed herself to smile, unrestrained, recognizing how much he and his father had in common.

Then, shrieks of laughter came from behind them. Lydia jumped to her feet, startled. Two young women, with strikingly similar features, held their sides and pointed to the three of them.

"Dylan, you cannot seriously think your father would approve of a mountain mole," one of the women breathed through her giggles.

"Mr. Prescot, you are being too nice . . . 'Oh, Miss Lydia.'" They spoke in unison and seemed to mimic Dylan. They could hardly say two words without laughing so hard they appeared they would burst or collapse if they didn't get some air.

In a blink, Dylan grabbed Lydia's arm and pulled her across the grass to the other side of the party. When he did, Lydia realized these young women were not acting in kindness.

Everyone had been so accepting of her up until that moment. Dylan seemed stunned, but something inside of Lydia wasn't surprised. One truth she knew from Mama's stories was that there was always someone set on destroying the happiness of another. Yet, tears still stung her eyes and streamed down her cheeks at the realization. She gathered her skirts and without letting Dylan say a word, spun on her heel and rushed through the crowd of dancing couples, wanting to get as far away from everyone as possible.

She ran down the hill into the graying light of the evening, unable to fight the anger burning in her chest toward Mama. She couldn't deny the anger, or the guilt that clung to it.

Why did I stop asking Mama questions so long ago? Why didn't I make Mama tell me more?

She hardly heard Dylan shouting out to her. She

hardly heard Hattie tell him to wait. She hardly heard her heart pounding against the hollow places in her chest. She returned to her room at the Inn breathless, and collapsed on her bed, unrestrained sobs jarring every inch of her.

THIRTEEN

Arms wrapped around Lydia's curled shoulders. Hattie whispered an unfamiliar melody, clinging when Lydia tried to pull away. She didn't let go until the sobs melted into soft cries.

"Maybe you're not ready, yet." Hattie consoled. "I can't imagine what this is like for you, not knowing anyone but your ma and suddenly meeting dozens of people over only a few weeks. Not to mention, your ma passing and all . . ."

"It's not that, Hattie. It's not all the people." Lydia drew in a deep breath, trying to avoid more tears. "They've always been a part of my dreams and a part of the stories Mama told me. I never thought I would be a part of their world, of your world." She sat up to face Hattie. "And I never thought I would feel so different from everyone. When I used to go for walks or work in the garden, I imagined what living with other people would be like. I imagined belonging with them. But those girls—I don't know how to explain it. They made me feel like . . . like I belonged in the barn with the cows."

"Oh, never mind them," Hattie said. "They're

only jealous of all the attention Dylan has been giving you. The Marks twins get bored when attention is not on them and they cause trouble. You might find it hard to believe, but if anyone stands out in French Corral, it's the two of them prancing around like they're royalty. Their papa is a miner like everyone else's around here, except for the store owners and Mr. Prescot." She whisked her hand across Lydia's back. "I'm sorry I didn't warn you, but I figured they would control themselves this evening."

"At least Mr. Prescot was nice." Drying tears tightened on her cheeks. Dylan's father did not see her as Mr. Sinclair had seen Mama. "But why isn't he a miner like everyone else around here?"

Lydia was now confident she could ask Hattie anything. Maybe her talkative nature would help to stuff down the thoughts Lydia had of going back to the Valley and forgetting she ever knew about French Corral. She silently thanked God for her curiosity. It seemed to save her from giving up in that moment.

"I don't know him very well," Hattie began, her gaze shifting to the window as if spotting Mr. Prescot outside would help her to answer. "His vineyards and orchards have been very profitable from what Dan says. He also travels a lot to the city to tend to his father's estate. If I were Mrs. Prescot, I would hate to be alone so much. She doesn't seem to mind. Your mama isn't the only one who's kept to herself around here now that I think about it. Women in these parts seem to embrace isolation."

Hattie continued, not allowing a moment of silence between them. Lydia began feeling drowsy, not sure she was up to more talking. Then Hattie mentioned that Dylan's mama had lived in San

Francisco before marrying Mr. Prescot.

"Hattie, can you read?"

With crossed eyebrows, Hattie jerked her head back. "Sure, I can. We have an excellent school here in French Corral. Why do you ask?"

Lydia drew the tattered diary out from under her pillow. "Mrs. O'Shea has been reading this to me. It's my mama's diary."

Hattie's jaw dropped and she giggled.

"I would like for you to read it to me. The last entry Mrs. O'Shea read was April 25, 1886."

Hattie took the diary without hesitation and turned the pages. "May I read the first few entries to myself before I begin?"

"Of course," Lydia whispered. She walked over to the window and waited.

Several silent minutes later Hattie cleared her throat and sighed.

Lydia shifted her gaze from the window and looked hopefully toward her new friend, ears opened with new curiosity.

April 30, 1886

I feel horrible. I never imagined something so terrible would happen to me. I have been so caught up fretting over Charles Sinclair, I have nearly ignored my parents. And now the unthinkable has happened. Our apartment caught fire and both Mama and Papa perished. They were trapped on the upper floor and had no way to escape. If only Charles hadn't walked me home the long way—I might have saved them or perished as well.

It will take weeks before family back home hears word and replies. In the meantime, the safest place to stay is at the church. I do not know what I will do. I have lost everything, and I would have lost you too, had you not been tucked into my apron like always.

Lydia cupped her hand to her mouth. "Read more," she whispered. "Please."

Hattie nodded and pressed her lips together before she continued.

May 23, 1886
Much has happened in the past few weeks. Charles has called on me several times, to the disapproval of the nuns, but I do not care. I thought I would never see him again.

Last night, he proposed—Yes, he asked me to marry him! I was surprised beyond belief. Just when I thought I had lost everything, God has come through. Charles says he doesn't care about his inheritance. He loves me—loves me! He has already made plans to take me to some property his father owns up North. He says his father will never know we are there, that the land was an investment and he doesn't plan to use it for years. I am not sure how I will fare out in the wilderness, but my sewing and cooking skills should suffice for a while.

Charles promises that we will learn to work the land together. We will make a life for ourselves away from the city and the people that want to keep us apart. I will write again soon. The nuns rang the dinner bell so I must go.

A blend of emotions suffocated Lydia. Her throat tightened.

Mama's parents had died in a fire. Was the land Mama wrote of the Valley? Did she really marry Charles and live there with him? Mama's stories about the angels helping her build the barn and the house came into focus.

She imagined a young man, with sweat at his brow, fine clothes tattered and stained while he worked long hours through heat and cold. Lydia saw him hacking huge logs, hauling away brush, hoeing unbroken garden soil with a younger, radiant Mama at his side.

Hattie's eyes glowed in contrast with her frown. "Oh, Lydia, it sounds so romantic, so tragic. It's like a forbidden novel. I think this Charles Sinclair must be your father. I wonder what happened to him and why he didn't stay on with your ma..."

"Father?" Lydia strained to utter the word. She must have a father somewhere. It made sense now, more sense than Mama's stories of the angels bringing her from heaven.

Lydia face grew hot at the thought, recalling how the sheep and cows made their young.

"Hattie . . ." her cheeks burned while she spoke. "Do people make babies like . . . like the farm animals do?"

Hattie smiled through her tears and pressed her lips together to form a crooked smile. "Well, sort of . . ." She stifled a laugh. "People go about their mating a bit differently, more—privately among other things." At that, she began to giggle uncontrollably and Lydia couldn't help but join in. She was comforted to know people didn't mate out in the open as their farm animals did.

Once they gained control of their laughter, Lydia's sides hurt. The more answers she got about Mama, the less their Valley life made sense. Mama had lived with people—in a huge city for that matter. Mama had also known the love of a man.

What had changed her to the point that she

would keep Lydia from the joys and pains of knowing other people? As grateful as Lydia was for all the friendly people of French Corral, her lack of knowledge irritated every inch of her. Would she ever understand the simple aspects of relationships?

Why was Mama so intent on protecting me?

Then, she considered another possibility.

What if Mama was protecting herself?

A soft rapping at the door broke her thoughts. Hattie stood to answer before Lydia moved.

Hattie opened the door only a crack, speaking to whomever it was in whispers too soft for Lydia to make out the words.

Hattie closed the door and turned to Lydia. "That was Mr. O'Shea. Dylan's here. He's downstairs and wants to speak with you."

"I can't, Hattie." She covered her lips with her finger. "Tell him I went to bed—and I'm sure you need to check on Olive anyway. Thank you for being a good . . . *friend* . . . but I need to be alone now. Goodnight."

Hattie appeared disappointed as she lowered her head and crept out the door.

Lydia shook her head and resisted the tears that welled up in her eyes once again.

After watching through the window to see Dylan and Hattie return to the party, Lydia changed into her nightdress and slipped under the covers. With one hand resting under the pillow beneath Mama's diary, and one hand resting on her heart, Lydia let the far-off sounds of the music at the dancing party lull her to sleep.

FOURTEEN

Lydia expected Dylan to attempt a visit the next day, but he never showed. After a week, she asked Dan about him. All he knew was that Dylan and Mr. Prescot had traveled to the city on an urgent errand a few days after the party. He assumed it had to do with the grandfather, but he wasn't sure.

Not exactly ready to handle the emotions Dylan's presence stirred, she took his absence as a reprieve and decided to put her efforts into mastering her tasks around the Inn.

Several days later, she lay up in her room, browsing the images of sewing tools in a catalogue Clara had loaned her from the general store. Mrs. O'Shea had relieved her of her duties for the evening since they currently had no guests.

A soft knock at the door surprised her. Hattie would not be over to visit until well after dinnertime.

Lydia's heart jumped as she opened the door and saw Dylan standing there with a fistful of dandelions.

"Miss Lydia," he nodded as he pulled his hat from his head to reveal his smooth, light brown curls, "I'd like to make amends on behalf of the town 'clucks'." His sincere smile coupled with white teeth and dimples made it difficult for her to reject his gesture.

"I-I did not realize you had returned from the city." She glanced at the dandelions in his hand, trying to hide the heat creeping into her face. "Dandelions?"

"All the other flowers stopped blooming weeks ago, but I wanted to bring you something."

"Thank you. It is a kind gesture. You don't have to apologize. I can't expect everyone to accept me as graciously as you and Hattie have." She took the dandelions from him and placed them in a glass of water on the nightstand. Then, she pulled out a chair from behind the door, gesturing for Dylan to sit.

The unexpected visit put a lump in Lydia's throat. She felt clammy and lightheaded. Why did his presence rouse such intensity within her? She gripped her hands together behind her back, trying to hide their shaking from his sight.

"Lydia? Is something wrong? Should I go?" Dylan stood and rubbed his hands together. "I should go. I am sorry for barging in on you." His dimples faded and his eyes grew dark.

"No, don't leave, but yes—something is wrong. I don't want you to go, but I . . . I don't know what you want from me." What was he hoping for her to say or do? Whatever it was, she was sure she couldn't give it to him.

Dylan's puffed up his chest, closed his eyes, and pressed his lips together before exhaling. "I don't want anything from you—except to try to understand what I am about to tell you, and why I didn't tell you sooner."

Beyond the Valley

Lydia sat down hard on the chair. Her heart raced and she clung to the sides of the seat to stabilize herself. What could he possibly have to tell her?

"You recall how we send messages to the outlying towns and the city through the telegraph line at the Wells Fargo building?"

Lydia nodded.

"You know I was looking into the Sinclair family who owned the land you lived on with your Mama. Last I told you—before the fire—I was waiting to learn more. With everything that happened since then . . . I haven't been able to find a way to tell you what I've learned. I thought I could resolve the problem myself . . ."

"Problem?"

"Yes, there is a problem and I can't resolve it without your cooperation." Dylan hung his hat on the nail by the door and took a seat on the edge of the bed facing Lydia.

"Just tell me—whatever it is I need to know. How will I ever make my way in this world with people keeping things from me all the time?" Lydia clenched her fists and crossed her arms. The stirring within shifted to familiar frustration.

"I understand—well, I'm trying to understand. We don't have a lot of time for me to explain all the details and I don't want to confuse you. So, please just listen for now. Agreed?"

"Agreed." She would burst if he did not tell her what was going on. Her breaths grew short while she anticipated his explanation.

After another deep sigh, Dylan continued. "Essentially, your Mama had been sending money to the Sinclair family for years as some type of agreement for her to be able to continue living on the property. The dilemma we are in is that she was sending the money pretending to be Charles Sinclair. After Emelyn's death, the summer payment was never made. As a result, Mr. Sinclair sent a telegram last month demanding payment or the property deed—which we now know still holds his name. I forged . . . faked . . . a response telegram—acting as Charles Sinclair—promising payment in the fall and explained that a fire had destroyed the crops so there were no summer profits."

She bit her tongue against the dozens of questions battling to surge forth.

"Did Mr. Sinclair reply?"

"Not exactly. My father and I actually went to the city to meet with him and discuss the matter in person."

"What?" She felt like Dylan was taking more control over matters than he should. *Why would he keep all this from me?*

"Against my father's better judgment, I insisted we approach Mr. Sinclair as investors interested in purchasing his property to expand our vineyards. We had hoped he would accept our offer and sign over the deed. We were careful to avoid mentioning you or your mother, our apparent interest strictly a business proposal. Of course, my father and I would have turned it over to you if we'd succeeded."

Lydia exhaled, unaware she'd been holding her breath. "What did he say?"

"The good news is that Mr. Sinclair was open to removing his name from the deed. But then he asked about Charles giving up the land, and why had he not come with us to make the proposal. My father stepped in at that point, making up something about a son's pride, and that Charles was too busy repairing the burned buildings on the property."

"All this and you still don't know what happened to Charles, my assumed father?" Mama's diary must hold some answers—and hopefully explain why Charles had left Mama alone and not contacted his father all these years. But Lydia wasn't sure she should tell Dylan about it quite yet. Not when he had already taken matters this far without her involvement.

Dylan waved his hands and shook his head. "That is one detail I cannot explain to you yet. However, what is more important in this moment is that Mr. Sinclair must have been suspicious about our story. He insisted on sending land surveyors to inspect the property at the start of spring. He also insisted that Charles accompany us back to the city to finalize the deal."

"What does that mean? What happens if Charles doesn't go?" This wasn't good. Lydia's hands started shaking.

"This is where the problem lies. Without Charles, Mr. Sinclair will put the property up for sale in the spring and will sell to the highest offer. My father and I talked through every possible solution and there simply isn't a lawful one. Mr. Sinclair has every right to take back his property. Once he finds out there is no farm generating income, there is no telling what he will do next."

"But it's my home . . . mine and Mama's." Lydia stood, tightening her fists at her side while tears burst, blurring her vision. Her blood surged. "What have you done, Dylan? How could you do all of this without talking to me about it?"

Dylan's eyebrows raised and he stood. "Wait,

Lydia. I have one more—"

"No . . . No. If you hadn't done anything, everything would be fine. Did you think I never wanted to go back to the Valley again? It is my home and all I have left of Mama. And now you've ruined any chance I have of living there again."

Wide eyes glistening, Dylan raised his voice. "I don't think you understand. I was trying to help."

"I don't think you understand. The only help I need is for people to tell me the truth!"

Dylan winced, and then snatched his hat from the nail on the wall. He stomped into the hallway. Spinning on his boot, he turned back to Lydia. His blotched face contrasted with its normally flawless appearance. "I guess I'm finished helping then. Good day, Miss Lydia." Clenching the rim of his hat, he bounded down the stairs.

Lydia shook, heart pounding, and palms sweating despite the sudden chill in the room.

Taking the back stairs to avoid an encounter with Mr. or Mrs. O'Shea, Lydia fled to the barn. Tears blurred her steps and no matter how many deep breaths she took, the shaking wouldn't stop. It wasn't until she buried her face into the thick, velvety rolls of Megan's neck, that she felt a slight serenity begin to calm her.

"Oh, Megan, I wish there were a way we could just go home. I've tried to fit in, tried to keep believing God has a purpose in all of this." Lydia wiped her face with her apron and realized Megan was due for her afternoon milking.

After grabbing the bucket off the wall, she settled into her usual position and continued sorting out her thoughts. "But now I wonder if this whole time, Dylan has had no interest in me. I know I am only beginning to understand how people in this world act, but what if all he wants is the Valley? Mama had tried to warn me about men, about evil motives . . ." Then Lydia recalled the dance and the dandelions. Dylan had seemed genuine, even nervous. He didn't need to pretend to like her. For all she knew, he could have arranged to buy her property without telling her a thing.

God, help me to make sense of this.
Be still and know that I am God.

Mama used to repeat this to her when they faced trials she could not explain. Eventually things worked out. Mama had also taught her to focus on what she could control and that worry would not add a day to her life.

FIFTEEN

By the end of September, Lydia had surrendered to the idea that her permanent home would now be French Corral. Nobody had offered to take her back to see the Valley, and she had not asked—afraid her request might somehow demonstrate she was ungrateful for all everyone had done to help her. Besides, Mama was buried in the cemetery here, a place Lydia often went to express the thoughts she was not quite ready to share with Hattie, or God.

One Sunday morning, Lydia joined Hattie and Dan in the French Corral schoolhouse, to hear a Methodist Elder teach from the Bible. Olive nuzzled against her, warming her legs, and drooling on her bonnet ribbon. When Hattie explained to Lydia how a Methodist elder would occasionally teach from the Bible for anyone in French Corral who wanted to hear, Lydia was amazed at the concept. However, she was not prepared for what he would teach that day.

"In the book of First Corinthians," Elder Scott continued, "Paul writes about his own imperfection regarding sharing the Gospel. Yet, confident in what Jesus did by the shedding of His blood, Paul has a guarantee of his salvation and that God's Will can be done through him. He writes in verse nine: *But as it is written, Eye hath not seen, nor ear heard, neither have entered into the heart of man, the things which God hath prepared for them that love him.* This means that if we have a heart, a longing to follow and know God, that God will prepare a way and a future for us more incredible than we could ever imagine . . ."

His words brought her thoughts to Mama's teaching about shedding of blood.

"We must shed blood to cleanse us of sin." Mama rubbed lye into Lydia's bed sheets, and vigorously scrubbed them against the washboard. Lydia was fourteen and had woken up soaked in blood. "Long ago, on the first Earth, God created people without sin, but because he also gave them free will, they soon betrayed him. You remember the story of Adam and Eve and the garden and the snake?"

Lydia nodded through her tears, confused, and frustrated at why Mama had not warned her. "I don't understand, Mama. Why do we have to pay for the sins of Eve?"

"We all fall short. We all have places in our hearts that do not honor God. One day you will learn of a way God has made for us to be cleansed forever. For now, we must accept this monthly sign that you are now a woman and that your sins count against you as they do me. And though we work hard here in the Valley, we can never make up for our sin."

A cool breeze stirred up dried leaves, their violent clicking ushering Lydia back to the present moment. As Lydia recalled Mama's explanation nearly three years earlier, a glimmer of hope filled her heart. The elder confidently referred to a man named Jesus, who had come to this one and only Earth to redeem every one of their sins. Jesus had paid the price!

Had she heard correctly? All she needed to do was have a heart to know God and live for him to receive this cleansing. It seemed too easy, especially after living for God the way Mama had taught her.

This must have been what Mama meant when she said God would make a way. So why then—if Mama had lied about what she called their "monthly", did Lydia still have to shed blood? She would ask Hattie about it later.

The more that Elder Scott spoke about the redeeming blood of Jesus, the more Lydia felt contempt for Mama. She had made her feel guilty for her sinful thoughts, for not being satisfied with the life God had given them. Whenever Lydia hadn't worked hard enough, Mama had made her feel ungrateful. She even made her feel like it was her fault God had not yet called her to deliver offerings.

Why would she make me feel so unworthy if she had known about Jesus?

She supposed that nothing about their life in the Valley would have made sense if Mama explained the truth about a man named Jesus.

Emotions tore at her heart. She was getting more answers, yet the questions that filled her mind were endless.

Then there was Dylan. He seemed to be an answer to her years of prayers for a man, a hero to rescue her. Yet, she could hardly tolerate his presence without some form of physical turmoil. Her heart broke at any thought she entertained about him losing interest. Yet, her heart burst at the thought that Dylan wanted something from her that she could not give.

Her mind continued to swarm. Lydia followed Hattie and Dan out of the schoolhouse. Holding Olive close to her chest, she thought if this babe could talk, she'd understand Lydia more than anyone else would.

They enjoyed a simple supper of bean soup and bread at the Inn, and then Lydia excused herself and went to her room for a nap. A cool breeze played with her cheeks as she rested facing the open window. Had she finally shed her last tear for Mama? Like the trees shedding their leaves outside, maybe it was time to let go of her past and look toward a future of new beginnings, a new life. Tightness in her heart confirmed her thoughts.

A gentle rap on her door startled her from what had almost been sleep. Lydia pushed herself up from the bed and smoothed out her dress.

Hattie smiled softly and leaned into the room.

"Olive fell asleep with Dan in the rocker, so I thought maybe you would like for me to read some more diary entries."

Although sleep beckoned, Lydia accepted the invitation, realizing the smile on Hattie's lips came from her own curiosity.

To distance herself from further turmoil, she silently resolved that she would immerse herself in Mama's diary as if it were only a story. Maybe she would understand Mama's intentions if she could ignore the notion that this Emelyn was the woman who'd lied to her for her entire life.

Hattie began.

June 5, 1886
Charles and I have joined a wagon train to Nevada County. Our final destination is a plot of land south of the town of French Corral that lies beyond Bridgeport. Eventually we will get our supplies and meet the town folk, but first, we will survey the land for the best place to build a barn and our home.

I am overwhelmed thinking about how different our life will compare to that in the city. I will miss the life my parents and I had. Yet it will be nice to start a new life apart from all that reminds me of what I have lost—and memories that only bring me pain. I must look forward now and be grateful that God has given me a husband to love.

I am frightened at the thought of harsher weather. I have never seen snow before. Will I be strong enough to do the work needed for us to survive? When I speak of my fears, Charles assures me everything will work out. I suppose I have no choice but to trust him.

We've stopped to camp for the night, so I must go prepare our separate beds at the back of the wagon. He is a gentleman and insists that we wait to spend our first night as husband and wife until we can spend it in the privacy of our own home. Though I long for the comfort of his closeness, I am grateful at

his discretion.
Goodnight.

Hattie raised her eyebrows as she read the last sentence, "Good thing we had that little talk the other day." She winked at Lydia and continued reading through her chuckles . . .

June 9, 1886
I simply cannot believe the heat here in the mountains. While Charles waters the horse—poor thing struggles to climb the steep terrain—I am taking a moment to write of the new and different scenery that surrounds us. The strong and strange scent of Manzanita bushes and the clicking and buzzing of insects overwhelm me. The air feels drier than fog-infused San Francisco. Yet, it is beautiful as well. Earlier today, we crossed the covered bridge at Bridgeport, paying an outrageous toll of one dollar to cross with our small horse and buggy. The shock dissipated as we balanced along a steep ledge and I dared to look down. The river rushed below to our right, tucked between enormous, jagged rocks with green, red, and golden oak leaves jutting from every crevice. It's like a completely different world . . .

We've just arrived at the property. After leaving the river's edge, we took a steep incline away from the ravine. Entering a cluster of trees now, I could hardly see the path where Charles guided our horse. Faint sunlight seeped between the branches until the opened into a clearing—
It is amazing! I am not sure I know the proper words to describe the vision before us. A small, green valley spreads out in front of us, bordered by trees on

every side. Wildflowers bloom in clusters of pink, purple, white, and orange. Charles stopped the wagon at the small pond surrounded by cattails to the east, to water our horse again. It will not take us long to know where to build our house. A small hill beyond the pond looks perfect.

Charles is urging me to put my pen and ink aside. We are home.

August 2, 1886

If it were not for the beauty of this valley, I would have given into death from heat exhaustion and physical frustration weeks ago. We have had days of such extreme heat, I thought I would melt into the dirt clinging to my toes. The work has been harder than I imagined. Every muscle in my body aches and my stomach longs for a nourishing meal that doesn't require me to spend hours to prepare. Yet, Charles assures me the worst is over. Finally, today I sit in the shade of the small oak tree we planted next to our home.

Yes, our home is complete, and of course, Charles agreed to build it on the small hill between the pond and the steep mountainside on the back end of the Valley. It has two bedrooms, a kitchen, and a living area. It is larger than the city apartment I shared with my parents, yet it seems a shame to use such a small part of this land for our home. Charles assures me it will be easier to heat in the winter. It is difficult to comprehend the harsh winters Charles described to me as I sit dripping sweat from every limb, but I trust he knows better than I do.

I do not have long to write, as Charles will be returning from French Corral soon. He is hoping to bring back at least one cow, a small flock of sheep and several chickens. I have only been into town once since there is always too much work here for both of us to go. Charles says it's best to avoid the town people until he knows for certain his father will not send anyone to find us.

Though I long for the counsel of a married woman to guide me in where I fall short as a wife, I find solace in working the land, no matter how difficult. It is hard to explain, but I sense I belong here. There is no one here to judge me. There is no one here to tell me I cannot achieve my purpose due to societal constraints. Between Charles and this glorious land, my every need is satisfied. Sometimes I wish this world consisted of only the two of us.

November 12, 1886

I came across you today, covered in dust beneath our bed. I cannot believe I have not written for so long. Our life here is good, though we were forced to stay isolated for several weeks when Charles got word his father had sent detectives to French Corral. Fortunately, the saloonkeeper told them a young couple fitting our description came through French Corral announcing it would soon be a ghost town and that they headed north to Boise, Idaho.

Ever since, Charles has insisted that I stay at home. If his father's henchmen happen to cross him again, he will claim I ran away and his father will likely let him be in hopes that Charles will come crawling back after winter.

Once October arrived, the weather turned cold fast. We harvested the garden before the ground grew hard. I learned how to make cheese and butter after reading a few manuals Charles purchased from the general store. I am keen at slaughtering chickens *now and the last time Charles brought home flour, I fried what he called the best chicken this side of the Sierras.*

I wish I had more time to update you on our life here in the Valley, but daylight is shorter now and Charles says the dark clouds in the east could mean snow by morning.

SIXTEEN

Lydia's mind swarmed with the events from Mama's diary. There was still no hint of her existence in the entries. Yet, she had to enter the story soon, for the last entry was dated November of 1886. That morning, when Elder Scott welcomed them to a fine, cool September afternoon, Lydia realized she had completely forgotten her seventeenth arrival anniversary only days after Mama's death. Lydia would have to ask Hattie how long people carried their young because if she was born at the end of July, Mama would need to become pregnant soon.

Thoughts of Mama and Charles shifted Lydia's curiosity to matters about Dylan. She wanted to forgive Dylan, assume his motives were pure. But when he continued to keep his distance and did not attempt to make amends, she consumed herself with working at the Inn and learning the ways of the other townsfolk.

When Dylan was needed at the Inn, he kept his manners, but spoke few words and remained somber.

"He must be really mad," Hattie said one afternoon while they enjoyed a glass of tea during

Olive's nap.

"I do not understand why he would be angry with me. He is the one who lied and could have ruined my chance to ever live in the Valley again."

"It is pretty typical of men from my experience," Hattie laughed. "They go behind a woman's back and then get angry when she doesn't agree with his choices."

Although it took several weeks, Lydia fell into a routine assisting those around town as needed. It seemed like nobody had enough time in the day, so when Lydia offered her help, they were happy to take it. With every task, she learned more about the life and people of French Corral and started to feel like she belonged there. In time, even the Marks twins learned to appreciate her talents. Their snickers turned into words of gratitude after Lydia learned to sew one of the newest dress patterns popular in the city. She felt a sense of purpose and healthy pride when her berry pies brought a smile to a lonely miner's scowl.

The school-aged children in town soon took a daily detour to indulge in a slice of Lydia's spiced bread slathered in butter. Seeing their delighted expressions reminded Lydia of a simpler time she was glad to pass on. When she wasn't in the kitchen, she fulfilled orders to mend or sew garments for Clara at the general store. Soon, Lydia was shelling out a dozen pies in the morning, scrubbing laundry with Lucy in the afternoon, and preparing supper with Mrs. O'Shea each evening. Nearly every skill Mama had taught her became useful once again. However, the one thing Mama hadn't taught her soon became Lydia's favorite task.

Helping Hattie care for Olive was a new adventure every day. Hattie was expecting her second child near the end of April and she could use the extra set of hands. Lydia couldn't imagine caring for two children at once. Despite the many messes a toddler managed to attract, Olive's delightful giggles and gibberish never failed to put a smile on Lydia's face.

Olive distracted Lydia in a good way, creating enough chaos to keep them occupied. When Lydia wanted to speak her mind, Olive listened intently and then graciously told her when to hush by shoving her fingers into Lydia's mouth.

After supper, while Olive and Dan were sleeping, Hattie would come to the Inn and continue to read Mama's diary entries. What Lydia learned softened her heart toward Mama, though it became more difficult for her to understand the reasoning behind Mama's choices.

November 13, 1886

I must sneak a quick entry to you as Charles sleeps soundly at my side. Last night we had a delicious supper of bean soup, rolls, and lamb. I made a strawberry pie for dessert and we took turns feeding it to each other as we sat in the light of the fireplace. The snow had begun to fall at dusk and the temperature in the cabin dropped severely with nightfall. Charles suggested we place our bedding in the living room and sleep in front of the fire.

Instead of worrying about what we would face in the morning, he embraced me. Refusing to let me clean up our meal, he began kissing my forehead. He whispered he loved me about a thousand times—then we joined as only a husband and wife can. I almost felt guilty whispering a prayer of thanks to God for such an amazing husband as we fell asleep in each other's arms.

I had to sneak this opportunity to write about it, in order to savor it forever. Oh, but it is cold! I should wake Charles soon to start a new fire. For the moment, though, I will nestle myself into his arms until I can no longer bear the chill brushing across my cheeks.

December 24, 1886
Merry Christmas. We've had a week of icy rain mixed with snow, which makes travel into town difficult. I do not think I will ever eat another strawberry. However, without berry jam to sustain us between store runs, I'm not sure how we'd survive. The bread is rock hard, but I've learned to boil it in chicken broth to make a sort of dumpling soup to eat it. Charles doesn't complain. He seeks the **LORD** *to sustain us each morning and asks Him to help us take it one day at a time. I have trouble keeping faith, as it seems our rations do not sustain me as they used to. It is hard to keep up my strength when I am hungry all the time. If it weren't for eggs and milk, I doubt my strength would last through a morning.*

Charles says we could still have two more months of winter, but that the clear skies mean no more snow for a while. I always wanted a white Christmas so I guess I cannot complain.

Oh, speaking of my amazing husband, he has just walked in the door with our Christmas tree!

January 15, 1887

I think I may now know why I have been so awfully tired and hungry. I dare not say a word to Charles, as his spirits seem low the past few days. I know at the right time, the news that we may be expecting a child will bring him great joy, but for now, we barely meet our own needs. I wonder if he might be coming down with an illness. He seems to be having a difficult time waking up yet is falling asleep long before me each evening. Because of this, he has probably not noticed my symptoms.

Tomorrow he is going to get the farming equipment out and put the ox to work if the ground is not too hard. I think it is too early yet to try to break ground, but Charles thinks we could get a head start on the planting if we can locate some soft soil. I think he is trying to stay busy. He keeps talking of going into town, but he won't say why. I have a feeling he may want to sit in the saloon and have a conversation with someone besides me. Strange, but I have no desire to talk to anyone besides Charles. Yet, I confess there were times in early fall when he worked in the pasture and I worked in the garden, that I felt more at one with the soil in my fingers than I do with him now.

The hope of a child growing inside of me has changed that some, but I still feel my husband growing distant. I hope he isn't having second thoughts and considering going back to the city to grovel to Mr. Sinclair. Perhaps with spring things will change. It is so difficult to keep up my spirits with gray skies and hard, colorless snow all around.

I imagine he must feel the same way.

January 31, 1887
The unthinkable has happened! I do not know what to do. I pray for help, as I cannot remember the way to French Corral. Oh, God, why must you take everyone that I love?—

Lydia gasped, afraid of what would come next. She took a breath and then nodded for Hattie to continue.

First, my parents and now Charles—I do not know how it happened, but Charles was caught in front of the plow and he is—in pieces. I am horrified. Lord, help me...

Lydia closed her eyes and tried to breathe, but the weight on her chest stifled her. "Does that mean that Charles was my father and that he died before I was born, leaving Mama all alone in the Valley?" Her head felt light as she slumped over on the pillow.
"Lydia . . . Oh, Lydia! That seems to be the case." Hattie cried.
Hattie hugged Lydia and joined her in soaking every handkerchief in the room as they sobbed together on the bed.
Mama had lost everyone.
The baby inside of her, who had to be Lydia, was all she had left in the world.

SEVENTEEN

Lydia's thoughts blurred between images of Mama living alone, her belly growing much like Hattie's, and the far reaches of her own memory as a young girl. She couldn't fathom how Mama survived without any help, especially since she seemed to depend so much on Lydia for as long as she remembered. Lydia worked methodically in the kitchen morning after morning. Her logical thoughts soon met with her old fantasy world. She longed to be that little girl again.

As hard as the work had been, Lydia never doubted Mama's love for her, never doubted she knew what was best. Now, Lydia didn't understand anything. Why wouldn't have Mama made every effort to move into French Corral, or to go back to the city to get help in raising her? Why make up so many rules to keep Lydia from knowing about other people?

For the first time in her life, Lydia hardly recognized the seasons change. Autumn would have come and gone unnoticed if Lydia hadn't needed to double the coal in the stove before noon by mid-October. She had to warm near-numb fingers in front of the flames before she could separate eggs for custard.

That same afternoon, Dylan silently stacked logs along the back of the Inn while Lydia husked corn alone, in the dining room. Would he come in to say hello? With a stern face, he moved methodically back and forth from the wagon to the porch, white puffs of air shooting from his tight lips. Even in his rage, he left her breathless. Should she still be mad at him, too? Hattie said it was just like a woman to forgive her man and just like a man to hold a grudge.

"A man's pride is more important than being right," Hattie had told her. "If a man doesn't have his pride, he may as well die. Don't take this wrong, but if he thinks anything like Dan, he felt foolish once he realized he'd upset you. He's probably angrier with himself than with you."

After learning about Charles dying on the farm, it was even harder for Lydia to speak with Dylan. She was torn between wanting to make things right with him and wanting to know the rest of Mama's story before deciding about how much he should know about where she came from. All the while, guilt ate away at her heart.

How many times had Lydia prayed for a life other than what she had with Mama? How many times had Lydia taken her for granted, unaware of all she had lost?

"Are you done shucking that corn yet, Lydia?" Mrs. O'Shea asked with an armload of flannel fabric bolts. "Clara's asked if you could make a dozen more dresses to help move inventory before winter brings travelers to a stop."

Lydia took one last glance at Dylan on the porch and then got up to help Mrs. O'Shea unload the fabric onto the dining table. She'd heard of a contraption called a sewing machine, which Clara had offered to purchase for her as a means to expedite her sewing projects. However, Lydia feared learning to use such a thing would only delay her process. Besides, sewing basic dresses by hand was simple compared to the gowns for angels that took her and Mama weeks to complete. Lydia easily completed two or three dresses a day when she hadn't other obligations.

"The corn is almost ready for the kettle, Mrs. O'Shea. With Hattie and Dan leaving tomorrow, I will have plenty of time in the evenings to sew. I'll stop by the store and get a list of measurements from Clara before I go to Hattie's this evening. Besides, with the last of the blackberries going into cobbler for tonight's dessert, I'll need something else to keep me busy." Lydia glanced toward the porch again.

Mrs. O'Shea nodded back with raised eyebrows and a partial smile. "Eventually, Dylan Prescot will come around. I've kept silent on this until now, but maybe it is time you made amends. Mr. and Mrs. Prescot are also heading into the city to visit his ailing grandfather, so Dylan will be alone for the next few weeks . . ."

Lydia stood there, astonished at the suggestion, and sighed. "I will think about it. Thank you for the suggestion."

Lydia went to work preparing the rest of dinner. If she didn't get all her tasks done earlier than usual, it would be too late to visit with Hattie. By the time the guests finished eating, Lydia resolved that she would try to talk to Dylan in the next week or so, but only if Hattie agreed it was a good idea.

Hattie promised to read a couple more diary entries to Lydia before leaving to visit her parents in Grass Valley. Lydia would pack while Hattie read.

"Shhhh. Olive just fell asleep," Hattie whispered, inching open the door while avoiding bumping into the small round table and two chairs nestled near the doorway.

"Where's Dan," Lydia asked softly. A wave of heat from the fireplace hit her frozen face like a hot towel as she entered.

"He's down at the saloon, having one last drink with the boys. My parents don't allow any alcohol, so he'll be awhile." She smiled and rolled her eyes. Then she took Lydia's coat and hung it on the back of a chair.

"All we need is on the bed," Hattie said as she opened the round-bellied black coal stove to the right of the door. Using folded linen towels, she pulled out a steaming pie and set it on the cutting block between a pile of empty tin loaf pans and a chipped, white washbasin. Muslin curtains hung below in place of cupboards where Lydia imagined Hattie stored the same washboard, lye soap and baking supplies as Mrs. O'Shea did in her kitchen.

"Go ahead and fold everything and fit it into that trunk by the bed while I read." Hattie tossed the towels into one of the four apple crates filled with linens and dishes beneath the window. "Then we can finish our evening with blackberry pie and some coffee before Olive wakes for her midnight feeding."

Hattie's eye filled with sorrow as she plucked the diary from Lydia's thawing fingertips. She glided between two rocking chairs and across a woven, cream-colored rug, which nearly filled the narrow floor. Tiptoeing around their bed and the small, hand carved cradle at the foot of it, she pushed some clothes aside and sank silently into a quilt-covered pillow. Lydia followed with the same caution and stood between a knotted-pine dresser and the trunk. Feeling her insides begin to turn and her hands shake, she began folding diapers.

"It'll be fine." Hattie smiled and reached across the bed to squeeze Lydia's hand. "We already know how it ends. She makes it through the next seventeen years. Now, let's get to reading and find out how."

February 5, 1887
I buried Charles today between the back of the cabin and the oak tree. The baby's bedroom window faces the tree. I could not think of a better place for Charles to lay to rest. I know his spirit is with the LORD, but I find comfort in his physical body remaining close. Maybe he will protect our child from all the heartache I have known.

I rummaged through Charles' paperwork and came across what I think is an answer to prayer amidst this tragedy. He had been in the process of arranging an agreement with Mr. Sinclair to ensure we can stay on this land. I found a telegram from Mr. Sinclair stating he will allow Charles to stay on the land—as a business partnership. All he requires is a small percentage of farming profits as proof he is improving the land.

If I send a telegram to Mr. Sinclair to let him know his son has died, he may want to take back the property. Where will that leave me? I have an idea, but I will need the cooperation of some of the people in town to make it work. The man and woman who run the Inn seemed like trustworthy people, so I will approach them first.

I will go into town to gather supplies and if it seems right, I will tell who I must about Charles and pray they will help me to figure out a way to stay on the property and in our home.

For now, it is easy to hide the fact I am with child. Will the town people accept a pregnant widow among them? I cannot risk anyone wanting to take my baby. If my calculations prove correct, the baby will arrive in early summer.

March 2, 1887
Praise God! Mr. and Mrs. O'Shea proved trustworthy and provided a solution. With more people packing up and heading into Grass Valley or to Sutter's Mill for work, the secret will be easier to keep. After begging for their help to find a way to stay in the Valley alone, they suggested I try to earn enough income on my own to send to Mr. Sinclair—and agreed that there is too much at stake to inform him of Charles' death. Another telegram also arrived from Mr. Sinclair, finalizing his agreement with Charles with terms that bring me relief and pain at once.

His conditions require Charles to cut contact with the rest of the family, as his marriage to "that girl"—me—is a disgrace along with any offspring.

Reading the words stung, but at least now, I can stay if I can find a way to generate income. After learning of my background in sewing, Mrs. O'Shea suggested I sew garments to stock the general store. With the right supplies, I can also spin yarn from our sheep's wool and use a loom to weave sheets of cloth. She could arrange to send a servant to pick up the goods at a halfway point, so I wouldn't have to make the journey all the way into town. We worked out all the details.

My bigger concern is hiding my pregnancy, but I think I may have found help for handling the birth.

While still in town, I overheard Mr. and Mrs. Prescot discussing preparations for the arrival of their baby. Mrs. Prescot gripped her back as she went on and on about the signs the midwife, a Miss Hastings, told her to be looking for. My ears pricked up as Mrs. Prescot asked her husband to go back and ask Miss Hastings about exactly when she should take the castor oil.

Mr. Prescot ran up the hill behind the General Store and toward a small, black cabin settled between two huge oak trees. I made a note of the path he took. I can easily come up from behind the hill to Miss Hastings's cabin during dusk without a soul in town noticing me.

I thanked the Lord again. I will need a midwife. I just must find a way to get her help without the town people knowing. I cannot risk another person learning of my pregnancy and thinking I am unable to care for a baby on my own—

Dan barged in the door, staggering into the chair holding Lydia's coat, and startling Olive into a high-pitched cry. As soon as he saw them at the back of the room, he pulled his finger to his mouth and spit out "SHHHH!" while he tossed his coat and hat onto the table.

"Dan!" Hattie whispered loudly as she scooped up Olive and pulled her under the quilt to nurse. She shook her head and then nodded at the pie cooling on the cutting block.

"That'll keep him quiet for another minute." Hattie curled herself around Olive on the bed and carefully propped the diary open on her hip with her free hand. "This next entry isn't long. Let's hope it holds us over until I get back from Grass Valley."

Lydia stacked the last of the clothes and linens into the trunk while she listened, disregarding the grunts and slurps coming from Dan at the table.

March 6, 1887

Miss Hastings is one of those people I have heard talked about as a "breed of her own." She hardly spoke as I explained my situation to her. She nodded slowly and pursed her lips, as if taking in each word and weighing its consequences. When I finished, her only condition was that I would not hold her responsible if anything went wrong. She told me her fee. I paid her immediately and then she performed a rather intimate "check" of me to determine if my pregnancy was in a healthy way. She asked me a few questions about my symptoms, and my last menses. Then she told me the baby should arrive in the first week or two of August.

She gave me some bitter tasting tea and a jar of dried leaves to make into my own tea to drink each night. She will visit me every month until July, and then she will check on me once a week until the baby is born. After giving me a list of supplies to collect by the middle of July, she grabbed my arm and locked her eyes with mine. Then she placed a pistol in my palm. In case I need her urgently, I am to shoot toward the mountaintop until it empties.

My heart thumped hard in my chest. I am on my own now. I am at the mercy of God and pray that Miss Hastings will be my angel in my time of need.

"I hate to stop reading, but I'd like to share my thoughts with you before continuing." Hattie slid a scrap of fabric between the pages and closed the diary before handing it back to Lydia. "It's getting late and now that Dan is home, we need to finish packing and rest before the journey tomorrow."

EIGHTEEN

By the time Dan finished his pie, Olive had drifted back to sleep. Dan snuggled in with the baby in bed. He started snoring before Hattie had a chance to pour the coffee. Lydia hung the coats and Dan's hat on the pine hooks behind the door and took a seat at the oval pine table.

Smiling in semi-silence, Hattie and Lydia sipped coffee and indulged in perfectly flaky blackberry pie. Though Lydia had been baking pies for weeks, she had not eaten a slice since her first night in French Corral. She ate slowly, letting the pieces of crust melt in her mouth while Hattie described her thoughts about Mama.

"I think your mama was scared of losing the baby, of losing you." Hattie slid her empty pie plate to the center of the table. "I think she might not have had her head about her . . . not been thinking clearly after all that time alone. I hope you don't take offense to that, but any woman in her right mind would have caught a train back to the city and moved back in with the nuns. They probably had places for pregnant widows in the city back then, places where they would have fed and clothed her."

Hattie paused, looking toward the flames in the

stove as if they would give her the words.

Lydia sipped her coffee, trying to understand Hattie's assessment.

"But then, they might have made her give you up for adoption. Yes—that must have been it. Considering Miss Hastings, well . . . I have always thought she was a little strange, but letting your mama live all alone through her whole pregnancy seems dangerous. No amount of money would have convinced me to let your mama do that."

Lydia pondered Hattie's words for several minutes, trying to ignore the distraction of pig sounds coming from Dan. What she said made some sense. But Lydia would have been more frightened of losing the baby *because* she was living alone. Lydia reached toward Hattie's belly and closed her eyes. Hattie rested her hand over Lydia's and they waited in anticipation. Then Lydia felt a gentle roll beneath the palm of her hand. They each squealed and then shushed each other, covering their own mouths. It was amazing, a miracle unlike Lydia could have ever imagined. She wondered what it would be like to have a baby growing inside of her, and then her thoughts shifted.

"Hattie, can I ask you something about Dylan?"

"Of course. It doesn't have to do with babies, does it?" She smiled and sipped her coffee.

"No . . . Mrs. O'Shea told me that Mr. and Mrs. Prescot are planning on taking the same wagon train you and Dan will be catching tomorrow. They are going to San Francisco to visit his sick grandfather. They will likely be gone for a couple of weeks." Lydia took a deep breath, trying to hold back a nervous smile. "Mrs. O'Shea suggested that maybe it would be an appropriate time for me to mend things between Dylan and I If I must stay in

French Corral, I can't keep pretending Dylan and I never met. Why does life have to be so complicated?"

"Slow down a minute." Hattie leaned over the table toward Lydia. "Honey, life is complicated no matter where you live. People make life complicated. I don't even understand my own life sometimes. Dan and I have our issues, yet we stay up here to keep distance from my parents despite another child on the way." Hattie stood and began to clear the table.

One person Lydia did feel she understood was Hattie. Cleaning up meant that she was about to give Lydia her answer and send her back to the Inn before she could argue.

"My point is that life is hard and complicated and no matter what we do to avoid it, the people we care about will hurt us—and the things they do might not make sense." Hattie rolled her eyes and shook her head at the bed holding her husband and child. "I have never known Dylan to stay gloomy for so long." She turned to face Lydia. "He cares about you. My guess is he can't hide the hurt it is causing him to live like you're not here."

Hattie leaned down and stared into Lydia's eyes. She balanced the stack of plates and cups in one hand, and patted Lydia's shoulder with the other. "I'm ordering you to pack a hearty lunch and find yourself at the doorstep of the Prescot home by the end of the week. I will look forward to a good report upon my return." Winking, she turned around and began washing the dishes.

Lydia buttoned up her coat and wrapped her scarf around her ears, neck, and mouth. What could she say? Her excuses were no good. What did she really have to lose anyway? She was making her way in French Corral. She would continue to do so, even if he rejected her. Lydia bit her lip to prevent the tears stinging her eyes from pouring down her face.

Mama would want this. Mama would want me to have the life she couldn't have. Wouldn't she?

But the thought of going to speak to Dylan alone made her queasy. She would have to find another reason to visit him besides bringing him lunch. She needed a better reason to convince herself to go.

Lydia desired to understand Mama's past—yet the threat of losing the Valley felt like she would be giving over all Mama had worked to preserve. Dylan had started to tell her he needed her help that day. Had her outburst prevented him from sharing a possible solution? With his resourcefulness and connections in the city—she believed Dylan had a way to help.

By Sunday, she knew that her visit to the Prescot home would be about far more than asking for Dylan's forgiveness.

Monday afternoon, an overcast sky and an overfilled basket of savory foods accompanied Lydia as she guided Jasper up the trail behind the Wells Fargo building. Her beloved "runaway" horse had appeared in the stables at the Inn in early autumn. Mrs. O'Shea had read the note attached to the gate and explained that the person who had originally purchased him as a favor to Emelyn had returned Lydia's horse. The person did not want their name revealed but offered Jasper as a gift of condolences on the loss of Lydia's mother.

Lydia had felt grateful to have another familiar animal friend to ease her into life in this town. Now, Jasper led the way up the uncertain path toward Dylan Prescot. With each rumble of the wagon wheels on the road, her hands shook, and her heart shuddered. Lydia prayed for God to guide her words carefully, and that she would not upset Dylan anymore.

The sky darkened as she steered Jasper around the final corner leading to the Prescot home. Clouds loomed above and wind whisked dry leaves until they spun into the air, nipping at her face and hands. Lydia snapped the reins and the wagon lurched, nearly knocking over the kettle of soup at her side.

When Lydia arrived, she tied Jasper to a whitewashed fence post, hung the basket of food on her arm, and carefully lifted the steaming kettle. A single drop of rain splattered the lid as Lydia stepped up onto the shelter of the wraparound porch of the Prescot home. A steady tap of raindrops mingled with rustling wind in the treetops behind her. A still silence filled the house before her. Perhaps Dylan was not even home.

She pulled on a cold, large, brass ring and thumped it against the smooth, white door. Each rap echoed followed by a silent response. Maybe he was out in the vineyard, preparing for the storm.

Lydia turned away, courage dissipating, ready to brave the rain and dash toward the wagon.

Then the door swung open, and warm air rushed up her back, fighting back waves of frigid air that assaulted her face. Lydia turned her head and prepared to step off the porch.

"Lydia?" Dylan whispered. "What are you—"

Without finishing his sentence, he grabbed the kettle from her grasp, and led her inside.

In the darkness of the foyer, the whites of Dylan's eyes glowed with the reflection of tree limbs and leaves tossing about in the large window beside him.

"What are you doing here?" He dropped her hand and set the kettle down next to an unlit lantern on a narrow table by the door. He crossed his arms and stood in firm silence.

"I . . . I . . . Dylan, I need something from you." Lydia pulled at her lip, hoping her cold fingertips would prevent her from speaking the wrong words. She looked down and squeezed her eyes closed in preparation for a harsh reaction. "Will you help me confront my father's family . . . convince Mr. Sinclair to allow me to keep the Valley . . . as my home?" Lydia kept her eyes closed, bit her thumbnail, and prayed she could be strong enough not to cry. Her heart vibrated in her chest.

Dylan's shoes scuffed the floor. Lydia opened her eyes as he turned to face the window. They stood without a word, without movement. Rain pelted the windows in bursts as the gusts of wind whipped around the house.

Finally, Dylan drew his hands up in a prayer position and pressed his fingers to his lips.

"These past weeks . . . have been difficult for me." His voice grew a little stronger with each word. "Yet . . . no matter what I have been going through . . . you don't deserve my silence."

He remained facing the window.

Is he talking to me or to God?

"What I am fighting is hard to explain. The day we met in the forest, I thought you were an angel, sent by God to give me a reason to live beyond working for my father for the rest of my life. My motives were selfish. All I did to help you was out of my need . . . my desire to be close to you and . . . some insane idea that if I rescued you, I would be whole."

Lydia crossed her arms. What was he saying? What did it have to do with her keeping her land? She kept listening.

"That night, in your room I realized how wrong I was to keep everything from you. I realized I was doing it all for the wrong reasons." He turned and took a step toward her. "I know everyone in town thinks I am mad at you, but the truth is, Lydia . . ." he approached her, and pulled her by the elbows into the gray light seeping through the window.

Lydia felt suddenly weak inside. Her stomach flipped and she sucked in a breath.

"The truth is, I have been mad at myself," he continued, seemingly unaware that Lydia was petrified. "I figured I don't deserve you or anything to do with you. I thought if I apologized, you would feel obligated to me in some way. I've gone on with my life as if you were not here. And it's been tearing me apart, Lydia . . ." His voice faded with her name. He released his hold on her and crossed his arms again.

She searched his eyes. How could he express in words what replicated so much of what she had been feeling but had not been able to articulate? The aching to be near him, the feelings that she could never become someone he could want . . . or need.

Lydia reached to touch his face and cupped his cheek in her trembling hand.

He leaned into her palm, despite how cold it must have been against his warm flesh. A tear slid down his cheek.

"I actually thought coming here to simply forgive you wouldn't be good enough." She smiled, allowing her own tears to fall. "And I do . . . I do forgive you. I have never been so confused about anything ... so uncertain of what the future holds. But I want you to be a part of it."

Dylan started to smile, and then his eyes grew dark. "There is something else you should know before you make up your mind about me."

Her stomach sunk. The picnic basket on her arm fell to the floor with a thud.

No more, Lord. No more surprises . . . please!

"I wasn't completely honest about why I went into the forest that morning we met, about why I wasn't afraid to go onto your property." He sighed, grabbing her hand from his cheek, but maintaining a hold on it. "Clara had sent me to check on Emelyn, concerned about her declining health since the previous fall. I was supposed to confront her, offer to accompany her to Grass Valley and cover the cost of a physician. None of us expected for me to find you, to find out she had been raising a child this whole time."

"Physician? What do mean . . . *declining health*?"

"She was ill, showing signs of disease . . . she needed tests, medicine—"

"I don't understand...she was fine. She was only tired from working so hard all those years . . ." Lydia shook her head repeatedly.

"Your mama was going to die if she didn't see a doctor . . . and it's my fault. All I could think of was that her illness would provide a way for me to be with you. I thought if I could rescue you both, I would get what I wanted—I would be your hero— saving your mama and showing you the truth about life beyond the Valley."

Lydia wrinkled her forehead—fear and frustration converging into anger. "What? My *hero* would have told me the truth from the beginning!" Her heartbeat accelerated with the tone of her voice.

"I'm sorry, Lydia. I realize now how wrong I was . . . delusional really, to think it would all work out. That I would end up with my perfect, faultless mountain girl without a reason to find fault in me. And then the fire happened." He turned away, grinding his palms into his eyes, and rubbing his face.

Lydia's thoughts swam, fury resonating. A suffocating wave of pain swam from throat to her chest. She pulled balled fists to her face, pressing them into her cheeks until it hurt to keep herself from screaming.

Was this what Mama had wanted to save me from? Was this what she had meant about the sin in our hearts, about not being content?

Her mind dug up bits and pieces of their conversation by the pond that moonlit night. He told her most people wouldn't go onto someone else's property out of fear of being shot.

Had he known that night that Mama was sick? Did he already know she could die?

The sky outside cracked. The windows vibrated and the room lit up for an instant.

"How?" She cried. "When did you know Mama was going to die? Why didn't you tell me so that I could convince her to see a doctor? Was that why she didn't make it out of the forest? Was she too sick to make it out alive?" Dylan's face blurred through her tears.

His brow wrinkled, his own tears falling freely.

"No, I didn't know for certain. I thought we had more time. I needed to find out why your Mama hid you. Miss Hastings had not yet revealed what she knew. I was being honest about wanting to make sure you were not in danger."

"But you knew I would have believed anything at that point. You could have taken us into town . . . you could have brought us here and paid the doctor to come care for Mama. I would have done anything to make her well again . . . anything!" Lydia shrieked and turned toward the door.

This whole time, she had blamed herself for Mama's death when Dylan could have done something to prevent it.

Men only bring pain, Lydia.

"This was what Mama was protecting me from!" Screams cut her throat. "She tried to warn me about men. She tried to tell me they would hurt me. Your *flawless mountain girl?* Is that some prideful act of men, to rescue the innocent and ignorant for their own satisfaction?" Her hand vibrated the doorknob, slipping with sweat while she struggled to open the door.

The raging storm might as well have been a calm morning mist compared to what raged inside of her. She felt stupid and betrayed. And this time, it wasn't by Mama.

She jerked the knotted rope from the fence post, gathered the reins, and pulled herself up to the wagon seat, nearly sliding off the slick seat. Jasper leaped and whinnied in response to Lydia's force, and in seconds, the wagon bound down the road.

Dylan's voice trailed faintly in the background, muffled by sheets of rain and thunder from above.

Between the storm's bellows, Lydia's wails permeated the darkness. She expected Dylan to come up beside her on his horse at any moment. But soon, she found herself disoriented between pouring rain and a steep decline covered in pine needles without a visible road or path in sight.

At the bottom, Jasper hesitated at another hill ascending before them. Near the top, a dim light glowed from the window of a small, black cabin, squeezed between the trunks of two oak trees. The horse wouldn't climb the muddy terrain.

Shaking and soaked through every layer of her garments, Lydia slid off the wagon seat, gathered the ends of her sopping dress, and trekked up the soggy trail of pine needles and soaked leaves toward the light.

NINETEEN

Miss Hastings opened her door with a faint smile and a twinkle in her eye. Knobby, wrinkled hands grasped Lydia's wrists and led her inside. Exhausted and bewildered that her unannounced visit required no explanation, Lydia allowed Miss Hastings to remove her soaked petticoat and pantaloons and wrap her in a wool blanket.

Without a word, the old woman turned Lydia to face the fireplace and nodded at the empty rocking chair. Had she welcomed Mama with as much expectation nearly eighteen years earlier?

Strange, yet familiar scents bombarded Lydia, bringing images to her mind from deep places in her memory. The aroma of cloves and strawberries drifted from the steam lifting off the pot of water on the stove. Drying garlic and fennel stalks hung on the wall, emanating a pungent and sweet odor that whisked Lydia back to days she played with cornhusk dolls on the floor of her cabin.

Lydia rocked nervously, staring into the fire while trying to make sense of the memories flooding her mind.

A moment later, Miss Hastings handed Lydia a cup of mint tea, as if she had expected a guest. The warmth flowed down her throat and soothed the damage from her screams and sobs. The reality of how tightly Lydia had steadied herself on the racing wagon throbbed in her legs and arms now that her sobs had transitioned into silent tears.

Miss Hasting took care to wash Lydia's face with a warm cloth, hushing her if she tried to speak. Then, she scooted around her tiny cabin for several minutes, pulled bread from her stove, hung wet clothes along the rope above the fireplace, and all the while hummed a tune that brought comfort to Lydia's weary spirit.

Then Miss Hastings began to sing the words softly—

"Safe in the arms of Jesus,
Safe from corroding care,
Safe from the world's temptations,
Sin cannot harm you there.
Free from the blight of sorrow,
Free from your doubts and fears,
Only a few more trials,
Only a few more tears!
Jesus, my heart's dear refuge,
Jesus has died for me,
Firm on the Rock of Ages,
Ever my trust shall be.
Here let me wait with patience,
Wait 'till the night is o'er,
Wait till I see the morning,
Break on the golden shore…"

Lydia's ears and heart hung on each word. A peace covered her as if huge arms were holding her together. All at once, she felt like an infant wrapped in the arms of an angel.

She remembered!

Miss Hastings used to care for her when Mama delivered offerings. She used to rock her and sing songs to her. Long ago Mama had explained that Miss Hastings was one of the angels. Lydia had forgotten about her, setting aside her memories along with her fantasies of living a life with other people.

"You used to sing to me," Lydia whispered. "I remember now . . . I thought I imagined you, but I remember now . . . I remember . . ." Tears turned into bawling again. Lydia trembled and clung to the blanket.

Miss Hastings dropped the muslin towel from her hand and came to Lydia's side. The light from the fire glistened in the tears that filled her eyes.

"Now, now," she whispered, caressing Lydia's back. "The good LORD reveals all things in due time. It is in these times we must trust Him and take only from the past that which will strengthen us for the future."

Suddenly, Lydia longed to be home more intensely than she had since Dylan had taken her to French Corral without a choice. Deep in her heart, Lydia knew Miss Hastings words rung true, but she was tired of being strong, tired of pretending she could go on without ever seeing the Valley again. She didn't need answers anymore. She only wanted something familiar.

As memories of Miss Hastings filled her mind, memories of Mama did too. *Oh, how I wish Mama were the one holding me.*

Lydia wanted to feel Mama's worn hands squeezing hers tightly while they danced circles in the garden. She closed her eyes for a moment, tears pouring down her face and soaking the edge of the blanket under her chin. She rocked slowly and imagined she was home again and Mama was sitting across from her, spinning wool, and telling her stories.

"I want to go home," Lydia sobbed, and reached out for Miss Hastings hand. "I need to go home—no matter how temporary it may be. Will you help me go home?" Miss Hastings would know the way back to the Valley.

The rain slowed to a tap on the roof. Dark-blue twilight crept through black tree branches through the window.

"You will stay here tonight." Miss Hastings stood. "In the morning we will go—before the sun comes up behind the mountain."

Lydia's encounter with Dylan faded into the back of her mind like a bad dream she wanted to forget. Sleep came more easily that night than it had in all the months since the fire. When Miss Hasting gently tapped Lydia's arm to awaken her, it took a moment to remember she was in the midwife's cabin.

She jolted from her slumber. She would finally be going back to the Valley.

Lydia rubbed her eyes and saw that Miss Hastings had gathered a few of her things from the Inn. She'd slept so deeply that she never noticed Miss Hastings leave. The creak of the door opening when she returned had sounded like a distant tree falling in the forest. Among Lydia's things, Miss Hastings had brought Mama's diary, Lydia's quilt, and her Bible.

Damp logs crackled and popped in the fire while Lydia changed into clean, dry clothes. She ate a soothing bowl of hot porridge. Miss Hastings worked outside, strapping her few belongings to the back of the wagon in a jiffy while Jasper munched on a pile of grass. How had Miss Hastings managed to get him and the wagon up the steep hill to the shelter of her porch?

"The sky is beginning to brighten," Miss Hastings whispered when she came back inside. "No more rain. Travelers will enter the road to French Corral soon. We must go now."

Lydia nodded. Her heart raced. She would be home soon.

It had been over three months since the fire. There would likely be a lot of work required to get the cabin back in livable condition, the garden ready for winter, and the sheep pen and barn prepared for new animals and Megan. But the work meant less time to notice the absence of Mama. For a while, Lydia would pretend Mama was delivering offerings.

She wouldn't worry one second about what could happen in the spring, when Mr. Sinclair sent his men to assess the land.

For now, the Valley was *her* home.

Brisk air brushed across Lydia's cheeks. Puffs of white escaped in short bursts from her lips and nose. Lydia followed Miss Hastings on her own horse, carefully guiding hers over slick, icy leaves and crackling, frozen mud puddles. The horizon glowed with an orange tint, lighting their way. By the time they crossed the road and began to climb the steep terrain leading to the top of the mountain, the charcoal gray sky was pale blue and thin rays of sunshine clung to black treetops.

It didn't take as long as Lydia expected to reach the peak and begin the decent on the other side. The path turned, and darkness seemed to fall again. Bare-branched oaks and groves of blackened, gnarled Manzanita branches gave way to a narrow passage bordered by clusters of charred evergreens.

How had Dylan ever managed to find their Valley through the thick foliage? If she didn't already know it existed, she would not have imagined a flat, open valley lie beyond the darkness of this forest.

No wonder Mama was able to keep her hidden all those years.

Then, twinkles of light broke through the slits between trunks and low branches. The terrain flattened and they crossed a gurgling brook. Moments later, the horses trotted into the light. Fog covered the Valley like tufts of wool ready for spinning. In the distance, the black rooftops of the barn and cabin jutted out above the mist.

Lydia's hands began to shake and sweat. She squeezed the reins and urged the horse on.

But then, Miss Hastings stopped at the pond's edge. "It is time for me to go back."

Was she leaving? "Won't you at least come with me into the cabin and let me heat you up some tea?"

"Hard to tell how long that will take."

Lydia shouldn't expect more of Miss Hastings. After all those years of keeping her and Mama's life here a secret, she was not about to ask her to do it again.

Lydia nodded, and bit her lip to stop stinging tears from escaping.

"Will you tell Hattie that I will come see her as soon as I can?" Somehow, she knew Miss Hastings would ensure Lydia would not be disturbed—at least for a few days.

Miss Hastings nodded. "You will do fine, Lydia. You have the strength of your mama."

Before Lydia had a chance to thank her, Miss Hastings disappeared behind the forest's edge.

Lydia snapped the reins and gripped her legs around the horse's belly, forcing him into a swift gallop.

The mist parted a perfect path before Lydia, reminding her of the first encounter with Dylan. She had clung to him instinctively as he raced his horse along this same path, headed directly to her porch. She had not once wondered how he had known the way.

While Lydia located enough dry wood to stoke a fire in the stove, sunshine and a bright blue sky dissolved the darkness and mist cloaking the Valley. It was then she saw the charred proof of the fire that had crossed here in the summer, reaping destruction like a huge black snake slithering between the pond and behind the barn, and miraculously missing the cabin by dozens of feet. She imagined the flames soaring above the roof while clouds of dark smoke frightened sheep and chickens clamoring to escape.

However, layers of ash and soot covered the surface of everything left behind, yet still in its place, throughout the cabin. Had Dylan also exaggerated the damage to keep her in town? Her home was still livable. It needed a good cleaning and a portion of the kitchen wall needed replacing.

Despite the finger-numbing cold, she kept the door and windows opened, to release the lingering stench of suffocating dust and smoke, while she cleaned. It took most of the morning for her to clean the things she would need to use. Anything else drenched in smoke odors went out to the barn. She washed her bedding and brought wet logs inside to dry by the heat of the stove. By the time the sun hung above the oak tree outside of her bedroom, Lydia was ready for a nap. She took the blankets Miss Hastings had supplied, along with her quilt, and slipped into the familiar comfort of her bed. Ignoring the lingering scent of smoke clinging to the mattress, her eyes grew heavy in no time.

Right before she drifted into a deep sleep, Lydia thought of Charles, her Papa, buried beneath the tree outside of her window. She had always found comfort and felt protected by that tree. Maybe it was the comfort and protection Lydia had missed from a life without a father.

After what seemed like only seconds of sleep, the sunlight seeping through her eyelids grew dark. More storm clouds. She jumped out of the warmth of her bed and rushed outside to secure Jasper in the barn for the night.

"It's cold enough that we might see snow tonight."

Lydia spun around, smacking the back of her head into the barn door.

Dylan stood only a few inches in front of her.

A lump formed in her throat, preventing her from speaking.

"Sorry to startle you, but I had to know you were

all right."

Lydia couldn't believe he would allow a smile to creep around his mouth. Shocked, she watched him lead his own horse into the barn. Then, he tucked her arm into his elbow and guided her to the cabin.

How was she supposed to respond to this? Her mind told her she needed to hate him for what he had done. But the pounding of her heart told her she could not go on without him.

TWENTY

Dylan drew her close once they entered her cabin.

"I can't do this," Lydia whispered, pathetically trying to push herself out of his arms. His presence gave her comfort, despite the pain that resonated from their earlier argument.

Tears warmed her cold cheeks and she avoided his gaze in search of a handkerchief.

"Do what, Lydia? Let me love you?" He grabbed her hands, holding them tightly with his calloused fingers.

"*Love* me? How can I let you love me when I don't even know who I am? I thought staying in French Corral would provide answers about where I came from, and why Mama did what she did. Instead, it has made me question my life even more."

"But I want to help you find those answers and be a part of your future. You have to believe I only lied . . . kept things from you—for your protection."

"Well, I'm tired of people trying to protect me from the truth, and I'm tired of feeling like answers will lift this burden when all they do is weigh me down. If it weren't for my Mama's diary, I would have come back here sooner." Lydia pulled her hands out of his grasp and poked at the fire with a branch.

"A diary? You have a diary from your Mama?"

"Yes. It was what Miss Hastings gave to me at Mama's funeral. But it doesn't help anything."

"It must be giving you some answers. When did she write it? Did she date the entries?"

Lydia sighed loudly, prodding the logs in the fire, trying to let him know she didn't want to talk about it. She didn't want him there, his presence suddenly a stark reminder of all she could not have.

"Lydia?" He placed his hand on her shoulder and softened his voice. "Please."

She sighed again, refusing to turn toward him. "Mrs. O'Shea and Hattie have been reading it to me. I thought it would explain why Mama kept me here, why she lied to me about life beyond the edge of the Valley. But all I have learned is that my Papa died here and that Mama may have been sick in her mind as well as her body."

Dylan backed away and paced in front of the stove. He pressed his hands together, drew them to his mouth, and then stared at the floor.

Lydia looked at him, trying hard to erase all emotion from her face. She crossed her arms, fighting the urge to ask him to leave. "Can we take a moment to talk about you? There is still something you haven't explained yet."

"What is that? Not that I haven't tried to explain things. You either yell at me or run off."

She could tell he was hurt. The men in Mama's stories seemed more resilient that he was. "Why me? What is it about me that is worth all this . . .

pain in your eyes?"

He grunted. "My father often chastises me for wearing my heart on the outside. I can't help it. I take after him."

"What do you mean?"

"Many years ago, my father rescued my mother . . . it is something nobody else in French Corral knows, so I tell you in complete confidence." Dylan adjusted both rocking chairs closer to the fire and gestured for Lydia to take a seat in Mama's chair.

Curiosity emerged. She wrapped herself in the quilt draped over the back of the chair and sat. "Rescued her from what?"

Dylan remained standing. "He rescued her from a horrible life in an area of San Francisco called Barbary Coast. He said my mother was worth more than that life offered. He also knew she could never live a normal life in the city. So, he sold his portion of the business to my grandfather and bought our home from a miner's widow. Ever since he has been devoted and determined to give my mother the life she deserved without the scrutiny of high society."

"That's amazing—*romantic* —is what I think Hattie calls it. It sounds a lot like my Mama's story."

"She was from Barbary Coast too?"

"No, but my papa brought Mama here after her parents died in a fire. His father refused to accept her since she wasn't from *high society*."

Dylan grinned. "Don't you see?"

Lydia was sure her heart stopped beating. "See what?" She looked around the room.

Dylan laughed. "No, not see with your eyes—see with your heart. Who else could understand where my family came from better than you? Who would accept my heritage—the son of a former prostitute—without a second thought?"

Lydia began to understand. Was all she and her mama lost a part of a bigger plan to bring her and Dylan together? Why? "I know you think you've been the selfish one, but you are wrong." She was overwhelmed with an unexpected need to make things right.

She pushed herself up from the chair and approached Dylan. "I'm sorry I didn't trust you. I'm sorry that at some point I forgot about that man who risked his life to save me from the fire."

He clearly needed her as much as she needed him. She could not deny it.

Determination replaced the longing in Dylan's eyes. "Do you have your Mama's diary with you here?"

"Yes." Lydia nodded, "It's in the flour sack over there on the table. Why?"

He retrieved the diary from the sack, dropped the sack onto the floor, and dragged his rocking chair over until it was side-by-side with Lydia's chair. "Are there more? Are there more entries in here Mrs. O'Shea and Hattie haven't read yet?"

"Yes." Lydia sighed, and sat in the rocking chair. "There are more."

"May I read it to you?"

Lydia never considered that Dylan could read Mama's diary.

Was this what loving her meant—helping her to understand her past so they could move forward together? She longed for healing from the pain in her heart. She longed for a final peace in her soul, knowing she had done all she could to make sure Mama hadn't died for nothing.

"Yes, please read it to me."

"Where did you leave off?"

Lydia briefly explained what Mrs. O'Shea and Hattie had read up to that point. She cried when she told him about Mama's pregnancy and how she hadn't been able to tell Charles before he died tragically. Then out of fear and nowhere else to go, she chose to stay here and raise her baby alone.

"If I remember correctly, the last entry Hattie read was from March 6, 1887."

Dylan nodded. Then his forehead wrinkled in concentration. He turned the pages, scanning them quickly until he came to the right spot.

"Looks like the next entry came at the end of March."

Lydia closed her eyes, leaned her head back, and slowly rocked as he read.

Would Mama have wanted it this way? Lydia prayed she would have.

Dylan cleared his throat and began.

March 27, 1887
I picked a bouquet of wildflowers today. I will ask Miss Hastings for a book about flowers so that I can learn their names. If I am going to make a life here for my child and me, I need to know all I can about this valley. The Valley. I have decided to give it a simple name. It looks as if it could be a world all in its own. I have everything I need here. When my baby comes, I will also have a chance to love someone once again. I must do whatever I can to make this the best home for us. I will do whatever it takes to keep my child here with me.

I have collected everything I will need for the baby's arrival. I have started sewing cut up, old flannel blankets into dozens of diapers. Once I'm finished, I have fabric for gowns and bonnets, and spun enough yarn for several pairs of booties and woolen caps. If anyone questions my ability to mother a child alone, I will be able to prove I can provide for all our needs.

The strawberry preserves are ready for jarring now, so I must go.

April 20, 1887
Once again, the weeks have gone quickly. I can feel my baby moving around within me now. Sometimes she (I am praying for a girl) keeps me awake even when I am exhausted. If I press my hand into the side of my belly, she will push it back out again as if to say, "I don't have much room in here to begin with, Mama!"

Other times, I will lay my hand gently on the center of the puffy bump that is my belly, and smile as she rolls back and forth against my palm. I am amazed that a life is growing inside of me! I pray every day that she will be healthy and strong. I pray that she will be able to overlook the many mistakes I am sure to make as her mama.

Thankfully, with it just being the two of us, my baby will never know when I mess up. She can't know. What if she learns that I could have given her to a family in the city? What if she learns that she could have had a Papa and a Mama? She may never forgive me.

Oh, why do I write in here? These thoughts never enter my mind while I am working in the garden or sewing—only while I am writing. Suddenly, I do not fear losing her to society and their idea of what I cannot give. Suddenly, I fear losing her to her own ideas if she ever finds out what her life could have been.

I must go now. The thought of losing another person I love is too much to bear.

Dylan nodded slightly, and his jaw twitched. "It seems like she truly believed that isolating the two of you would somehow prevent more loss . . . and pain."

Lydia filled the kettle with water and placed it on the stove for tea. She slid the loaf of rising bread dough in the stove and started to add a log to the fire. "It's as if all she feared came to pass no matter what she did to stop it."

Dylan reached over and grabbed the log before she could. "Why don't you let me keep the fire going? I don't mind helping to keep us warm."

She returned his smile and then glanced out the window at the darkening sky, suddenly aware of the imminent storm and the late hour.

"Perhaps you should be heading back. Like you said, we could be getting snow tonight."

Lydia had learned enough from the people in French Corral to know it was not proper for an unmarried young man and women to be alone and secluded. If the snow fell hard and fast, he would have to stay the night. Did anybody even know he was here?

"I will be fine. I have fared snowstorms before. There are only a few entries left. I thought you wanted me to finish it?"

Her curiosity once again won over common sense.

"The clouds are making it really dark in here." She lit several candles in the center of the kitchen table.

Lydia didn't care what the townspeople thought. She would finally know Mama's entire story. *The good* LORD *reveals things in due time . . .* Miss Hastings' words echoed in Lydia's mind. Had the Lord's hand been guiding them this entire evening?

Dylan continued.

May 1887

I am not sure about the exact date. It is somewhere in the middle of May. Spring is in full bloom. Miss Hastings came to visit today. She quietly came and left like an angel. Maybe that is what she is after all. She said the baby and I are doing fine.

My baby doesn't really have a need to know anyone besides me. I can give her everything she needs right here. Whenever she asks about our life here, I will tell her we are living for God and God alone.

June 1887

It would be a miracle if my baby never knew heartache or the pain of losing someone she loves. It is peaceful here. It's just God's presence among His glorious creation.

The angel visited again today. She said the baby is growing well. She told me that when it is time for her to be born, I might see a little blood on my undergarments. After that, my belly will tighten and my back will ache in waves. She told me to fire the gun ten times once the tightening and the pains are strong enough to prevent me from moving about the cabin.

But God will tell her when to come help me have the baby. She is probably having me use the shotgun to set my own mind at ease.

July 1887

This is not how she said it would be. It's too early. It's not August yet. I had just chopped the last of the kindling for morning. I thought it was too hot to make a fire, but that I needed to make enough bread to last for after the baby comes. Then something started leaking down my leg and I couldn't hold it back. It wasn't blood, so I figured she finally kicked me hard enough to make me wet myself. Then the tightening came as the angel said. Now I can hardly write these words. I fired the pistol moments ago. I pray my baby is not coming too early.

Dylan's cheeks grew red and he cleared his throat.

Lydia set his tea down in front of him and took a seat beside him at the table.

"Thank you." Dylan set the diary, open and face down, on the table. "This is chamomile, right?"

"Yes, picked and dried from the Valley last summer. Is this making you uncomfortable reading about childbirth? I can't remember why, but I think Hattie told me men are not usually present at such events."

"Well," he cleared his throat again, "in the city, men physicians or midwives attend births depending on the resources of the mother. But . . . that's not what is troubling me." He took a long sip of his tea.

"What is it?"

"It sounds like your mama started to believe Miss Hastings was an angel. Whether intentional or not, it seems your mama was beginning to believe in her own version of a solitary world in the Valley.

Did you notice how she stopped referring to Miss Hastings by name? I wonder if she honestly thought she was an angel."

TWENTY-ONE

Lydia chewed her thumbnail. Was Dylan confirming what she and Hattie had begun to suspect? Was Mama sick in her mind? If so, how did she reconcile going to town for her offerings and how did she know what to lie to Lydia about? What troubled her more than anything was how Miss Hastings ever arrived at the decision to allow Mama to raise her alone.

Once again, Mama's diary brought more questions than answers.

"But she went into town eventually. We know she went into town, lying to me about delivering *offerings*. She had to have known what she was doing to some extent—"

Suddenly, gusts of freezing wind burst open the door of the cabin. It snuffed out the candles and blew a thin layer of snow across the floor.

Dylan jumped up, forced the door closed, and pulled down the wooden beam, securing it shut with a rope knot tied to a nail on the wall.

"Whew! That should keep the wind out for now. Where are the matches?"

With the door closed again, the cabin grew dark. The orange glow coming from the fireplace hardly lit up the outline of Dylan moving about the cabin.

Lydia searched blindly along the counter, trying to recall where she had put the box of matches. She found the box drenched in kerosene. "Oh, no . . . I found the box, but it is soaked in kerosene."

"Spill the box out onto the table. There must be at least a few dry ones in the middle."

Lydia dumped the box and felt around for a dry match.

Dylan nudged up beside her, his warm, strong arm brushing against her shoulder. After a moment, he stopped searching and placed his hand on hers, curling his fingers gently between her own.

He stood close enough that she could smell the chamomile and honey on his breath, despite the odor of kerosene floating in the air. It felt like a dozen butterflies were flying around in her stomach.

She couldn't move. She could barely breathe. Her heart pounded in rhythm with the snowflakes tapping against the window.

He pulled her hand down in front of the table and then turned her body to face his. Standing in the dark in such proximity felt worlds different from the brief embrace they had earlier while daylight streamed through the windows.

He cupped his hands around her cheeks and drew her face to his until her mouth felt the warmth of his breath. He tenderly pressed his lips into hers. She grew limp, but somehow remained standing.

What was happening? Had Mama felt like this with Charles? Was this why she was willing to go wherever she had to be with him? For one awfully long moment, nothing else seemed to matter.

Then, Dylan pulled away, and gasped. "I am sorry, Lydia...this isn't right . . ."

"But wait, for the first time—to me, it is. It feels right. I have never felt . . . I don't know if there are words. Is this what . . . *love* . . . feels like?" She tried to hold back her grin, even though she knew he couldn't see it.

She reached for him, longing for his embrace again.

But he stepped back. "Yes, love begins like this—and it can become much more than feelings in time. However, love can make you want to do things before the time is right. Lydia, we can't do this. These feelings you are having—I am having—they can lead to things that are not proper between a man and woman who are not married." He recovered a dry match from the pile on the table and lit it on the edge of the stove. "As a gentleman, if you still believe I am one—I must stop this right now."

Warm light flooded the room a little more with each candle until it encompassed most of the room and revealed Dylan's flushed face and sweat glistening across his forehead.

Lydia didn't care about what was proper. She didn't understand why he couldn't hold her again, why he couldn't kiss her again. How could something that felt so good and so right be wrong? Lydia could see in his eyes that he struggled along with her.

She took a deep breath. "I don't care how long it takes to understand what things should be like between a man and a woman. But if this is what love feels like, then . . . I love you." Lydia reached for his hands, needing to touch him in some way.

He squeezed her hands. "Only God understands

the depths of my love for you. Sweet Lydia—you have opened my eyes and heart to this world in ways you will never know. When I set out to rescue you, I never thought that you would rescue me. You rescued my heart from selfish desires and now you are compelling me—in a good way—to put your needs ahead of my own." He gazed deeply into her eyes, keeping hold of her hands, but stepped back far enough that she could not reach to kiss him again. "And that is why I need to do this the honorable way."

It was worse than the gnawing feeling Lydia would get in winter when food rations ran low.

Dylan pressed his lips together as if to hold back the agony he too must be feeling. "But first, let's read the rest of your mama's diary. I think it is best to resolve what we can about her past before we start talking about the future."

Lydia sighed deeply, feeling a twinge of guilt about their unplanned embrace causing such a distraction. She had momentarily forgotten the last thing Dylan read was that Mama was about to have her baby.

Back in their seats at the table, the aroma of baking bread filled the room, and snow blanketing the blackness while Dylan read on.

August 1887
Her name is Lydia. She came into the Valley with a rush of unseen angels by my side. Her skin is like rose petals, her breath sweet like the air after it rains, and her cry is like a newborn lamb. She is lovely. She is perfect. I am overjoyed that I can meet her every need. She needs me and she wants me. Her delicate fingers wrap around mine as she nurses and

her dark blue eyes open wide as they stare at me and sparkle. I feel like we are in heaven, until my stomach cries for food of its own.

Miss Hastings brought a cradle for Lydia on her last visit. I told her Lydia was doing fine in my bed. She said it is safer for me to keep Lydia in the cradle while I tend to the needs of the garden and animals. One day, Lydia will learn to roll over and the cradle will keep her from falling.

Miss Hastings tried to convince me to move into French Corral. She says the town people are nice and they will not see a problem with me raising Lydia without a father. I cannot do it. I cannot risk Lydia wanting to leave me for a better life. If she finds out about the world beyond the Valley, then she surely will want to explore it.

No. I cannot bear to let her learn anything that could cause her to want to leave me. I know I won't live forever and that one day she will need to live on her own. For now, for this time when all she needs is me—I can give her everything. There is no point in telling her what she does not need to know.

October 1887
Lydia smiles at me all the time now. She is such a happy baby. I use a large piece of muslin cloth to hold her to me while I work. She loves to face out and watch all that I am doing. Her hands and arms and legs are plumping up and dimples dot her wrists and knees. This is a good sign that she is getting plenty of milk from me. Eventually, I will give her goat milk and other foods, but for now, I am all she needs.

Miss Hastings came by earlier today. She was impressed at how orderly the cabin was and she said

Beyond the Valley

I am back to myself again. When I asked what she meant, she said I called her an angel several times toward the end of my pregnancy and that she was concerned I wouldn't be able to care for Lydia.

I took the opportunity to try to convince her to keep Lydia's existence a secret. She says she cannot come to the Valley indefinitely. Eventually people will become suspicious. Perhaps, she suggested, I can go into town alone once Lydia is weaned. Miss Hastings will watch over her while I go to personally trade my goods.

I think this plan will work...it must. But one day, Lydia will be old enough to engage with Miss Hastings. Will Miss Hastings be willing to keep the outside world a secret from Lydia? I will have to convince Miss Hastings that she will no longer need to come to the Valley once Lydia can manage alone while I am gone—but before she is old enough to remember Miss Hastings.

November 1887

I have decided to get rid of all my books when the time comes to end Miss Hastings' visits here. Having books is proof of an outside world. As curious as an infant as Lydia is, she will no doubt want to know about everything she explores in our home and outside. I must not leave anything here that I cannot explain is something we need to survive in the Valley. This means I will not teach her how to read. Instead, I will teach her how to garden, sew, and cook—all the things that will help her to take care of herself in the Valley for as long as we both live.

Regarding Miss Hasting' part in all of this, she has promised not to tell anyone about Lydia as long as I keep an orderly home and maintain the property. One day, I will give her this diary and other proof of a world beyond the Valley for safekeeping until it is time for Lydia to know how we came to live here.

In the meantime, I pray God will give me the words to convince Lydia our life here is all we need, and that He is our source for everything else.

Dylan sighed and closed the diary with hesitation. "That is the last entry."

"What?" Lydia shouted, shocked at how her voice cut through the silence following Dylan's statement. "That's it? How did she convince Miss Hastings to leave us here alone? Did Charles's family ever come to check on him? Maybe there are pages missing. Maybe Miss Hastings still has them in her house . . ."

Dylan examined the inside of the diary. "No, it looks like Miss Hastings took good care of this. There are no missing pages. However, we still have many answers. She loved you and cared for your every need in the ways she believed were best for both of you."

"She met my every need besides my longing for other people. I used to lay awake at night and pray for God to bring us other people. I would beg Mama to tell me the stories about people on other worlds so I could imagine myself living their lives. How could she continue to keep the outside world a secret? How could she convince herself she was all I needed for so many years?"

"We will probably never know, but we know enough to move forward."

Dylan got up from the chair, and then leaned down and began to unstrap her boots. "It is time for you to go to sleep, young lady."

Seconds later, he took her hand, and after verifying which room was hers, tucked her into bed in the way Lydia imagined a father would do for his child.

He kissed her forehead and blew out the candle. "I will remove the bread from the oven, and keep the fire going for the night. Don't worry about anything out here. I'll sleep on the floor by the fire."

TWENTY-TWO

In the morning. In the morning.
Lydia tried to recall the hymn Miss Hastings sang the other night.
...*Here let me wait with patience, Wait 'till the night is over, Wait 'till I see the morning, Break on the golden shore*...

As exhausted as every ounce of her was, Lydia tossed and turned all night. She searched her memory of Mama, searched for a hint that she wanted Lydia to know the truth eventually. Did Mama's stories hold any answers? Maybe, she knew what she was doing was wrong. Maybe Mama knew that if Lydia understood that people failed that she would forgive Mama's failures more willingly.

Out of all of it one thing that did not make any sense was why Mama had failed to teach her how to love a man. Why couldn't she have told her about her father? She could have explained that God made the three of them and that Charles had died. Then Lydia would have known about the love between a man and woman.

Was she afraid I would leave her to seek love of my own?
The morning sunlight shone bright, reflecting

white light off the snow and onto her quilt, and radiating the worn corner that had been her papa's handkerchief.

It was then she knew why Mama couldn't tell her about the love she had for Charles—it would hurt too much. Even though Lydia was beginning to realize the love she felt for Dylan, she could not fathom the thought of losing him.

Then, a fleeting thought twisted her stomach into knots. What if Dylan decided to go back to French Corral while she slept? She sat up, shoved off both quilts, and ignored the biting cold that clung to her nightgown and stung her bare feet hitting the floor.

"Dylan?" Her voice quivered.

No answer. She raced into the living area. A wool blanket lay crumpled up in front of the cold, blackened ashes of the fireplace. The plank of wood holding the door closed had been untied and put back up against the wall.

"Dylan . . ." Lydia snatched up the blanket, wrapped it around her shoulders, and headed for the door. Dank cabin air gripped her hands and legs, making it difficult to move. Keeping a hold of the blanket, she blew hard into her freezing fingers, trying to warm them enough to grasp the door handle.

Right when she reached for the door, it swung open. She jumped back, slammed into the table, and fell onto the floor in a heap.

"What are you doing?" Dylan chuckled, rolled the stack of logs he held onto the floor, and then pulled Lydia into his arms.

"I thought . . . I thought you had gone." Tears streamed down her face, warming her numb cheeks.

"I thought you'd still be sleeping for hours. I'm

fine, and I'm here." He wrapped the blanket around her in secure layers and kissed her forehead firmly. "Now, go and get dressed in one of those nice dresses I saw lying on your dresser last night. I plan on making you breakfast."

Sighing, Lydia smiled. She wiped the tears from her face and followed Dylan's instructions.

Flaky biscuits with strawberry jam and fried eggs never tasted so good. Maybe food tasted better when coming from a man's hands. Long after their plates were empty, Lydia and Dylan sat across the table from each other, sipping tea. She waited for him to speak, glancing between his face, and the crackling fire behind him.

The diary entry where Mama described a night by the fire fluttered through Lydia's head. She imagined herself and Dylan, wrapped together in a blanket and cuddling by the fire. Heat crept into her face when Dylan caught her stare with his eyes.

"What's next?" Lydia asked, shaking the thought from her mind.

"Well . . ." He smiled, absorbing her full attention with his dimples and willow-green eyes. "If you would like to stay here until spring, there is a lot of work to be done to make it habitable again. I can't let you do it alone."

Her shoulders fell. Maybe she had only dreamed about their embrace in the dark...his kiss. She decided she liked his passionate side better than the practical one, but she did want to stay.

"This house, this land . . . they are my only connection with my mama and papa. And I need time to let everything that has happened set in. I would be grateful to you and anyone else willing to help me make this my home again...even if it's only until spring."

"Then it is settled, but on one condition."

Her belly flipped and she bit back a smile. "What condition?"

"That you will not isolate yourself as your mama did. I am not the only one who has come to care for you in the past few months. I am sure I speak for us all when I say we would like mutual visitation . . . you come to us and us to you whenever the weather allows. To make sure you are faring and to visit as well."

Her home and property open to friends and neighbors like any other in French Corral?

"I would not have it any different. I have come to depend on all of you too much to want it any other way."

"All right then." Dylan stood and clapped once. "We still have time before winter settles in. If you're fine with it, I would like to assess the condition of the roof and the barn and bring back supplies and a few more hands to help you fix things up."

Weeks of mild autumn weather allowed plenty of time to complete the work needed for Lydia to have a safe and warm winter. Mr. O'Shea, Mr. Roberts, Dan, and Mr. Prescot spent many long days repairing the damaged barn and kitchen wall, putting up a new sheep pen, and completing the tasks and toil Lydia used to dread.

She and Mama had failed to properly repair the sheep fence after a hard rain the previous spring. Lydia shook her head in disbelief as Dylan effortlessly wacked new posts into perfect position. It used to take Mama and Lydia all day to chop and stack firewood. Mr. O'Shea and Mr. Roberts cut and piled logs halfway up the wall in only a couple of hours.

Was this what her life would have looked like if her father had lived?

In the first week of December, Dylan brought a flock of sheep, a half dozen hens, a pig, and Megan back to the Valley. A few days later, the men declared the buildings were fully repaired and ready for winter. That evening, Clara, Hattie, and Mrs. O'Shea came with ample supplies to feed the dinner party in addition to a cartload of salted meat, jarred vegetables, and a plentiful supply of ground coffee to sustain Lydia through the winter. Mrs. Prescot offered regrets that she was overcoming a mild illness and would be unable to attend.

Lydia's house filled with laughter and warmth, one sight she had never imagined happening in the Valley. Dan played his banjo while Olive swayed at his knee. Dylan told jokes that Lydia didn't understand, but she laughed along with everyone anyway. Hattie tried to teach Lydia to dance, but they soon doubled over with giggles. Lydia felt a satisfaction in knowing her home could bring joy and comfort to more than just her and Mama.

Later, the women helped clean up the meal while the men loaded up wagons with their tools and other supplies Lydia no longer needed. A stab of disappointment turned in her belly as one family at a time loaded into their wagons and waved farewell.

Dylan and Mr. Prescot were the last to leave. After making sure the barn and sheep pen were secured for the third time, Dylan went to Lydia, who stood on the porch regretting his departure.

He gently kissed the top of each hand and smiled, before mouthing the words, "Goodbye for now," with a wink.

Then, he joined his father sitting on the wagon, and grabbed the reins. Mr. Prescot tilted his hat and smiled sideways. "Miss Lydia . . . have a good evening. We will be checking on you in a few days."

"Thank you, Mr. Prescot." Lydia waved and then watched them until the moonlit path took them into the forest. It was the same path Mama had taken to deliver offerings. The men had also cleared the entrance to the Valley from that road to ensure easier passage to and from town. There would be no more trekking up the steep mountain on a secret path into French Corral. There would be no more life of seclusion in the Valley.

TWENTY-THREE

It was the mildest winter in a decade. Cooler days were dry or rainy at their worst. Secure in the comfort of knowing Dylan, Hattie, and others from French Corral would visit her often, Lydia settled into a routine much like what Mama and she once had.

When Dylan traveled with his parents to the city for Christmas, Hattie and Dan offered to celebrate Olive's first Christmas with Lydia. The traditions and rituals they shared mimicked much of what Mama and Lydia had done to ring in the season. But this year, Lydia learned what part Jesus symbolized, bringing deeper meaning and joy to this time she had long looked forward to as a child.

In turn, Clara and Jason hosted a New Year celebration at their house, as a way of welcoming a fresh resolve for the year 1905. Though some in town chose to spend the evening at the saloon, the Roberts' home was open to those willing to confess their wrongdoings and choose to improve themselves and their focus on God in the coming year. Lydia relished the time, soaking in the prayers and worship of others. It did her soul well to know that others strived to do good in the future, even if they had failed in their past.

For one reason or another, Dylan's mama never appeared at any of the social gatherings. Lydia was sure she understood that nobody else in French Corral knew of Mrs. Prescot's past. Yet, Dylan always made up a reason she could not attend. Dylan promised that at the right time, he would introduce Lydia to his mother. That time had simply not presented itself yet—not even on his eighteenth birthday in March—when he explained his parents had a private celebration planned for only the three of them.

Though Lydia wondered if he was holding back the full truth again, she stopped pressuring him about it. Everything else was going well, aside from the pending approach of spring and what to do about the arrival of Mr. Sinclair's men. No matter what occurred, Dylan was willing to accompany Lydia to confront her grandfather with the full truth about the life her and Mama lived on the land. They hoped once he knew everything, he would hand over the land without a fight.

Shortly after the hillsides turned green and bare branches grew buds, Dylan announced he had something important to tell Lydia. With a twinkle in his eye and smile beaming, he assured her it was not bad news, and for her to meet him for an early lunch by the pond the following day.

Bursting with curiosity and anticipation, it didn't take long for the gentle tapping of the oak tree branch on her window to wake her the next morning. Lydia pushed open the window above her bed, smiling up at the robins chattering among the trees.

"Good morning, Papa." Lydia smiled, looking at the tight, green buds on the tips of the branches.

Sweet air blew around her cheeks. Lydia closed her eyes for a moment, imagining the gentle kiss of her father.

Damp blades of grass clung to the bottom of her feet as Lydia tiptoed to the barn to milk Megan. As milk streamed into the bucket, Lydia wondered what Dylan had planned for their morning picnic. He told her all she needed to bring was fresh butter and a small kettle of coffee. Lydia was supposed to meet him behind the cattails, at the same place they had met nearly a year earlier.

No matter how much Lydia tried not to imagine the possibilities, she couldn't stop smiling at the thought of kissing him again. He had not allowed such an embrace since that cold autumn evening, months earlier. Lydia imagined the sun warming their backs while they sat on the picnic blanket, with legs crossed and knees nudging.

Then her toes tingled, drenched in warm milk. Lydia had given in to daydreaming again and overfilled the milk bucket.

She set the bucket outside of the barn and took a moment to observe the morning sunlight that streaked across the Valley in shimmering golden and yellow hues. Lydia topped-off water troughs and scattered feed for the chickens before skimming the cream off the top of the bucket. While she poured cream into the butter churn, she decided to wear her green and brown calico dress with the green bonnet.

She would leave her braid falling down her back instead of turning it into a bun. She would use the small mirror Clara gave her to ensure every strand was in place, and that her face wasn't soiled from morning chores.

Dylan greeted her with a kiss on her hand and then spread out the blanket for their picnic. He arranged their supplies and then sat, peering behind Lydia before catching her eyes with his and smiling.

A concerto of buzzing bees, whirring wings, and babbling birds ushered in spring and all that was bursting to blossom around them. The sun's reflection glided from the edge of the pond to the center, flooding it in golden glimmers.

His presence and the memories of this place awoke the butterflies that Lydia had tried to keep from fluttering during her morning chores. Lydia smiled back at him, nervous about how silly her words would sound, but what she prayed was a prompting from God on her heart.

"I have something to say before you tell me whatever it is that we are here for."

Dylan cleared his throat and relaxing his shoulders. Then he began to pour a cup of coffee for each of them. "All right. After I say a blessing for our meal, go right ahead."

She held her breath as he prayed, not hearing a word of it while she went over what she was about to say in her head.

Swallowing hard, she began. "I think my mama wasn't perfect. She loved me and did everything she could to give me a life she felt was best for both of us. She also loved my papa to the deepest parts of her being and I see now how I had become all she had left of him. As hard as it would have been for her to show me the world and let me go, I believe in time, she would have given me her blessing to..."

"To what?" Dylan's forehead wrinkled and his smile faded.

Lydia realized her words and expression might be coming across as more serious than nervous. She sighed and made herself smile despite the lump in her throat.

"To have my dreams realized . . . to know love. Mama would have wanted me to know and receive love—and all that comes with it." Lydia took a sip of her coffee, still adjusting to the bitter taste, and waited patiently for Dylan to realize what she was saying.

"Amazing." Dylan shook his head and grinned. "That will make what I have to tell you . . . ask you . . . that much easier. But let's eat first."

Lydia smiled and sighed, afraid that if she said more, she might spoil his announcement.

When their meal was over, Dylan moved their picnic supplies to the edge of the quilt. Then he crawled over to where Lydia sat, and leaned up on one knee.

He took her hands in his and searched her eyes.

She could feel the pulse on his wrist racing against her fingertips.

The deepness of Dylan's gaze engulfed Lydia in shades of green and flecks of gold reflecting from the sunlit pond.

What is he doing...or about to do?

"Would you tell me already?" The anticipation left her breathless.

"I planned on reasoning with you, telling you it would be necessary for our plans to journey to San Francisco and confront your grandfather." Dylan cracked a wry smile. "But this is about more than formalities."

Lydia bit the inside of her lip.

"We've already confessed our love for each other in private, but it is time to profess it before God and men." Dylan drew a small band of silver from his pocket.

Lydia's head felt light, but she could not will herself to breathe.

Dylan's voice grew deeper. "I love you . . . and everything about you. Your zest for life and curiosity . . . your willingness to continue to trust in me and this world despite all you did not understand . . . your continued belief that God has a purpose, and that I could be a part of it—all of it leads me to one conclusion." He cupped his free hand beneath hers and grasped one of her fingers.

Her hand shook at his touch. But his hands were shaking too.

Dylan swallowed and then moistened his lips, his smile suddenly fading. "It is time for us to begin our life together. Lydia Sinclair, will you . . . give me the honor and pleasure of being my wife? Will you marry me?"

Finally, Lydia exhaled. Although she had imagined what her life would be like as Dylan's wife many times, she never thought this was how it would begin.

"How am I . . . supposed to respond?" Lydia stuttered, wanting to provide him with the response he desired.

Dylan grinned. "Just say yes. I'm sure Hattie will be glad to fill you in on the details of what comes next."

"Yes!"

Dylan slid the silver ring on her finger, stood, and pulled her into his arms.

Without warning, his lips met hers with a deep kiss.

Lydia kissed back until she had to pull away to breathe. Dylan laughed, and lifted her off the ground, then spun her around until they collapsed, side-by-side, onto the picnic blanket. They lay there holding hands and staring at the sky until their delirious giggles faded into content smiles. Thin, white clouds inched across a bright blue sky.

Finally, Lydia felt the heaviness on her heart lifting to fly away with the clouds. Regardless of what came of their journey to San Francisco, she felt certain of one thing. If their love for each other—and God—remained true, his purpose for their life together would prevail.

A short time later, they walked hand in hand back to the cabin. Naturally, Lydia scanned the swaying grasses for wildflowers, many of the typical ones already in bloom. Orange poppies and purple lupine grew abundantly among tufts of dandelions. Then, she spotted a rare cluster of purple and white petals. She loosened her hand from Dylan's and strayed from the path to get a closer look. They were anemones—the flower of anticipation and protection from evil. Plucking one stalk of each color, she joined Dylan on the path again.

PART 2

TWENTY-FOUR

Lydia dabbed a damp cloth along Hattie's temples and forehead. Dark curls clung to the sweat on Hattie's blotched cheeks and neck. The room stood silent aside from Miss Hastings' slippers whispering across the floorboard, and the gurgle of water she poured into the kettle on the stove.

A long, deep groan came from within Hattie. She shifted to her side, and gripped Lydia's arm. Lydia reached over with her free hand, and making a fist, pressed it firmly into the small of Hattie's back for the twelfth time that hour.

Miss Hastings looked up from her task and nodded. "It's time for this mama to push." She scooped up a basket of torn rags that had been warming by the fireplace and brought them to the bed.

Lydia froze at the reality of what was about to happen. This was far different than assisting a sheep or cow in birthing young. Hattie appeared to be in far more pain than the animals. All the preparations concerned Lydia as well. Adhering to Miss Hastings' instructions, she gathered hot water, clean rags, heated a knife over the flame, and then wrapped it in a sterile cloth on the table near the bed. Was this normal preparation for a human birth?

Miss Hastings didn't explain—she gave orders. "Take that bedroll and place it behind Hattie. Then pull off what bedding you can from under her and slide that old quilt under her bottom—"

Hattie groaned again, protesting as Lydia worked quickly. Then Hattie wailed and grunted.

Miss Hastings flung Hattie's gown back over her knees and instructed Lydia. "Take her arm in one hand and hold this knee back with the other, Lydia. Now Hattie, look at me...breathe in deeply and hold it. When the next urge comes, bear down as hard as you can."

Hattie nodded and tears flowed down her cheeks. She looked a Lydia and somehow managed a smile as she locked arms with her friend.

Not two seconds passed and the grunting began again.

"Good . . . good . . . there's the head." Miss Hastings pressed her lips together and nodded with approval.

Hattie gasped for breath and another wave hit within seconds. She sucked in, held the breath, and pushed again.

Amazed at her friend's strength and focus, Lydia ignored the fingernails that dug into her arm, the strain in her back as she held Hattie's knee to her chest.

"All right, the head is out. This one is coming much faster than Olive . . . you will have a baby in your arms in one more push. Lydia, lay that small quilt on Hattie's chest and get ready to wrap the baby in it quickly."

Hattie leaned her head back and inhaled once again.

One . . . two . . . three . . . four . . . —

"You have a son!" Miss Hastings placed the infant onto Hattie's chest and assisted Lydia in wrapping it tightly.

The infant whimpered and then wailed.

"Is it good that he is crying?"

Hattie and Miss Hastings laughed. "Yes, it is good," they said together.

Lydia sighed with relief. She had more questions, but this moment wasn't about satisfying her curiosity. She was here to support her friend and joined her in admiring the new life Hattie now held to her bosom.

Brian Philip Logan demanded every moment of Hattie's attention. His wails only ceased while he was eating or sleeping. Lydia longed to help with his care but chasing around a toddling Olive took most of her time. Although Hattie never came out and asked for help, she was obviously overwhelmed. As excited as Dan was to have a son, he seemed at a loss. He had to travel to the Empire Mine for work, a safer and better paying job than local mining offered. Often, he would stay in Grass Valley for weeks at a time, leaving Hattie all on her own to care for two babies.

"My mother will be arriving from Grass Valley the evening before the wedding." Hattie lay Brian in the cradle by the fireplace and reached to take Olive from Lydia's arms.

Olive clung to her mother instantly and nestled her head into the crook of Hattie's neck.

"I don't mind staying with you until then." Lydia took advantage of a moment with free hands and gathered up soiled diapers and gowns for washing.

"I can manage for a day or two without your help. Besides, I'm sure Clara and Mrs. O'Shea will stop by more regularly once they know you've headed back to the Valley. You, my dear friend, have a wedding to plan!"

Lydia closed her eyes at the thought.

A wedding?!

Helping to care for two babies seemed a less demanding prospect. "Consider it a trade, then. At least you have a clue about how to care for these little ones."

"How am I going to convince you that the wedding is one of those days most young women dream about from the time they can talk? Women have babies every day—but the wedding is only once in a lifetime for most of us." Hattie shook her head, giggled, and adjusted Olive on her hip.

"I know it's a big deal. My belly flips every time I think about it. I am going to be Dylan Prescot's wife. *His wife?* It seemed like the perfect plan that day by the pond." Lydia started for the door. "If only my mind would stop swimming with questions about how it will all work out. I haven't even met his mother yet."

"Well, that will change soon enough. Didn't you say you are attending a formal dinner at the Prescot house this week? It is strange how she has managed to avoid meeting you all this time. Now that I think about it, I can't remember the last time I saw Mrs. Prescot in town." Hattie took Olive over to the table and placed her in the highchair, shushing her whines. "Anyway, I'm going to feed Olive some lunch while you do the wash. We both know Brian won't be sleeping for long."

The sun warmed Lydia's back as she crouched over the large washtub. She sliced off a few pieces of soap and swished them around in the warm water. Birds twittered and chirped from a dozen different trees and the occasional bee buzzed in Lydia's ear. Every time she swatted one away, she'd splash murky water on her face and bonnet. Soon, stray, damp hair clung to her cheeks. Her shoulders burned. She scrubbed each item on the washboard until her knuckles stung.

Lydia stood and faced the sun. She closed her eyes and reached up to stretch out her weary arms and back before she knelt back down to rinse. The sunshine dried the soapy water on her face in moments. She tucked the now crisp strands of hair back behind her ear and beneath her bonnet. Despite feeling fatigued after a week of helping to care for Hattie's household, this moment brought peace to Lydia's soul. She felt content, even with all the unknowns she and Dylan were about to embark on.

"I was beginning to think you changed your mind." Dylan's squeezed Lydia's shoulders from behind.

Lydia spun around, feeling a different form of heat fill her cheeks. "Are you ever going to stop sneaking up on me like that?" She couldn't hold back her smile as he stole a quick kiss. "And I'm a

Beyond the Valley

mess . . . is it really proper for you to see your bride-to-be in such a state?"

Dylan cleared his throat. "I don't know what you mean." He grinned. "You look fine to me—the prettiest young woman in town—even with dried soap on your face." He laughed.

Lydia crossed her arms, shook her head, and tried to wipe off her face with a damp edge of her apron. "Well, I am happy to see you anyway. This week has gone by fast—or has it been longer? Hattie's new baby requires much more attention than I imagined. The poor woman is exhausted. Olive only wants her mama and doesn't seem to understand why this little screaming thing gets all her attention."

"I figured as much. I have plenty to do, securing things at the vineyard so we can cherish whatever time we can as newlyweds before Mr. Sinclair interferes. Of course, Father used to run things on his own, but he's gotten accustomed to me being his right-hand-man." Dylan stepped back into the shade of an oak tree and removed his hat.

"What about the dinner at your house? How has your mother been taking all this? I get concerned when you don't talk about her." Lydia poured a few drops of blue brightener into the rinse bucket and arranged herself on her knees so she could keep working while facing Dylan.

"My mother? You have nothing to be concerned about as I am sure she will adore you as much as father—and I—do. She is actually looking forward to meeting you."

Lydia sighed with relief. Why did she assume that his mother was avoiding her? "Does she know you told me about her and your father? About how he rescued her from that place in San Francisco?"

"No, neither of them knows I told you anything. My father reminded me indirectly that I should keep a careful watch on you when the time comes for us to go to the city. Orphaned young women tend to be prey for the madams."

"Madams?"

"Uh . . . the older women who run the . . . uh . . . homes where the businesses are run." Dylan clenched his fists at his sides. "Sorry, Lydia, it is so hard for me to resist trying to protect you. But you should probably know a few things about life in the city before we go."

Dylan remained with Lydia until she completed the washing and assisted her in hanging up each piece on the line to dry. While they worked, he explained there were many kinds of people in the city. In addition to plenty of kind and well-meaning citizens, there were also those looking for any chance they could to get the better of someone else. Some of what he said jolted her. It seemed San Francisco was home to the evil, depraved, and sinful people Mama had told her God wiped out of other worlds. How could God allow these humans to continue living in these ways?

"God gives us a choice to live for him or live for the world. The choice is rarely an easy one, as you will see when we get there. Life in the city can be captivating, but as your *husband . . .*" he paused until they made eye contact. ". . . it is my job to protect you from the city's seductive practices, while still showing you all the incredible sights and activities that only a city like San Francisco can offer."

Excited about exploring more of this world with Dylan at her side, another thought occurred to Lydia. "That makes me think of something else I would like to see when we go there. If there is a way to find it, I have thought about trying to locate the area where Mama used to live. Maybe there's someone still living there that can tell me more about her."

Dylan laughed, and dumped the soiled water into the ditch behind Hattie's cabin. "Your curiosity never ceases, does it? Of course, we can try locating Emelyn's old neighborhood. I hadn't thought of that. But first, we will need to tackle the challenge of facing your grandfather."

Lydia shuddered, uncertainty replacing her enthusiasm. She couldn't imagine life without the Valley as her home, yet she didn't want to fight Mr. Sinclair for it.

Brian's screams followed by Olive's howling came from the back window.

"Lydia," Hattie yelled.

Dylan stacked the washtubs by the well and handed Lydia the water bucket. He removed his hat, kissed her forehead, and then replaced his hat, grinning. "I expect you will be cleaned up by the time I pick you up for dinner tomorrow?"

Olive's howls turned into screams.

"You will hardly recognize me, Mr. Prescot." Lydia curtsied and then hustled around to the front of the cabin.

TWENTY-FIVE

The next morning, Clara delivered gifts from people in town, in honor of Brian's arrival. Normally, a delivery boy would complete the task. Lydia and Hattie joked that Clara's real motive was to help Lydia get ready for the dinner at the Prescot home.

"This is a special day for you, Miss Lydia. Of course, I want to assist you—although Hattie is perfectly capable." Clara retrieved a large paper parcel from the seat of her wagon. "You may as well get used to it, since you will require more than the two of us to help you prepare on your wedding day." Smiling, she handed Lydia the parcel.

"You are welcome to help all you want since I have no idea what to do. I want Mrs. Prescot to like what she sees. I can't bear even a hint of hesitation from her. Besides, I'm certain Dylan desires her approval more than I do." Lydia began to place the parcel with the other gifts for Hattie.

"That is yours, Miss Lydia." Clara pinched the edge of her dress and curtsied. "There are three dresses in there, delivered from Grass Valley earlier this morning. Any one of them is sure to impress Mrs. Prescot in an instant."

Dresses she did not make herself? She had not worn one of those since . . . since Mama's funeral. A blend of emotions surged. "Oh, Clara . . . I . . ." Lydia sighed and pulled on the twine tied around the paper wrapper.

Simple, yet elegant, each dress was made of smooth fabric, each one in a different deep shade of navy, red, or green. Two crisp, white, lace blouses, and a black overcoat could accompany any one of them.

Lydia's finger snagged the fine stitching. "These are beautiful Clara. Thank you. Do you have a pair of gloves I can wear as well? My hands are as rough as the side of the cutting block."

"Of course, Miss Lydia. There are two sets of gloves on the bottom of the package. Now, what else does Hattie need before you can get ready?"

Clara helped Lydia stoke the outside stove for biscuits and pull the laundry off the line. Mrs. O'Shea brought over cream of potato soup and fresh berries, so Lydia did not need to prepare supper for Hattie and Olive.

While Olive took a late afternoon nap, Hattie rocked Brian under the shade of the front porch. Sitting at an angle facing the doorway, she participated by providing suggestions to Clara about Lydia's hairstyle, and making conjectures about Mr. and Mrs. Prescot.

"The Prescot's hardly ever have dinner guests." Hattie patted Brian's back in unison with her rocking. "I don't think I've been to their home since Mrs. Prescot stopped giving piano lessons back when I was still attending school. Mrs. Prescot is an amazing pianist ... and her voice ... I wonder if she will sing for you."

"Oh, good gracious, Hattie!" Clara shook her

head. "She isn't going to serenade her future daughter-in-law."

"What are piano lessons? A certain way to sing?" Even after nearly a year in French Corral, Lydia was still learning.

Clara pulled an iron rod from the stove and wrapped a section of Lydia's hair around it. "A piano is a musical device, like the banjo or drum. Only it remains indoors and takes up more room than a standard kitchen table. In fact, one is at the schoolhouse too. Not only does it sound like angels singing on Earth, but a well-cared for piano is also a beautiful piece of furniture."

Hattie set Brian on her lap, pulled his gown over his toes, and tightly wrapped a small linen blanket around his shoulders and under his feet. "All the children of French Corral used to get regular piano lessons from Mrs. Prescot. But when the state outlawed hydraulic mining, families left to find work, and left her without many students."

Olive stirred and began to whine. "Ma…Ma…"

Lydia turned to make sure Olive was not trying to slide off the bed. But she yanked back, her hair still in Clara's grasp and the iron rod. "Ouch," Lydia whined.

Clara apologized and loosened the rod's grip on Lydia's hair. "Almost finished. Olive will be fine for another minute."

A little while later, Dylan arrived in his wagon.

"Miss Lydia." Bowing at the doorway, he reached for her gloved hand and led her to the wagon.

The hat he wore was much different from the wide-brimmed one he wore for work. This one only had a rim along the front, and it appeared to be made of wool. The top portion rolled slightly over the rim and fit snugly around the back of his head, right above his ears. Lydia had seen other men wearing similar hats. However, those men appeared aged and tired. Those men Clara and Mrs. O'Shea said were the city *elite*.

A crisp white shirt and pale green vest brought out Dylan's sparkling eyes. Was that a glimmer of mischief she saw as he helped her into the wagon? A small smile formed but did not allow his dimples to emerge.

Lydia gathered her skirt in layers and piled the excess into her lap to give room for Dylan to sit beside her. She'd chosen the crimson crushed velvet dress with white lace and satin collar and sleeves. She couldn't think of anything to say, confused at how a change in their clothing made her feel so different as they began the ride to the Prescot home. Cupping her hands and resting them on her lap, she admired the scenery and observed the evening routine of the townsfolk.

They ascended the trail up a sharp incline behind the main town. Familiar faces smiled at them along the way, each person busy with their evening tasks. Mr. Roberts and two school-aged boys led cows in from the pasture. Lucy waved while she shook out bedding from behind the teetering shack she shared with her cousins and uncle behind the Saloon.

Tall, green grass swayed among speckles of orange, pink, purple, and white wildflower petals. Groves of oak trees marked the way, branches stretched into the sky with bright green, baby leaves fanned and clustered in every direction like huge broccoli crowns, their shadows growing longer along the road as the terrain steepened.

The wagon hit a dip in the road, nearly tossing Lydia off the side. Dylan released one of the reins and looped his arm around her waist, pulling her close. "Are you trying to get out of dinner?" He chuckled, keeping a firm grip on her while using a free finger to hook the loose reign into his other hand.

"Of course not." Lydia frowned. *Why would he think that? Why is he laughing about it?* "The wagon jerked—"

"I'm only teasing. You are normally good at knowing that." His fingers squeezed her waist for a moment.

"Why would you tease me about meeting your mother?" She didn't want to be teased. The butterflies in her belly were beginning to feel like bees in a hive.

"Why are you so nervous? My mother can't wait to meet you. Yes, she does keep to herself. I don't know what Hattie or Clara have told you, but my mother is one of the few *cultured* women left in French Corral. Her life in San Francisco wasn't all terrible." He released his grasp on her side and took both reins in his hands. His eyes stayed focused ahead.

"Keep talking about her." That small bit of information began to calm her nerves. "You've kept this a secret for too long. I think I will feel better if I know more about her."

It took a few moments for Dylan to begin, but then his words rolled out like leaves floating on a gentle breeze, eager to feel the freedom of the open sky. With the silence filled, they pulled up to the front of the Prescot home in no time. All previous notions about Mrs. Prescot vanished. In minutes, Dylan's words had transformed her from a helpless and insecure woman, to a strong and courageous one.

Lydia couldn't wait to meet this woman who would be her—what did they call it . . . *Mother-in-law*.

Lydia tapped her foot against a lose wagon floorboard. Dylan seemed to take longer to tie up the horses than he did to guide them up the hill from town. He smiled and shook his head while helping her down. She would have asked him to elaborate on his amused look if she didn't think it would delay their ten-step journey onto his front porch.

Memories wisped through her mind as she recalled the last time she'd approached his front door. She forced them to fly away in haste, determined to form a fonder memory this evening—one worth remembering. Before Dylan could turn the doorknob, Mr. Prescot pulled open the door and greeted them.

"Welcome, Miss Lydia." Mr. Prescot pressed his palms together prayerfully. "You look almost as stunning as my wife does this evening." He winked and stepped aside to allow the couple through.

"Doesn't she, Father? You know how Clara is—any excuse to pretty up another girl in town." Dylan returned his father's wink, and guided Lydia into the foyer.

This time, golden lamps lit the room from windowsill to ceiling. Paintings of flowers and other scenery, Lydia had yet to behold in person, covered the walls and filled her mind with wonder. If paintings of such glorious images could take her breath away, how would viewing them in real life affect her? She had to stop and take a closer look at one that appeared to have water flowing from one edge to the other and into the skyline. In front of the water, children played in pale-colored dirt with miniature tools and clothes covering their pudgy bodies from shoulders to knees.

"Come, Lydia." Dylan tugged on her hand. "Mother is waiting."

"I've never seen anything like this, Dylan. It is so much different from the Valley or French Corral. There are no trees, no grass . . . and the water. I have never seen water carry on into the sky before. And why are those children playing in the dirt and wearing next to—"

Dylan pulled a hand to his chest and a let out a low laugh before he clamped his lips closed and shook his head. "Oh, sweet Lydia. That, my dear, is a painting of a beach in San Francisco. The *dirt* is sand and the water is called the *ocean,* and you will get a chance to see it with your very own eyes one day very soon." With a bit more force in his tug, he pulled Lydia away from the wall and into the dining room.

Lydia turned away from her ocean view, hoping to spend more time learning about all the paintings after dinner. She followed Dylan through a wide doorway where a vast table stood gleaming with sparkling plates, flaming slender candles, and gleaming covered dishes steaming with a blend of savory aromas.

Was this woman standing at the far end of the table truly Mrs. Prescot? She did not only appear younger than Mama had been—she appeared vibrant, as if every day filled her up instead of draining her dry. She stood in a manner that Lydia determined as wise, yet gentle. Chestnut brown ringlets circled a smooth complexion and fell onto her shoulders. A hint of pink along the top of each cheek brightened her green eyes, nearly the same shade as Dylan's, which glimmered in the candlelight reflecting from the table. She wore a maroon, crushed velvet gown bordered in black lace.

"Mother, you were not supposed to out-do our guest this evening." Dylan beamed as he grasped both Mrs. Prescot's and Lydia's hands in his own and glanced from one face to the other. "But I will have to disagree with Father and call it a tie."

Mrs. Prescot smiled on one side and shook her head. "Dylan, that is not the way to introduce me to your future bride." Her smile evened out and she tilted her chin toward Lydia.

Dylan's smile vanished. "Pardon me, Mother." He cleared his throat. "I am privileged to introduce you to the next Mrs. Prescot. Mother . . . Lydia Sinclair. Lydia . . . my mother, Mrs. Prescot."

"Jaina. Please, call me Jaina." Mrs. Prescot took Lydia's hands in her own, squeezed them hard and then pulled Lydia into a hug. "I am so glad to finally meet you."

Lydia exhaled and returned the embrace, not sure if she were about to laugh or cry.

"You do speak, right, Lydia?"

Lydia cleared her throat. "Yes . . . yes. Mrs. Prescot . . . Jaina. It is nice to meet you."

Mr. Prescot and Dylan made their way to opposite ends of the table, each pulling out a chair. Mrs. Prescot glided over to the chair her husband held and sat like a dandelion tuft landing on a soft patch of grass. Lydia did her best to mimic the older woman's graces throughout the meal.

Lydia hardly spoke a word while she consumed the incredible meal. Sliced meat dripped in dark red-brown juice, whipped potatoes seasoned in a way she'd never tasted, steamed vegetables slathered in tangy herbs, and rolls so light and fluffy they practically melted in her mouth. She enjoyed every bite until she feared her dress would burst open at the seams. In between bites, she tried sips of the wine—a drink made from the Prescot vineyards—but she did not care for its bitter taste. It was almost worse than coffee.

Choosing to remain quiet unless called upon, she observed every detail of Dylan and his parents as they took turns chewing and speaking.

Dylan and his father bantered often, Mrs. Prescot shaking her head and waving her hand while smiling at Lydia. Mrs. Prescot did not contribute much to the discussion, yet her few words seemed to weigh heavily on the men, who gave each syllable their full attention. They clearly adored her and appeared to enjoy working her into a fuss as well—but all in good fun. When Lydia thought they were serious, someone would break out in laughter.

Would she ever learn to read the subtle cues of sarcasm or jeering?

While Lydia took her last bite, a petite girl with straight black hair and narrow, petal-shaped eyes entered the room and began clearing the table.

"Thank you, Lin." Mrs. Prescot dotted the corners of her mouth with her napkin and set it on her plate before the girl stacked it on top of the others. Then she set her hand on Lydia's and smiled. "Lydia, would you like to see my rose garden?"

Lydia nodded. "Yes, I would love to . . . but isn't

it getting too dark outside to see it?"

"Not at all. Sunset is the perfect time to visit the garden. Almost as peaceful as that moment right before sunrise."

Lydia couldn't decide if she was more enamored with Mrs. Prescot or her rose garden. More than a few small rose bushes, the garden contained rows of shoulder-high, square-cut bushes of dark green clusters. Jagged leaves cupped thorny stems topped with closing rose buds in every color imaginable. Pink, red, white, yellow, white with magenta edges, and orange in every shade of the sunset danced between fading light and stray rays of golden sunshine. The fragrance of pungent, yet sweet, petals emanated the air and overwhelmed Lydia, coating her senses like silk dripping in heaven's kisses.

Between the even lines of rose bushes, several paths of flat rock, fanned out toward the back of the garden. The smooth paths came together in the center like spokes of a wagon wheel. Here, a wood-slated bench sat facing a rock-walled well.

"What do you think, Lydia? Do you like my rose garden?" Mrs. Prescot sat on the bench and patted the empty space beside her.

"Yes. Yes, I do." Lydia sighed as she gathered her skirt and took a seat. "But why keep such a beautiful garden hidden from view?"

Mrs. Prescot folded her hands in her lap and looked off beyond the edges of the garden into the darkening cluster of oak trees bordering the back of their property. "Sometimes beautiful things are not meant to be shared."

Lydia pondered the words for many moments. Feeling at perfect ease in the silence, she didn't concern herself as the minutes passed. She would wait for Mrs. Prescot to determine the direction of their conversation. They shared a love for God's creation at the very least. For a moment, that was enough to ease Lydia's nerves in the quiet.

Rose petals exchanged their rainbow hues with the sky and then turned shades of gray as the sun retreated below the tree line. The round, light of the moon soon covered the garden in a glowing, ashen calm while the sky grew black behind it.

Still, Mrs. Prescot sat without uttering a word while cricket chirps and frog croaks filled the air. Was she waiting for Lydia to speak?

Mrs. Prescot stood straight-faced and smoothed her skirt. "Shall we go back inside and make sure those men of ours are behaving themselves?"

"Of course." Lydia stood, disappointed, and confused.

What happened to the woman who had greeted her with a smile and hug at the start of the evening? Lydia had expected a slew of questions about her life with Mama—or at the very least, an attempt to share some of the cultured life Dylan had described earlier. Was Mrs. Prescot even curious about Lydia's life in the Valley? Did her silence symbolize acceptance or rejection?

After a brief tour through the lower part of their

home, Mr. and Mrs. Prescot saw Dylan and Lydia to the front door. Distraught at the lack of conversation at the garden, Lydia had not given much attention to the other paintings or the piano. Besides, Hattie would begin to fret if Lydia were not back soon. Lydia's eyes grew heavy as she said good-bye. Turning to follow Dylan down the porch steps, she sighed.

"Everything all right?" Dylan helped Lydia onto the wagon but held onto her hands. Moonbeams veiled his face, lighting in his eyes enough to show his concern below knitted eyebrows.

"Everything is perfect." She forced a smile. "I am exhausted, that's all."

"Or full. My mother's cooking tends to do that to the best of us."

Now she smiled without effort.

Lydia was relieved that the ride back to Hattie's house didn't seem to take as long as the journey to the Prescot home.

The Logan's house was dark and quiet as Dylan walked her to the door. Had Hattie mastered putting two babies to sleep on her own?

Dylan embraced Lydia. His face lingered a moment between her head and shoulder, and then he kissed her forehead. "Good night, my sweet Lydia. Sleep well."

"Good night, Dylan." She returned his gaze and smiled as she considered that in a matter of days, they would not need to part ways come evening.

TWENTY-SIX

Two days later, Dylan came to see Lydia, announcing that a telegram had arrived from Mr. Sinclair addressed to "Mr. Andrew Prescot and Son."

They discussed the details as they walked, hand-in-hand, along the road between the Inn and Hattie's house. This would be the last time they would see each other before their wedding, only four days away.

"His land survey team will not arrive until the beginning of May." Dylan explained. "They expect to meet with Charles, my father and myself to review ledgers and other documents. Mr. Sinclair regrets he is unable to make the trip due to unforeseen business complications in the city. However, he will be financing the expense for all parties to meet at his estate in San Francisco in late June . . ."

While Dylan continued, Lydia weighed each word, trying to grasp the implications. Although she had not forgotten that Mr. Sinclair promised to send surveyors in the spring, a part of her had hoped he would dismiss the idea. Why couldn't he let the land go? Even as the thought entered her mind, she knew the answer. This was not about the Valley at all. Mr. Sinclair wanted to see his son again. At least that is what convinced Lydia. If what she saw between Dylan and his own father was any indication, the relationship between a father and his son was indelible.

Lydia could hardly contain the emotions whipping about as she considered all the unknowns between her wedding and a visit from Mr. Sinclair's men. Depending on where her thoughts and curiosity trailed, a lump of unease would either lodge in her throat or settle hard in her stomach. Was it necessary for her and Dylan to perform this ritual of proclamation to the whole town? Thankfully, Hattie assured her part of the tradition included Elder Scott providing her the words throughout the ceremony. Hattie refused to reveal the details that followed the wedding party—when the new husband and his bride traditionally spent the better part of ten days getting to *know* each other. Hattie had winked and giggled, assuring Lydia that Dylan would take the lead. Yet, Lydia found it difficult to imagine the possibilities. After their wedding, they would only have one week before the surveyors arrived. It was enough uncertainty to make a young woman lose her mind.

"What happens when they get here and discover my father has been dead for years and the Valley is nothing but a small farm built for two?"

Dylan slowed his steps. "I will speak with my father and we will handle the details. The rest, we will entrust to God." Dylan took Lydia's hand in his and tightened his grip. "You are not alone in this. I confess I am not sure how things will go, but even if we face trouble, we will face it together."

She kept her thoughts to herself over the next

few days and allowed her friends and the other women in town to fuss over the details of her wedding day. She welcomed their chatter and excitement, which loaded her with more details than she could fathom—distracting her from thinking too much about the unknown future. For the ceremony, Mrs. Prescot would supply the bouquet and other flower arrangements. Mrs. O'Shea would lead the choir and play the piano from inside the schoolhouse. The ceremony would take place outside, allowing plenty of room for family, friends, and other guests, in a location not far from the oak tree where Mama's funeral took place.

Mama. Lydia had not visited her grave since before winter. She had thought about it often, but there was always something or someone else needing her. With the thought fresh in her mind, she decided to make a special trip to visit Mama's grave before heading to Clara's house for her *bridal* shower.

The next morning, Lydia woke before the birds to complete her morning tasks. She latched the hen house door, brought the eggs into the kitchen, and then paused in a moment of solitude.

Would she change her morning routine once Dylan was here? After spending nearly six months in the Valley on her own, sharing this space and the workload with Dylan brought relief and discomfort. What would she do with a man's help every day? She could always assist Hattie if she had

Beyond the Valley

nothing else to do. But it was time for Lydia and Dylan to make this their home together—even if Mr. Sinclair decided to make things difficult.

Lydia pulled the window shut and drew the curtains closed. A gift from Clara and Robert in the fall, the heavy wool fabric kept the heat in and the cold out through the winter. Clara said they would also provide privacy, especially if unexpected visitors came by after their wedding day.

With the cabin secure, Lydia mounted Jasper and led him to the road west of the pond. She was still amazed that she'd spent her whole life here and never knew this road existed behind the clusters of blackberry bushes. It took some persuading, but the men had managed to train the remaining bushes to grow alongside the road instead of across it—but only after burning two cartloads of vines and putting up a low fence.

An unusually warm morning, the occasional breeze caused the branches of baby trees to tap together in bursts, serenading her while she crossed the Valley. The sun shining off the pond grabbed her attention and she stopped Jasper for a moment. Breathing deeply and smiling at the idea of a post-wedding picnic entering her mind, she urged Jasper into a trot. With patches of meadows strewn with oaks to one side and warm air beating off the mountainside to the other, Lydia absorbed it all. Simply knowing she would soon see and experience what the world was like below this mountain filled her with excitement.

What would the land look like beyond the clusters of mountain trees? How would she feel when everything surrounding her was new and different? Would she see places like those in the photographs and paintings at the Prescot home and the Inn?

When the Wells Fargo building came into sight, Lydia slowed Jasper to a walk and released his mane, several strands tangled in her grip on the reins. She pulled one leg over to sit sidesaddle—the *appropriate* form for a woman to ride. While she made her way through town, it seemed like everyone outside made a special effort to greet her.

Then, in a moment, when she passed the Saloon, the road emptied of passersby. Lydia tugged the reins to the left, taking the opportunity while nobody was watching, and led Jasper off the road toward the cemetery.

After climbing off her horse, she guided him by the reins and walked through the grave markers. Mr. O'Shea had ordered the stone marker for Mama only weeks earlier, since the ground had to settle through the winter before they could place it. When she came upon the simple, white rectangular stone, it took her a moment to realize it was Mama's. Then she recognized the lines as the same ones etched into the front of Mama's diary—the ones Hattie had told her read *Emelyn Sinclair*.

The breeze kicked up, played with the hem of Lydia's skirt, and then rolled up her side and onto her face before tilting the front of her bonnet off her forehead. She tightened the ribbon beneath her chin and lowered to her knees.

"Mama." As soon as the name left her lips, tears sprung from her eyes. "Oh, Mama . . . I know this is only a stone slab, and that somewhere in the unseen you are singing praises with the saints." She pulled the handkerchief from her apron pocket and wiped her eyes and nose. "Yet, whether the Lord takes this message to you or only the birds and butterflies hear it, I need to do this. I need to talk to you and pretend you are here listening. Mama . . . how I wish you could be here with me today and tomorrow. I pray somehow you are watching me and that you are happy and content knowing Dylan will be caring for me from now on."

She blew her nose and continued.

"For a time, I had many regrets and thought somehow if I willed it, I could change the past. I wanted to be able to tell you about meeting Dylan. I wanted to go back and be bold about making you take me with you that day. I wanted you to be honest with me and to trust me that I would still love you forever as my mother—even when love and life beyond the Valley came my way. Now I see that was not God's plan. I will never understand why he would allow all these things to happen to us. Why would God take your parents and then Charles from you? Yet, he allowed you to raise me all these years without interruption from the outside world. He kept Mr. Sinclair away as far as I know . . . and he kept us from harm for many years. I hear about all the accidents on farms, of Indians killing at random, of disease—and realize that even though we have both lost so much, God still kept us safe in many other ways."

A sparrow bounced about, pecking at stray twigs and stones, its silky, striped head jutting side to side. Lydia paused, hoping not to frighten it before it found its nourishment. It flew off, a small beetle in its in beak.

Lydia went on. "Mama, if I could have one prayer answered, it would be that you would have had more faith to believe God's plan for you was more than you could see with your own eyes. I feel foolish saying such things, as if I know anything of living in this world. Yet, something tells me that all of this is happening exactly as God planned. There is something bigger going on and I feel God's invisible hand pulling me toward a larger purpose. And Dylan is part of that plan—"

Jasper stepped back, tugging at the reins. The gesture made Lydia aware of the sensation of the sun's heat on her neck and how the pain of pebbles grinding into her knees had grown more intense. She stood and rubbed the dents out of her knees before pulling the legs of her bloomers down and then flattening her skirt.

Sighing, she straightened her bonnet. "Okay, Mama, I better get myself over to Miss Clara's house before the ladies send the men out to search for me." She leaned down and pressed her palm into the etched stone. Eyes closed, she, paused in silence before re-mounting Jasper. Lydia clucked and clenched mane and reins in her hands, forcing her horse in a gallop across the field of grazing cows in the direction of the Roberts' home.

TWENTY-SEVEN

Clara and Jason Roberts' home came into view. The white house sat above a low hill of goat-nibbled grass at the center of a meadow. Purple leaves fanned the tops of plum trees dotting the land. Along the back edge of the property, even rows of grape vines lined up to the edge of a ravine. Chickens clucked in the hen house while to the left of the porch, horses hitched to two wagons, munched on a pile of hay.

Lydia tied Jasper to a porch post shaded by the fat leaves of a fig tree. She petted one of the other horses and scooped up a fistful of hay for her own. Women's voices chattered with excitement inside, and then hushed when Lydia's steps creaked on the porch. Before Lydia made it to the entrance, Clara pushed the screen door open, a huge smile emphasizing her round eyes and full lips.

"You took a day and forever!" Clara clapped and laughed. "Come in. Come in. Everyone is here aside from the blushing bride-to-be."

Aromas of a variety of food and more voices than Lydia could follow filled the room. The dining room table sat under the window, filled with platters and bowls of bite-sized sweet and savory treats. The dining chairs, a bench upholstered in floral fabric, a sofa and two rocking chairs sat in a circle in the center of the living room.

Mrs. O'Shea, Hattie, Lucy, Mrs. Prescot, and the Marks twins sat in various locations holding plates of food. A pile of gifts wrapped in brown paper or patterned fabric lay in front of the unlit fireplace beside the seating arrangements.

Clara stood behind one of the rocking chairs, gesturing for Lydia to take a seat. "Make yourself comfortable here and I will make you a plate of food. We already said a prayer over our meal as well as blessings over our conversation."

Smiling and nodding at each lady, Lydia made her way to the rocking chair, chest tightened in anticipation at what this "shower" would entail.

Hattie set a plate of food on her lap, and then shook small fists and bounced—a huge grin across her face. "I get to go first. You ladies have no idea how hard it has been for me to contain myself while Lydia has been helping me with the children." Beaming at Lydia, she took a deep breath and waved her hands in front of her face. "We decided to go a bit out of the ordinary since you are no ordinary bride. Normally, a bridal shower is fun, food, and providing the bride with anything she may need to care for herself, her husband, or her home. But today is special—not only because you have given so much of yourself despite losing your mama and adjusting to life here in French Corral—but also because we have the privilege and honor of passing on our own wisdom to you regarding your future role as a wife."

Clara handed Lydia a plate holding a miniature lemon tart, a narrow slice of berry pie, and a triangle-shaped cheese sandwich. "Each of us, aside from the twins, has experienced marriage in our own unique ways," Clara added. "We have decided on the important and not-so-important insights we pray will allow you to enjoy every minute as a new bride and bring you into many blissful years as a wife and a mother."

Hattie moved one of the larger gifts from the pile, and picked up a smaller, rectangular one wrapped in floral fabric. "So, with each gift, each of us will share a story about our first days of marriage and another from a more recent experience." She leaned forward and handed it to Lydia. "Now, open it so I can tell you what it is."

Lydia unfolded the fabric from the shorter ends and pulled open the layers wrapped around the gift. It was a book of some sort, but the pages were blank. She tittered, not sure what to make of it.

"It's a scrapbook. I am envious of you for being able to go to San Francisco. I confess this gift is partially for me. It is for you to fill with photographs, playbills, train tickets or whatever else will fit in those pages so you can remember—and share every detail with me upon your return." Hattie continued to bounce on the bench with each word. "I know one of these days you would like to learn to write, but this way, you can record your memories now."

Lydia ran her fingers across the smooth pages, amazed at her friend's thoughtfulness. "Thank you, Hattie. I love it and promise to fill every page with . . . whatever those things are." Everyone belted out in shrill laughter at the comment, including Lydia who felt her face grow hot.

"Now, for my story, before the babies wake from their naps." Hattie peered into the hallway behind Lydia. "I have never been a particularly good cook. Apparently, my mother was optimistic that I'd marry into money and be able to hire kitchen help. During the first few weeks of our marriage, Dan got ill three times after eating dinner. I cried every time I had to prepare a meal after that—afraid he would die from my horrible cooking."

She sighed and smiled, shaking her head. "Then one day, I realized Dan kept eating my cooking anyway—and I knew his love for me meant more to him than a tasty meal. As soon as I stopped worrying about how the food turned out, he never grew ill again."

"Mrs. Prescot, you may go next." Clara announced.

Mrs. Prescot nodded and her eyes brightened despite her straight mouth. "I have no gift you can hold. For you, Lydia, I am giving you the gift of reading and writing. After your days as a new bride are over, you will come to my home once a week for reading and writing lessons. And call me Jaina . . . please."

Lydia pressed her lips together and drew her hand to her mouth, trying to hold back grateful tears. "That is kind of you . . . Jaina. Thank you. Thank you. I will be your best student." Lydia decided she would secretly cherish this gift above anything else she received.

Jaina sat up, aligning hips and shoulders in a way that made her appear higher than the other women seated in the circle. "I do not have a story to share about being a new wife. However, as the mother of the groom, I will share something with you about my son . . ." She closed her mouth, lips straight and chin up while she peered at each woman in the room. Pointing her finger into the air she said, "I know you ladies love to gossip, but before I continue, I must have your word that what I am about to share will not leave this house."

Each woman's smile faded as she nodded with somber obedience to Jaina.

Jaina turned to Lydia and smiled. "Since the day my Dylan met you, I have watched him mature from a boy into a gentleman." She folded her hands over her chest. "It brings me joy to see my own son love and cherish another woman while striving to care for her and protect her no matter the cost. It is not easy for a mother to let her son become dependent on the love and care of another woman." Jaina's chest heaved. "Yet, I cannot deny the unwavering love he has so willingly given you—even when he was hurting and doubted the choices that he'd made following the fire."

Lydia's chest tightened. *How much did Jaina know of what transpired between us?* Visions of the afternoon she and Dylan argued in his foyer during that spring storm swept through her mind. Had a servant told Jaina of their confessions and about Lydia screaming at her son?

The only sounds in the room for several moments came from the henhouse outside.

Jaina brought her hands down to her lap and leaned in toward Lydia. In slightly above a whisper, she spoke. "I expect nothing less than for you to love him back with the same fervor."

Lydia nodded and looked around at the other women. Each of them sat strangely silent and still. Hattie's eyes were wider than usual and the twins' mouths were half-open and frozen.

Olive's high-pitched wails suddenly echoed from the hallway.

Hattie hopped up and her plate crashed to the

floor. The clatter seemed to prompt everyone into movement and whispers among themselves. Mrs. O'Shea followed Hattie down the hallway, offering to take the baby after Brian's cries joined Olive's. Clara swept up the plate shards, took Lydia's empty plate, and refilled everyone's teacups. Jaina addressed the Marks' twins, inquiring of their parent's plans to relocate to Oregon by summer's end.

As the morning grew into afternoon, each woman continued to share a story of heartache and wisdom she had learned through her years of marriage. Every story helped Lydia understand that although everyone had something different to share, they all had one common thread. Each woman had come to honor and respect her husband. Each of them felt deeply loved—even when their husbands occasionally made choices that hurt them.

When it was time for the party to end, Lydia knew why this was called a bridal shower. Not only was she showered in physical gifts including kitchenware, a large cotton quilt, a rosebush, and jars of preserved food—she had been showered in the unmeasurable gifts of wisdom and love.

Overall, the afternoon brought relief and joy in anticipation of tomorrow—despite the uncertain weight of Jaina's implicit advice. Regardless of all she would still have to learn, Lydia intended to fulfill her role as Dylan's wife beyond everyone's expectations—especially Jaina's.

TWENTY-EIGHT

That evening, Clara and Jason delivered Lydia's bridal shower gifts to the Valley. While Jason fed and watered the horses, Clara joined Lydia by the well.

"It didn't seem appropriate to mention earlier, but I wanted to explain Mrs. Prescot's words to you." Clara's smile faded into a frown. "It is difficult for all of us to imagine a life without observing and interacting with others from our earliest memories…" She glanced toward the barn, her gaze resting on Jason for a quiet minute before she sighed. "But there is something the other ladies and I think needs clarifying."

A large lump grew in Lydia throat, making it impossible to swallow. She clutched the water bucket handle until her nails dug into her palms.

Clara grasped Lydia's wrist and drew close, speaking in a loud whisper. "Mrs. Prescot's words may have appeared kind, but I would take them with caution. I don't mean to damper your glorious day tomorrow, but I think you should know she was quite serious. None of us has ever heard her speak so many words at one time."

Lydia's heart rate sped. "What do you mean? She

was smiling and offered to teach me to read and write."

"I don't want to presume too much, Lydia. However, guard your words while you are in her presence. A young bride does not need to share every detail of her marriage ... especially any problems . . . with her mother-in-law—"

"We better get going Clara." Jason swept up behind his wife, resting his gloved hands on her hips.

Clara stepped to the side, shooed his hands away and rolled her eyes. "Feel free to visit me at the store anytime." The lace trim of her wide sunhat fluttered in the evening breeze. She tightened the bow of the pale blue ribbon beneath her chin.

"Yes, I will. Thank you, Clara . . . Jason . . . for delivering my gifts. I should have thought to bring the wagon—"

"Nonsense, Lydia. You had no idea what to expect. It was no trouble at all. I will be back in the morning." Clara slid her arm through her husband's and they walked to the wagon.

Jason turned back to Lydia for a moment, tipping the brim of his hat. "Have a restful evening, Miss Lydia."

Restful it was not.

It felt as if a bucket of pebbles had settled in Lydia's stomach. What was she thinking? How could she ever be a good enough wife to Dylan— or good enough for his mother? No wonder she had been so nervous before their dinner. There was more to this woman, Jaina, than Clara was telling her. Lydia may not have had experience around many people, but she had learned the telling signs of lies that covered the truth by watching Mama for seventeen years.

Beyond the Valley

When she tried to shift her thoughts to something else, she imagined the worst possible scenarios in meeting her grandfather. Could she even call him that? Grand . . . Father—he had been neither. He was a faceless, greedy, selfish man for all she knew. Yet, until this restless night, she'd made him a kind man with a broken heart—too prideful to face his son and ask him to come back home.

Why did everything feel different now that it was happening? Why had the possibilities never entered her mind until now? Where was all this fear and hopelessness coming from? She wished Dylan were with her now holding her tight and saying he would take care of it all while kissing away her tears . . .

A rooster's crow woke her.

Then the clicking of horse hooves and the rumble of wagon wheels echoed from the edge of the Valley.

Was Clara here to get her already?

She wrapped the quilt around her and went onto the front porch to check the position of the sun. A veil of light gray clouds coated the sky, and the hazy silver glow of the rising sun filtered through tree branches above the mountain line.

She had overslept on her wedding day.

Lydia found little time to speak in the blur of activity over the next few hours. A heavy heart and thick thoughts of doubt weighed her down as she forced smile after smile, finding only the strength to say "thank you" as Clara and Hattie helped to prepare her for the ceremony.

Before she knew it, bright-white lace and ivory satin decorated her from head to toe. A round, lace-trimmed hat sat upon tight ringlets of hair resting above puffy-sleeved shoulders. Her dress fit uniformly from bust to waist, then billowed out in layers behind and around her. Low-ankle, white shoes with pointed toes and jeweled-leather straps poked out from the embroidered border of her skirts. Outside the open window, a pale blue sky and golden sun had long replaced the dreary morning. Birds chattered away, flitting between treetops as if they too anticipated the ceremony.

Tears glistened in Clara's eyes as she stepped back, looking over Lydia from head to toe. "You look like an absolute angel!" She beamed and clapped her hands quickly, yet quietly.

Hattie smiled through tear-stained cheeks. "I feel like I am sending off my little sister to wed. I couldn't be happier for you and Dylan. Thank you for allowing me to be a part of this special day with you." She hugged Lydia, lingered for a moment, and then sighed as if she hesitated to let go or say something more.

Lydia could not imagine getting this far without Hattie's constant guidance and companionship. Hattie needed thanking, but words alone didn't feel enough. Lydia didn't know what else to give. She squeezed Hattie harder, aware that the embrace could muss up her carefully placed curls. "Thank *you*, Hattie," she whispered, her throat thick with her own tears. "You have done more for me than I can put to words and I cannot imagine doing this day without you."

Clara blew her nose in an unbecoming manner. Lydia couldn't help but laugh and Hattie joined in.

The three of them giggled through salty tears. Elder Scott knocked at the back door of the schoolhouse. The ladies wiped their faces and straightened their gowns in a hurry, stifling a few more chuckles before Hattie and Clara slipped out the front door to take their places.

Lydia joined Elder Scott behind the schoolhouse while they waited for Mr. O'Shea to accompany her for the first part of the ceremony.

"Do you have any questions for me regarding your vows?" Elder Scott's short-brimmed black hat did not shade his face enough to prevent the sunlight from reflecting off his spectacles.

Wishing she could see his eyes, she did her best to look straight at him. "I always have questions, Elder Scott, but I am prepared to follow through with the promises my vows entail. If I stray, it will not be intentional." Could he tell her smile wasn't sincere? Hopefully, he would credit it for nerves, not deceit. Was it right to intentionally lie about her insecurities in this important moment?

"Very well. There is one more thing we have to take care of before I commence the ceremony."

The rock in her belly seemed to grow larger at his words. "What is it?" She swallowed hard to shove the lump down her throat, only to feel it settle in her chest.

"You have been quite the student of scripture these past months. I am impressed at your knowledge and understanding of God's Word, despite the mixed messages your mama gave you. However, the one thing you told me she did not and could not—I presume to deter you from questioning further—was to explain the meaning of salvation."

Lydia exhaled and nodded. She thought she

understood his intent. She hadn't realized Elder Scott had paid that much attention during the past months. After hearing one of his first sermons shortly after the fire, she had not only heard the name of Jesus for the first time but realized Mama had kept this detail a secret—this idea that she did not have to earn her salvation—in order to maintain her rules of life in the Valley.

According to Mama, God had wiped out all of humanity and larger worlds because of human sin. Bringing the life, death, and resurrection of Jesus into the story would have demolished the reasons behind their entire purpose.

"I have no doubt your faith is strong, Miss Lydia. You have a servant's heart and a trust in the Lord not many in your situation would continue to embrace. However, it is important that you verbalize your dedication. I am going to lead you in a prayer of recognition about Jesus Christ and your commitment to follow Him, no matter the cost. This promise will allow his Holy Spirit to fully dwell in you and to provide strength and direction in your marriage and in your other endeavors."

Relief washed over Lydia, and she nodded faster, eager to receive whatever this promise would entail.

A few moments later, Elder Scott left her side to join Dylan in front of the schoolhouse. Although Lydia did not sense an instant change in her mood after confessing Jesus Christ as Lord of her life, she believed the Spirit of the living God would strengthen her faith in time. She understood she no longer had to earn her way to heaven by thought and deed. Every part of her desired to prove her dedication to living for Jesus but putting her all into everything God called her to—beginning with being the godly wife Dylan deserved.

Within seconds, Mr. O'Shea poked his head around the corner and then joined Lydia.

"You look very nice, Miss Lydia."

As did Mr. O'Shea. He somehow looked shorter than usual in his crisp collared shirt and black vest. The top of his black hat lined up with Lydia's ear as he led her around front.

They stepped in unison. A melody from the piano floating from the open doorway of the schoolhouse, timed their steps.

Wooden chairs and benches, filled with the citizens of French Corral, lined either side of a path leading up to the shade of the large oak tree. Beneath the tree, Dylan and Elder Scott stood facing Lydia and Mr. O'Shea.

Though her heart pounded and her hands trembled, Lydia's steps did not falter. The closer she came to Dylan's comforting smile, the further her thoughts, and awareness of everyone watching her faded into the distance.

Mr. O'Shea kissed the tops of Lydia's hands and delivered them into Dylan's. Then he stepped back and took a seat in the front row near Mrs. O'Shea, Clara, and Jason.

Elder Scott looked out at the crowd and began. "Dearly beloved, we are gathered here in the sight of God and in the presence of these witnesses, to join this man, Dylan Prescot and this woman, Lydia Sinclair, in holy matrimony . . . which is an honorable estate, instituted of God, and signifying unto us the mystical union that exists between Christ and his Church, which holy estate Christ adorned and beautified with his presence in Cana of Galilee.

"It is therefore not to be entered into unadvisedly, but reverently, discreetly, and in the fear of God. Into this holy estate these two persons come now to be joined."

Elder Scott shifted his focus to Dylan and Lydia, who now stood facing each other. "I require and charge you both, as you stand in the presence of God, before whom the secrets of all hearts are disclosed, that, having duly considered the holy covenant you are about to make, you do now declare before this company your pledge of faith, each to the other."

Dylan squeezed Lydia's hands and winked.

Elder Scott continued. "Be well assured that if these solemn vows are kept inviolate, as God's Word demands, and if steadfastly you endeavor to do the will of your heavenly Father, God will bless your marriage, will grant you fulfillment in it, and will establish your home in peace."

Fullness overflowed within Lydia, and the heaviness in her chest dissolved. She felt an authentic smile press into her cheeks.

Elder Scott turned to Dylan. "Will you have this woman to be your wedded wife, to live together in the holy estate of matrimony? Will you love her, comfort her, honor, and keep her, in sickness and in health and forsaking all others keep only to her so long as you both shall live?"

Dylan's dimples deepened. "I will."

Elder Scott turned to Lydia and nodded. "Will you have this man to be your wedded husband, to live together in the holy estate of matrimony? Will you love him, comfort him, honor, and keep him, in sickness and in health and forsaking all others keep only to him so long as you both shall live?"

Lydia bit the inside of her lip and breathed deeply, returning Dylan's grin. "I will."

"Lylia! Mama, is Lilia!" Olive bellowed from the

back row.

Lydia turned to see Olive standing on Hattie's lap, pointing and bouncing while she squealed.

"Shhhh, Olive!" Hattie shook her head, red-faced while she pulled Olive to a seated position.

Elder Scott waited until the forgiving giggles faded before he continued.

"You may now repeat your vows. Dylan, you begin." Elder Scott nodded once and folded his hands around his Bible, then drew it down in front of his waist.

Dylan, voice shaking, spoke slow and sure. "I, Dylan Prescot, take you, Lydia Sinclair, to be my wedded wife, to have and to hold, from this day forward, for better, for worse, for richer, for poorer, in sickness and in health, to love and to cherish, 'till death us do part, according to God's holy ordinance, and thereto I pledge you my faith."

Elder Scott nodded. "Now, Lydia, you may begin. Look to me if you need a reminder of the words."

Lydia nodded and smiled at Elder Scott. She would not need a reminder. She'd run the words through her mind and repeated them to herself . . . to Megan . . . to the chickens . . .

Heart pounding, she began. "I, Lydia Sinclair, take you, Dylan Prescot—" her voice cracked and a tear spilled down her cheek. "To be my wedded husband . . . to have and to hold . . . from this day forward, for better, for worse, for richer, for poorer, in sickness and in health . . . to love and to cherish . . . till death us do part . . . according to God's holy ordinance, and thereto I pledge you my faith." Lydia dared not break her gaze with Dylan.

Soft sounds came from the onlookers. Sniffles, a short cry. Lydia thought she heard someone softly clapping.

"The wedding ring is the outward and visible sign of an inward and spiritual grace," Elder Scott continued. "Signifying to all the uniting of this man and woman in holy matrimony, through the Church of Jesus Christ our Lord."

He pulled two silver bands from his vest pocket. One, Lydia had provided him from Dylan's proposal. The other had come from Mr. Prescot.

Elder Scott continued. "Bless, O Lord, the giving of these rings . . . that they who wear them may abide in thy peace and continue in thy favor . . . through Jesus Christ our Lord. Amen."

Elder Scott handed the smaller band to Dylan who slid the ring on Lydia's trembling finger.

Repeating after Elder Scott, Dylan said, "In token and pledge of our constant faith and abiding love, with this ring I thee wed, in the name of the Father, and of the Son, and of the Holy Spirit. Amen."

Elder Scott provided the larger band to Lydia and prompted her. She slid the band onto Dylan's left hand and repeated, "In token and pledge of our constant faith and abiding love, with this ring I thee wed, in the name of the Father, and of the Son, and of the Holy Spirit. Amen."

Dylan joined hands with Lydia once again. Elder Scott wrapped a small linen cloth around their hands and nodded.

Dylan and Lydia turned toward the crowd seated before them. Some held handkerchiefs to their mouths. All of them smiled with glistening eyes and nods of approval.

To the people, Elder Scott raised his voice over the shifting breeze and completed the ceremony. "For as much as Lydia Sinclair and Dylan Prescot have consented together in holy wedlock and have witnessed the same before God and this company, and thereto have pledged their faith each to the other, and have declared the same by joining hands and by giving and receiving rings, I pronounce that they are husband and wife together, in the name of the Father, and of the Son, and of the Holy Spirit.

"Those whom God hath joined together, let no one put asunder. Amen."

Mr. O'Shea brought out a folded quilt and set in on the ground in front of Dylan and Lydia. Forgetting for a moment about this part of the ceremony, Lydia looked at Dylan, shaking her head. Smiling, he tugged their still entwined hands downward, bringing them into a kneeling position over the quilt. Then he whispered in her ear, "Elder Scott will pray for us now . . ."

She nodded, feeling a bit of heat creep up her neck, then bowed her head and closed her eyes with Dylan. The breeze blew the scent of boiled beef and cabbage their way and Lydia realized she was starving. She was grateful that these people of French Corral made sure plenty of food came along with every celebration.

Elder Scott cleared his throat. "O eternal God, creator and preserver of us all, giver of all spiritual grace, the author of everlasting life: Send thy blessing upon Dylan and Lydia, whom we bless in thy name, that they may surely perform and keep the vow and covenant between them and may ever remain in perfect love and peace together and live according to thy laws.

"Look graciously upon them, that they may love, honor, and cherish each other, and so live together in faithfulness and patience, in wisdom and true godliness, that their home may be a haven of blessing and a place of peace, through Jesus Christ our Lord. Amen."

Dylan squeezed Lydia's hands and helped her stand. Elder Scott removed the cloth connecting them and smiled. "Dylan, you may kiss your bride."

Dylan wrapped one arm around Lydia, and untied the ribbon from her chin, letting her laced hat fall to the ground. He wrapped his other arm around her and pulled her so close—she thought their hearts would meld into one. Warm peppermint breath enveloped her as he pressed his lips to hers.

The crowd cheered, hooted, and hollered.

A few minutes later, the wedding guests helped to rearrange the chairs into clusters across the meadow. Dan and Jason pulled their banjos from the back of a wagon and began to strum and sing. Mr. O'Shea attended the barbeque and Mrs. O'Shea and Lucy arranged an assortment of breads, pies, and baked vegetables on top of a long table set in the shade against the outer schoolhouse wall.

The celebration went into sunset, a blur of smiles, songs, dancing and so much food, Lydia had to have Hattie loosen the strings of her petticoat.

During a break in the music, Dylan whispered it was time to leave, and pulled Lydia away from the crowd. She followed, almost breathless at keeping with his pace, as he led her by the hand toward the road.

Bailey and Jasper waited patiently near the road, grazing on grass and weeds, seemingly undisturbed by the noise on the hill above them. The wagon attached to them swayed and creaked in protest of the breeze.

"Are you sure we should leave while everyone is still celebrating?" Lydia panted.

Dylan stopped, turned to face her, and laughed. Cupping her face, he gave her a quick peck on the lips. "Yes, my darling ... Mrs. Prescot ... it is quite customary for the bride and groom to leave the party early. Besides, I can't think of a better moment to bring my bride home than while the sun is setting, and colors are still dancing along the Valley floor and reflecting in the pond."

TWENTY-NINE

How could she protest? She allowed her husband to help her onto the wagon's seat, not realizing how weary her limbs were from dancing until she attempted to climb up on her own.

Once they were seated and the horses were trotting along, Lydia snuggled up to Dylan. She closed her eyes, cheeks sore from smiling for what seemed like hours. She rested her head against his shoulder, not allowing her thoughts to stray to what lie ahead or behind them. She believed every word and promise they spoke to each other during the ceremony.

Every concern from the night before faded into distant memory. Tonight, she would finally feel the comfort and safety of Dylan at her side.

Exactly as Dylan predicted, brilliant hues of honey orange, plum purple, and dandelion yellow danced along tips of dried grass while deeper hues swirled among wisps of clouds reflecting in the pond. Crickets and frogs serenaded them while birds, settling in their nests among clusters of oak trees, bid goodnight coos to their neighbors.

Pulling the wagon up to the edge of the porch

slowly, Dylan hopped out and around to Lydia, and covered her lap with a quilt. "Wait here. I will only be a few minutes." He smiled and winked.

Lydia's insides danced with curious anticipation. She sighed and nodded, keeping her eyes steady on the front window after Dylan entered. In moments, the window glowed gold. Dylan's shadow moved from the living room window to the bedroom, where a faint glow emanated from the side of the cabin. Then he drew the curtains closed and Lydia realized the setting sun had disappeared and left her in utter darkness since there was no moon.

The front door creaked and Dylan emerged, having removed his overcoat and hat. His tousled curls clung to his forehead and his white shirt appeared damp in the dim light. Without a word, he approached Lydia, with an almost serious expression, but for his dimples and the glimmer in his eyes giving away the smile he contained.

With a gentle, single swoop, he lifted Lydia from the wagon's seat, and held her close to his chest. His heart pounded into her side as he stepped onto the porch, pausing at the open doorway.

"Is something wrong?" Lydia was getting used to going along with unusual customs, but this?

Dylan laughed, his warm breath, laced in sweet apple cider, swept up her face. "I assumed Hattie would have filled you in. It is simply a tradition for the groom to carry his bride across the threshold. I like to see it as a final act of dedication to protect and love you in our new home. Shall we?" He nodded toward the kitchen.

Lydia caught her breath, not realizing her eyes had not strayed from Dylan's until now. A dozen candles lined a wide path along the floor, set on small plates or inside canning jars. They led directly to the bedroom doorway, where the curtain was tied back with what looked like her apron string.

With slow ease, Dylan lowered her to the floor, and then keeping his hands on her waist, circled around the front of her to stand with his back to the bedroom.

"Are you okay?"

Lydia tried to take a breath but found it difficult to inhale past the pounding of her heart. Heat seeped up her neck and into her face. "I . . . I'm fine. Give me a moment to realize I am not dreaming."

Taking both her hands in his, he pulled her toward him. "Take as long as you need. I will wait right here until you are ready."

For some reason, his words released the fear within her and the rush of feelings returned from the last time they stood here.

Only now, he wasn't holding her back at arm's length.

Loosening one hand from Dylan's grasp, she placed it along the back of his neck and drew herself up to his face. "I think I have been ready for a while, Dylan Prescot."

Grinning, she kissed him, holding nothing back.

Morning came too soon. Twerps, trills, and bird whistles called through the open window. Leaves rustled in the breeze and Megan mooed. Reluctant to untangle herself from Dylan's limbs, she nudged her elbow into his side, memories of their evening imparting a smile even though she kept her eyes closed.

He moaned and removed his arm from her waist. He squeezed his eyes closed further, scrunched his face, and inhaled deeply, then groaned. Opening his eyes, he grinned and kissed her. "Is it morning already?"

She pressed her lips together, holding back the larger smile wanting to stretch across her face and nodded. "Mmhmm . . . and Megan needs milked."

He kissed her again, signaling he didn't care. Several minutes later, they made their way outside to attend the morning chores. Dylan let the sheep and horses out to graze while Lydia reversed her usual routine and milked Megan before collecting the eggs.

Her daydreaming this morning encompassed reliving her wedding night. She had freely given herself to her husband and held nothing back. Desire she'd forced dormant for well over a year sprung forth like tender shoots through warm soil after a long winter. The way in which Dylan had embraced her with both softness and strength was overwhelming. She did not think it was possible to love him more. Once they had joined as one ... love overflowed from depths she did not realize lived within her.

She laughed with ironic pity at Megan, thinking of the bull on its way to the Valley for the sole purpose of creating offspring with her cow. How incredible that God allowed humans to join for reasons beyond reproduction.

For once, she didn't care to understand why. She was simply grateful that as Dylan's wife, she could succumb to her feelings without guilt.

However, she and Dylan had other challenges before them. In only ten days, Mr. Sinclair's men would arrive to assess the condition of the Valley. Amid newlywed bliss, they would work hard to clean up the property and the house in hopes of convincing the men to return with a good report—despite discovering Charles and Emelyn had died and the land was now occupied by Mr. Sinclair's granddaughter.

Back-to-back beautiful spring days made it easy to labor long hours under the warm sun and forgiving shade. Thin layers of clouds came and went, with an occasional afternoon sprinkle giving Dylan and Lydia the excuse to take a break indoors.

Each evening after dinner, Dylan would read scripture to Lydia by candlelight. He explained that one of his husbandly duties was to cover his wife in the washing of the Word. He began with Psalms, which soon become Lydia's favorite *book*, though she didn't understand how a single book could contain so many within it. Many of these Psalms were similar, if not exactly the prayers Mama had said over Lydia as a child.

The night before the surveyors were supposed to arrive in town, Dylan read from Psalm 86 and Lydia felt God speaking to them through the prayers of David. His firm, scruffy voice somehow added power to the words as he read them.

"...*O God, the proud are risen against me, and the assemblies of violent men have sought after my soul, and have not set thee before them. But thou, O Lord, art a God full of compassion, and gracious, longsuffering, and plenteous in mercy and truth. O turn unto me, and have mercy upon me, give thy strength unto thy servant, and save the son of thine handmaid..."*

"Tell me what it means," whined Lydia. "I understand some of it, but those words are much different from how people speak here in French Corral." Lydia set her palm over the open Bible in Dylan's hands.

They were sitting together on a sofa Mr. Prescot had given them on loan from his own parlor furniture. The plush upholstery and border of golden silk cords brought welcome color to the contrasting dullness of the wooden and wicker rocking chairs and table. Dylan said it looked out of place, but Lydia didn't mind. She relished the soft seat and the fact that she could sit beside him while he read to her.

"Well, in that last part I read, King David is being pursued by men who don't appear to consider God's will in the matter. David expresses his fear and then reminds God—rather reminds himself— that God is compassionate and gracious. Essentially, David is encouraging himself through this prayer by reminding himself of all God has already saved him from. He is asking for strength to continue to believe in God's mercy and for a sign to demonstrate God's hand of protection."

She pondered his words. "We can pray this way too, can't we?"

"Yes, we can . . . and we should."

"Then let us pray right now. I don't know if these men coming tomorrow plan to harm us, but I will feel better knowing we have asked for God to show us His favor."

"That sounds like a perfect plan. I so often read

these scriptures and never consider how I can apply them to my current circumstances. One more thing I love about you, my sweet Lydia. We will pray at our bedside after we secure the house and subdue the fire in the stove."

THIRTY

They rose early the next morning, ensuring all was in order before Dylan went into town. It would be best for Lydia to stay at the property, acting her part as a hardworking pioneer woman. Dylan said he didn't like forcing her to keep quiet but felt that these men needed only know the basics of her life prior to marrying him. The fact Emelyn had kept Lydia secluded was of no consequence. She was simply raised here by her mother after her father's death. Nothing more.

Dylan would stay in town until the surveyors arrived and then accompany them back to the Valley from the main road. Lydia would have fresh biscuits and stew ready to serve them and would do her best to wipe any worry from her face.

Shortly after Megan's second milking, Lydia heard the clatter of horse hooves and wagon wheels. Exiting the barn, she watched two odd looking wagons approach. The worn wooden wagon she and Dylan used paled in comparison and nearly blended into the grassy field near the road. The other wagon matched glimmering black horses. A canopy shaded the men sitting in the back.

Lydia rushed the milk bucket to the kitchen,

planning to skim off the cream after the men settled in the living room. She exchanged her soiled apron for a clean one hanging on the wall and dipped the edge of the used apron in the dishwater basin. Using the slight reflection of herself in the window, she wiped the dirt smudges from her cheeks and brow.

Dylan hollered at the horses and brought their wagon to a halt. Lydia pulled the curtains back from the front window so she could steal glances at everyone while they approached the porch. Then, she stirred the stew and dumped the cooled biscuits into a basket lined with embroidered muslin. She hoped there would be enough food.

There were three men aside from Dylan. The man driving the wagon was dressed more casually and tended to the horses while the other two men followed Dylan to the cabin. They were dressed in fine attire—clothing Lydia had only seen drawings of in the catalogue at the general store. Their faces, with short-trimmed beards, held flat expressions. One held a black, rectangular case at his side, and listened intensely to Dylan. The other seemed more interested in the Valley. He observed the surrounding buildings, animals, and land. He held a large book in one hand, and would stop, stare off, then use his pen to write something in the book.

Dylan pointed to the barn and continued speaking. Then he pointed to the sheep pasture, garden, and out to the pond and talked some more. After several minutes, he finally opened his arms in a sweeping motion, gesturing toward the cabin. Hardly stopping for a breath, he continued to speak while they gradually approached the porch.

Lydia was dying from anticipation. Why didn't they come in already?

Coffee! She'd forgotten to start the water for the coffee. Did she have time to go out the side door and pump a bucket of fresh water before they came inside? As soon as the thought entered her mind, Dylan and the men stepped onto the porch.

She tucked stray strands of hair behind her ears and smoothed out her apron for the third time. Folding her hands in front of her, she stood still, waiting for the door to open.

A moment later, Dylan and the two men entered, and their conversation halted. Both men removed their hats, the one with the black case revealing a nearly bare head that shined in the sunlight streaming through the kitchen window. Dylan removed his hat, took those belonging to the surveyors, and then hung each hat on a nail on the wall.

"Gentlemen, my wife, Lydia." Dylan extended his arm and nodded. "Lydia, these men are from the Firm of Baldwin and Howell. Mr. Laufenberg—" he gestured to the hairless one. "And Mr. Thomas."

"Ma'am." The men nodded at Lydia and spoke in unison.

Lydia nodded back and curtsied like she and Dylan had practiced.

"My wife has made her famous stew and fresh biscuits for us to enjoy while we continue our meeting." Dylan glanced at the empty water pot on the stove and raised his eyebrows at Lydia.

"And I was about to fetch some water for our coffee. I would have already had it boiling—"

"But you were not expecting us so early," Dylan tilted his head at the side door. "Gentlemen, please take your seats at the table and make yourselves comfortable."

Lydia dashed outside, not realizing she was shaking until she couldn't grasp the well pump handle. *Dear Lord, help me to keep my ears open and my mouth shut. Help me to trust that Dylan...and You, have this under control.*

The meal went well. The gentlemen marveled at the stew, taking second helpings, and devouring every crumb of Lydia's biscuits. After cleaning up, Lydia took her place at the rocking chair near the bedroom doorway, pretending to focus on her embroidery. The gentlemen sipped their coffee on the front porch, alongside Dylan. He talked a lot more than Lydia expected, but stuck to the plan of only answering their questions and telling them nothing more. They wrote their notes, nodded, and occasionally hummed in thought. They gave no indication what they were thinking or how Mr. Sinclair would take the news that her father, Charles, was dead.

By evening's end, Dylan assured them his plans would bring "greater value to the property." The only element of surprise they displayed was when Dylan told them about his father's vineyards and that he planned to use the land to the east of the pond to begin new vines in the coming winter. They seemed impressed for all Lydia could tell.

After gathering their hats and bidding farewell to Lydia, the men joined the wagon driver at the barn and they parted. Dylan lingered by the barn, watching them leave until their *carriage,* as they referred to it, was out of sight. Lydia stood on the front porch, watched him bring the sheep and Megan in from pasture, and then secure the barn and pen gates.

The tasks took longer than usual, or maybe it only seemed that way since normally Lydia would be busy tending to other things. For the moment, she couldn't think of a thing she needed to do. She wanted to know if he thought the meeting was a success.

Her heart fluttered while he approached her, grinning. "You must be bursting with curiosity." He gathered his arms around her waist, nudging her enough that she walked backward into the house. He caught the side of the door with his boot and kicked it closed before planting a firm kiss on her mouth. "You were perfect. The men asked me to give you their condolences on the loss of your father and mother."

Lydia stepped away from him enough to make room for her hands to cross over her belly, trying to calm the bees knocking around inside of her. "What happens now?"

"Now, we make the most of waiting. Mr. Laufenberg will report their findings to Mr. Sinclair and after he has time to consider his decision, he will reply by telegram. I am certain summer will be well underway before we hear from him again."

THIRTY-ONE

The following week, Lydia took special care during her bathing, and put on a new dress Dylan had purchased from the general store catalog as a wedding gift. A deep midnight blue with white lace trim, it seemed almost too nice to wear for a reading lesson. Nevertheless, Dylan had insisted his mother would no doubt be teaching her the "ways of a lady" as well.

She pulled coordinating gloves over her calloused fingertips and then climbed on the quilt-padded wagon seat. She tittered and tried to snatch the parasol from Dylan's tight grasp. He dangled by his boots and leaned over the edge of the wagon, insisting on a dozen kisses before he would relinquish the umbrella.

Trying to be firm with him, she couldn't help but smile, kissing him back between her words. "Would you let me go? I am already nervous enough to be alone with your mother . . . I don't need . . . my face breaking out in a rash . . . from your whiskers to top it off!"

Dylan let the parasol go and threw his head back. Dirt glistening on his neck and chest, his laugh echoed across the Valley floor. He jumped off the side of the wagon and waved. "Go on, my bride. Enjoy your lessons."

"I will be home before sunset—my groom." Lydia rolled her eyes and snapped the reins, urging the horses forward in a steady jaunt. Turning her head, she called back to him, "Your supper is on the stove ready to heat as soon as you are hungry."

It was a mild spring afternoon, so Lydia took to her usual daydreaming. Every tree, every rock, was so familiar. She could even predict which birds would chirp from which branches along her ride. What would it be like to journey along a road where everything was new? Where everyone was new? She'd met and seen dozens of people over the months she'd been in French Corral. After a while, she stopped noticing the differences among individual travelers. Most of them looked tired, worn. Some tried to hide their weariness with clever remarks or the latest fashions. Somehow, Lydia saw past all that. Aside from the people she'd come to know well, most everyone else seemed . . . lost and sad.

She had heard about gold fever. Once they caught it, it held onto them. Was it something about life below the mountain, a life where God may not be evident at every turn? From what Dylan said about the city, it sounded very much like the stories Mama had told. A city filled with greed, violence, and men out for their own interests. Lydia couldn't imagine living a life where she thought only of herself. Of course, she had her curiosity, which Mama had told her could lead to sin if it kept her from fulfilling her purpose or focus on God. Mostly, she wanted to learn new things and experience the world to understand it and maybe find her place in it one day soon.

The rewards of living and helping at the Inn brought amazing fulfillment, beyond any task or duty she had accomplished with Mama in the Valley. Knowing that other people enjoyed her cooking, quilting, and crafting abilities, filled her with a sense of purpose. The more she found ways to help others, the higher her spirits lifted, and the closer she felt to God.

Now, she would learn to read and to write. She couldn't imagine what these new skills would offer her in the ways of helping others. Not needing to ask someone else to help her read something as simple as a letter or telegram—or being able to read Mama's diary again on her own—the thought elated her.

Sheets of clouds moved across the sun, forming a gray cloak of still air over the road leading to the Prescot home. Birds grew silent as the huge home came into view. The only sounds were clopping horse hooves and the grind and squeak of wagon wheels turning into the hardened ground. Heaviness grew in the hollow space between Lydia's ribs and stomach.

Images of hundreds of pages filled with letters and words filled her mind. How would she ever learn to decipher them all? What if she couldn't? Would she lose Jaina's approval if she proved to be the simple-minded "mountain mole" the twins had called her? What about her grandfather—would he accept her as family without her having mastered the skills to read and write? She'd heard enough chatter at the Inn and among those in French Corral to know these skills led to opportunity and the ability to live an abundant life—whatever that meant she wasn't sure—but it seemed important, especially to those from the larger towns and cities.

Lydia's stuffed away her worries when Jaina opened the door and descended the porch. She floated across the uneven ground like a petal on a breeze and joined Lydia as she climbed from the wagon. Jaina wore a tan shirtwaist with miniature navy dots that matched a navy skirt, the pleats in the back flowing down her back in layers to no more than a finger width above the worn grassy path leading to the road. Jaina's elegant, confident movements only stirred the tension within Lydia.

Jaina smiled, grasping Lydia's gloved hands firmly. "Good afternoon, Lydia. I don't think you saw the library on your previous visit, but you will come to know it well by the time your lessons are complete. Our farmhand will water and feed your horses, so we can begin right away."

Jaina led Lydia into the house and down the hallway into a room that seemed nearly the size of a barn. Jaina pushed the ceiling-tall doors into the walls at either side of the doorway. A long, dark, wooden table with cushioned chairs sat centered in the room. Instead of flat walls containing paintings or candle sconces, the walls held shelves filled end to end with books.

How I will ever learn enough to read even one shelf of these books?

Lydia ran her fingers across the bindings, each bump holding a story, a fact about humanity, perhaps even photographs of people, places, and things she had yet to learn or understand. Did they hold made-up adventures or Bible stories? Were there pictures? How many people did it take to create each one?

She dared not ask her questions aloud. For some reason, Lydia did not feel Jaina would accept her curiosity.

"Please, take a seat here. This is your pen and ink, and here are your composition books. This slate and chalk will serve as practice during the lesson. Then you will write it again in the book, practicing at home until next week . . ."

Jaina continued talking at a rather rapid pace—leaving no room for Lydia to speak aside from repeating the instructions to demonstrate her understanding.

When it came time for Lydia to use the pen and ink, Jaina drew back, taking in a long sigh. "It didn't occur to me you would also need a lesson in using a pen." She reached over and ripped out the page Lydia had soaked with a large circle of ink. Jaina cleared her throat, giving Lydia a small smile with tight lips. "Again." She nodded at the blank page.

Lydia bit the inside of her lip, tasting blood as she fought tears that welled up and began to blur her vision. She dipped the metal pen tip into the ink well and tapped the tip before holding it at an angle above the page. Holding the pen rod steady and hoping Jaina didn't notice her hand shaking, Lydia attempted to draw the letter "L" again—a feat far more difficult than using the chalk and slate. The ink tried to pool with any hesitation in her stroke.

By the time she repeated the motions across and then down the page, she'd finally formed a near-perfect resemblance of Jaina's example. This letter, symbolizing the first part of Lydia's name, was quite beautiful on its own—with a small curve and loop at the top and a larger loop and curve at the bottom. Maybe she could learn this task of writing after all.

Lydia looked to Jaina for approval.

"A good start. You will need to practice and

Beyond the Valley

master this and the other letters of your name by our next lesson. Shall we break for tea?" Jaina spoke with tight lips.

Was the dullness in Jaina's eyes due to the overcast sky outside, or did they mean she was disappointed in her new pupil?

A few minutes later, they sat on hard, iron chairs under a large umbrella on the back porch. A stream of sunlight shot through the clouds and landed along the edge of their skirts on the wide-wood-slatted floor. A servant Lydia didn't recognize brought out a tray holding dainty white cups with golden edges and pastel flowers painted on the sides. A matching teapot and platter covered with pastries filled a second tray.

Jaina sipped silently for several moments, looking out on the sheep-spotted meadow below. Beyond a grouping of low hills, dozens of rows of grape vines lined the elevating slope, stopping at the foot of a steep mountain of mixed evergreens, oaks, and maples. Sunlight reflected from the back window, forming a soft glow around Jaina's face. Her lips softened right before she broke the silence.

"So, tell me, have your first days as a bride to my son been everything you'd hope they would be?" Jaina's smile grew with each word.

Lydia cleared her throat, trying not to spray tea across the table. Clara's warning blared in her mind loud enough she feared Jaina could hear it. "I . . . I really did not know what to expect—"

"I trust Dylan has been a gentleman . . ." she raised her eyebrows. "And that he has removed the awful burden you and your mother bore of doing a man's work on that farm."

Lydia released the breath she realized she was holding. "Yes." She nodded, forcing a smile. "Yes, it is nice to have a man around. That is one thing I had longed for ever since Mama told me . . . told me about men in the Bible stories." The words sounded foolish, like something a child would say.

Jaina nodded and set her cup down. She lifted a pastry from the platter with two fingers, treating it like an obligation rather than nourishment. After nibbling a portion, she placed it on her plate and dotted the corners of her mouth with the napkin from her lap. "And the food . . . he . . . pardon me . . . both of you have enough food?"

What an odd question. Of course, they had enough food. Why wouldn't they? "Our food stores are plentiful. You remember all the jarred goods I received at my bridal shower? Besides, the hens produce and abundance of eggs and the garden is overflowing with herbs and vegetables."

"You were sure to leave Dylan a suitable supper knowing you wouldn't return until later this evening?"

"Of course, Jaina." Where was she going with these questions? "I left a fresh batch of biscuits and a kettle with the lamb and root stew left over from last night on the stove."

Jaina nodded, continuing her line of questioning about every aspect of what Lydia assumed were normal daily tasks. Didn't Jaina know Mama had not deprived her of the customs of everyday people? Why was she making Lydia feel as if she wouldn't know how to care for the needs of another person? It wasn't so much different from helping Mama, aside from understanding which tasks were more suitable for a man than for a woman.

Though Lydia did not understand Jaina's intent, she did not see the harm in sharing the daily routine she and Dylan had established. While Lydia explained, Jaina seemed to relax. Her smile even seemed truly genuine by the time the sun fell back behind the clouds, which now settled between the trees on the mountains to the west.

After tea, Lydia gathered her composition books, pens, and a sealed bottle of ink. At the wagon, she filled a satchel with her "homework." Lydia thanked Jaina, who stood waving from the front porch. Mr. Prescot appeared from the doorway and waved as well, asking Lydia to remind Dylan he was due to start work back at the vineyard in the morning.

Keeping the horses at a steady pace, the trip back to the Valley always seemed faster. The declining terrain helped, but somehow Lydia's thoughts managed to speed time. She reviewed the conversation with Jaina over in her mind. Had she said something Dylan wouldn't want his mother to know? Had Jaina truly been pleased with Lydia's report, or was there something else behind her smile? How much of their conversation should she share with her husband if any of it? She prayed God would hold her tongue and help her avoid a single word which may cause strife between her and Dylan.

THIRTY-TWO

The next day, working alone in the Valley seemed an entirely new experience for Lydia. Chores took on new meaning as she admired all the specific things Dylan had repaired or improved. The barn door no longer squeaked. In addition, Dylan had applied a fresh layer of pitch between the slats to keep the cool air in during hot days. He had coated the outside walls with oil mixed with skimmed milk, lime, and red iron oxide, explaining to Lydia that the oils in the paint would protect the wood as well as absorb the sun's rays in the winter, keeping the horses and Megan warmer. The reddish color brought contrast against the green valley grasses and clusters of wildflowers. Lydia stared in awe. A practical solution could also have beautiful results.

When Lydia went to pull weeds and bring water to the garden, the moist soil was clear aside from the sprouts of seedlings. She smiled at first, and then wondered what she could do instead? Wandering behind the grove of small oak trees Dylan and Dan had planted the previous fall, Lydia inspected a hedge of blackberry bushes. There were plenty of berries for pie. Hustling back to the kitchen, she grabbed an empty basket, lined it with a muslin cloth, and went to gather berries. She would surprise Dylan with a blackberry pie for dessert. Surely, after a long day on the vineyard, he would have worked up an appetite.

A light spring rain began to patter on the roof while Lydia completed dinner preparations. She'd decided on fried chicken and pickled potatoes. Soon, the stove piped with hot steam from the bubbling pie. Peach-blossom patterned plates from their wedding gifts, matching embroidered napkins and a teapot filled with coffee sat in perfect arrangement, glowing in the candlelight from the center of the table.

She was about to grab a few more logs for the fire, predicting the rain would bring a cooler evening, when Dylan walked through the door. The gleaming grin she expected to see was a solemn look of concern instead. Dylan held a piece of paper Lydia now recognized as a telegram.

She walked up, ignoring the paper long enough to grab his collar and kiss him hello. He hardly responded to her, stepping back.

A dull feeling settled in her gut.

"What is it?" Tears welled up even before she knew the answer. Whatever it was, it was not good.

"Your grandfather . . . Mr. Sinclair . . . has sent an urgent request for you and me to catch the next train to San Francisco." He lifted the paper up between them. "He has an *important* matter to discuss that cannot wait."

The following two days passed in a blur. Few words and even less physical contact came between them. Lydia hoped Dylan was not angry with her. She could not read the telegram and worried there was more to it than what he shared with her. What if she had done or said something that those men reported to Mr. Sinclair and led to his urgency? Rather, she felt Dylan might be disappointed in his own words. He had talked a lot. Much of it she did not even hear.

She didn't want to bring up anything to upset him more. Instead, she quietly followed his orders. During the evening before their departure, he started writing something on a paper in the kitchen, then suddenly crumpled it up and threw it in the fire. Dylan combed his hands through his hair, beads of sweat glistening on his forehead as he smirked in conflict with his wrinkled brow. "What am I thinking?" He mumbled. "I was about to make you a list of what to pack of our personal items." Then he started to laugh.

Frozen at first, Lydia let out her own giggle once she realized he was laughing at himself.

"I guess I have faith that one day soon, you *will* be able to read a list I write for you." Their laughter grew until they held their sides and caught their breaths.

Dylan drew Lydia close in a tight embrace.

Lydia pushed the damp curls from Dylan's forehead, searching his eyes. "Please don't concern yourself with what tomorrow may bring. I have yet to learn what your silence means in times like this. But I hope you know that no matter what happens, my love for you will not falter."

He looked away, the flame from the fireplace dancing in his eyes. "Even if I did something to cause you to lose this land . . . the Valley . . . as your home?"

Lydia drew him closer, wrapping her arms under his and gripping the tops of his shoulders. She pulled herself up to press her lips into his bristled cheek, pushing back thoughts of what would be happening if it were still only her and Mama, and she never met Dylan. "I don't want to lose the Valley as my home . . . our home. But losing the husband I am getting accustomed to, feels worse." She drew an arm free and turned his face toward hers. "From what the ladies in town tell me, land is plentiful around here. It's a good husband that is hard to come by." With a smile, she kissed him until she felt his body relax into hers.

He groaned, returned the kiss deeply, lifted her up, and carried her into the bedroom.

The long shadows of tree limbs dissolved into dusky blue light by the time Dylan adjusted his suspenders and slid on his boots. Lydia allowed a cool breeze from the open window to whisper along her bare shoulders while she sat on the bed, befuddled by her husband's improved mood. He rattled off the list he had started writing in the kitchen, his dimples deep, and his voice almost jovial at discussing the final preparations before they departed for Sacramento to catch the train.

Lydia smiled, thinking how odd his demeanor could change so easily. Men were different from women. Her mind still swirled with the possibilities of their future, but she held firm not to reveal any concern to Dylan. She did not understand how his pain filtered to her own heart. Yet, she was determined to demonstrate she had her full faith in him. No matter what happened in San Francisco, she would do anything in her power to avoid causing the ache she had seen in her husband's eyes earlier that evening.

Lydia lit candles inside and topped off the kerosene in the lanterns before helping Dylan finish packing, desiring to minimize their tasks before climbing into the wagon come morning.

Long after dark, they fell into bed, confessing their utter exhaustion to each other in sleepy whispers. Regardless, Dylan tossed and turned, keeping Lydia awake. Several times through the night, she found herself staring out at the stars—the moon only a sliver in the sky. Eventually, she gave up the idea of actual sleep, and allowed her mind to wander back through the previous months and all that had led her—and Dylan—to this day. The stars dimmed and the indigo sky faded into a bluish, nearly colorless white behind crooked tree branches and clusters of leaves. For a few brief moments, the sky was still and silent. Then high-pitched chirps assaulted the calm, bringing Lydia to the present.

Lydia turned to face Dylan, now sleeping solid. His mouth slightly opened, she grinned at the drool hanging from the corner of his lip.

No wrinkled brow. If it weren't for his size and the sprinkle of stubble along his jaw, he could have passed for baby Brian sleeping in his cradle.

Tempted to caress his face, she resisted, and slid out of bed and into her slippers. She lit the stove and placed the kettle water on for coffee. Lifting the bar from the door with care, she tiptoed across the porch, and glided across the grass to the barn. She rubbed the tops of her arms, not thinking it could be so cold this close to summer. Grateful, the barn was slightly warmer, she sat in her usual spot beneath Megan.

"I hope you don't mind, but Violet Marks will oversee milking you while we are gone. Now don't confuse her with her sister. Violet is the nicer and quieter one—at least when she is not around Rose. She may even board with us this summer, as she is interested in learning the loom and the secrets to my berry pie recipe. Mr. and Mrs. Marks and Rose will be heading to Oregon over the summer. Mr. Marks is in search of a new job. But Violet doesn't want to leave French Corral." Lydia leaned up to whisper in Megan's ear. "According to Clara, Violet has an eye on one of the young men living near Bridgeport."

It occurred to her she had not seen another person talk to an animal in the way she talked to Megan. She shrugged her shoulders, thinking of what they were missing. Farm animals were blessings from God. Besides providing various forms of food, they could be trusted confidants.

She expected to see Dylan tying down their belongings to the wagon by the time she'd churned the butter and collected eggs, but the house and yard around it appeared untouched since she'd snuck outside. Inside, only the roar and crackle in the stove filled the room. Lydia filled the coffee press with grounds and added hot water. Then she peeked into the bedroom to check for movement. After a few seconds, Dylan's soft snores floated to her ears. She relaxed her shoulders and sighed. He could rest a little longer.

Hoping not to wake him, she pulled the curtain closed over the doorway, wanting to keep out some of the noise making breakfast would cause. Dylan had hinted at getting a door for this room, but there wasn't time or money to order one yet. She would try to remember to remind him while they were in the city. Hattie said they sold everything in the world there. Shops and stores of every sort sold anything from basic farming tools and equipment to elegant furniture and clothing.

Lydia returned to the kitchen, only to feel a rush of air behind her and Dylan's arms looping her waist. He nuzzled her neck, causing her skin to prickle in a pleasing way. "Why didn't you wake me?" He whispered and nibbled her ear.

"You were sleeping so soundly . . . I . . . you're not upset, are you?" She bit her lip, turning to look at him before he answered her.

"Upset at you? Never, my sweet Lydia." He leaned in for a kiss. "Now—" He released his hold on her and clapped his hands. "What have you done already?"

"My normal tasks . . . and the coffee is ready. I still need to boil the eggs and pack our breakfast and lunch."

An hour later, they were sitting snuggly at the front of the wagon, making their way down the mountain. At first, the terrain was relatively flat, rolling hills dotted with fig, apple, and oak trees on either side of the road.

Then, around a corner, the road dropped in a sharp decline, and wound back and forth between a wall of rocky mountain and a chasm so steep, Lydia could not see the bottom from her place on the wagon. Around another corner, the chasm opened wide, revealing steep tree-covered mountains overlapping in the distance.

A deep, manzanita-lined ravine bordered the descent on the roadside of the gap. Where the hills broke in two a wide body of water crashed against boulders and broken tree limbs. It looked as if the rushing water had cut into the side of the mountain like a dull knife through a clump of clay. Green-blue and sparkling against bright white rocks like the jewels on Jaina's pale neck, the water surged. The water flowed around rocks and formed white, foamy rings before moving along at great speed to the next cluster of rocks. Lydia's mind began to fathom the vastness and beauty Dylan had tried to explain to her. For a moment, she was lost in her senses.

Lydia's eyes followed the flow coming from the mountain behind them until manzanita bushes blocked her view. Grasping the edge of the wagon, she leaned over to see where the water emerged around the next bend.

The rooftops of several buildings came into view. A long, covered bridge linked the ends of a narrowing in the ravine at the foot of the hill. Lydia had only heard of the Bridgeport Bridge until this moment. As they came to the foot of the mountain, she marveled at its length and size. Like a stretched-out barn, it hung above the river waters that had slowed and pooled into a calm flow. The bridge defied the invisible forces that should have forced it down into the water as a home to fish long ago. How could something so large stay steady over the water and still bear the weight of travelers crossing its planks?

Before they entered the covered bridge, Dylan glanced at Lydia. "Are you worried about something?"

"No." She shook her head, looping her arm tightly around Dylan's elbow. "I'm fine." She hoped he didn't notice her holding her breath as they crossed.

By early evening, they had passed through Penn Valley and entered Grass Valley. Lydia took in what she could of the buildings and bustle of people. Wagons and buggies of many kinds clamored for space on the narrow street, and Lydia thought she would surely see a small child or pedestrian pummeled, but somehow everything and everyone stayed clear of the other's path. Dylan fed and watered the horses, which they would leave at boarding stables until their return. Lydia prepared their lunch on a grassy knoll near the stagecoach station.

Over a simple stew dinner and rolls, Dylan made light conversation, trying to explain to Lydia some of the things they had seen on the journey so far. She tried to follow along, nodding, and pretending to understand. She loved him even more for his efforts, but exhaustion made it hard for her to focus. Their unfamiliar surroundings and buzz of people's chatter and laughter distracted her.

Yet, once they were in their room, lying in a bed that felt softer than a billow of clouds, Lydia found sleep difficult. Although every bone felt weary and she could hardly roll to her side without extreme effort, her thoughts would not slow down.

She wanted to ask Dylan more details about Mr. Sinclair but feared he would sense her concern. Mr. Sinclair had wanted nothing to do with her mama, so why would he want anything to do with her? Why would he insist on her and Dylan going all the way to San Francisco? She searched her memory for Mama's stories that might reveal an answer—a hint of what to expect.

Rising early the next morning, they ate breakfast in haste, and boarded the coach, joining another couple heading to Sacramento. But first, they would spend the night in Auburn, a full-day's journey ahead.

At first, Lydia grew excited at the idea of getting to know more people, but the couple didn't seem interested in talking. After the customary greetings, they sat across from Dylan and Lydia, looking solemn and bored.

The trip to Auburn nearly replicated Lydia's discomfort, overwhelming her senses and the discord within her soul. Thankfully, Dylan did not prompt her to explain her silence. Whenever she glanced his way, he seemed caught in his own storm of emotions and thoughts, jaw strained and eyes peering out at the distant mountain peaks or sky.

THIRTY-THREE

Lydia rose to a silent and still morning. Dylan slept undisturbed while she slipped out of bed. She dressed, careful not to wake him, and snuck outside onto the porch of the hotel. A wooden board creaked, and a small creature scurried between the flower stems below. Across the yard, a winery with rock walls stood, a faint orange glow reflecting off the window. She couldn't tell if the light came from the rising sun or from something else around the side of the hotel.

She knelt anyway and turned her face toward the dusky sky above the rooftop. She and Mama had always done their morning prayers facing the rising sun . . . *to welcome the day and the glory of God onto the land* . . . so it felt strange to attempt a morning prayer without the rising sunlight warming her face.

She wove her fingers tightly and pulled them to her chest. "God . . . Savior Jesus . . . please take this weariness from me. Help me to trust you for the remainder of this journey. Give Dylan peace no matter what happens . . . and . . . show my grandfather the right thing to do. Keep our hearts secure and safe. Amen."

A hand rested on her shoulder, but she didn't

budge. She knew it was Dylan. "Amen." His voice sounded deeper in the morning, as if his own burden lay lodged in his throat. "The stagecoach leaves within the hour." He squeezed her shoulder gently and went back inside.

They shared a stagecoach with two businessmen on the leg to Sacramento. Dylan had suggested they reveal few details of the purpose of their journey with strangers. Mr. Sinclair could send lookouts to pretend they were travelers in hopes of gaining information. Lydia kept quiet again, and with gloved hands folded beneath her chin, she stared out the window and took in the scenery. The land shifted from endless, flat wheat-colored prairies to rows upon rows of orchards. She thought they were apple trees, but some of them held orange-colored fruit as well.

"Lydia," a voice called her from far away. "Lydia . . . you've fallen asleep." The voice whispered and a hand rocked her shoulder.

Lydia pulled her mind forward from a sleep so deep, she shuddered. Her hat felt as heavy as a bag of flour while she lifted it from the back of the seat . . . the seat . . . She'd forgot she was sitting in a stagecoach. It was no longer moving. She squeezed her eyes and forced them open. It was dark and she barely made out Dylan's face in the odd light shining through the window.

"Lydia, you slept all the way to Sacramento." Dylan scooted back and stepped down from the coach on his side. "Do you need me to carry you to the carriage?"

"Hmmm . . . No . . . I . . . I'm fine. I only need a moment to come to my senses." She smiled at him and reached up to stretch her arms, but her knuckles knocked into the roof before she could straighten them. Annoyed at her sense of space, she tried to hide her error. Dylan was already on his way around to her side of the coach and opening the door before she could rub the sting from her fingers.

She looked at their surroundings in a daze, finding it hard to take in. Lights attached to ornate poles stood on a street that intersected another street and then another. Dozens of buildings, and carriages sat mostly still and silent. The hour must be late as very few people walked the street. Only those she'd seen arrive by another stagecoach wandered nearby. A large gentleman with a small black hat helped them load their trunk and other belongings into a carriage. They would stay the night at a boarding house on the other side of the city, closer to the train depot, which was across the river.

Unaware she was famished until she took her first bite ever of fried fish, she couldn't avoid moaning in response to the incredible flavor. Dylan smiled with his mouth full, seemingly amused at her reaction. "Do you like it?" he asked, after swallowing.

She took another bite, enjoying the crunch and then let the buttery flakes melt on her tongue before swallowing. "This is delicious! I wonder if Mrs. O'Shea knows a recipe for this. I've heard the miners catch fish along the river at Bridgeport. But I never thought of how they would cook them."

Dylan laughed and nodded his head at a glass

holding a pale-yellow beverage. "It goes very well with dry white wine."

Lydia hesitated, inhaling the strong scent of the wine, and then sipped enough to wet her lips. Slightly bitter with a sweet lingering flavor, she decided white wine was something she would not mind drinking on occasion. She took a few more sips and finished eating her fish.

Dylan winked, never taking his eyes off her. "That wine might help you fall asleep as well. After napping all day, you might need it."

He was right. By the time they made it up to their room, Lydia felt relaxed and her mind felt fuzzy. Safe in her husband's arms, she nuzzled into his chest and let her mouth speak freely. "Orange apple tree s . . . fried fish . . . a fat man in a little black hat . . ." she giggled. ". . . never thought I would see so many odd things." She closed her eyes and sighed. "Will you tell me about those tall lights on the poles in the morning, Dylan?"

"Of course. Tomorrow we will have more privacy on the train. Rest now, my sweet Lydia . . . rest." He kissed the top of her head and pulled her closer.

To Lydia's dismay, they did not get to do much talking on the train. Within an hour of boarding the enormous and loud contraption, Lydia grew dizzy. She did not say anything to Dylan at first, taking in deep breaths, and keeping her eyes focused on the scenery outside. The speed at which everything passed brought a lump to her throat. Her mouth filled with saliva and her stomach turned.

She reached over and grabbed Dylan's hand in desperation, feeling a flush up her neck and sweat masking her face. She pressed her lips together, pleading to Dylan with her eyes. Before he could respond, she bowed her head between her knees and heaved. Head in her soiled skirt, she didn't move. Dylan called one of the train porters over discreetly and within a few minutes, a half a dozen hands and rags were cleaning up the mess. Her head in a fog and feeling another wave approach, she groaned. Someone placed a bucket on the floor in front of her, and she gratefully let her body expel every trace of food and liquid. Thinking it was over, she tried looking up at Dylan but the motion made her head spin.

"Keep your head down, Lydia. Let it pass and then you can lie down on the other seat."

Even lying down, it didn't pass. She had to lie completely still, with her eyes closed, or she would heave. With nothing left in her stomach, her throat and mouth burned.

Eventually, sleep took over, her mind and body too exhausted to do anything else. Without effort, Lydia's thoughts fled to the Valley, to the still and quiet of a simple, predictable life with Mama . . .

"Mama, tell me again why God doesn't give us a man to help us in the Valley."

"God provides for us without the need of a man. Though our work is hard, God has seen too many men use their power to harm, their greed blinding them of what a woman can offer on equal ground. Men can't . . . could not . . . see past their pride in those other lands."

"But how could a man's pride hurt us here, Mama? Why couldn't he share the work, and the land as God requires us to do?"

"Men didn't see things God's way in those lands. No matter how He provided, no matter who he sent to speak on His behalf, men would always try things their own way. And the women would suffer for it...So now God has made a way for us to live apart from that suffering. Now stop asking questions and get back to your needlework . . "

The scene repeated in her mind, only Mama seemed to grow older and sadder with each repetition. The words echoed as if Mama sat beside her . . . *greed blinded them . . . can't see past their pride . . . women would suffer . . .*

Then suddenly, she understood what Mama meant. *Other lands...could Mama have been speaking of San Francisco? Of someone who had caused her to suffer? Who else could it be aside from Mr. Sinclair? He had rejected Mama and that rejection had led her and Charles to French Corral . . . and her ultimate isolation.*

The train came to a stop. It took several minutes, but eventually her head stopped spinning and she opened her eyes. Dylan sat on the floor, head bowed and hands resting on Lydia's, which lay folded across her belly.

"I think I can sit up now," she said.

After sleeping during daylight two days in a row, Lydia found no rest that night. A black sky sparkled with hundreds of stars through the window of their car. Relishing the calm within, she stared at the sky and took in the quiet around her. An occasional rustle from another passenger startled her as she began to drift. When the train car sounds faded, she lay in awe of the expanse of sky she could see through the small window. Once again, the stars dissolved into pale blue, and then a thick fog floated in.

When the train began to move, the waves of nausea returned. Giving into her demise, she found strength to ask Dylan to read to her from Mama's diary to help distract her. Pulling the book from her satchel, Dylan nestled into the seat at Lydia's feet, and read in a faint voice. By the time they arrived in Oakland, he had read through to the part where Mama wrote about Lydia's first days. "I suppose it is a good thing that Mr. Sinclair only paid for train tickets from Sacramento. My father offered to purchase train tickets from Grass Valley, but I thought you would enjoy taking in the scenery at a slower pace to start." Dylan stood and replaced the diary in the satchel. "Are you feeling better now that the train stopped again?"

Gathering her senses for a moment, she determined she was fine. "Yes, I think so." She sat and took a deep breath.

It was late morning as they stepped off the train. People crowded around them and Lydia didn't have a chance to look further than her own two feet as she clung to Dylan. Like a flock of sheep, they shuffled between trains, and down a wide dirt path. Then a massive building, floating on a cloud of fog, towered over them.

"That is the ferry," Dylan said. "It will take us across the channel and into the city." He patted her hand, which refused to lose its grip on his arm.

Discouraged, her body rejected the motion on the ferry as well. This time, though, Dylan found a private bench along the backside of the ferry. Using a few stray crates to raise her up, he arranged Lydia so that she could vomit over the side of the boat into the water if needed. It was hardly comfortable, her ribs grinding into the railing, but at least she didn't soil another dress. The cool foggy air brought chills but refreshed her face between waves of nausea. Soon, she was shaking and Dylan

Beyond the Valley

wrapped her in his coat to warm her.

The ferry ride didn't take as long as the train ride, and soon she and Dylan stepped onto solid ground, fog fizzling away in the dim sunlight.

Dylan pulled Lydia against his side and kissed the top of her head. "Here we are, my sweet bride—San Francisco—a city that people from the entire world flocked to for a new and better life."

Lydia shuddered, confused at why anyone would want to come to a place with so much chaos and no room to breathe. Her first impression likely warped by a weary mind and worn body—she didn't understand the appeal.

Herded like sheep once again, and fighting for strength to take each step, strange people, sights, sounds, and smells assaulted Lydia's senses. People spoke in words she didn't understand. Babies screamed in the distance. Animals protested. Carts, carriages, and wagons swept past them at high speed. She held tight to Dylan, and soon he waved down a carriage. Helping her up, he told her to wait there while he paid the man at the dock to deliver their trunk to his grandfather's house. They would be staying at Mr. Prescot's mansion on Russian Hill, located on the other side of the city from Mr. Sinclair's estate.

Frightened Dylan would never find his way back to her, Lydia kept her eyes stuck on his hat as it bobbed between the crowds and other obstacles. She didn't draw a breath until she made eye contact with him on his return. He climbed up alongside her and rattled off a number and name Lydia didn't recognize. The carriage driver urged the horses along and soon they were riding along a street that appeared to lead straight into the layer of fog above them.

Chuckling, Dylan handed her a brush and mirror from her satchel. "You'll want to tidy up before we get to the Sinclair estate—especially after our long journey."

One look in the mirror and Lydia understood what Dylan meant. Her grandfather's first impression had to be a good one.

Lydia removed her hat, and untangled strands of hair from the ribbon. She pulled the brush through her hair, finding it difficult to steady her hands between the jarring of the carriage and the rattling of single-car trains streaming past them.

Dylan leaned over, raising his voice above the clanking of wheels against rails. "Cable cars. You will get used to them in no time." He brushed his lips across her cheek and settled his hand into the small of her back.

As they ascended the steep hill, fog fell behind them and a blue sky emerged. Narrow, yet tall homes stacked one against the other lined both sides of the street. Each one different from the pillars and gates at the entrance to the colors of trim and intricate patterns engraved into doors and around windows. The higher the carriage climbed, the larger each building grew, and the more elaborate the foliage and items surrounding them became. They looked more like grand hotels than houses and were nothing like the simple living quarters in French Corral. A moment after Lydia reached into her satchel to grab a pair of white gloves, the carriage came to a stop in front of a home that seemed to take up the entire length of the street and around the corner.

"This is it, Lydia. The Sinclair Manor on Nob Hill."

THIRTY-FOUR

Lydia felt no taller than two-year-old Olive as she stood before the ivory-white steps, each as tall and wide as a watering trough, leading up to the front doors. Dylan took her shaking hands in his, folding one of them securely into the crook of his elbow. The iron gate, a tapestry of jointed rods and star-like patterns, connected two white pillars before a flat landing and another flight of cobblestone stairs leading to a darkened doorway.

With each step, Lydia's heart raced. Perspiration clung to the back of her neck despite the cool air. She felt like Dylan was pulling her, though he stepped alongside her.

Two massive, nearly black doors loomed in defiant silence. There was nothing welcoming about them. Before Dylan could reach his hand to press the bell, one of the doors cracked open, and a hazy stream of light flowed across the porch floor.

Standing beside the door, an older man dressed in a crisp white shirt buttoned to his neck and a black coat short in the front but long in the back, nodded with a long face and straight expression.

"Mr. and Mrs. Dylan Prescot, I presume?"

Dylan removed his hat, loosened Lydia's grip on his arm, and bowed without a word.

"Mr. Sinclair is expecting you. You may wait in the parlor while I announce your arrival."

After they entered, the man closed the door, pointed to the parlor, and then disappeared into a dark hallway. Lydia did not want to sit, aware of the soiled hem of her dress and the grime coating her clothing. Though she had changed out of the skirt and wrap she'd worn on the train, she still felt residue from her motion sickness dried along the inseam of her petticoat. She'd never felt filthy before. Yet, it seemed unfitting for her to be standing in such a grand home in her pitiful state.

Dylan's small smile and shadowed eyes didn't help her. She wished he would say something, but he seemed as insecure and uncertain as she was in this moment. Certainly, if he knew what to expect, he would have told her by now.

"Mr. Sinclair will see you now." Lydia jumped at the voice as the man emerged from the shadow like a mouse in the doorway.

The couple followed him down a short hallway and around a corner through sliding doors.

A desk twice the size of their kitchen table sat in the center of the room. Behind it sat a white-haired man, with deep hard lines etched into his forehead and around his nose. Thin lips wrinkled and pursed as if his tongue would betray him at any moment. His hands lay folded like gnarled tree branches on the blotter.

Dylan and Lydia crept toward thick-armed chairs facing the desk.

Without changing his expression, Mr. Sinclair stood, held out his hands stiffly, and gestured to the empty chairs.

Dylan and Lydia sunk into the oversized, plush seats. Lydia swallowed hard, afraid she would gag on the saliva collecting in her throat.

Mr. Sinclair sat and refolded his hands. He glanced at Dylan, blinked, and bore his gaze into Lydia without a single sound.

Something about his eyes seemed familiar to her, but the fright pounding in her chest prevented her from placing it. Why didn't he speak?

"Mr. Sinclair . . . I . . . we—" Dylan's voice shook.

"Enough." Mr. Sinclair drew his up hand, flattening it toward Dylan. His chest heaved and he slapped his hand on the desk.

Tears sprung from Lydia's eyes, and a sob escaped her lips. Dylan grabbed her hands and held them tight, but she continued to shake.

Mr. Sinclair caught Lydia's eyes in his own, the familiar fleck replaced with the hardness of two black coals. "I am not interested in explanations or reasoning. You may or may not be the child of my deceased son, Charles. With no way to prove it, I have simply called the two of you here to clear up the matter of my property—property, that until two weeks ago, I assumed Charles was managing with his wife Emelyn."

He shifted his glare to Dylan. "Without mention of a child in any of the letters or telegrams I received from Charles or Emelyn, I must conclude that I have no heir. Since I am forced to accept that Charles is buried on that land, my lawyer has drawn up the necessary paperwork to ensure the property remains in my possession."

Another man, donning a mud-brown suit and matching hat, stepped out from the shadows behind Mr. Sinclair. He placed a stack of papers on the desk blotter.

Mr. Sinclair retrieved a pen and inkbottle from a drawer and began scratching it along the pages. "Mr. Prescot, you and your wife are heretofore banished. My signature confirms my repossession of the property and requires both of you to remove your personal belongings and to vacate the property immediately upon your return." He stamped a waxy mark on the pages and handed them back to the man in brown.

The shadows in the room closed in around Lydia. She tried to breath, but darkness cloaked over her. A stabbing pain hit her temple and her surroundings vanished.

A cool cloth on Lydia's forehead coupled with Dylan's gentle voice woke her. She cracked one eye open, the drum of her heart steady against her chest.

"Shhhh . . . don't speak." Dylan kissed her forehead and cheeks. "We are still at the Sinclair Mansion. You fainted right when Frank Sinclair entered the room—"

"Ma'am," said a deep, slow voice.

Lydia faced the voice, prying her eyes open to peer behind the back of the couch she lay on. Straight, short, gray-streaked brown hair framed the square face of a man she had not yet met. Soft lines surrounded sparkling eyes, and a thick mustache curved above gleaming, white teeth.

"Hello." Lydia did not know what else to say.

"I am your uncle, Frank, brother to your father, Charles." The kind-looking man nodded toward her. "I am gravely sorry the way my father chose to treat the two of you and this entire matter. Had he told me you were arriving today I would have arranged for a more civilized meeting."

"We appreciate your efforts, Frank," piped Dylan. "But it is obvious Mr. Sinclair has made up his mind. I am sorry we could not come to a different arrangement, but I take full responsibility. I was dishonest with your father upon our first engagement—I was foolish to think I could handle this . . ." He sighed as Lydia squeezed his hand. ". . . this matter with a simple offer to purchase the property."

Frank waved his hand and laughed. "My father is angry he couldn't control his number one son. Lucky for me, as number two, I can pretty much do as I please and he hardly blinks."

"Well, that is still no reason for him to be so harsh with Lydia—proof or no proof that she is his granddaughter—a gentleman should never speak that way in front of a lady." Dylan's voice grew louder with each word. He let go of Lydia's grip, stood, and walked around the couch until he faced Frank. "If you could arrange for my wife to have a cup of tea before we part ways, I would be much obliged."

"Of course," said Frank, reaching for Dylan's hand and shaking firmly. "I will have the kitchen staff prepare a basket of food for you as well. Will you be staying in the city tonight?"

"Yes, we are staying at my grandfather's house on Russian Hill. Once my wife rests, I hope to take her on a tour of the brighter parts of the city, maybe even take in a show at the theatre."

"Have you never been to San Francisco?" Frank raised his eyebrows and looked down at Lydia with a wry smile.

"No . . . I have not. This is my first time—" She still felt dizzy and the echoes of her grandfather's booming voice made it hard for her to think of anything else.

Frank clapped. "Take her to the Cliff House then...and the Sutro Baths." He reached into his coat pocket. "I am not one for formalities but keep this between us in case my father decides to make an issue of it. Take this money here and give your wife a night she will never forget. San Francisco is like having the entire world at your fingertips, if you have the means to indulge." Frank winked, seemingly pleased at his obvious defiance.

Dylan tried to wave away the roll of bills.

Frank stuffed them into Dylan's vest pocket and patted his back. "It's the least I can do to make up for my father's obstinate state. How long have you two been married, anyway?"

Dylan cleared his throat and dabbed his handkerchief across his forehead. "Err . . . we were married three weeks ago—"

Frank slapped Dylan on the back hard, causing him to lung forward. "Newlyweds! Here, take all I've got." He pulled more crumpled bills from the inside of his coat. "You're still practically honeymoon'n! I should pour you a drink."

"No, thank you. We should be on our way soon. Thank you." Dylan glanced at the wad of cash in his hand, looked at Lydia and shrugged before flattening out the bills and adding them to the others in his vest.

Whirling with emotions, Lydia found words difficult. She followed Dylan's lead as they exited

Beyond the Valley

the mansion and made their way back down the hard, white stairs and into the carriage. Dusky light made each step a chore to locate. Thick clouds had rolled in and replaced the bright sunlight with a silver haze—much like her grandfather's words had obliterated any ray of hope she'd had left and cloaked it in despair.

Though she had feared she would face an angry man, she had hoped Mr. Sinclair would exercise some sort of self-control. His hard, coal eyes, and the echo of his hand slapping the desk ran repeatedly in her mind. Each time, the reality of his words sunk in deeper, and tears streamed freely, soaking into the collar of her blouse without restraint.

The Valley would no longer be her home. Where would she and Dylan live?

A strong stench wafted up from the street and Lydia thought she would be sick again. She held her breath, hoping they would pass into fresher air soon.

Why didn't Dylan say anything?

Dylan held her tightly. She looked over at him, his face hiding in the shadows for a moment before muzzled light seeped through in-between buildings and revealed moist trails of tears streaking his cheeks. Instead of acknowledging her discovery, she nuzzled into his side and numbly noticed the sights and sounds that seemed to belong only to this city.

The carriage careened up and down, then down and up fog-filled streets like something out of a bad dream. Some streets were clusters of activity—wagons without horses, rumbling cable cars, music streaming from buildings bursting with crowds of brightly dressed women, and men smoking cigars.

People scurried or moseyed, laughing or grumbling in every direction.

Other streets hardly held a soul, aside from a lone passerby begging for coins. Once, grimy hands and missing teeth grabbed for Lydia's sleeve, only to be batted by the end of Dylan's umbrella at the sound of her shriek.

Finally, they arrived at the Prescot home and Lydia sighed with relief.

Modest in comparison, but beautiful in its design, Lydia admired the cone shaped corner roof pointing into the gray sky. Fancy bright-white shapes strung in a neat row around the top of the second story windows. Lacey-white loops bordered the roofline in an inviting and cheery appeal. Below the lower windows, a long row of bushes dotted with tiny flowers with red, purple, pink, and white petals, bordered the base of the house.

A weight lifted from Lydia's heart as she and Dylan climbed from the carriage and made their way to the entrance. Servants greeted them with large smiles and shining eyes. Inside, at least a dozen bronze candle sconces lit up white and cream striped walls. An enormous crystal chandelier hung from the ceiling, measuring at least twice the size of the one in the dining room at the Prescot home in French Corral.

A staircase with a white banister wound up a red-toned wall and around to a landing above them. After a few moments, she looked over at Dylan, hoping he'd been able to dry his face.

Dylan smiled, dry-eyed, and walked with her to the base of the staircase. "I wish you could meet my grandfather, but his illness prevents many visitors. He cannot risk catching any minor ailment. Even I must stand at the far end of his room to speak with him. Miss Gracie will show you to our rooms and draw your bath. I will meet you in the parlor when you are ready." Dylan smiled as he spoke, his gaze softening from the furrowed brows he held as they crossed the city.

He kissed her gloved hands and then pulled her close, pressing his lips firmly on hers. Several moments passed, and then he drew back only enough to gaze into her eyes, his grip around her waist remaining firm.

She could melt into the green pools of his eyes and for a moment, their troubles vanished.

Dylan whispered, "My love for you has only grown these past few hours, Lydia. Tell me you believe me and that you believe I will do whatever it takes to change your grandfather's mind."

She blinked away tears and kissed him again. "Yes, I do . . . I believe you love me, even if Mr. Sinclair's words and that paper stand firm. But for tonight . . . if there is a way for you to make me forget tomorrow's worries, that is all my heart desires."

Dylan raised his eyebrows, raining kisses from her forehead to her neck. "I'm sure I can find a way to erase our troubles for the night." He faced Miss Gracie, her face flustered while she stood silent on the first stair. "Miss Gracie, please help Mrs. Prescot dress in the finest gown you can find. If there isn't one nice enough in our trunks, then perhaps there is something of my mother's that she left behind during a past visit."

"Yes, sir, Mr. Prescot. I will make certain your wife looks like royalty before she joins you this even'n."

THIRTY-FIVE

Miss Gracie assisted Lydia in scrubbing every bit of filth from the top of her scalp to the bottoms of her feet. When finished, Lydia could not remember ever feeling so clean, fresh, and free. She almost thought she would float down the stairs.

"You look like a princess, Miss Lydia," whispered Miss Gracie.

If she looked like a princess, then surely, she must feel like one too. Careful to drape the train of her gown across her arm to avoid tripping, Lydia descended the steps, one at a time. The soft, elegant satin fabric fit snugly across her back and hugged her sides. Layers of cream-colored lace entwined with silver beads fell around the tops of her otherwise bare shoulders. Pearly white, satin gloves stretched from fingers to elbow. Pink petals, embroidered with silk and cotton thread, blended with silver strands and glass beads to form a garden of flowers and stems on the front bodice. The pattern continued down the sides of the satin, pale-gray skirt, collecting in a dense cluster along the bottom of the skirt, which trailed behind her for several feet when not over her arm.

Beyond the Valley

At the bottom of the stairs, she followed Miss Gracie across the wide entry hall and into the parlor. Dylan jumped from his seat, the hat on his lap falling to the floor. His jaw drew open for a silent second.

Then his smile emerged on one side and grew into a grin so large it nearly hid his dimples. "And I thought the mountain girl was a sight to see. Whew . . ." He shook his head. "I better keep you close at my side this evening. You look absolutely stunning . . . royal doesn't seem a worthy enough word . . . *heavenly* is more like it."

Lydia took in a sight of her own. Dylan wore a gray suit, with a matching vest and checkered bow tie. His unruly curls smoothed down in a curve across his forehead, making his green eyes pop and sparkle. His normally stubble-strewn cheeks and chin were smooth and glowing. Lydia nearly removed a glove to caress his face.

Miss Gracie curtsied and scurried down the hall.

With nobody else in sight, Dylan strode toward Lydia and pulled her to him by the small of her back. Lips hovering before hers, he whispered, "May this kiss melt away all your troubles, my sweetheart, even if only for the night."

In that moment, Lydia decided this night was a dream. She would experience it all without a care, so long as Dylan remained at her side. He was all she had left in the world, and she would be all he needed and wanted, no matter the consequence.

Minutes later, they strode arm-in-arm out the front door. The massive homes and gardens lining their path seemed distant and unimportant. They walked for several blocks and then climbed aboard an electric streetcar. Dylan acted as her guide, pointing out the different elements that made San

Francisco stand out from other large cities. They rode through Golden Gate Park—plants, trees, and flowers from around the world filled the landscape with glorious shades of green and colors brighter than any Lydia had ever seen. She stared past the open window, taking in every detail.

Beyond the park, they traveled around sand dunes, and approached a tunnel within the jagged cliffs. Brisk, salty air plucked at her cheeks and chilled her bare arms, but she didn't care. Twists and turns caused a slight twinge in her tummy as the streetcar entered the mouth of the tunnel. Chatter from the other travelers in the full car echoed in the rounded walls, and then ceased with roaring water crashing along the rocks on the other side. The sea rolled in great waves far out into the distance and Lydia began to understand the true vastness of this world.

When the Cliff House came into view, nothing could have prepared Lydia for what she saw. More like an enclosed city, *house* hardly seemed the correct word. Three rows of at least twenty tall windows lined the outer walls and sat atop the jagged cliffside. On top of it, another level looked like houses lined one against the other, with steeply pitched roofs in the center and reddish cones on the top of each corner.

By the time they climbed down from the car, Lydia couldn't contain herself. Giddy with excitement, she entwined her fingers with Dylan's and skipped toward the entrance. She ignored the strangers that stared at them with wide eyes or wrinkled brows. Somehow, her gown made her feel bold and undaunted by what others might think. She didn't look like a mountain girl who knew nothing of a night in the city. Besides, Dylan didn't seem bothered by her excitement. In fact, he appeared amused and followed along, tipping his hat with a smile to anyone who tried to gawk.

Lydia stopped at the entry and craned her neck to follow the immense white walls to the steep red roof. The tiles and rods at the tallest parts reached into a sky swirling with streams of fog and hues of sunset oranges and pinks. She felt like a lone, fragile poppy facing the trunk of one of the massive redwoods they'd passed in the park.

"The gingerbread palace," Dylan announced bowing and extending his arm toward the entrance.

Lydia clapped, curtsied, and mimicked the arrogant steps of the woman who walked in before her. She raised her chin high and narrowed her eyes at onlookers. Then, like a little girl, she pulled Dylan inside and insisted on seeing every inch of the humongous building . . . and having him read every word plastered along the walls, under glass displays, and on signs placed along the walkways.

They started at the fourth-floor parlors and galleries. Each displayed elaborate arrays of life-sized items and animals from around the world. From wrapped dead people called *mummies* to finger-sized versions of everyday items supposedly belonging to tiny human called Tom Thumb, Lydia giggled at the strange sights. In another room, she shrieked and jumped at the sight of a gaping mouth of sharp teeth on a large, spotted lion. Dylan laughed, telling her it was only a stuffed jaguar.

Lydia's stomach rumbled. "There is so much to see, but I don't think I can wait much longer for dinner." She smoothed gloved fingers over her stomach.

A few minutes later, a waiter seated them at a table for two by the window. Outside, crashing waves rumbled below a large glass building with a domed roof encasing the bathhouse.

"Tell me about the baths," Lydia insisted. "I want every detail about what to expect."

Between salad, lobster, pasta, and a watered-down glass of sweet wine, Dylan described the Sutro Baths—the largest public bath house in the world. Holding seven pools of salt water, the bathhouse could hold up to 100,000 people. There were platforms for sitting and watching, slides, diving areas and even live entertainment on select evenings.

After having only taken turns bathing with Mama in their small mountain cabin, Lydia could not fathom what it would be like to bathe among hundreds of strangers. They would be provided bathing suits, assured Dylan. These baths were for swimming, not cleaning. She still didn't understand, but the wine made her chuckle at her ignorance instead of wallowing in it. Shrugging her shoulders after finishing off the last bite of cake from her plate, she stood and announced she was ready to, "head to the baths!"

A cold breeze whipped around them as they walked up the road to the bath entrance. Sobering, invisible specks stung Lydia's face. She buried her head inside Dylan's coat.

He pulled her close, chuckled, and sped his stride. "Sandy wind is never pleasant, a downside to the castle on the cliffs."

Lydia's toes hardly touched the ground as they

flew up the rest of the sidewalk.

After entering, they walked up and then down two wide-rounded flights of stairs, Dylan handed her a few coins and pointed her down a hallway. "That is where the ladies change into their swimming suits and caps. I will be in this direction where the gentlemen change. Of course, I have not been in the lady's side, but the changing rooms cannot be too different. Follow the steam and watch your step. The floor can get quite slippery when wet. I will meet you at the outside of the door, so stay put if I'm not there yet."

Lydia nodded with an exaggerated, "Yes, sir." She scooped up the end of her dress that dragged on the floor behind her and flung it over her arm. She stumbled, then found her footing and followed a group of giggling girls down the hall. Taking a deep breath, she stood inside the changing area for a moment and observed. Rows and rows of stalls lined the narrow corridor. Women and girls of all ages and sizes pranced in and out of the swinging doors. A second later, someone plucked the coins from her palm, handed her a suit, and pointed to where she could change her clothes. How would she ever remember which room was hers upon returning?

"First time?" One of the giggling girls said with a smile.

"Yes . . . I'm . . . not from around here." Lydia hoped the statement wouldn't cause too many questions. She wasn't ready to hash up her reality now.

"Oh, well, welcome! You will have a killer time. It's easy to figure out. There are hooks in the changing room, and that buzzer there will call an attendant to assist with what you cannot reach.

Don't forget your number painted on the door. If you need help with anything, give me a holler. I come here all the time with my sisters. Are you here alone?" The speed at which this girl spoke made Lydia dizzy. On the other hand, maybe it was the wine.

"I am here with my husband. He said he would wait on the other side of the door."

"Oh, well men don't take nearly as long to get changed, so you better hurry before he gets worried."

After a bit of a struggle, Lydia buzzed and attendant who assisted her in removing the many layers of her gown and underclothing. The swimming suit consisted of a short-sleeved, black, knee-length dark wool dress and black stockings, leaving her feeling oddly unprotected despite nearly covering her from neck to toes. She wrapped her hair in a handkerchief in the same fashion as the other women, and slipped on flat, black shoes.

The group of girls, who failed to share their names, led Lydia right out the door, where Dylan stood waiting. "If that is your husband, you are in good hands. Congratulations and have fun. Ta-ta . . ." the girl waved and joined her sisters as they scurried along the edge of one of the pools. Squealing, they latched hands and jumped in with a splash.

Lydia's face grew hot at the sight of Dylan in the form-fitting full-piece men's bathing attire. Yet not a smidgen of his charm seemed daunted. His sideways grin deepened the dimple on one cheek when she grabbed his hand. Feeling safer in his company, she took in the vastness of the bathhouse.

Steam hung in the air, floating far above their

heads, and clinging to hundreds of windows that formed walls on every side. Larger than any building Lydia had ever seen, let alone been inside, it seemed at least the size of French Corral. Hard, narrow green and golden beams adjoined and jutted out from corners of the ceiling, forming a hatched look, like over-sized stitches across a sky-sized quilt. How could such narrow poles hold up the weight of glass walls?

She counted seven rectangle-shaped ponds filled with blue-tinged water—each lined one behind the other across the center of the room. "These are not like the pond or the river. What did you say these were called?" Lydia shouted over screams and splashing.

"Pools. Man-made and heated too," Dylan shouted into her ear.

They chose one of the warmer pools and found a spot to sit and soak their feet over the edge. People and children of every age splashed, screamed, and flailed their arms and legs while somehow staying afloat. The commotion caused Lydia's head to spin. The energy from everyone's enthusiasm was exhilarating.

Then Dylan pushed himself off the edge and flew into the water hands and head in front of him. Lydia's heart leapt and then she laughed when he bobbed up between the ends of her feet.

"You are not getting away with simply sitting there. I will keep you from sinking, don't you worry." He pushed the water aside and glided closer to her, then grabbed her waist and pulled her down into the water.

She kicked her feet hard, but still started to sink. Salty water splashed into her mouth and she forced it out with her tongue, not wanting to spit.

Laughing, Dylan provided further instruction. "Move your arms and legs slowly, like this. Big motions, pushing the water under you . . . there you go."

Soon, she relaxed and floating came more easily. Dylan stayed right with her, close enough to the edge that she could grab on if needed. A light feeling came over her and the noise around them faded into the background. She pulled herself to Dylan, floating like a cloud on a gentle spring breeze. Then, she wrapped wet fingers around the back of his neck, twirling a loose strand of his hair while she pulled his face to hers. She pressed her lips to his, but he pulled back, eyes wide.

"Darling . . . Lydia . . . not here."

She pushed away and threw herself to the edge of the pool. Heat rushed into her face and she felt light-headed. *How foolish of me, I've embarrassed Dylan.*

Dylan was at her side in a moment. "It's fine. It's been a long day. You're probably not the first lady to let some wine and heat get to her pretty, little head in these pools. We should head back to Grandfather's and try to get a good night's sleep."

THIRTY-SIX

Visions of their evening excursion danced through Lydia's mind during the ride back to the Prescot home. She tried to keep her eyes open to observe the sites of the city at night, but her lids grew heavy long before their ascension of Russian Hill. The rumble and clicking of hooves on the cobblestone path became a monotonous rhythm and a deep sleep took over.

Somewhere between awake and asleep, Mr. Sinclair's eyes seared away any glimmer of hope. The Valley would no longer be her home. He had not even recognized she was his granddaughter. Hardness filled her heart. This man was the reason for all the pain Mama endured. He had created the fear in her that caused her to hide Lydia all those years. He had probably pushed Charles to fear as well—a fear that may even have caused his death. Did this man have any good in him? Why would God allow him to live and her parents to perish?

Now, she could not even remain on the land she only knew as home—a world that for however short a time had made her life seem significant. Then, a question that had never occurred began to dominate her thoughts.

Is my life important to God at all?

Dylan's hand squeezed her shoulder and the carriage came to a halt.

She shook her head and opened her eyes to reassure herself it was her husband whose arms held her. He smiled and winked at her. Then he hopped over the carriage door and opened it in one fell swoop.

She sighed and placed her hands in his, allowing him to lead her in silence from the carriage and up the walkway to the front porch.

Before they entered, he cupped her face in his hands. The porch light illuminated his face, his eyes dashing back and forth across her face. "You will rest in my arms tonight, dear wife. I do not want a single worry to cross your mind. I promise, I will do whatever it takes to provide you with the life you deserve . . . a life void of rejection and requirements."

She lost herself in his embrace, allowing his kiss to erase all doubt. Whether she mattered to God or not, she mattered to this man who wrapped her in his arms. A man whom she could see and feel—and who cared for her beyond her ability to comprehend.

She followed his lead up the winding staircase and into their room. Standing beside the bed, Dylan drew up behind her. His fingers unclasped the top of her dress. He tugged at it for a moment, the layers falling to the floor without resistance. Lydia stepped out of the skirt, kicking the layers beneath the bench at the foot of the bed.

Dylan now stood in front of her. He removed his hat and vest, his gaze remaining on her face.

The bed, framed in an ornately carved head and footboard, welcomed them with layers of satin bedding and soft pillows. Lydia allowed her husband to explore her every curve, and then she willingly explored his. She ignored any notions about what was possible or proper. What they shared belonged to the two of them, and no one else.

A bird whistled in short bursts, waking Lydia with a start. Gray light, muzzled by the heavy curtain, hinted at daylight. Was it morning? She lifted her head, which was nestled in the crook of Dylan's elbow. A throbbing pain emanated from her neck and she dropped her head back, wincing.

Dylan stirred. "What's the matter?" His eyes remained closed, his voice thick and groggy.

"My head . . ." Lydia whispered, afraid her voice would intensify the throbbing.

Dylan cleared his throat. "Traveling, wine, and heavy food will do that. I should have warned you to take it easy, but you were enjoying yourself too much."

He removed his arm and replaced it with a pillow beneath her head. Soft lips nuzzled each of her cheeks before he pulled himself up on his elbows. "Stay here and rest some more. I will alert the kitchen staff to prepare a light breakfast and some strong coffee. Perhaps we should stay another day before heading back home . . ."

Her eyes burned and her nose tingled at his words. "Home?"

He sighed deeply and rubbed his forehead. "Never mind about that. I promised you I would handle it."

He left her in the company of the whistling bird. She pulled a pillow over her face—the shrill squawks clawing at her aching head.

During breakfast, Dylan announced they would stay another day, but would leave before morning light the next morning. He explained to Lydia that wine might have been why she had motion sickness on the way down and did not want to risk another miserable journey back up the mountain.

After her headache subsided, Dylan suggested they take a stroll through the neighborhood. The fresh air revived her and removed any remaining heaviness from the night before. Soon, the challenge of steep hills and learning to walk in strange shoes among cobblestone sidewalks invigorated her limbs and cleared her mind.

Visions of the large city did not overwhelm her as much the second time. Walking, she was able to stop, observe, and ask Dylan about each unfamiliar sight. From Russian Hill, they had an incredible view. Dylan pointed out important buildings and various neighborhoods. Once the fog lifted from the bay, sunlight shimmered on the water beyond the structures.

She tried to imagine what the land looked like before man had littered it with layers of buildings and streets. Their meager attempts provided an illusion of creation by planting their own trees and flowers between man-derived constructions. It was as if they had tried to improve upon God's own handiwork. As enthralled as she was with the intricate designs of homes and statues, she could not remove a sense of sadness for those who built this city. If they erased the physical trace of God, replacing it with the work of their own hands, did they also erase His influence on their lives? Recalling her thoughts from the previous evening, she saw how easily a single night immersed in the city offerings could draw one away from God.

"What is that mind of yours thinking?" Dylan looped his arm around her waist. They stood between houses before an iron fence, which bordered the top of a grassy hill descending into rows of much smaller houses along the streets below.

"More than I can put into words." Lydia chuckled. She smiled at her husband's curious look. "But they are futile thoughts—nothing that really matters." She sighed and leaned up to kiss his cheek.

"Well then if you won't share . . . we should make our way back to my grandfather's house. I should check on him before dinner." He squeezed her waist. "And we will need to do our best to get to sleep early tonight."

His words caused her insides to flutter and she bit her lip to hold back a grin.

As planned, they rose before the birds the next morning. Much of the city still slept while they climbed into the carriage. The clatter of horse hooves echoed in the streets until they joined the clamor of cable cars and merchants swarming the dock. A thick cloud of fog blocked the view not more than a few steps in front of them, but Lydia trusted Dylan as he led her to the ferry.

Afraid her belly would swoon at the motion, she kept her eyes on the water flowing beside them. After a few deep breaths, the speed of the ferry steadied, and she relaxed. Her nose and throat tingled in the cool, ocean air. She leaned back against Dylan and enjoyed the brief journey across the water.

Fortunately, the train ride back provided complete enjoyment, at least from a visual perspective. Relieved to see the more natural setting, she hardly contained bursts of joy as rolling hills, steep mountainsides, and a wide rushing river streamed past. Far more breathtaking than the hard, square, crammed structures of the city, the landscape beyond the train window demonstrated a gradual, artistic flow of beauty. As the train drew closer to Sacramento, the air in the train car grew hot and thick. Lydia longed for the cooler mountain breeze, the smell of sweet flowers and sour pine refreshing her senses. The wagon train for Auburn did not leave until morning.

They stayed at a farm belonging to Jason Robert's uncle, located beyond the center of town. The two-story house set against rows of apple orchards. An elderly couple welcomed them with a meal of fried chicken and apple pie. After making light conversation about their travels, Dylan and Lydia retired to their room. The day's heat lingered and they slept with the balcony door wide open, pushing off their bedding so the slight breeze would keep them cool enough to sleep.

Lydia could not get comfortable on the narrow bed. Perspiration clung to her neck and chest, making it hard to breath. Her thoughts mingled between the events of the previous days. Tomorrow, they would return to French Corral.

Dylan refused to tell her his plans and the possibilities flooded her mind.

Would they live with his parents?

She shuddered at the thought of Mr. and Mrs. Prescot sleeping down the hall. She desired the freedom she'd felt with Dylan in San Francisco. Would she feel so free with his parents under the same roof? What about Clara's warning that Mrs. Prescot did not need to know about every aspect of their marriage?

She longed for peace and resolution—for a finality and predictability to her life once again. Nothing was certain now. Nothing but the love between Dylan and her. Yet, she feared something unseen could take that as well. She buried her face into Dylan's chest, hoping to bury her thoughts. She would not let anything come between them— not like her grandfather had forced upon her parents. Even if that something turned out to be Mrs. Prescot herself.

Where did that thought come from? God, all this time away from the familiar is gnawing at me. Take these thoughts away…why am I finding it so hard to trust you now?

Lydia didn't care if she slept. As soon as the rooster began to crow outside, she jumped up and pulled on her skirt and shirtwaist. Tugging at Dylan's arm, she woke him. "Wake up. It is morning and I want to get back to French Corral. I need to get back home . . . however short a time I have left there."

THIRTY-SEVEN

Instead of taking the stagecoach from Auburn the following day, Dylan arranged for them to take the train into Grass Valley, courtesy of Uncle Frank's generosity. From there, they would take their own horse and wagon home.

Several hours after sunset the following day, they crossed the covered bridge, the lantern glowing in a half-circle along the creaking wooden boards. Darkness cloaked them. Only a sliver of a moon lit the way. Moments later, the river roared below on their right. Lydia prayed that God would prevent the horses from slipping on the loose rocks bordering the road. The buggy rounded the mountainside in tight curves before the road opened, veering away from the chasm. Finally, a pale line of moonlight streaked across the split in the road that led to the Valley. Lydia exhaled, dropping her shoulders in relief as they entered the canopy of trees welcoming them home.

Though they did not speak much while they unloaded what they would need for the night, Lydia felt Dylan's thoughts churning along with hers.

Did he really have a plan about what they would do? How much time did they have? Days, weeks?

What could Mr. Sinclair do if they refused to leave the land? That did not seem like an option.

Ultimately, Lydia felt useless as Dylan hurried along, his jaw taught and eyes focused on something in the distance he could not possibly see.

She made her way inside the cabin. The rocking chairs sat empty by the cold and dark fireplace. Long shadows of each frame hardly noticeable aside from running in the opposite direction of the floorboards. Memories of her and Mama working by the firelight flooded her mind.

Tears stung her weary eyes.

She turned to the stove that Dylan had lit upon their arrival. It was now hot enough to boil tea water and to break the midnight chill. As she went to place the kettle over a burner, she recalled the time Mama taught her how to use the stove. Lydia had been barely tall enough to reach the back without the front of the stove burning her chest. Mama's instructions were kind and patient. She had trusted Lydia at a far younger age than the mothers in French Corral would have allowed.

She had trusted me.

All those years, Mama had kept them safe and far from harm. All those years, she had trusted Lydia alone while she went off to bring offerings to the angels. She had trusted that Lydia would continue to believe her and the reasons the Valley would be—should be—the only home they ever needed.

"Lydia, Sweetheart...don't cry." Dylan dropped the satchel he held and rushed to Lydia's side. "We must not let hope die . . . the Lord will provide. He will . . ." His voice trailed off as if he were speaking to himself.

"I have so many questions that will never get

answers. How do you know God even cares?"

Dylan wiped away her tears and drew her face into his shirt. "I know . . . because he would not have taken us this far if he didn't." His chest rose with a deep breath. *"The Lord also will be a refuge for the oppressed, a refuge in times of trouble. And they that know Thy name will put their trust in Thee; for Thou, Lord, hast not forsaken them that seek Thee . . ."*

Lydia lifted her head against his grasp, catching a glimmer of moisture in Dylan's eyes, reflecting in the candlelight. "Where have I heard that before?"

"It was from our Bible reading the night before we left for San Francisco."

"So, we must trust God, even in times of trouble?" The more she trusted God, the worse things seemed to become.

"Yes, we must."

It's you I trust, the one I can see and feel.

But if Dylan wanted to trust God, she would do her best to honor his request.

The next afternoon, a muggy gray sky led the way to Mr. and Mrs. Prescot's home. Strange how different everything looked under a colorless sky, how much less magnificent this home appeared after being on the streets of Nob Hill.

The fluttering in Lydia's chest almost hurt at the prospect of what was about to transpire. Dylan hadn't revealed details but insisted that she accompany him while he presented his plan to her and his parents.

Within moments of entering the home, the four

of them stood in the parlor.

"Father, Mother, please sit." Dylan nodded for Lydia to do the same.

Dylan took a deep breath, fingers white along the brim of the hat he held at his side.

Jaina waved a blue and white fan before her face and huffed. "Well, it is far too early for you to be announcing a pregnancy, so I assume this is not good news?"

"Jaina . . ." Mr. Prescot patted his wife's knee. "Let our boy speak."

"Thank you, Father." Dylan sighed again. "Lydia and I come to you with dire news. As you know, Mr. Sinclair hastened us to the city to discuss the property . . . and . . . well . . . he—"

"He what?" Mr. Prescot's tone was sharp.

"He ordered us off the land. He had the paperwork drawn up, his lawyer present and everything." Dylan's voice cracked.

Jaina stood, approached her son, and pulled him in a long embrace. "That devil of a man...how dare he?"

"I should have known, son—after he wouldn't sell us the land. I should have known. I sent you right into the lion's den. I am sorry son, sorry . . ."

Lydia sank deep into the chair and watched Dylan's parents console him for several minutes. She remained quiet, obeying Dylan's request that he do the talking.

Jaina returned to her seat, hardly glancing at Lydia while Mr. Prescot and Dylan discussed their options.

Not a single word from any of them about Lydia losing the Valley, and the only place she had ever called her home.

"Father, I have a plan. And it does not include

us moving in with you." He chuckled, though it sounded forced along with his slight smile.

"Well, what is it? What is your plan?"

"I would like my full inheritance. Grandfather has approved. You only need to sign—"

"Absolutely not." Mr. Prescot stepped away and turned his back to Dylan.

"But Father . . ." Dylan's face fell and his voice squeaked.

"How dare you take advantage of your dying grandfather to contrive such a ridiculous plan?" He spun back around, somehow appearing taller than Dylan. "What do you expect to do with it?" Mr. Prescot spun around to face Lydia and Jaina and cleared his throat.

Jaina stood wide-eyed and looked at Lydia. "Shall we take a walk in the rose garden while the men sort this out?"

Startled, Lydia shook her head, and then nodded, clenching her shaking hands at her sides to try to hide them. "Yes, I . . . could use some air."

Sunlight peeked in and out of clouds as the two women strolled along the rocky path. The fountain water drowned out any distinction in the men's shouts echoing from indoors. Jaina seemed intent on discussing anything and everything besides what the men may be hashing out. After a while, Lydia didn't hear a word of it. Her thoughts wandered to Dylan's unspoken plans, and how once again, his attempt to rescue her seemed to be failing.

Yet, she trusted him in a way she could not explain. As much as leaving the Valley forever cut at her heart and caused her soul to ache, she believed that if Dylan were by her side, she could endure anything. He was her rescuer. He was all she had dreamed of and more. He was willing to risk everything for her—just like her father had for Mama...

"Mr. Sinclair sounds like an awful brute." Jaina voice raised an octave, pulling Lydia out of her thoughts. "His kind is one of the many reasons Mr. Prescot and I chose to make our home in French Corral. Though I must say, as the years pass, I miss many things about city life. This isolated life is no longer suiting me."

"The city life." Lydia nodded, pretending that she had been listening all along. "Now that I have been there, I know what you mean."

"Oh, but I would never go back to San Francisco. I am thinking smaller, yet still plenty of people and happenings to keep things interesting."

"Are you thinking of leaving French Corral?" Lydia said in a shrill, yet unintended tone.

Jaina's steps slowed and she tapped the handle of her parasol on her shoulder. Then she laughed. "You know, it is a funny thing. We *were* thinking of leaving—"

"What about my lessons?" Her words felt foolish, but they were all she had in response.

"Lydia, you have to realize something. French Corral is dwindling. There is nothing here for most of us. Families are packing up and leaving by the week. The miners can make far more and travel less in Grass Valley. And us, well...with the failing health of Mr. Prescot—Dylan's grandfather..." Jaina stopped walking and speaking.

"What are you saying?" Lydia said, surprised that Jaina would reveal so much.

"Never mind . . . never mind." Jaina shook her head, pivoted her heel, and walked toward the house.

Confused to tears, Lydia remained in the garden. What was happening here? She was apparently not the only one facing changes and difficult choices.

The still air shifted and a cool breeze blew across Lydia's face.

Maybe nobody's life was meant to stay the same. The urgency inside of her that had longed for change all those years wasn't bad . . . it wasn't a sin . . . it was a part of the human condition. It was because of change that she had encountered Dylan in the forest that evening. Everything that followed that moment meant that her life would never be the same. If she honestly believed, as Dylan did, that they had a purpose together—the possibilities seemed too many to know which direction they should turn.

Suddenly, Jaina appeared on the balcony. "Lydia, come inside!" She waved in a circular motion, a huge grin across her face. "They have found you a new home."

THIRTY-EIGHT

Two weeks later, Lydia sat on the floor of Mama's room, fighting tears with each item she placed in a crate. Mama's room had remained untouched since the fire that took her life. Even while living here alone last winter, Lydia couldn't bear to explore her mother's possessions, as if doing so would reinforce the fact Mama was gone for good. Like the oak tree planted outside of her bedroom stood as a firm symbol of her papa's arch of protection, this room—remaining as Mama left it—reminded Lydia of her mama's constant care and guidance.

Lydia folded each dress, apron, and nightgown with care, smoothing the fabric with her fingertips and recalling a memory each one held. Strawberry juice stains on the sleeve of one dress stirred memories of a sweltering summer afternoon when Lydia swatted at a bee that landed on Mama's shoulder. Instead of scolding Lydia for not realizing her hands were in the middle of mashing strawberries for jam, Mama had surprised Lydia by laughing her way to tears.

On the table near Mama's bed, dusty, brass plates held melted candles. Solid wax drips froze along the sides and ended in hardened puddles at the bottom. How many nights had Mama prayed while those candles remained lit long after Lydia fell asleep? Taking the cloth scrap she was using to dust, she cleaned the plates and gently rubbed the dust from the hardened wax.

Beneath a shelf on the wall, bunches of dried wildflowers hung upside down, each tied with a remnant of ribbon. At first, they appeared only as a decoration. As she pulled each one down and looked closer, Lydia's memory surged. There were thirteen bunches, each a different array and number of flowers.

Lydia drew her hand to her mouth. These were more than random groups of flowers. These were the first flowers of spring—the flowers Lydia had gathered on their first walk of the season—a bunch for each year going back to when she was four years old.

Mama had kept each one.

A tear dropped on the dust coating the bunch of purple lupine, yellow mustard, and white lily she held. Lydia sniffled, and wiped her face with the sleeve of her free arm.

Mama, you had cherished those walks just as much as I did.

"Is everything all right in here?" Dylan's voice echoed in the near-empty room.

"Yes . . . I . . . came across these flowers Mama kept from our walks." Lydia turned toward the doorway to show Dylan her discovery. "I didn't know she saved these. Is there another crate or box we can keep them? I would like to find a way to display them in that hutch with the etched-glass doors we ordered for the kitchen."

Dylan embraced her and kissed her neck. "Of

course, we can. There is an empty tin box in the barn that will work perfectly. It looks like you are about finished in here. Do you need help with the bed?"

Lydia shook her head, smiling at his thoughtful gesture. "I think I can manage if you can take the quilt."

She set the dried flowers on the bedside table. Then she tugged carefully on the quilt, trying not to disturb too much of the layer of smoky dust atop it.

Dylan gathered it with care and hurried outside to shake it off.

Lydia grabbed a hold of the edges of the mattress, pulled up, and shoved it into the wall. A spider flung from a single thread connected to the underside of the mattress, then slid through the air as it released enough web to take it to the floor. Lydia watched, finding comfort only when the creature fled to the wall and climbed into a shadow.

She looked down and kicked the mattress steady, and then stopped when she noticed a strange black square outlined the floorboards. She made sure the mattress wouldn't fall and then crouched for a closer look.

It was not an outline—it was a door in the floor.

A small metal hinge, nearly hidden along a knot in the floor, lay pinched between floorboards. Lydia ran her fingers along the line until she could dig her nails far enough under the edge to lift the boards. The wood creaked and groaned, resisting her efforts, and dropped back into place. It was too heavy to lift with her nails alone. She needed something stronger. Everything from the kitchen and barn was already packed.

"Dylan!" She jumped up and raced outside,

scanning the side of the house for her husband.

He was still flipping the quilt into the air. Dust flew about and joined bits of flower pollen in the sunlight. "What is it?"

"I need a tool . . . something hard and flat. There is a door in the floor under Mama's bed."

Dylan folded the quilt in haste and flung it onto the stack of crates on the back of the wagon. Reaching beneath the wagon seat, he pulled out a flat iron rod and followed Lydia back into the house.

Within seconds, he had the door open.

A shallow, dirt-lined hole lay filled with a myriad of items—most of which Lydia didn't recognize. Her legs wobbled and she brought herself to the floor, crossing her legs and reaching in to examine each treasure.

From inside a burlap sack, she pulled out an infant gown, tied together with a knitted hat and booties. Pairs of shoes Lydia had long grown out of were stacked on the inside wall of the hole. Another wall was lined with a half-dozen tattered books and a Bible. Two picture frames stood snug between the Bible and a tapestry-covered box.

Dylan removed the frames. "A certificate of your parent's marriage." He set it on his lap, revealing a photograph in the next frame.

Lydia leaned over to get a closer view. A young man and woman stood in wedding attire. Lydia immediately recognized the woman, as a far younger version of Mama. The man, holding a slight resemblance to Frank Sinclair, stood tall, his face straight though Lydia thought she saw a twinkle in his eye.

She snatched the frame from Dylan's grasp and pulled it to her chest.

Looking at Dylan through blurry eyes, she sobbed. "It's Mama and my . . . papa . . . Papa."

"He looks so proud . . . happy." She laughed. "And Mama looks scared out of her wits...very much like I was on our wedding day." Tears gushing now, she glanced over at Dylan.

Dylan sat still and silent and nodded—a small smile veiling sniffles and wet eyes.

The breeze rushed through the leaves outside as if her Papa were whispering words of comfort to her soul.

She inhaled the fresh air that blew in and nodded with assurance at the small voice speaking inside of her. Glancing outside at the waving branches, she thought the leaves looked like they were clapping in approval of what Lydia had resolved in her heart.

She could accept their new life now. God had provided everything down to a remnant of her parents' past.

The blur of the previous two weeks become clear. What else could explain the ranch that became available only the day before they had returned to French Corral? The widow, in search of someone who would maintain it, had run the ranch with her husband for over fifty years—her asking price nearly matching that of Dylan's inheritance to the last dollar. According to Dylan, Mr. Prescot had shifted from rage to rejoicing the moment he realized it.

"Dylan," she said past the tears in her throat, still clutching the image of her parents.

He looked at her, his gaze enveloping her like rapids over river rocks—refreshing and powerful. Tears poured from his eyes.

"We could have gone years before discovering these if we had been able to continue living here,"

Lydia sobbed.

"Or maybe not at all," he sniffled, and then wiped his face with his sleeve. "But now you have a way to take a part of your parents with you . . . no matter where we live." He gathered the books in his arms, examined the bindings briefly, and then stood.

"Wait, there is more. What about the box here?" Lydia pulled a floral-covered box from its nesting place and brushed off a layer of red dirt.

Dylan glanced at the box, and then nodded at the books in his arms. "I will be back after I rearrange some of the boxes to make an empty one for your discovery."

Impatient, she lifted the lid before he returned. Startled at first by the sounds that came from it—her heart settled when she realized it was music. A soothing melody rang from the box. Velvet-lined compartments held two metal wedding bands, a curled lock of golden hair tied with a pink ribbon, and a small key. Nudging at the items, she felt the velvet give. There was a space beneath the compartments. Pinching the edge, she lifted the middle out of the box and discovered a pile of folded and worn papers.

Dylan's eyebrows rose when he returned. "I am surely as curious as you are, sweetheart. But we've got to finish up the other packing before we lose light."

Curiosity ate at her. "You're right," she said, bowing her head to place the box carefully next to the floor opening.

THIRTY-NINE

With a sudden burst of energy, they were able to finish their packing right before sunset. After eating what would be their last meal in the Valley, Dylan and Lydia sat on the porch, the fabric, floral box between them. The sun dropped below the treetops, casting deep golden streaks of light onto the Valley floor.

The barn, sheep pen, and hen house looked odd void of tools, supplies, and wandering animals. Every rope, bucket, and tool that normally had a place against a wall or draped over a fence post, lay piled in the back of the wagon.

Though they had sat on this bench many times since, memories of their first meeting flooded Lydia's mind. The present sky was clear of clouds, yet she could almost hear the rain rattling the roof. Dylan's knee nudging against hers had sent waves through her body. This is where the truth came forth for the first time—the truth that would bring her relief and grief all at once. Truth that had led to the loss of her mother yet gained answers and provided this man at her side—a man she felt she somehow knew long before they met face to face.

Now, they sat here for the last time. In minutes,

they would climb aboard the overloaded wagon and make their way to a new life. Was Dylan thinking or feeling any of the same things? He had a look of longing in his eyes—his silent gaze tracing the borders of the Valley. He hummed, nodded, and rocked, causing the legs of the bench to creak. Then he reached for the box, set it on his lap, and opened it.

Gentle chimes strung a melody around them.

He handed the top compartment—containing the rings, the lock of hair, and the small key—to Lydia. She held it secure in her lap and scooted toward Dylan so that they sat leg against leg. With her free hand, she held the lantern up to provide the additional light Dylan needed to examine the items.

Dylan did not say anything. He took his time to look over each piece of paper. He expelled an occasional "Hmm," or nod, wrinkling his forehead, or squinting at some of the pages.

Lydia wiggled and nudged him. "So, what are they? What do the papers tell you?"

Dylan cleared his throat, folded the paper in his hand, and then placed it back in the pile. "Most don't tell me much." He pointed to another stack of folded papers on the bench. "Those are travel documents, possibly from your mother's parents." He lifted a stack of tattered, browning pages tied with twine. "This looks like a ledger of some sort, maybe from your grandfather's tailor shop. And this booklet here could be from the convent your mother stayed at after her parents died in the fire."

"What about the key? Any of those papers tell you what the key is for?" Lydia's heart pounded. Could these items help her to learn more about Mama's life before she came to French Corral?

"No." Dylan shook his head. He lifted two stacks of yellow papers. "But these are the telegrams sent between Charles...or...your mama and Mr. Sinclair." A smile emerged. "These other papers are letters your mama wrote to an Uncle Moses. These may have some answers, but the light is too dim to make out the faded text. I will read them to you after we settle into our new home. However, we should probably be on our way. It will still take us an hour or more to get to the ranch with the loaded wagon."

Lydia sighed and nodded, then pressed her lips together. This was promising news that brought her hopes high. As much as she wanted to know what the letters would reveal about Mama's past, she was also ready to start her future with Dylan in their new home. What could they do with the information the letters held now anyway?

Dylan kissed her cheek, his lips lingering, then trailing around to meet hers. "I hate to confess this." His head tilted and a wry smile emerged. "But I am a bit eager to take you home."

The thought of losing herself in Dylan's arms sounded heavenly. Finding the treasures below Mama's bed sparked hope within her once again. Not only hope in discovering where she came from, but also hope that she and Dylan could somehow achieve the dream of love her parents could not.

After one last look across the Valley, Lydia snuggled up close to Dylan on the seat of the wagon and turned to face the road ahead.

She pondered her grandfather's motives while the full moon lit the road. Leaving also cut ties to him, a matter that did not settle well. She wouldn't believe his heart hardened for no reason. A man who appeared cruel from the inside out could not father two endearing sons.

Maybe there was a way to gain his love. Wouldn't it be amazing, if after all this time, Lydia could find a way to make peace with him? Perhaps her Uncle Frank could help.

She shifted in her seat, excited at the challenge and the prospect of learning about yet another uncle.

Exhilarated at her plans, any remaining doubts flew from her mind like dandelion seeds in the wind. She hugged Dylan's arm, his bulging muscles flexing beneath her fingers.

He looked at her sincerely—a wide smile, and deep dimples emerging. Then he clicked his tongue at the horses.

Lydia giggled. He probably took her gesture as a desire to get home sooner than later.

Sometime later, the moon set high in the sky. Blue-gray beams streamed into the upstairs window and across rumpled sheets wrapped around Lydia and Dylan on the bed. Lydia kept her eyes fixed on Dylan's perfect profile while she drew circles with her finger across his chest. His eyes closed while a smile played with his lips.

"I love you, Dylan Prescot," Lydia whispered.

He pulled her closer, turning his head toward hers. "Oh, sweet Lydia, this is only the beginning. We were brought together for a purpose and with God as our guide—we will surely find it and succeed."

Eye hath not seen, nor ear heard, neither have entered

into the heart of man, the things which God hath prepared for them that love him.

The promise echoed as if Elder Scott had spoken it only a moment earlier.

It seemed like a promise of hope, of blessing, of justice even. Yet, it required her to love God for it to happen. At that moment, loving anyone more than she loved Dylan seemed impossible.

"How am I supposed to love God when I can't see him?" Lydia said the words more to herself than to Dylan.

Dylan took a deep breath. "If you look close enough, you will see him in the everyday things...people, places, how circumstances merge to lead those who are willing to pursue his perfect purpose. It is then your love for him will bloom, and your trust in him will stand firm."

Her chest filled with unexplainable joy and hope beyond measure. God had indeed made a way so far. It had not been what she imagined—but these words promised so much more than she could see or hear or dream on her own. With Dylan at her side, and their fate in the hands of the ever-faithful God, what could possibly shake her faith now?

Acknowledgments

In the near thirty years since the idea of this story set root in my young writer's mind, many people have cheered me on in my journey. My high school creative writing teacher, Ms. McDaniel, believed in this story even in its rawest, infant stages.

Next, my mother, Christina Ivazes has always believed in my writing and continues to support me in many ways. Having lived in and visited San Francisco over the years, our tour of the city and public library proved valuable for this book and for Book 2.

My faithful husband, Mike, has also been supportive through decades of writing courses, piles of writing magazines and writing craft books, and even when I've had to set aside my writing dreams due to the demands of raising our five children, multiple moves, and helping to run our business, he doesn't hesitate when I say it's time to write! Though the sacrifices, expenses, and inconveniences are more than we can count, there is no way I can continue to pursue my writing goals without his support and understanding that this is God's calling for my life.

Thanks also to our five children who are now all nearly adults—Elora, Tayler, Dawson, Jared, and Parker. I hope I have set an example of perseverance and dedication, even if it has taken me all your lives to finally publish this book series!

Next, it's difficult to encompass the important contributions of the other writers who have come alongside me during the process of writing this series. Thanks again to the Inspire Christian Writers critique group of Roseville, California and to Dana, John, Don, Tracilynn, Beth, Ruth, Ricky, and Susan. Your honest edits, suggestions, and praise gave me the confidence to pursue a professional writing career. The first edition of this book would not have been completed without you.

I also want to acknowledge the volunteers at the Searls and Doris Foley Historical libraries in Nevada City, California. Your enthusiasm and knowledge provided important historical details that allowed me to weave authentic details throughout this fictional story.

Finally, I thank God for putting the spark in me to write for His glory in a way that has stretched my faith, increased my talents, and provided a path to realizing my dreams in Your perfect timing.

Author's Note

In this official "second edition", I had to decide on what to change and what to keep the same. In consideration of those who already read the first edition, there are only a few minor changes besides the inclusion of the Prologue. As I pondered ways that I could create a different story the second time, it occurred to me that we only get one chance at this life. Like the character of Lydia learning about life beyond the Valley, this story is also my learning curve. To stay true to Lydia's character and her narrow points of reference, I avoided excess variety in her thoughts and descriptions of the world around her.

This is a unique, yet simple story of a girl finding herself despite having an unusual upbringing. In Book 2 – *Below the Mountain,* things get a lot more complicated! Knowing her limited life experience from Book 1 is necessary in understanding the emotional complications many of us take for granted or are taught from a young age. I encourage you to grab a copy and continue the journey with Lydia and Dylan.

Thank you for devoting a small part of your life to escaping and exploring the world "beyond the Valley" through Lydia's eyes!

Made in the USA
Las Vegas, NV
18 January 2021